10/12   ASL

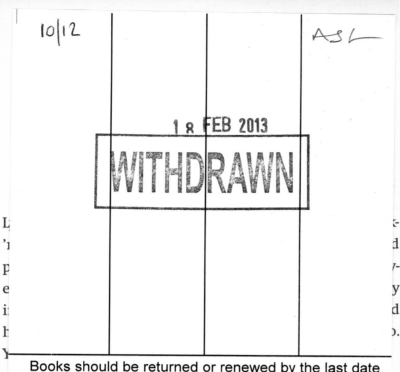

Also by Lynda Hilburn

The Vampire Shrink

BLOOD THERAPY

LYNDA HILBURN

Jo Fletcher
BOOKS

First published in Great Britain in 2012 by

Jo Fletcher Books
an imprint of Quercus
55 Baker Street
7th Floor, South Block
London
W1U 8EW

A CIP catalogue record for this book is available
from the British Library

ISBN 978 0 85738 722 6

10 9 8 7 6 5 4 3 2 1

Typeset by Ellipsis Digital Limited, Glasgow

Printed and bound in Great Britain by Clays Ltd, St Ives plc

To my son, Daniel, who makes life interesting

CHAPTER 1

'But she's fat, Doctor Knight!' The lithe vampire was wringing his hands compulsively in his lap as he whined, 'You *know* fat women remind me of my mother—'

'Yes, Nicky. I know.' I took a deep breath and struggled to keep my expression neutral. He'd repeated this story several times in earlier therapy sessions. 'It's very unfair that you were turned by a . . . large female vampire and that she insists you share her coffin – and other things.'

Even vampires think it's okay to denigrate people of size – well, why not? They used to be human.

He leaped off the couch and paced the lush blue carpet in the space between us. 'Just so you know, it ain't that I've got anything against my mother. She was a nice lady. She did the best she could. I guess it wasn't her fault she had a disease or condition that made her blimp up to three hundred pounds.' He strode to the window and stood staring out silently for a few seconds, his hands clasped behind his back. 'She didn't mean for all the kids in the neighbourhood to make fun of me for having a hippo mom. I'm not blaming her. I tried not to be disgusted by her.' His voice softened. 'I was sorry when she died.'

Setting my notepad and pen on the table next to my chair, I rose and joined him at the window. Sometimes just being with a client is the best I can do. We stood together, watching the lights of Denver glitter from our lofty vantage point.

Maybe I should change my title to Dr Kismet Knight, Vampire Whisperer.

I studied his frowning reflection in the glass. He was an attractive young man, closer to pretty than handsome – the word 'winsome' came to mind. His dancer's body and long, silky light-brown hair gave him a decidedly androgynous appearance. He looked to be in his early twenties, but I knew he'd been a vampire for fifty years.

Good thing new vampires couldn't read minds for decades – sometimes centuries – or I'd go crazy trying to censor myself around clients like Nicky.

'Last week you said you were going to tell Wanda why you have strong negative reactions when she tries to have sex with you, or wants to keep you in her coffin all night. Did you talk to her?'

He gasped and his gaze shot to mine, his deep-green eyes wide. He looked as horrified as if I'd come at him with a sharp stake. 'N— No, no! I could never talk to her about those things – I could never disobey my moth — I mean, Wanda.' Glazed eyes now transfixed on the window again, he hugged himself tightly for a moment, then raised a slender wrist to his mouth and began gnawing furiously.

'Nicky!' I jumped aside as blood spurted from the holes he'd made in his arm, splashing onto the window, fouling my black trousersuit and oozing into the carpet. 'What are you doing? Please stop!' What the hell? He'd never done anything like that before.

He stopped chewing on himself long enough to speak. He

turned to me, blood dripping from his fangs, and said, 'It makes me feel better, Doctor Knight. I saw this TV show about a girl who cuts herself with razor blades. She said it relieved her anxiety. I tried cutting, but the wounds healed too fast – but this works for me. I've been doing it for a while. It really takes my mind off whatever I'm worried about. You said I should learn different ways to cope, didn't you?'

Holy crap. Be careful what you ask for . . .

'Hurting yourself wasn't what I had in mind, Nicky. Please stop.' My heart was still racing and my breath came in shallow bursts. I was sure I looked shocked as I surveyed the red stains on the wall and carpet and examined my soiled trousers. I was definitely going to have to start wearing blood-repelling leather clothing.

He reluctantly lowered his arm, which had already stopped bleeding. The holes disappeared as I watched. Still sniffling, he covered his face with his hands, then mumbled, 'I'm sorry, Doctor Knight. I didn't mean to be bad. If you tell Wanda, she'll punish me.'

Does he think that's a good thing or bad? Knowing Nicky, it could go either way.

'We don't have to tell Wanda anything about what happens in our sessions, Nicky.' I recognised the familiar pattern: progress gained in one hour usually evaporated in the next. Every time I met with Nicky I felt like we'd stumbled into an old *X-Files* episode: we were stuck in an endlessly repeating time loop – although he didn't appear to notice. Apparently he'd been cycling through this approach-avoidance pattern with his maker for the last five decades. I didn't know enough about the bond between a vampire and his creator to make even an educated guess about what would help him – hell, I'd only been officially counselling vampires for a few weeks

– it was less than three months since I'd blundered into the bloodsucker underworld. I was lucky I hadn't become an unwilling evening snack or coffin-toy yet.

His eyes now glued to my face, his fangs fully extended, he slowly raised his arm towards his mouth again. He thrust his tongue out in quick darting movements, licking the dried blood from his arm, all the while shifting his weight from foot to foot. He inched his arm closer to his teeth.

Gee, what a surprise. He wants to see what I'll do, how far he can push me.

'Nicky?' I layered my *I'm an authority* tone into my voice. 'Don't even think about it.' Crossing my arms over my chest, I examined the spatter. 'Who's going to clean up the blood on the glass and the carpet? It's only fair that you should take care of it, don't you think?'

He dropped his arm, his chin trembling. 'What?' A tear spilled down his cheek. 'You want me to *clean*? I don't know how to get blood out of stuff – Wanda always does that. See how messed up I am? I can't do anything! You have to help me, Doctor Knight!'

Same song, same verse ... 'I'm here to teach you to help your-self, Nicky. If you keep coming to therapy, keep practising your skills, I promise things can get better.'

A muscle jumped in his cheek and he frowned, then he turned back to the window and stared out, clearly uncon-vinced.

Nicky was young for a vampire, at least compared to some of the other multi-century specimens I'd had on my couch, and he was struggling through an extended undead ado-lescence. I'd discovered the greater the time since the turning, the more autonomy the undead acquired. Nicky would prob-ably figure things out eventually. Maybe. I intended to speak to Devereux, the Master of the local vampire coven and my – what? Boyfriend? Significant other? Friend with benefits? None of those descriptions quite fit – about my conflicted client.

For safety – mine – and confidentiality, I insisted that all my supernatural clients sign a Release of Information form giving me permission to consult with their leader. I didn't want any pointy surprises. But Devereux had been so busy and so out of sorts as he recovered from being captured and subjected to a black-magic ritual orchestrated by a demented offspring – the bloodsucker formerly known as Bryce – that I hadn't had time to broach the subject.

'It'll be okay, Nicky,' I said softly. 'You'll work things out with Wanda. You always do.' I raised my hand to pat him on the shoulder, then thought better of it. Vampires couldn't be counted onto have human-like reactions, and I was still learning to alter my behaviour with my nocturnal clients. Nicky was too immature to be completely trustworthy.

Maybe I need to bring Wanda in for some couples' therapy. Note to self: buy rubber sheets for the furniture.

'*How* will it be okay?' He turned sad eyes to me. 'She's my maker, so I'm tied to her for ever. She'll never let me go.'

'I don't know,' I glanced at the clock, 'but I'm going to ask someone who might have some advice for you.' *Where's a blood-sucking clinical supervisor when I need one?*

'Someone?' He tilted his head, confused. 'You mean a human?'

'No, not a human, a vampire. Someone powerful.' I stepped back from the window and walked towards the door to the waiting room. 'That's all the time we have for tonight, Nicky. I can't promise anything, but I'll tell you what I discover when I see you next week.'

He skipped across the room, swinging his arms, a wide smile on his face. 'Do you mean you'll ask the Master?'

Everyone in the local vampire community knew I had a unique relationship with Devereux – in fact, my undead main squeeze had been graphically clear about what he'd do to any vampire who laid a fang on me. So far, his threats had kept me off the menu.

'Wait.' Nicky stopped, the corners of his lips turning down. 'Is the Master even the Master any more?'

'What do you mean?' *Why would he ask such a thing?*

I turned the handle and opened the door.

Ensconced on the white couch in my waiting room sat the blond god in question, decked out in his usual body-skimming high-fashion black leathers. His thick platinum hair flowed down his well-toned chest in the most touchable, inviting manner. Blue-green gemstone eyes sparkled.

A fallen angel.

He gave a devastating grin and Nicky gasped and fell to his knees, question forgotten. 'Master!'

As always when Devereux was near, my body developed a mind of its own. My heart pounded, my mouth declared a drought and my knees weakened. I blinked to clear the sudden fog and clutched the doorknob for support. I didn't know what it was about him – perhaps it was his mystical vampire vibe, or maybe his personal charisma and raw sex appeal – but once again my brain cells refused to report for duty and my libido dimmed the lights.

My mouth fell open as a sharp pain radiated across my brow. I stared at him, and the room temperature suddenly spiked. Sweat beaded on my forehead and trickled between my breasts.

Whew! Did somebody turn up the heat in here? Maybe I should just take off a few of these clothes ...

'Good evening, Doctor Knight,' said the gorgeous nightwalker, widening his dazzling smile as he rose in a fluid motion. 'I hope I am not interrupting.'

Interrupting? Am I doing something? Oh, yeah. Counselling. Client. Psychologist. I remember. I leaned towards Devereux and inhaled deeply. *There's that amazing aroma. Spicy. Earthy. Sensual. Edible. Wait – what's happening? Snap out of it, Kismet! Why does he always scramble my senses?*

As I tried – and failed – to form coherent words or thoughts, Nicky speed-crawled across the floor and wrapped his arms like fleshy shackles around Devereux's legs. He pressed his face against the supple leather. 'Master! I can't believe I'm in the same room with you. What an honour.'

Devereux arched an eyebrow, his disturbingly sensual lips gently lifting at the corners as he stared down at his devotee. 'Rise, child.'

Nicky lurched to his feet as if he'd been yanked up by invisible hands. A look of adoration on his face, he stared into Devereux's eyes.

'Say goodnight to Doctor Knight and be on your way,' the Master crooned in his deep, vibrant voice.

His eyes still locked on Devereux's, Nicky mumbled, 'G'nite, Doctor,' then he turned, zombie-like, and shuffled out through the door into the hallway.

The usual struggle took me hostage: my body instinctively wanted to move towards Devereux like a flower bending to the sun, but my brain – at least, the tiny part that wasn't missing in action thanks to his innate vampire juju – reminded me that I barely knew this attractive, scary male, and that I was tired of other people deciding what I should and shouldn't do.

I shook myself and blinked to break the spell Devereux's appearance always cast on me, then I sucked in a deep breath and licked my dry lips. The pain in my head morphed from a bonfire to a simmer.

Why am I having so many headaches lately? Maybe I should have my eyes checked.

'That's incredibly annoying, you know.'

'Annoying?' he asked, looking deceptively innocent. 'To what are you referring?'

'Yeah.' I took a step back from the doorway, and from Devereux, in a vain attempt at self-control. 'As if you didn't notice the pseudo-lobotomy-without-anaesthesia my brain gives itself whenever you show up. I thought you said I'd get used to your vibration, or your *aura* – whatever the vampire version is – and I'd stop turning into the village idiot in your presence. Oh, wait, no, I mean the *hormone-riddled* village idiot. But what am I saying? You probably like it.'

He laughed, which was even more annoying, and propped a shoulder against the doorjamb. 'I promise you will acclimatise.' He pretended to pout, which wasn't very effective because his mouth kept twitching as he fought a smile. 'Soon I fear you will have no reaction at all to my arrival and I shall be reduced to competing with all your human suitors.'

I didn't have any human suitors at the moment and he knew it: he'd cleared the decks. But that wasn't anything I'd admit, or a subject I wanted to discuss, so I switched channels. 'What did you do to Nicky? Why was he walking so strangely?'

Devereux chuckled. 'His body resisted the command I sent to his brain. He is too young to understand the futility of fighting a directive from one so many centuries older than himself. He will learn.'

He thinks mind control is amusing?

He moved effortlessly, with surreal vampire grace, stepping

inside my office and closing the space between us. He sniffed the air. 'Umm. Such an enticing aroma.' His eyes tracked down my body to the invisible-to-humans bloodstain on my black trousers. 'Why do you have vampire blood on your clothing? Did Nicky misbehave?'

'Er, not really. Just a little messy self-soothing.'

He leaned down to me until we were almost touching, then slowly skimmed his lips over my skin down to my neck.

My heart was slamming against my ribs like the drums of a marching band while my imagination was rolling out the red carpet.

He licked along my pulsing jugular. 'Of course, nothing can surpass the scent of your sweet blood, my love,' he whispered into my ear, then straightened and gave me the full effect of those baby blue-greens.

A feeble groan escaped my lips just before he kissed me. He gently pried my fingers off the chair I'd grabbed onto and pulled me tight against him as he took the kiss deeper. A low growl rumbled in his throat.

Without conscious thought my arms closed around his waist and my lips settled in for the duration. For some reason, whenever Devereux touched me, nothing mattered but him. My brain pressed the *pause* button and all competing impulses disappeared in a haze of yearning. My bones melted along with my resistance as his spicy, intoxicating aroma overwhelmed my senses and made my head spin.

He whispered in my mind, 'Yes, I desire you also. We are finally together.'

Finally together? Like a bucket of cold blood his words snapped me back to full awareness and I stiffened. He'd been saying things like that since I first met him and I still didn't understand what he meant. He appeared to be experiencing a different reality: to my mind, there was no *finally* involved. We'd known each other just over two months, and for part of that time he'd been in some kind of mystical near-death coma. He'd only rejoined the land of the living – so to speak – a few weeks ago. Maybe he'd suffered a form of undead brain damage while he floated 'between the worlds', as he called it. I didn't know how else to explain his strange fascination with me. What could an ordinary Denver psychologist possibly offer to so intrigue an 800-year-old vampire? Even my blood type was average.

'There is nothing average about you, Doctor.' As he raised his mouth from mine to answer my silent question his enticing voice caressed my ears. 'On the contrary, you are indeed special. I have waited for you my entire life. My heart belongs to you.'

What?

'I really don't know what you mean.' I pushed back from him and raised my eyes, although I kept them firmly anchored on his chin. I didn't want to become any more entranced than I already was. The subtle pounding in my head picked up its pace. '*How* am I special? Why does your heart belong to me? Did I miss the first chapter of this book?' I took another step back and bumped into my potted ficus tree. *Damn. So much for a graceful retreat!* I recovered and shifted over to lean against my desk. *Why do I always act so weird around him?*

'Okay, I get that you painted a picture of me a long time ago and you believe we were destined to meet, but something else is going on. You have another agenda.' My voice held all the frustration I felt about his ambiguity. 'When exactly are you going to explain all your cryptic remarks?'

In a blink, he was standing in front of me. 'Be patient, my love.' He pulled me close again and kissed the top of my head.

'It would not be wise for me to overload your brain with such esoteric information.'

Does he mean to be condescending, or does it just come naturally?

'We must take things slowly,' he murmured next to my ear. 'All will be revealed in time.'

Goosebumps crawled up my arms: another evasive answer, not to mention an anxiety-producing one. Overload my tiny little brain with esoteric information? I met his eyes for a second, then quickly fixed my attention on the photograph of the Denver skyline visible over his left shoulder. I had no intention of being pulled into his magnetic laser beam again. I had to clear my throat a couple of times before I managed to speak. My knees were still threatening to buckle as I said, 'I wasn't expecting you tonight. I thought you said you'd be busy with coven business.'

'Yes.' He ignored my unspoken question. 'I did say that. And I must apologise.'

Involuntarily, I found myself falling into those turquoise eyes as the familiar fog engulfed my brain. I forced myself to focus on his lips. Big mistake. The tip of my tongue eased along the edge of my teeth as I remembered the feel of his mouth against mine.

Warm, soft, sensual, delicious ... orgasmic ...

I had to will myself to trigger any still-functioning neurons and finally released him, stepped to the side, and mumbled, 'Apologise? For what?'

His lips curled into a devilish grin and amusement flared in his kaleidoscopic eyes. He'd obviously read my embarrassing thoughts.

Damn mind-reading vampire.

Refusing to panic, I fought to regain control of myself. What the hell was wrong with me? Would I never be able to handle being in the same room with Devereux without acting stoned? Trust me to attract a male who's a walking recreational drug.

He inclined his head and his platinum curtain of hair swung forward. He raised his hands, palms out. 'Sincerely, you will get used to me. I will not always have this *intoxicating* effect on you. You may gaze into my eyes without fear.'

I must have looked sceptical because he locked eyes with me and . . . nothing happened. Or at least, nothing *more*. I was still fuzzy and slow from his last dose.

'So, uh, you said something about an apology?' I cleared my throat. 'I'm all ears.'

He quirked a brow and studied me intensely, probably looking for the elusive extra ears. Modern slang often confused him, though I was pretty sure I'd explained this phrase wasn't literal when I'd used it before. He never appeared convinced, though. He'd lived in Denver for only thirty years and hadn't made much of an attempt to Americanise himself, or to join the twenty-first century. Since he could move effortlessly through time and space merely by thinking and preferred earlier centuries and European countries, he tended to spend most of his time there. He'd admitted that he couldn't imagine vampires adopting 'passive' human activities like television- or movie-watching; the undead usually chose more active pursuits. Yeah, like draining mortals and clawing their way out of coffins.

Humour has always been my best defence. I smiled at the unlikely image of Devereux digging through clumps of earth – under any circumstances. The Master with dirty or blood-stained fingernails? No way!

'Yes, apology.' He frowned, apparently choosing to disregard my singularly unflattering train of thought. 'In my attempt to organise my various enterprises after the . . . *unpleasantness* on Hallowe'en—'

'Hmm. About that. We haven't had time to discuss Lucifer. I know you said I'm safe and you have your people protecting me twenty-four/seven, but he's one scary bloodsucker. How is it he's managed to stay away from you? What's going on with the search for him? I still have nightmares . . .'

He straightened, his expression and voice flat. 'You have nothing to worry about. I am completely in control of the situation. Now, as I was saying, I allowed my priorities to become skewed. Instead of arranging time alone with you, which is what I truly want, I found myself swept up in a mass of vampire bickering and infighting, and now I cannot find a moment of peace without someone insisting I settle a disagreement or deal with one problem or another.'

His chin lifted. 'In olden times, no one would have dared bother me with such nonsense. But today a Master's role is more diverse.' He clenched his fists. 'And I have had a pressing matter on my mind.' His eyes went cold. 'I have unfinished business with someone who overstepped his bounds: a situation I have vowed to rectify.' He relaxed his hands and stared out into the night. Then he shook his head and visibly calmed himself.

Whoa! That was an impressive mood shift – too bad psych meds don't work on the undead. And why the hell didn't he answer my questions about Lucifer?

I moved around my desk and sat in my chair. 'This might sound like a cliché but I'm here if you want to talk about whatever's going on with you. Obviously somebody's pissed you off.'

And apparently you have one hell of a temper.

He sauntered around behind my desk and bent to run a gentle fingertip across my lower lip. 'Yes, someone did indeed *piss me off*, and I am having difficulty keeping my anger under control.' He stood, giving me the not-so-subtle signal that the topic was now closed. 'I appreciate your willingness to listen, but he is not worth our time. This is the longest we have been together in days without interruption.' He smiled wryly. 'And had it not been for a human customer at The Crypt inquiring about the club's plans for New Year's Eve, I would have completely forgotten the importance mortals place upon this date.'

Momentarily confused, I blinked to slough off the last remnants of Devereux's eyeball voodoo and his emotional ping-pong. 'Oh, yeah – this *is* New Year's Eve, isn't it?' I laughed. 'Obviously I'm not one of those mortals who mark the date on my calendar.'

Although after the week I've had, tossing back a few glasses – or bottles – of bubbly sounds pretty good.

Surprise flashed across his face, followed by disappointment. 'This is not a holiday you celebrate? Have I misunderstood yet another contemporary custom?'

'Oh no.' I patted his arm. He took everything so deadly seriously. 'You didn't misunderstand: it is a big deal, for lots of people – it just hasn't been on my radar for a couple of years. Basically, I can take it or leave it. Why would you feel the need to apologise?'

Doubt flickered in his eyes as he lifted one of my long curls and tucked it behind my ear. He sat on the edge of my desk. 'I should have made plans with you for this important evening. It was my responsibility to create a memorable occasion for you and I almost failed in my duty. For that, I apologise.'

'Your *responsibility*?' I frowned and rubbed my forehead. 'Where did you get that idea?' I grew up with people deciding every aspect of my reality: been there, done that.

His eyes widened at my stern expression. We'd had this

discussion before. 'Perhaps "responsibility" is too strong a word. Let us say instead it is my *pleasure*. I realise a modern woman neither expects nor wants her mate to arrange her life. But might I assume you would enjoy a surprise were I to offer one?'

I decided to ignore the 'mate' reference. He was exceptionally clever about sneaking that word into our conversations, although without ever explaining it, of course. I was beginning to realise that Devereux was astoundingly single-minded.

'A surprise?' My stomach tightened. Even the notion of what might constitute a *surprise* for a vampire made my mouth go dry. 'What kind of surprise?' I did my best to keep suspicion out of my voice.

'Something that will appeal to your professional curiosity and provide you with additional information about my world,' he said, ignoring my inner fear-fest.

Hmm. That sounded reasonable enough – but I remembered the last time he'd offered to educate me about the vampire universe: by taking me to a protection ritual around Hallowe'en he'd organised on my behalf that completely destroyed every idea I'd ever had about the nature of reality. The bizarre mix of bloodsuckers and magic and the appearance of Devereux's dead mother totally rewrote my inner script about *possible* versus *impossible*. And I was pretty sure it had permanently fried a few brain cells in the process.

'Yes.' He responded to my unvoiced concerns, frown lines once again creasing his brow. 'The ritual was challenging for you. My world – the world of the vampires – bears little resemblance to that to which you are accustomed.' He smirked. 'But as you have often said, you set yourself upon this course, so it behooves you to learn as much as you can about your preternatural clients.' He did that nifty Old-World head-bow thing again. 'I am pleased to be able to assist in that endeavour.'

He still hadn't told me what the surprise was. Why did I think I wasn't going to like it? 'This surprise will appeal to my professional curiosity? What does that mean, exactly?'

'You shall accompany me to a vampiric handfasting ceremony, the bonding of two important immortals – a pagan wedding. The rite is ancient and intimate. You will witness things no mortal has ever seen.'

And lived to tell about it, I'll bet . . .

I became temporarily distracted by a mental horror movie featuring hundreds of vampires feasting on the blood of enchanted, unwilling humans. Then the scene quickly shifted to another, this one of hapless mortals being thrown into pits filled with ravenous bloodsuckers in a feeding frenzy—

'Kismet?' Devereux tapped my shoulder, his face a mask of distaste. 'I fear you are doomed to disappointment if that is what you are expecting to find at the gathering. It is for all intents and purposes a simple party.'

'A *simple* party?' My laugh held a sardonic incredulity that I suspected would tick him off. 'Like the last event you brought me to was a *simple* ritual?'

Clearly impatient, he rose, circled to the front of my desk and shook his finger at me. He'd just opened his mouth to respond when a familiar bloodsucker-moving-through-time-and-space *pop!* preceded the arrival of a beefy long-haired vampire.

The unexpected visitor materialised near Devereux and bowed from the waist, sending purple-streaked black hair cascading to the floor. 'Excuse me, Master, but your attention is needed in the shipping area. The coffins you ordered have arrived.'

'Why does that require my attention?' Devereux barked.

'Deliveries of all kinds take place every night. You may sign for the merchandise, as always.' He flicked his fingers in dismissal.

'There's a problem, Master.' The messenger fidgeted, twisting his hands together, his eyes wide. 'It appears the coffins are already ... occupied.'

'Occupied?' Devereux stared at the messenger for a few seconds.

It took me a moment to realise he was reading the other vampire's mind. 'What's going on?' I asked halfheartedly. As curious as I always was about the things vampires didn't say out loud, I really couldn't get too enthusiastic about anything having to do with coffins – especially occupied ones. I had started to realise there were things I *really* didn't need to know – at least if I wanted to stay sane. Could a human brain even process such an unnatural experience as the one I'd stumbled into? I wondered what would happen to mine if I kept trying. Maybe that was what Devereux meant by *esoteric information*. Could someone truly be driven mad by exploring a nonhuman reality? There'd been no mention of that possibility in any of the popular vampire movies.

'It looks like there was a mix-up at the mortuary and instead of sending six empty coffins as usual, they mistakenly delivered the remains of half a dozen humans who perished in the recent cult suicides here in Denver.'

I cringed at the reference to the grisly event currently saturating the daily news. Yet another charismatic guru had convinced his flock that death was the answer. Funny thing, though – the leader himself hadn't smoked any of the tainted marijuana.

Six empty coffins? *As usual?* I wondered what story Devereux had told the mortician to explain why he needed regular deliveries. Of course, he probably didn't have to say anything – he could use his handy little mind-control trick. Or maybe the funeral home director wasn't human. I still wasn't used to how many vampires nested in the Mile-High City.

'I am sorry, Kismet,' said Devereux, sighing, 'but once again duty calls. It is important for me to confront the mortuary director in person. He has been creating problems, behaving erratically. We will exchange the coffins and erase the memories of any mortals involved.' He lifted my hand and kissed it. 'I shall call for you at your home soon. I look forward to sharing many uninterrupted hours together.' He sent a silent message to the other vampire, who disappeared, then turned back to me. 'Until then.'

'Wait!' I hurried from behind the desk and grabbed his arm. 'What should I wear to this *simple party*?' I imagined something floor-length, with long sleeves and a high collar. A very high collar. Or maybe a hazmat suit. Hopefully I wouldn't be the entrée. I trusted Devereux to keep me safe from his less-civilised minions, but I'd learned that his ideas of 'normal' inhabited a far different galaxy from mine.

'Ah, yes, thank you for reminding me. Your clothing for the event has been transported to your bedroom. You will find everything you need. And please, wear your protective pentagram. Now, if you will excuse me—'

Why did he mention the pentagram if this is just a simple party?

He vanished.

CHAPTER 2

I was surprised and pleased to find my townhouse pretty much as I'd left it.

No bodyguard vampires camped out in my living room. No undead handmaidens ordered by Himself to attend to my every need. No snarly Luna – Devereux's personal assistant and evil human-hating bigot – waiting for an excuse to relieve me of my O positive.

I'd had a talk with *the Master* about his tendency to be over-bearing, to assume he knew more about what was best for me than I did, and he'd sworn to respect my personal space. Of course, what that meant to a vampire was anybody's guess. In his defence, it had to be a challenge to stop giving orders after centuries of doing so, but I could tell he was trying.

He was true to his word about my clothing, though: a stunning silver dress shimmered like liquid mercury on my bed. I lifted the silky moonlight by the shoulders and held it up to eye level. So much for my high-collar fantasy. The only way to transform this beyond-plunging neckline into something less fang-tempting was to wear a turtleneck sweater underneath it.

I was thankful my mother's contributions to my DNA hadn't

started to droop yet, because apparently a bra was out of the question.

Despite the plunging neckline, I had to admit the dress was beautiful, and my wish for a floor-length skirt and long sleeves had been fulfilled.

A matching hooded cloak lay draped over the back of a chair. Silver stiletto-heeled sandals sat conspicuously next to my dresser. I'd just pulled my hair up into a bun and pivoted to head into the bathroom for a quick shower when something glittery caught my eye. I moved over to the nightstand to find an antique-looking necklace, a large cross – at least three inches long – made of what appeared to be diamonds.

Devereux never ceased to amaze me.

He'd explained religious symbols had no effect – negative or positive – on vampires, so it wasn't likely he expected me to fend off his bloodsucking colleagues by waving the necklace at them. But as clever and intelligent as Devereux was, he didn't have much of a sense of humour, so why would he give me a cross? I scooped it into my hand to test the substantial weight. I didn't even want to think about the fortune that would be dangling in my cleavage.

And he needn't have reminded me to wear the pentagram necklace. At my request he'd removed the spell he cast on the symbol that had made it a permanent accessory, thereby forcing me to wear it. But after the insanity with Lucifer, one of the evil personalities of the maniac who'd stalked me and almost killed Devereux, I never removed the charm from around my neck. I'd take any edge I could get.

The fact that Devereux forgot I always wore it provided more evidence of his distracted state of mind. I hadn't known him long enough to have any meaningful opinions about his *normal* behaviours, but he'd been setting off my therapist's alarm since he recovered. I knew the crazed Lucifer wouldn't give up so easily – I'd become a psychological fixation for the mad killer – and I was glad to have magical protection while I studied everything I could about the various forms of Dissociative Identity Disorder, formerly known as Multiple Personality Disorder. Not that gathering knowledge would keep me safe from the horrifying lunatic, but delving into familiar subject matter gave me the illusion of control in the midst of the chaos.

After I finished my shower, I wet the ends of my long hair so the curls would re-form and reapplied my makeup – opting for a more dramatic look than usual, given the circumstances. I focused on accenting my sky-blue eyes, which stood out against my pale skin and dark hair. I'd noticed mascara was plentiful at vampire gatherings. Maybe the undead owned stock in some of the various cosmetic companies. Studying myself in the mirror, my reflection reminded me of Margaret Keane's 'Waif' paintings. The subjects of her portraits expressed both wide-eyed wonder and stunned horror. I wondered which description applied to me.

I was halfway through shaking several aspirin into my palm when I realised the headache had almost vanished. Only a vague, spacey sensation remained, along with a slight tension at the base of my neck.

'Well, yay! The hot shower did the trick!'

Had it really been less than three months since I'd fallen through the vampiric Looking Glass and landed in a dark night of the soul? I didn't understand why such frightening things fascinated me. Why in the world would I choose to hang out with predatory blood-drinking creatures? Did I have a death wish? If I were my client, I'd wonder if I had something to prove.

But then, how many therapists ever got the opportunity to explore a nonhuman species and write about it? Wouldn't it be professionally irresponsible of me to pass on the chance? Scientists put themselves in harm's way all the time. No guts, no glory.

Thinking about the bizarre research lottery I'd won made me wish I could tell my therapist, Nancy, the truth about my vampire clients and my new . . . *boyfriend*, for lack of a better word. That conversation would be worth recording with my cell phone camera. 'Oh, by the way, Nancy,' I said aloud. 'I forgot to tell you I've been treating actual vampires. Authentic fanged nightwalkers. The so-called bloodsucking fiends we all know and fear. Despite their negative PR, turns out they aren't all horrible monsters. Some are actually afraid of the dark or terrified of blood.

'And not only are vampires real, I'm having mad, passionate sex with the Grand Pooh-Bah. Not to mention the fact that I let him drink my blood. And I like it!' I laughed, thinking about the expression on her face. Of course, I'd only be laughing until the men with the straitjacket and the butterfly net arrived. After that, I'd be making clay animals, staring out of the window and swallowing my meds like a good girl in one of Denver's psych wards.

Needing someone to talk to had become a serious problem. There was always Lieutenant Bullock, the cop I'd worked with during the paranormal murders back in October. She knew the truth about the vampires. As did Cerridwyn, a savvy tarot reader whose psychic abilities were second only to Devereux's. Or maybe my trusty FBI friend, profiler and forensic psychologist Alan Stevens. But I didn't feel I could confide totally in any of them, Lieutenant Bullock and Cerridwyn because I didn't know either well enough to share intimate details, and

Alan because, well, Alan and I had some unfinished personal business of our own. I doubted if he'd enjoy hearing about Devereux.

Maybe there'd never be anyone I could talk to.

I took a breath to dispel the morbid thoughts, clicked on the radio and stepped into the silver gown. The snug fabric moulded to my upper body and hips, then flared out into a fluid skirt. It fit perfectly. Of course, it would. Devereux never missed.

The stiletto heels added inches to my usual five feet eight. I'd become better at walking in the wobbly shoes but appreciated not having to when I was with Devereux, thanks to the vampire ability to move via thought. There was nothing like the fear of falling off one's footwear to heighten the appeal of flashing through time and space.

The mercurial gown's daring V-shaped neckline plunged down below my navel. If the material hadn't been so tight, Mother Nature's bounty would have been in danger of bursting free, causing me to draw more attention to myself than I already would by being mortal. Just to be safe, I decided to apply two-sided tape on the inside of the dress to keep the fabric anchored on the modest side of my nipples.

The radio station played number thirty-five of the Top 100 songs of the past fifty years. I couldn't resist spinning in a circle, enjoying the sensation of the silky skirt floating out around me as I sang along with an old Beatles tune my parents often listened to. Not being particularly graceful, I wasn't much of a dancer, but it was fun to move.

Singing louder, I lifted the long chain of the cross necklace over my head, letting the relic fall just below my breasts. The moment it touched my skin, heat radiated from it. I palmed it to see if I was imagining things but found the warmth noticeably there.

Suddenly the familiar fuzzy sensation commandeered my brain as a dull pain gripped my skull.

'You are truly beautiful, my love.'

I startled and choked mid-lyric, released the cross and turned towards Devereux's voice. I pressed my hand over my pounding heart and hurried to turn off the radio. 'Hey! No sneaking up on me. You know I'm still a little paranoid after the horror show we went through on Hallowe'en. Cough or clear your throat or something, okay?'

'I am sorry.' He bowed his head. 'I did not try to sneak up on you, but I was so engrossed in watching you dance that I forgot to announce myself. Forgive me. I will say again, you are truly beautiful. I knew that dress would suit you.'

'Thank you, for the compliment and the dress.' My cheeks warmed with discomfort.

Speaking of beautiful . . . Now that my heart had resumed its normal rhythm and my brain had turned off the 'flight or fight' warning, I studied the gorgeous vampire in front of me. He wore a black European-cut tuxedo with a shirt made of the same fabric as my dress. Although saying he 'wore' it didn't begin to cover the situation. Like a high-fashion model, he displayed the suit. His platinum hair flowed down the front of his chest like a silky veil. The blue-green of his mesmerising eyes looked amazing contrasted against the dark of his lashes and eyebrows. Perfectly sculpted bones framed a flawless face. Full, expressive lips parted in the most inviting manner before white, fangless teeth flashed in a breathtaking smile.

I felt like a teenager going to the prom with the school heart-throb. Thanks to his brain-numbing effect, my mouth went slack and I hoped I wasn't drooling. As his spicy scent filled my nostrils, I hyperventilated and wondered why we were standing so far apart when we could be skin-to-skin and doing so many other interesting things.

He must have noticed my eyes glaze over because he stepped close, lifted my chin with his finger and stared at me. The skin between my eyebrows – what Devereux called my *third eye*, of all things – tingled and itched before pain crisscrossed my forehead. 'Ouch! Dammit.' I rubbed my finger across the painful area. 'What the hell did you just do?'

There'd better not be a lightning bolt on my forehead!

'I have once again added a layer of protection over your sixth chakra so you will not become so easily entranced or affected by me, or any vampire.'

I opened my mouth to take issue with his New Age reference to my *sixth chakra*, but the fog and discomfort in my brain had already started to clear so I kept my thoughts to myself. Or at least as much to myself as was possible around an intrusive mind-reading immortal.

He laughed, letting me know he'd picked up my mental monologue.

His mind-reading and the fact that he found me amusing were fast losing their charm. I was willing to put up with a lot to meet my professional goals, but he'd crossed a line.

'Listen, dammit!' Shaking off a few more mental cobwebs, I put a no-bullshit expression on my face and put my hands on my hips. 'Knock it off. This isn't funny. I mean it. It's bad enough that my brain turns into candyfloss whenever I'm near your neuron-melting energy, but you need to stop invading my privacy. It's disrespectful. Chauvinistic.' I poked my finger into his chest, forcing him to back up in surprise. 'If you want us to spend time together, my brain can't be an open book to you.' *Poke.* 'I'm a separate person, not one of your minions.' *Poke.* 'You need to make a new decision because I'm not going anywhere if you won't discipline yourself. If you need to exert that much control, I'm sure there are many other women – besides me – who'd be happy to accommodate you.' Whirling, I plopped down on the edge of the bed, adjusted the high-heeled sandals and tried to hold onto my anger.

'My apologies,' he said, his tone contrite. 'You are correct – I have been indulging myself and that was wrong. I will respect your wishes. In my defence, it is challenging not to notice that which is broadcast so strongly. Thoughts are powered by emotions, and yours are exceedingly potent—'

'What?' I stood slowly. 'Are you saying you're forced to read my thoughts because they're strong? That it's my fault? You can't be expected to restrain yourself?'

'No!' His brows rose over wide eyes. 'Certainly not.' The shocked expression on his face was worth the price of admission. I'd bet it had been centuries since anyone questioned his behaviour. He paused a few seconds before speaking. 'I was merely explaining, but I understand what you are saying and I am truly sorry. I swear I will try my best not to intrude.' He lifted a finger into the air, which often preceded one of his mini-lectures – in addition to giving him the added benefit of shifting the topic – and began pacing back and forth. Sensuality in motion. Devereux valued the acquisition of knowledge and enjoyed his role of teacher. 'I would like to correct one thing, though. The notion of *chakras* is much older than any New Age practice.' He saw my lips tighten and he stopped, thrusting his hands towards me, palms out. 'Do not be angry. I picked up that thought before you insisted I stop reading you. And since you often ask me to share bits of my history, I thought you might be interested in the fact that working with the energy centres in the body was common among the Druids of my time, as well as in other cultures.'

'Druids?' My acceptance of his lane change let him know I realised he hadn't intentionally broken his word, but the jury was still out about his willingness to avoid ransacking my head. 'Oh yes, of course: you said there are secret Druid groups still in existence, groups we humans aren't aware of. You'll have to tell me more about that sometime. I know nothing about Druids, outside of human sacrifices.' As the dots connected in my mind, I frowned. 'Hey, wait – are you saying that Druids were vampires?'

'Human sacrifices?' One perfect eyebrow arched. 'Druids were far too advanced to participate in anything so primitive. You must be thinking of the Incas, who – if I recall my time there – did indeed practise the death arts. But it is true that many Druids were vampires. In fact, it was a highly revered state of being. Many a young Druid, myself included, lusted after immortality before we realised what it meant. We worked very hard to join the ranks of the undead.'

My brain screeched to a halt. *What? His time with the Incas? Death arts? Vampire Druids?*

'You *chose* to be a vampire?' I asked, half-afraid to hear the answer. 'Why would you choose that?' *But then, his deceased mother did tell me it isn't easy to become a vampire. One has to have 'pure intention' – whatever that means.*

'Yes,' he said softly with a frown, looking uncomfortable. I didn't know if he'd gone back to reading my thoughts or if my judgemental tone had given him all the information he needed. 'I was ... mentored by a powerful immortal from a neighbouring clan. To my people, living for ever – or at least for a very long time – was the next evolutionary step. Drinking human blood was understood to be a way to pass knowledge from one being to another. All wisdom and experience held by the donor is transmitted to the recipient. It was considered a sacred rite.'

Drinking blood passes knowledge? What kind of knowledge?

And the media thought the sensationalist notion of aliens landing in spaceships to probe human orifices was the hot story. Devereux had just shared enough strange material to fill hundreds of episodes of *Unexplained Mysteries*.

I wanted him to talk more about how one became a vampire. He'd been very mysterious about it so far. 'But what do you mean—?'

He stepped forward, helped me to my feet and wrapped me into his arms. He kissed my forehead. 'Let us not spend our brief time together tonight discussing such weighty topics,' he coaxed. 'There will be ample opportunity for you to learn more about my history. For now, the celebration awaits.'

Was he avoiding the subject again? What was the big secret? I inhaled his signature fragrance, sighed with pleasure and decided it didn't matter. For some reason, talking about his background made me tense and anxious. I'd rather enjoy my Date Night with the Vampire.

He released me and strolled over to the chair holding the silver cloak. He lifted the shining fabric, arranged it around my shoulders and fastened the ornate Celtic knot clasp at my throat. His lips curved in a soft smile. 'I will be the most envied male at the gathering tonight. You are truly a vision.'

After a lifetime of being the quintessential nerd and therefore invisible to men, I sometimes found Devereux's compliments overwhelming. It was very frustrating to be so confident in my professional abilities, yet so insecure about the personal. 'Thank you,' I said, meeting his gaze, then averting mine. Such intensity was blazing from his face that I searched for a topic to distract him from whatever he was about to say. I'd seen that look in his eyes before and wasn't ready to navigate the emotional minefield lurking there. I couldn't handle talking about my being his *mate*. 'So why did you give me a cross to wear?' I wrapped my fingers around it. 'I thought religious items had no effect, one way or the other.'

'Ah,' he said, 'yes, indeed. Back to light and pleasant conversation. I gave you the cross, which is an heirloom from my birth family, because it marks you as mine.'

And here we go again . . .

'Yours?' I reached to remove the antique chain from around my neck. 'I thought we came to an agreement about your possessive tendencies. No woman—'

'Wait,' he said, gently grasping my hands, 'that is not what I meant. Once again, you are interpreting the situation from a human viewpoint. This is not about possessiveness. We will be among some of the most powerful of my kind. The fact that you accompany me will send a clear message to everyone about your standing in the vampire hierarchy. But I do have enemies, those who would find it amusing to challenge me – as Bryce did – by focusing on you. The cross holds my essence, and my family's, so no misunderstandings can occur. No vampire with any ability to perceive will be able to ignore the fact that you and I are extensions of one another. At least while you wear the totem.'

'I see,' I said, not seeing at all. 'How is it different from my pentagram?'

'The pentagram protects you specifically. As you discovered, it responds to hostile touch. The cross, on the other hand, alerts me to any danger you might be in, any change in your physical or psychic state – even faster than my sensing your emotions first hand. While wearing it, you are always in my consciousness, even if I am elsewhere. So, needless to say, please do not remove it tonight.'

'That sounds ominous.' His serious expression raised my

heart rate. 'Are you sure you don't want to dab some of your blood behind my ears to fend off your undead comrades?' I laughed at what I thought was a ridiculous notion.

He obviously didn't share my opinion because he stared intently at me. 'You want my blood?'

'No!' Had I said something important without meaning to? 'I was just kidding. Yuck. Lighten up, Master Devereux. Isn't this supposed to be a fun evening?'

'It will be, but you have raised an interesting option.'

'Seriously?' *Oh my God!* 'You want me to go out in public painted with blood? No way!'

'Not painted, but if you would consent to drink another sip of my blood, our connection would deepen – you would be strengthened. And I would be able to sense you even more easily than with the cross alone.'

'What do you mean, *another* sip?' This absurd discussion was getting way out of hand. 'I've never drunk your blood before. What's the matter with you?'

'Nothing is the matter with me. In this case, it is *your* memory that is faulty. At the protection ritual you drank from a chalice that contained not only my blood but the blood of many other powerful vampires.'

I froze as the horrible realisation hit home. *My God! He's right. No matter how much I want to deny it, I can't.*

'Well, so much for the so-called protection ritual. I drank that horrible concoction for nothing!' I ratcheted up my anger to mask emotions I didn't want to deal with. 'Lucifer got me anyway!'

His expression darkened as he straightened. 'Yes. He did. I apologise yet again. You may trust that he will be dealt with. If you would take more blood—'

What is wrong with him?

'No!' I shook my head theatrically. 'Really, Devereux. No! No more talk about me drinking blood. I'm weird enough as it is without starting to act like some of my vampire-wannabe clients. You'll just have to settle for the cross. Now, please,' I touched his arm, 'can we at least pretend this is a normal date and not scare me any more tonight?'

His expression relaxed instantly. He smiled and extended his elbow. 'Certainly. Shall we go?'

I linked arms with him and realised I hadn't asked an important question. 'Wait. Will I be the only human there?'

He lifted one shoulder. 'Perhaps—'

Where's the garlic?

'Perhaps? Are you saying I'll be the only food source in the room?' My stomach contracted so tightly I felt as if I'd swallowed rocks.

'No.' He patted my hand. 'Had you permitted me to finish my sentence, I would have assured you that while you might be the only mortal guest and therefore off-limits, there will, of course, be donors present. Did you assume otherwise?'

'Donors.' I sighed. 'Of course.'

How silly of me to think this would be a blood-free nightmare.

CHAPTER 3

A gentle breeze blew the hair back from my face as Devereux mentally transported us into a tunnel wide enough for a school bus to drive through. I experienced the familiar dizzy sensation as my physical body struggled to adjust to the new location. Travelling via thought was extraordinary, but unnerving. I doubted I'd ever get used to it.

We moved a couple of feet along the smooth cement, footsteps echoing, before I felt steady enough to let go of his arm. The passage smelled of moist earth, its walls painted a dull institutional green. The spooky place reminded me of a horror movie I'd seen where zombies invaded New York City and barricaded themselves in an underground mortuary. I shivered from the memory, as well as the cold and damp, noting that the eerie tunnel gave off a subtle creepy sensation.

'This doesn't look much like a party spot,' I said, hugging myself to ward off the inner and outer chill. I surveyed the long, empty corridor as we walked. Motion sensor lights flicked on ahead of us. 'Are you sure we're in the right place?' I asked, an edge of suspicion in my voice.

'Yes, this is the private entrance—'

I shivered.

He stopped walking and gathered me against him, his arm tight around my shoulders. 'How thoughtless of me to forget you would be sensitive to the cold in your lightweight cape. Inexcusable. Here.' Frowning, he released me, slipped out of his jacket and draped it over my shoulders, pulling me close again. 'Does that help?'

He looked so appalled at what he obviously considered his *faux pas* of forgetting I would experience the cold as a human rather than a vampire that I had to smile. He really could be a sweet man, if the word *man* could be used to describe an 800-year-old immortal.

'Yes.' I snuggled into the jacket. Warmth from his body lingered in the fabric along with his enticing fragrance. Since I knew drinking blood raised his physical temperature, I wondered where he'd got his meal. It hadn't come from me and I realised I didn't know how I felt about that. Was I jealous? Did I want *my* vampire only to suck blood from me? The absurdity of that question made me mentally roll my eyes. How deep into insanity had I sunk? 'Thanks. If I'd known we'd be tromping around in the cold, I would have worn long underwear and,' I lifted a foot to display a silver sandal, 'hiking boots.'

He smiled and began walking again, propelling me along. 'I sincerely am sorry. I have so much to learn.'

Either he really hadn't read my silent question about who he had drunk from, or he chose not to address it.

'Hey, everything's fine. I'm not that fragile. So where are we?'

'Aspen.'

Having his velvet voice so close to my ear caused a visceral reaction in several of my body's erogenous zones. *Steady, Kismet.* 'Aspen? Colorado?'

BLOOD THERAPY | 34

'Indeed. On the outskirts of the town, in the forest.'

'Well, huh.' I pulled the edges of his jacket closer around me and angled sideways, slipping out from under his arm. As nice as it felt to be tucked against him, I knew what happened when I spent too much time breathing in his vampire pheromones and I didn't want to have sex on the cement floor of a tunnel. 'I guess she was right.'

'Who was right?'

'I had a client last year who came down from Aspen for a session. She told me Aspen is full of vampires. I assumed she was referring to the psychic-vampire variety, but now I'm not so sure. She said I should look for the beautiful people wrapped in politically incorrect furs and wearing expensive cowboy boots the next time I explored the nightlife up here. According to her, those are the vampires.'

'I shall inform my associates that they are being noticed. It is never good to become too comfortable in a human environment. Drawing attention to oneself tends to have *sharp* consequences.' He grinned.

'Hey!' I bumped his hip with mine as we walked. 'You made a joke. I'm impressed.'

He eased his arm around my waist, holding me gently. 'I frequently say amusing things. I am told I have an excellent sense of humour.'

'Yeah. Told by your adoring devotees, who worship every pearl that drops from your lips. I've yet to see much evidence of this alleged sense of humour.'

'Ah, you wish to see evidence? I will take that as a personal challenge. Although you might discover that vampire humour is quite different from the human sort. It involves a lot more blood—'

Yuck. Of course it does. Change the subject . . .

'So.' I freed myself from his grasp again and put a few inches between us. As attracted as I was to him, I didn't want him to think he could control me as easily as he had Nicky earlier in my office. He had to remember that my life didn't revolve around him. 'What is this place? Do your friends live in some kind of underground bunker?'

'In a manner of speaking. You will appreciate this, Doctor Knight.' He sailed a hand through the air to indicate our surroundings. 'We are now in one of the sub-levels of an abandoned insane asylum – quite an infamous institution, if I recall – built in the early nineteen hundreds. Thirteen humans were murdered here under mysterious circumstances.' He no doubt heard my intake of breath. 'And before you assume the deaths were caused by vampires, let me assure you that was not the case. As a matter of fact, those thirteen deaths were not the first to occur in this cruel location.'

'What do you mean?'

'Between the notorious murders, other suspicious fatalities and the building having been erected on Pagan ritual lands, ghosts abound. I believe the homicides were committed by a delusional patient claiming to be possessed by several resident spirits. The current owner of the building tells me the haunting continues.' He stroked my arm. 'After hearing about your experience with the ghost in the mirror during my unfortunate confrontation with Bryce and Lucifer, I am sure you will enjoy communicating with our incorporeal guests tonight.'

What? Am I part of the entertainment? Me and the fortune-tellers?

'You could have warned me,' I grumbled, glaring at the amused vampire. 'Discovering I can see ghosts again wasn't good news, although I didn't realise that was what I was seeing as a child. The last thing I need is another so-called ability to add to my innate weirdness. Now I'm not only a nerd – I'm a paranormal nerd. Lucky me!'

I turned to look behind me to make sure we'd actually been moving forward. 'Have we stepped into a never-ending tunnel? Some vampiric wormhole through the fabric of time and space?' This place had started to feel like one of those bad dreams where the hallway just keeps extending and you never arrive anywhere. The motion-activated lights brightened as we approached and dimmed after we passed, leaving both ends of the passage in darkness. 'What's up with this tunnel? We've been here a long time. Are we caught in a time-loop?'

He glided in front of me and walked backwards, his movements as graceful as if he were on ice skates. His eyes sparkled mischievously. 'What is the hurry? I am thoroughly enjoying this undisturbed time together.' He grazed my lips with his. 'Tell me more about *nerd*. You have mentioned the term on other occasions, but there was no opportunity for me to ask questions. What is a *nerd*? And why do you believe you are one?'

In our short acquaintance, it was unusual for him to be so playful and I couldn't help but smile. 'I didn't think up the title for myself. It was bestowed upon me in childhood. I skipped grades in school a couple of times and wound up being much younger than my classmates, which meant I didn't have the socialisation skills normal for that grade level.' Sadness washed through me. 'Being a nerd means to be socially strange, focused on unpopular activities, and bookish. That was a perfect description of me. Plus I heard and saw things nobody else did. All in all, a recipe for a miserable childhood.'

Devereux reached out and took my hands, still effortlessly gliding backwards. 'I am sorry you had to endure such discomfort, but all those challenges made you the woman you are today and for that, I am very grateful.' He stopped suddenly and my forward momentum propelled me against his chest. He pulled me in for a hot, sizzling kiss. Then another. My toes curled in my stiletto shoes. *The man really does have marvellous lips.*

The kiss ended much too quickly.

'Okay. Kissing is good. Very good. No bloodstains. Do we really have to go to the party?'

He stepped back, his eyes mesmerising in the dim light. 'I gave my word that I would attend this handfasting, so I appreciate your willingness to accompany me. But please do not forget where we left off . . .' He traced his fingertip along my lower lip. 'We will leave early enough for other activities.'

Yikes. The words *other activities* caused my nipples to harden.

He stepped to the side and pointed to a set of wide, ornate double doors at the end of the tunnel, which we'd finally reached. 'We have arrived.'

'Why didn't you just think us into the place? Why did we have to take the tunnel?' I'd become very conscious of my toes going numb in the uncomfortable stilettos.

'First, I wanted time alone with you before we joined the others, and second, it is considered disrespectful and rude simply to pop into another powerful vampire's lair. This location is owned by a master vampire, Valentino, who is older than I am.'

'Valentino?' I held back a snicker. 'That's an interesting name for a vampire.'

'It is a nickname that reflects both his chosen profession and his romantic tendencies – like his namesake, he is an actor and an icon. His real name is quite difficult for English-speakers to pronounce. Many vampires refer to him as Louis, the character he played in a well-known vampire movie. He will never live that role down!' Devereux hooted. 'He said it was fun to play such an angst-ridden bloodsucker when he is actually much more similar to Lestat, who enjoyed the kill. Valentino wanted to try his hand at theatre again in the modern world. The last time he acted was in sixteenth-century England, where he was equally famous. He tells me he is thoroughly enjoying himself. Especially since he turned his latest wife.'

'Wait.' My mouth dropped open. 'Are you talking about who I *think* you're talking about? He's a vampire? And his wife—?'

'Indeed.'

'No way. That's absurd. Is this you showing me your sense of humour? Okay, you win. That was pretty good – you almost had me going.'

'I do not understand what you mean. What is absurd?'

'Please. The idea that ... Br – er, Valentino – is really a vampire. I've seen lots of his movies and they all have scenes shot in the daylight. How does he pull that off without bursting into flames?'

'Ah.' Devereux gave a half-shrug. 'You find it hard to believe someone so famous could hide his truth from the world. I suppose it does sound impossible. All vampires must be discreet. The movie scenes that absolutely must be filmed during the day feature a very unique body double. Valentino seeks out humans who resemble him at whatever age he is pretending to be and entrances them. They undergo surgery to become more perfect duplicates, which the attending doctors assume is merely celebrity obsession, and take over for him during the filming when necessary.'

'He *collects* humans? Like the vampire version of an entomologist?' *Oh. My. God!*

'Hmm. Perhaps. Of course, he controls their minds and even

possesses them psychically during important parts of the script. I told you we are able to communicate through dreams and the unconscious. It is very easy to manipulate humans, especially if the humans cooperate. You will likely notice several of Valentino's *doubles* here this evening. He takes very good care of them.'

Oh, yuck. He takes good care of his clones? Why do I keep expecting vampires to have human ethics?

'Will I be meeting Valentino himself tonight?'

One of the most famous actors in the world is a vampire who owns a haunted insane asylum in the mountains outside Aspen. His wife is a vampire, too. What's next? Werewolves, zombies and faeries? Bigfoot?

'Of course – Valentino and his wife are looking forward to it. They know how important you are to me.'

'Do they know *why* I'm important to you?'

'Certainly.'

'Well then, maybe I can ask them about it and they'll tell me.' I removed his jacket from my shoulders and handed it to him.

'There is no need.' He slipped the jacket on, leaned in and kissed my forehead. 'You may trust that I will tell you everything when the time is right. Come.'

But will the time ever be right? And why are you resisting?

His slippery response gave me an idea. Since we were going to be surrounded by Devereux's immortal chums, what would be the harm in asking a few innocent questions? Finding out what they knew about his real motivations? He didn't seem shy about sharing his thoughts concerning me with his otherworldly pals. What was the use of being a trained therapist if I couldn't manipulate – er, encourage people to tell me their secrets?

Devereux took my hand, stepped up to the door and knocked.

The doors magically opened to reveal a beautiful young woman dressed as a servant from an earlier century, who curtsied politely. 'Welcome, Master Devereux. Enter.'

We stepped inside and my senses boggled.

The interior of an immense castle stretched out before us – but not just any castle. I'd taken several professional trips to England over the years and my favourite place was Warwick Castle. While I experienced an affinity with many locations in Britain, visiting Warwick made me feel the most *at home*, as if I really had lived there. Not that I truly believed in reincarnation, but it was a pleasant fantasy. And now someone had replicated the historic landmark, right down to variations of the antiques and paintings.

I couldn't comprehend how such a gigantic castle had been constructed underneath the asylum. They must have had to dig deeper into the rock than my intellect could grasp. The spacious entryway flowed into a grand dining hall on one side and an elegant salon on the other. Copies of the artwork, tapestries and ancient weapons similar to the ones I remembered from the actual castle – and the piles of postcards I'd purchased – adorned the walls and exquisite furniture filled the space. Suits of armour lined the hallways. An exotic mix of sandalwood and patchouli scented the air. And equally amazing were the hundreds of stunningly dressed vampires milling about the place.

My midsection tingled, signalling that my Vampire Alert System had gone online.

Bloodsuckers of all shapes, sizes and colours mingled throughout the breathtaking estate, acting like *normal* party guests. Nearby, a short, fat, bearded male dressed like a Viking stood talking with a woman in a black burka, along with a tall, lovely Latina wearing the costume of a flamenco dancer and a regal dark-skinned male who looked like an African king. It was a freaking meeting of the Undead United Nations.

Still speechless, I glanced at Devereux and found him beaming at me.

'I recalled you mentioning your love of British castles once, so I knew you would be pleasantly surprised. Valentino's family actually owns Warwick, and he built a likeness here. Of course, one can never be sure which castle holds the original art and furnishings. He commissioned such good copies of everything, it is simply impossible for most to determine the real from the fake. We may very well be in the presence of the originals.'

I'd been so flabbergasted I hadn't noticed the young woman who'd opened the doors still standing there, waiting for me to relinquish my cloak.

'Oh, sorry,' I said as I snapped back to awareness and released the clasp. Devereux handed the wrap to her and she curtsied again and walked away.

As soon as I removed the garment, I felt exposed. Vulnerable. Tasty. I unconsciously placed a protective hand around my throat.

'You are perfectly safe here, my love,' Devereux said, either noting my discomfort or breaking his promise.

'If you say so.'

I feel like I just parachuted into the Serengeti, dipped in bloody gravy.

Safe? I didn't feel safe. Why had I agreed to come? Why did I keep putting myself in danger? After all the terrifying things I'd seen in the last three months, any sane person would have realised she was in over her head. What was it with my need to lift up every rock to see what's underneath? I suddenly remembered what curiosity did to the cat.

Devereux took my arm and we strolled into the ornate salon. Red and gold brocade covered the walls and a hand-crafted golden fireplace dominated the room. Large portraits of men and women in regal attire hung neatly, side by side. I scanned the area, looking for the donors he'd mentioned earlier, half-expecting to find them chained to walls or spread-eagled on dining tables with rubber tubing transporting the crimson elixir from their veins into collecting basins.

'Where are the donors being held?'

Devereux made a *tsk* sound. 'You are letting your imagination run away with you again, Doctor Knight. I told you there would be nothing unpleasant. Look.' He pointed to a section filled with individuals dressed in white sleeveless scoop-neck robes. 'Those are the donors. As you can see, they are enjoying themselves.'

That did appear to be the case. They laughed among themselves while circulating around a large wooden table heaped with a banquet of human food. The aromas wafting from the feast made my mouth water. Platters of roast beef, turkey and ham were complemented by almost every side dish a hungry human could ask for. Champagne flowed freely. Vampires certainly knew how to throw a party.

The words 'fattening up the cattle' suddenly popped into my mind.

Am I being paranoid or perceptive?

I tapped Devereux's arm. 'I don't think I ever asked you about human food. I know you said vampires don't eat it, but is that because you *can't* or you just don't want to? Does the smell or taste of it make you sick?'

He angled his arm around my waist and moved me closer to the banquet. 'Our bodies are not made for solid nourishment. Newborns discover quickly that attempting to ingest human fare always turns out badly. The smell can be unpleasant, but most of us have grown accustomed to it and no longer notice. Here.' He picked up a small crystal plate from the table and handed it to me. 'Have something. You probably have not eaten much today.'

Nodding in agreement, I sidled alongside the table and selected various appetisers and added them to my plate. He was right. It had been hours since I'd eaten anything.

Sampling the delicious options, I moved back to stand with Devereux, observing the two-legged cuisine. As I watched, a tall bald male approached one of the female donors and reached out his hand. She set her drink on the table, walked over to the man and exposed her throat. He eased behind her, snaked his arms around her waist and sank his fangs into her neck. Judging by her erect nipples, she appeared to be enjoying it. Her head dropped back against his shoulder and her facial muscles visibly relaxed.

I'd certainly seen my share of vampires feeding, but each time it took me by surprise. There was just something so *wrong* about it. Humans weren't supposed to be food. Unless, of course, it was me willingly donating to a certain blond-haired immortal. But that was different. Wasn't it?

Watching such an intimate thing began to feel creepy and I was glad when the bald man retracted his fangs and released the woman. He eased around in front of her, lifted her hand and kissed it before he bowed and drifted away. She breathed deeply, retrieved her champagne glass from the table and raised it in salute, then rejoined her companions as if nothing unusual had happened. The donor didn't look any worse for the experience, which had been oddly sterile.

Devereux tapped my shoulder. I turned to him and moment-arily wondered if watching the feeding had made him hungry.

'I have asked Anne, an old acquaintance, to help watch over you in case I must deal with unexpected business,' he said.

An old acquaintance? A female old acquaintance? Hmm ...

'Unexpected business?' I set my empty plate on an antique side-table, probably worth more than my house and car together. 'Are you planning to work tonight? I thought this was supposed to be time for us to be together. Isn't this a wedding?' I tensed and my heart stumbled. *Oh my God! He's going to leave me alone in a den of bloodsuckers!*

'Yes.' He stroked a finger down my cheek, undoubtedly having heard the blip in my heartbeat. 'It is a ceremony, which will begin soon. But when many master vampires are together in one place, often a little business must be transacted. You will be completely safe,' he continued. 'I asked Anne to stay near you to fend off overzealous suitors and to entertain you with her outrageous personality. I trust her – she is old and strong. As a matter of fact, she might also interest you from a therapeutic point of view, since she is quite self-absorbed. I believe you would diagnose Anne with Narcissistic Personality Disorder, at the very least.'

He'd obviously brought up a comfortable topic to soothe me.

Forcing myself to focus on his words instead of my dark imaginings, I said, 'You've been reading the *Diagnostic and Statistical Manual of Mental Health* again.' He was such a sponge for knowledge.

'Yes.' He draped his arm around my shoulders and guided us to a full-size statue of a knight in armour – it really was shining – riding a horse on the other side of the room. 'I enjoy learning new things, and the realm of the mind is especially fascinating. Narcissism, in particular, is prevalent among vampires, as you will no doubt discover in your professional work. And, of course, I wish to know more about whatever interests you.'

'Self-absorbed?' I snorted. 'Vampires? Gee, I hadn't noticed. Are you saying that also applies to you?'

He flicked his fingers in a dismissive gesture and grinned. 'Of course not. I am self-aware, which is an entirely different thing.'

'Uh-huh,' I said solemnly, 'we'll pretend that's true. So, you're sticking me with a chaperone who can't talk about anything but herself? What a pal. It's every therapist's dream to be saddled with the client from hell. I'm really jazzed about attending this party now.' I put a serious expression on my face. 'I'd appreciate if you'd try very hard not to leave me with anyone for long. Surely business can wait.'

He pulled me close. 'I will make every effort to remain by your side, but it has been my experience that vampire business often forces itself upon me at the most inopportune times. Just in case, allow me to contact Anne so I might introduce you.' He paused for a few seconds. 'Ah, yes. There she is.'

As I turned to look for my undead babysitter, my attention snagged on a man dressed in a filthy ankle-length baggy garment. He was running back and forth across the room holding a huge knife dripping with blood. His face was contorted with rage and he appeared to be chasing someone.

What the hell? Was he one of the donors, gone berserk? Or part of the entertainment?

My breath caught as he crashed directly into a large group of party-goers who were chatting in small circles in the centre of the crowded space.

CHAPTER 4

Waiting for the vampires to react to the man, for the screams and outrage – for the carnage – I steeled myself . . . but nobody noticed him. I blinked to make sure I'd seen the maniac, and there he still was, zigzagging through the crowd.

'Did you see that guy with the knife?' I asked Devereux, the pitch of my voice rising as I frantically tapped him on the chest.

'A guy with a knife? Where?' On full alert, he turned his head from side to side, his voice saturated with menace. Coiled power, ready to spring.

'There!' I gasped and pointed to the corner, where the fren-zied man tackled and straddled a woman dressed in the same kind of dirty loose-fitting nightgown he was wearing. He repeat-edly stabbed her, the bloody knife slicing through her chest with a wet, sickening sound. My stomach lurched. 'You have to stop him. The knife! He's killing her!' I grabbed Devereux's arm.

The woman's screams pierced the air, soaring easily over the Celtic music wafting from the kilted ensemble performing on a raised stage in an adjacent room.

'What man? I do not see anyone,' Devereux said fiercely as

he searched the area. 'And I do not smell spilled blood. Where is this attack? Take me there.'

Was he kidding? It wasn't like Devereux to be so insensitive. To refuse to help. How could he not see the man's crazed assault?

I tugged on Devereux's arm, pulling him towards the bloody scene. 'They're over here. You have to—' I stopped. As I stared at the murder unfolding before my eyes, I suddenly noticed that the man and his victim were superimposed on top of the group of vampires standing in the same spot.

Ghosts. Spectres only I could see. Great. But they looked so solid! Not wispy in the least. Almost as if I could reach out and touch them.

'Something is wrong,' Devereux whispered urgently as he turned towards me and grasped my upper arms. 'Your heart is pounding like a trapped animal. Your skin is hot. Fear emanates from you. I do not know how to help. I simply do not see the man to whom you are referring.'

'What?' I shifted my focus from the vision and met Devereux's concerned eyes.

He was staring at me, confused, worried. 'Perhaps I should not have brought you to such an intense place so soon. You were not ready. The energy has overwhelmed you.'

I can't argue with that.

I took a few deep breaths and forced myself to relax. After my heart rate calmed, I pressed my palm against his cheek. 'Sorry about that. You're right. Everything about vampires is intense and I might never be totally equipped to deal with the madness. But right now it isn't this place – it's me, my weirdness.'

His brows contracted into a 'V'. 'What do you mean?'

'I thought it was real.' I peeked once more at the ghostly

scene before looking back at Devereux. 'The murder. The blood. You said this place is haunted. I guess I get to witness ghosts all evening in addition to every other outrageous thing that happens at a vampire wedding.'

'Ah.' Understanding lit his face like a child's, all distress gone. 'Ghosts. You are seeing more incorporeal echoes from the past. Such a rare and wonderful gift. Extraordinary.'

Extraordinary? Try extraordinarily weird. And exhausting. I rubbed my arms to get rid of the goosebumps.

'Will you show me?' Devereux asked.

'Show you what?'

'The ghost. Picture the man with the knife and his victim in your mind – let me see how they appear to you.'

'Why couldn't you see them in my mind before?'

'I did not look there – you asked me not to intrude. I thought something had happened in the room that I could not see. And besides, like everyone else I can only give my attention to one thing at a time.'

'Okay, I guess that makes sense. Tune in. I'll show you.' I shifted my attention back to the butchery in the corner, dissecting every detail. The vision replayed like a repeating tape loop.

'Yes, I see,' he said eagerly after a few seconds. 'That must be the notorious tormented mortal killer. I am sorry you must witness such a miserable thing, and yet even you must admit you have admirable talents. But for now . . .' He closed the distance between us. 'Let me distract you from the gruesome sideshow.' He pressed his lips to mine and the room disappeared.

I sank into the blissful softness of his lips and mindlessly wrapped my calf around his. He did always manage to rouse my hormones.

'Devereux, you naughty boy,' said a smoky female voice. 'You call me over and then you make me wait while you play with your human.'

The sound snapped me out of my lust trance and I jerked back, startled by the proximity of the woman who was standing much too close. A quick jab of pain behind my right eye radiated through my skull-bones and my vision clouded. I took a couple of steps back to reclaim my personal space. She had to be old, because in my experience, the older the vampire, the less the social niceties matter.

The woman was petite, no more than five feet tall, wearing a low-cut burgundy gown displaying her ample assets to good advantage. Thick light-brown hair spilled over her shoulders. Her green eyes sparkled impishly in her pale face and a wide smile spread her full lips.

'Anne,' Devereux said, 'it is good to see you. It has been too long.' He kissed her on both cheeks, then took her hands briefly. 'Let me introduce you to Kismet.'

'Well, well.' She turned to me, one eyebrow raised. 'I have heard about you. The mortal who has captured the mighty Devereux.' She closed the still-too-slight distance between us and inhaled deeply. 'Oh my – she does smell delicious. I do hope you intend to share, my friend.'

Despite the lingering brain-fuzzing effects of Devereux's preternatural kiss, the hairs on my arms rose and my throat tightened. This vampire wasn't even pretending I wasn't food. I was sure every bloodsucker in the room sensed the spike of fear that burst off of me.

And, to prove it, hundreds of eyes turned in my direction.

A ghostly slaying and a hungry predator. Are we having fun yet?

'You know better than that, Anne. Behave yourself,' Devereux said, an edge sharpening his voice as he moved to stand at my side with his arm around my waist.

He kissed the top of my head, then looked around coolly at those staring, and all the gazes shifted away from me. Saved by the Grand Pooh-Bah Vampire.

'Oh yes.' Her laugh was a little hysterical-sounding. 'That was excellent, Devereux. Warning off the entire herd of them all at once. You certainly haven't lost your touch.' Anne gave an unabashed grin. 'I'm only teasing. I didn't mean to scare her. You're always so serious, my lad. I just wanted to get a rise out of you. She is lovely.'

'Yes, she is,' he said, his tone taking no prisoners.

'And feisty, too, I hear. A sword-wielding avenger. Bravo, Devereux. It's about time you took a mate.'

'Please don't talk about me as if I'm not here,' I said, exasperation allowing me to finally form coherent words. I looked back and forth between them, blinking to clear my hazy vision. 'It's very rude.' That sounded brave, didn't it? Now if only my hands would stop shaking . . . Why did I keep believing Devereux when he insisted I'd be safe in these bizarre situations? Seriously, how much preternatural terror could my mind handle?

'I apologise, my love.'

'Devereux!' said a smooth English-accented male voice behind me. 'There you are. I've been waiting for you to arrive. And how marvellous – you've brought your woman.'

Devereux turned us towards the speaker. 'Valentino, allow me to introduce Doctor Kismet Knight. The very same Kismet whose arrival I foretold eight hundred years ago with my painting.'

Shit on a stick. The pain in my temples throbbed. I swallowed hard and tried to speak, without success. It really was him. With an English accent. And fangs.

A vampire movie star knows about Devereux's portrait of me? How the hell am I supposed to respond to such weirdness?

I stared at his teeth and played with the antique cross around my neck – not because I thought it would ward off an undead actor, but because it gave me something to do with my hands.

'Oh, the fangs. Forgive me,' Valentino said, making excellent eye contact while gliding his tongue over his pointed teeth.

I shifted my eyes to stare at his nose. According to the strong tingle in my midsection Valentino was a very powerful vampire and I was having enough trouble staying focused as it was.

'I just ate and forgot to retract the buggers,' he said. The sharp incisors vanished into his gums. His famous dimples appeared. 'There. Much more politically correct.' He lifted my hand and kissed the back. 'I can't believe this elusive bachelor is finally making a commitment.' Raising a brow, his lips spread into a wicked grin. 'You simply *must* tell me how you managed it. Some of us have had a bet going for aeons.'

I cleared my throat and finally managed to say, 'Hello, it's nice to meet you.'

He's much better looking in the flesh ... such as it is.

He laughed heartily. 'I'll bet it's damn strange to meet me, since you didn't know about my true nature. And I'm sure our tight-lipped Devereux never said a word until tonight. No wonder you're a bit tongue-tied.'

Several of Valentino's doubles crowded in behind him, smiling and drinking champagne. One who looked like the long-haired sex object from *Thelma and Louise* stood next to an older *Inglorious Basterds* version. They raised their glasses in salute. I nodded politely.

Just when I thought I'd seen everything ... There are obviously no limitations on the creepy scale.

Devereux tightened his hold around my waist, reclaiming my attention. 'Kismet is remarkably resilient. She has a marvellous ability to acclimatise to our preternatural world.'

I kept the strained pseudo-smile on my face, feeling like the only exhibit in an alien zoo. Acclimatise? Was he referring to the fact that I didn't run screaming every time I thought about it?

I studied Valentino's face. He looked much younger than he had in the last few movie roles I'd seen, about the age he was when he played Louis in that hit movie. I'd loved that film.

'It doesn't take a vampire to know what you're thinking.' Valentino said. 'Yes, I was able to play myself as I actually appear in that movie.' He laughed. 'In fact, I scared the blood out of the fellow who played the reporter when I spent an evening with him, giving him an up-close-and-personal experience of having one's neck sucked. No wonder his performance was so good.'

Geez. Devereux was right about vampire humour being bloody. I'll never get used to this.

Valentino cocked his head as if listening to something I couldn't hear. 'You'll have to forgive me again, dear Kismet – my wife just reminded me that we require Devereux's presence for a moment. I trust Anne will keep you amused while he takes care of a little coven business?' He turned to Devereux. 'De Sade is acting up again.'

'The Marquis is here? Will he never learn?'

'He's demanding to see you. He says he's heard the rumours and wants to see for himself if you're still the mighty warrior you used to be. I told him—'

'Let us not discuss that here.' Devereux interrupted, his tone brusque.

Valentino looked at me. 'Ah, yes, of course.'

'What's going on? What rumours?' I asked. *The Marquis de Sade? Really?*

Devereux shifted his gaze to me and pressed his soft lips to mine in a quick kiss. 'Nothing important, but if I do not handle de Sade now, I will be forced to clean up a mess later. The Marquis has a bad habit of drawing human attention to us. I will return as quickly as possible.' He brushed his fingers across the pentagram and the diamond cross before tracing my collarbone. 'In the meantime, you are completely safe with Anne. And if you need me, just hold the cross in your hand and say my name.'

Before I could respond, Devereux and Valentino vanished.

I turned to Anne, who exposed her teeth at me with her fangs fully extended. I gasped. Such long fangs for such a tiny woman.

She laughed at my startled reaction. 'I'm sorry.' Her fangs retracted into her gums. 'Just couldn't resist. I hardly ever get the chance to frighten a human these days.'

I blew out a breath, calming myself, and grasped the cross again. 'I see.' *No, I don't.* 'Well, if it's all the same to you, I'd appreciate it if you wouldn't do that. I don't know if you can understand, but it's extremely strange trying to fit into a world so different from my own. It's been a pretty steep learning curve, and mostly I'm just trying not to have a heart attack.'

As Devereux had so blithely abandoned me to the asylum inmates, what else could I do but use my therapy skills? Provide a little personal disclosure to create a bond? Noticing my headache had increased, I pressed my temples with my index fingers, trying to remember which meridians in Chinese medicine helped with pain relief. Maybe a migraine was being triggered by the strong incense.

Of course, she'd probably prefer I open a vein.

A fangless smile curved her lips. 'No open veins required. I actually do understand – there were many times when I lived as a swan among ducks. In fact, during my most notorious life experience, I was executed for being different.' She paused and pointed at the donors. 'Let's go and sit near the humans and you can have some champagne while we chat. At least I can watch you enjoy it. A good glass of wine might be the only thing I truly miss about being mortal. You know,' she pointed at my head, 'you really should take something for that headache. Everyone in the room can read your pain and it's rather enticing to the undead.'

'Really? Everyone can sense it?'

'Well, not everyone, but certainly those of us who are accustomed to reading victims' – er, mortals' energy.'

Victims?

'I don't have any pain medication with me.'

'Pity.' She gave a half-smile. 'I suspect our host doesn't have a well-stocked medicine cabinet.'

'Why didn't Devereux notice I wasn't feeling well? He's usually very perceptive.'

'Probably because he never kept humans close before he met you. He likely doesn't even remember what a headache feels like since we don't experience them, or how one might incapacitate you.'

I accepted a glass of champagne from a server and smiled at the donors, who were still standing in small groups around the buffet table. They acknowledged me as I followed Anne to a nearby couch and sat.

'You have a question about Valentino. Go ahead. Ask.'

'What?' It took me a few seconds to realise Anne had been eavesdropping on an inner dialogue in which I'd been speculating how the famous vampire had kept his first wife in the dark about his true nature. 'Well, you obviously already know what I was thinking. How was it possible for him to be with his first wife without exposing his secret? Did he turn her, too?'

'No. He has the gift of precognition and he knew a more suitable mate would appear. Some humans are much more susceptible to being entranced than others. He had to do very little to retain the mystery. Enough said?'

'Yeah, I guess so. I just can't imagine how he pulled it off.'

'Many famous vampires have human wives at some point.' She scanned the crowd, then nodded towards a group of vampires standing nearby with their backs to us. 'Look over there. I'm going to send them a mental message.'

A gorgeous dark-haired male standing next to a blonde woman wearing bright-red lipstick turned and lifted his goblet to Anne. The man on his other side raised his glass as well.

They all looked familiar.

Anne bobbed her head in acknowledgement and waved.

'It appears most of the cast of that infamous movie is here tonight. It's rare for them all to be in one place at the same time. I believe one of them, the one you know as Lestat, is celebrating a birthday – or, more accurately, a re-birthday. It has been four centuries since he transformed.' She made a purring sound. 'I'd like to give that Latin lover's wife a run for her money. She never leaves him alone for a minute.'

'Wait. Are you saying that's really them? They're vampires, too?'

I stared at the group, unbelieving, and as if he sensed my gaze – and probably my lustful thoughts – the absurdly hand- some actor who'd played Armand turned his head, smiled with fangs showing and winked.

I gasped, then said, 'Oh, wow' like a teenager, loudly enough for the entire room of hearing-enhanced bloodsuckers to hear, and pressed my palm against my chest, totally lost in the moment and oblivious to the fact that I was making a fool of myself.

Vampire insanity aside, I'd just seen one of my all-time movie lust-objects. And he looked so young! The fact that he was undead didn't seem important. I briefly wondered if Devereux could get his autograph for me before I shook the stars out of my eyes and took some deep breaths.

Anne watched me sip my drink and swallow, her attention on my throat.

Startled by her focus, and not wanting to discuss my fan-girl reaction to the sensuous actor, I quickly brought the discussion back to her. 'So, you said you were killed – how is that possible if you're still here?'

'Good question. The answer is' – she stood and curtsied theatrically – 'I faked my death, made it look as if I'd been beheaded. I entranced them all. No one knew I was a vampire, not even my husband the king.' She returned to her seat.

'You were married to a king? What king?'

'Why, Henry the Eighth, of course. The second monarch of the House of Tudor. He was crazy for me, until my political enemies poisoned his mind. I was angry to have to give up the throne so soon. I adored my role as queen.'

Queen? The identity of the woman sitting next to me slammed into my brain. 'You're Anne Boleyn?'

She twirled her hand in the air. 'At your service.'

'But I've seen paintings of you . . .' My eyes examined her face then involuntarily shifted to her cleavage. 'You looked . . . different.'

She laughed. 'Of course you know that we can appear as we wish. It's fun to mix things up every so often.'

'Well, it's a pleasure to meet the notorious Anne Boleyn.' I held out my hand and she shook it.

'I haven't used that name since,' she said, 'but I might just have to dust it off and present myself to another king in the future – all that court intrigue was simply too much fun. Maybe I'll wait for one of William's children to grow up, then I'll pay a visit. Who knows what delightful trouble I might get into?'

Before I could respond, she was off again. 'Devereux actually spent some time at Henry's castle with me. We'd already known each other for a century or more, and he came at the king's invitation to foretell the future. It was Devereux who warned me of my husband's lack of loyalty and prepared me for the unfolding drama. We had some time together in Paris after that.'

'Time together?' *Is Anne one of Devereux's old flames? Am I really safe with her?*

'Ah, yes.' She folded her hands in her lap. 'You're wondering what kind of relationship we had. I really can't blame you – the lad is quite the catch. I admit I gave it my best shot, but we weren't destined to be together for long. I was too much of a wild card, never could keep myself from stirring up trouble – the kind that draws mortal attention. But it was deliciously romantic while it lasted. And to answer your question, you are quite safe with me. I have no desire to make an enemy of my friend. He has enough to worry about right now.'

Frowning, I drained my glass and set it on a nearby table. Vampire mind-reading was getting very old and the ability of most ancient vampires to invade my brain whenever they felt like it had become unacceptable. No matter how important my research might be, it wasn't worth giving up my autonomy. Devereux had told me the night of his first visit to my office that he could teach me to shield my thoughts. If I intended to continue exploring this preternatural world, I'd need to take him up on his offer. Or find someone else who could educate me. And he'd said something intriguing – thoughts are fuelled by emotions. What if I kept my mind calm? Would that make me harder to read? But how did one remain calm around night-walking bloodsuckers?

But if I was honest, I had to admit I'd begun to reconsider my career choice. How much of myself was I willing to lose just to write a few books about vampire wannabes? Did I really want to set myself up for more media exposure and ridicule? Vampires didn't strike me as an Oprah-endorsed sort of topic, anyway.

Anne smiled, clearly aware of my inner monologue. She'd made no promises to stay out of my thoughts. 'Considering giving up? I had no idea. That is a serious option – and the lad won't like it. But be logical – even though you aren't a *normal* human, you can't expect to share our reality without compromise.'

'What do you mean, I'm not a *normal* human? What compromise?' I sat straighter and looked at her, eager for the chance to gather information. Maybe she would answer some questions. 'I don't understand.'

She made a loud snorting noise. 'You're not going to psych me into divulging Devereux's secrets, so put away your bag of therapy tricks, Doctor Freud. But I am willing to give you whatever general vampire information I can. As I said, I do know what it's like to be the outsider.' She relaxed back into the couch cushions. 'Ask away.'

My attention was diverted by the arrival of another vampire seeking food. The tall, thin female chose a donor and followed the same routine as the male sucker I'd observed earlier, the experience looking just as bland as the previous one.

'Kismet?' Anne tapped her finger on my leg.

'Uh, yeah.' I turned my focus back to her. 'Sorry. My brain just jumped the tracks for a moment.' I paused for a few seconds, choosing my words carefully. 'You seem to know what happened on Hallowe'en. The fact that Devereux went into some sort of vampire coma after surviving a battle with his offspring, Bryce, and a demented monster calling himself Lucifer. You're aware of that, right?'

'Of course,' she said, her expression serious as she leaned in to whisper, 'every vampire in the world knows about that – it sent a shockwave through the entire community. Nobody thought Devereux could be defeated, even with a death-magic ritual. The vampire hierarchy has been rocked to its foundations. Doubts have surfaced about Devereux's leadership.'

'Damn.' I said aloud, more to myself than to her. 'I hadn't considered the ramifications to Devereux and his position in the hierarchy. Maybe that's why he's been so distracted lately. And so moody.'

'Indeed. From what I understand, he's enraged because he hasn't been able to find this Lucifer creature, who was apparently a mental defective even as a human. My friend has become obsessed with seeking revenge. His pride is wounded – he's never had his omnipotence questioned in such a way before and I haven't seen him this bloodthirsty for centuries. I pity the idiot when Devereux uncovers his lair. Quite frankly, he isn't himself and he's stubbornly refusing to talk about it. He tends to dig his heels in. I mean, look at the way he refuses to join the twenty-first century. Unless it suits his purposes and makes money, of course. He's the hot topic at every vampire gathering. Listen.' She touched my ear with a finger and suddenly the volume knob for my hearing turned up several notches.

'Oh yeah. Big, bad Devereux brought to his knees.'

I turned my head towards a group of male vampires dressed like meth-lab refugees.

'I can't believe he had the nerve to show up here,' a Keith Richards look-alike said, 'acting like everything's fine. Everyone knows he's been put in his place. About time, if you ask me.'

'Yeah, nobody's going to listen to him now,' agreed a fat, greasy-looking man with extensive facial scars and orange hair. 'Always so high and mighty, telling us who and what we can kill. We should just throw his sissy ass out and find a new Master.'

Anne touched my ear again and, like a speaker clicking off, my hearing returned to normal. I brought my eyes back to her. *Holy shit!*

'See what I mean? Devereux's made many enemies in the vampire community because he takes a rational approach. He insists we remain hidden, keeping our existence secret. Others don't agree. In fact, there's a growing number who want vampires to be free to kill again, to be the predators we truly are. If it wasn't for Devereux and those who follow him, humans would die by the thousands.'

'Jesus.' *What?* 'I had no idea Devereux was so pro-human and he was keeping us safe.'

'Not pro-human,' Anne said, shaking her head. 'He's pro-vampire. He doesn't want things to go back to the way they were in earlier times, when vampire slayers made it difficult for us to share the world with humans. Devereux enjoys his elevated position and mingling with humans like you. His ego is taking a beating and he isn't handling it well.'

'That's awful. He didn't tell me.' My gaze followed another vampire approaching the donors, but I looked away before I could become distracted again by the bizarre scene. I dragged my eyes back to Anne's. 'I noticed something while Devereux was unconscious, or whatever he was. During those three weeks, even though he communicated with me in my dreams, I didn't have the same overwhelming desire to be near him that I'd experienced previously and have again since he regained consciousness. It was as if I'd been set free, in some strange way.'

She raised a brow, surprised.

'I know,' I said, 'that probably doesn't make any sense.'

'On the contrary, it makes perfect sense. While Devereux was out of commission, his influence over your brain diminished. In essence, you became yourself again.'

I tensed and sat silently for a few seconds, letting her words sink in. Her statement felt very important. I barely noticed when the ghost with the bloody knife darted through my peripheral vision. How exciting that I'd become used to him so quickly.

'Are you saying that when I'm around Devereux I'm not myself?' My stomach clenched. 'That I'm under his control?'

She tilted her head, looking confused. 'Well, of course. How could you not be? He is very powerful.'

'Do you mean he manipulates me on purpose? He lied to me?'

'Vampires control humans – it's what we do. What do you mean, he lied to you?'

'Devereux told me shortly after we met that he's always in charge of his powers, that he never influences me so I can make my own decisions about him. If he lied about that, how can I possibly trust anything he says?'

She shocked me by laughing. 'Men! What are we to do with them? Devereux didn't lie to you – that was his ego speaking. In his mind he's all-powerful – he simply isn't aware that his abilities are too strong ever to be completely under his control.

He doesn't know you're influenced by him to the degree you are. The ever-popular psychological state of *denial*. Not that he doesn't prefer you to do as he wishes. He simply takes obedience, from everyone, for granted.' She chuckled with delight. 'I'm sure he feels very magnanimous about your supposed *free will*, but it's easy for me to sense the ways your brainwaves have been altered.'

'What? My brainwaves?' Bile rose in my throat.

'Certainly – you can't expect to be around someone as dominant as Devereux without repercussions. Vampires entrance humans without even meaning to, and our influence causes actual physiological changes in the brain's wiring. It isn't something we have to think about. The more talented the vampire, the larger the effects to the mortal.' She patted my arm. 'I'm surprised you can even remember your own name at this point. Why do you think you're having so many headaches?'

Ice slid down my spine. I had been going through a lot of aspirin lately.

'So as long as I'm near Devereux, I'm a puppet?' My heart rate doubled, my head spun. 'Is that what you're saying?'

She reached out and squeezed my hand. 'Relax. It wasn't my intention to frighten you. Quite frankly, I assumed you knew what it would mean to devote yourself to a master vampire. They are a rare breed. Devereux could affect every individual in this castle simultaneously if he chose to, even as young as he is.'

'Young? He says he's eight hundred years old.'

'Like I said, a mere youngster. Regardless, no vampire can ignore his power. He's unique.'

I breathed to calm myself. 'How could I possibly know what it means that he's a Master? Nobody told me. He said I would acclimatise to him and not be so overwhelmed. That I wouldn't always feel so ... *intoxicated*.'

She gave a quick shrug. 'I'm certain he believes that and perhaps it's true. You really are more talented than you know.'

'I wish people would stop saying that without explaining what they mean.'

She stared at me for a few seconds and appeared to come to a decision. 'I can't help you with that, but here's what I *can* do. Close your eyes.'

'What?' My heart rate accelerated again. 'Why do you want me to close my eyes?'

'What have you got to lose? I already told you I won't hurt you. Really. Do you think I want Devereux to rip my head off? But I will use one of my abilities to temporarily clear all vampire influence from your mind. It'll be better than pain meds.'

'What are you talking about? How can you clear the influence? If you're really telling the truth and I'm being affected anyway—'

'Oh, bother. You can thank me later.' In the blink of an eye, Anne pressed one hand against my forehead and her other on the crown of my head. A subtle vibration pulsed through my skull-bones for a few seconds, followed by a quick blast of heat.

'Yikes!' The heat swam through my head and sizzled down my spine. 'What are you doing to me?'

'Exactly what I said. All done. Open your eyes.'

I slowly raised my lids, afraid of what I'd find. What if her vampire zap had made me blind, or worsened the pain in my head? It wasn't much consolation to know that Devereux really would kill her if she hurt me.

Anne studied me, curious. 'Well? Notice anything different?'

Blinking a few times to verify my eyes were still functional, it took a few seconds but I began to recognise a subtle change.

It was as if I'd been a little drunk before, but was now sober. The light was brighter, harsher. My headache was gone. Completely gone. I surveyed the area, noticing the vampires chatting in groups didn't look quite as beautiful as before, their voices not as compelling. A trickle of fear slithered into my awareness. My palms went damp and I turned to her with wide eyes.

'Yes,' Anne said. 'Fear. Without the filter – the cumulative effect of being around powerful vampires – you're sensing what we really are and you're having the normal human reaction to encountering a predator. Or, in this case, hundreds of us.'

I ran my tongue over my dry lips and tried to catch my breath. My hands shook. I felt suddenly trapped and terrified. My fight-or-flight instinct engaged. 'I don't understand. I didn't experience this when Devereux was unconscious. I wasn't frightened then.'

'No, I'm sure you weren't. You spent enough time sitting with him and sharing dreams that his influence was merely diminished, not completely negated. You continued to meet with vampire clients and while they're not as strong as what you're accustomed to, their energy can still alter you.'

'How do I know you didn't just create this fear in me? Apparently you have some serious skills yourself – I've never felt anything like this before.'

'You're right about my skills, but what would be the benefit to me of creating a false emotion? You *have* felt this before. You've simply forgotten what it was like the first time you encountered one of us. Think back to the night you met Devereux. What happened?'

What *had* happened? I remembered being inappropriately attracted to him and angry that he showed up in my office uninvited. But she was right. First I'd felt fear. Irrational fear. 'Oh.'

Anne looked around the room then returned her gaze to me. 'I've given you a brief opportunity to remember what your life was like before you connected with any of us. It won't last very long – no more than a few days, a week at most, especially when Devereux returns and floods your brain with his essence. I've also made you harder to read. Maybe this reprieve will help you decide how involved in this world you actually want to be. I think you should be free to choose for yourself.' She laughed. 'But that's not why I did it. I simply live to stir up trouble. Devereux would expect no less. He'll remember our history and why I've liberated you, and he'll be so superbly angry. It's simply too much fun to pass up.' She rearranged her breasts in her snug bodice. 'Prepare yourself. I sense him approaching.'

On cue, Devereux materialised in front of me. He reached out a hand and pulled me up from the couch. He searched my eyes, his expression cold. 'What has happened? Why are you afraid?'

'Nothing happened,' Anne said, speaking before I could. 'Kismet is just having normal human reactions to being exposed to this many vampires. Sometimes you forget how difficult all this is for her.'

Pressing his lips tightly together, he stared at her for a few seconds, probably reading her mind. I wondered how upset he'd be if he discovered the 'gift' she'd just given me. But he quickly blinked and turned back to me, his mood unchanged. No doubt she'd blocked her thoughts. I hoped she was right about making me harder to read.

Suddenly the idea of sitting in my office with vampires felt ludicrous. Out of the question. Professional suicide. What madness had overtaken my mind? Or, more accurately, *who* had taken over my mind?

'It is odd for you to be so suddenly terrified.'

'I'll be fine,' I said, hoping that was true. 'So many vampires in one place can be a little overwhelming, that's all.'

Devereux wrapped his arms around me and pulled me close. His exotic aroma wafted into my nostrils, still pleasant, but it didn't cause my brain to spin or my libido to flare. His body felt almost hot. He must have fed again recently. Did he have an unlimited supply of donors? The horrible realisation hit me that I'd never bothered to ask him if he was one of those vampires who needed to kill to feed. Just because he hadn't hurt me didn't mean he wasn't dangerous. What did I really know about him and his frightening world? Almost nothing.

He released me and pressed his palm against my chest, worry etched across his features. 'I have never heard your heart beat so quickly. This cannot be healthy. Come. We will leave now. I will take you home.'

Just then an unusually pale robed vampire glided through the rooms, striking a gong. The sound reverberated off the walls and vibrated the pyramid of champagne glasses stacked on the buffet table. Without a word, everyone followed him.

Anne winked at me over her shoulder before stepping away.

'What's going on?' I asked.

'The ceremony is about to begin. We are being escorted to the ritual site' Devereux gave me a hard look. 'I am concerned about the level of fear in your body. Despite what Anne said, someone has done something to cause your reaction. We do not need to attend the ritual if you are not up to it. Just say the word and we will leave.'

He watched me, waiting for an answer. Part of me wanted

to go home, to curl up in my favourite chair in my pink robe and give serious thought to my future. But the rest of me wanted to discover as much about Devereux and the other vampires as possible, to sort out whether anything I'd experienced in the last three months had been true. To see if I could trust him to keep his word.

Anne had said the effects of her clearing wouldn't last long. I felt in charge of myself at that moment and wanted to memorise the feeling. I was aware of Devereux's mystical vibe but it didn't influence me.

'We can go to the wedding. I'm much better already.' The fear remained steady but manageable, as if my instinct-brain remembered being prey.

'Yes.' He brushed a finger along my cheek. 'You do seem to be recovering. Very well.' He extended an arm and we followed the throngs through a long, empty narrow room that opened into a vivid hallucination.

A full-size replica of Stonehenge – except it looked as it must have when first constructed – stretched out impossibly on a vast expanse of green grass. Somehow the illusion of a star-lit sky had been projected overhead. Beautiful mediaeval music floated on the air.

Three naked figures – presumably the bride and groom plus an official-looking woman – were waiting in the centre of the stone ring, clustered around a small altar decorated with astrological symbols.

Devereux and I joined the other guests pressed tightly into concentric circles. Even the donors attended. They huddled in a group directly across from me. Suddenly the background music stopped and all was silent except for the steady rhythm of the gong.

Being in physical contact with the vampires inflamed my

fear. I breathed deeply to calm the impending panic attack, thinking I must have been outrageously entranced by Devereux since I'd met him for me to have been unaware of this level of constant terror.

At that moment, I knew my involvement with the vampires would never be the same. Even Devereux's physical charms weren't enough to balance the scales. Nothing could undo the events of the last half-hour.

I practised self-hypnosis and riveted my focus onto the happy couple centre stage, refusing to allow my acute dread to keep me from witnessing the unique event.

At some invisible signal, the night-time sky overhead morphed into a brilliant sunrise and a collective gasp rose from the crowd as everyone looked up. My eyes tracked the faces, some of which held such expressions of yearning that I almost felt as if I was intruding on a private moment. A keen reminder that this was the only kind of sunrise they would ever see.

Hundreds of tiny floating balls of light materialised, illuminating the scene with a soft glow. Devereux squeezed my hand and I shifted my gaze to his face in time to see him staring up at the mock sunrise with wonder.

At that moment, I felt fortunate. No matter what powers vampires could command, there were equally profound losses.

My attention was drawn to the bride, whose exceptionally long bright-green hair flowed down her body like neon seaweed, curving around the mounds of her very large serpent-tattooed breasts. She smiled at her intended, displaying impressive fangs. The groom turned out to be the tall bald fellow I'd watched feed from the donor when we first arrived. Since he wasn't naked then, I hadn't noticed the intricate tattoo on his chest that matched his soon-to-be wife's. Joy radiated from his face.

I wondered what kind of vampire royalty they were to rate this kind of turn-out.

I was happy for them, but couldn't concentrate. Despite using my most potent visualisation techniques, fear crashed against my mental defences, rendering them useless. I scanned the crowd again, seeking to reassure myself that it wasn't a foregone conclusion that the monsters sensed my panic and would devour me at any moment. Devereux wasn't reacting to my intensity. Whatever Anne had done appeared to be effective. She caught my eye and gave an amused grin. I didn't know if I was grateful to her for the painful reality check or angry because she'd destroyed all my comfortable delusions. Delusions I hadn't known were there.

Counting backwards to soothe myself, I thought about the fact that I had an entire career to restructure. A whole life to reconsider. *I'm in charge of my choices. I don't have to do anything!*

The official woman – priestess? – at the altar began speaking in a soft voice, flailing an amethyst wand through the air. The wand created a vortex of sparkling gold energy around the couple like something out of a Disney movie. I strained to hear but couldn't make out anything she said. After a few seconds, I finally caught a couple of words and realised the ritual was being conducted in German.

Perfect. Even if I had any clue about what vampire wedding vows might be like, now it was useless to pretend to have a grip. But focusing on the ceremony kept my panic at a manageable level.

Every so often the official raised both her hands in the air and sang a word that drew affirmative responses from the spectators.

A chalice appeared out of nowhere and was passed from

the priestess to the bride and groom. Having seen such a cup before when Devereux created the ritual for me before Hallowe'en, I knew what it held. What else would vampires drink, anyway? The couple traded the chalice back and forth until it was empty.

After a few minutes of the participants talking to each other, probably saying all the appropriate 'I dos', the couple held out their wrists and the priestess bound them together with a red cloth.

Just as the groom bent forwards for the traditional biting-of-the-wife's-neck, a familiar disgusting odour filled the air and a tall, emaciated male in a filthy long black coat materialised in the middle of the celebrants, knocking the three participants and the altar to the grass. Coal-black eyes in his bald, malformed, veiny head turned slowly towards me. He sneered, showing brown teeth and fangs, pointed a finger in my direction, then lunged at me.

Everyone started yelling at once and what looked like a million vampire eyes turned towards me.

Devereux clutched my arm so hard I yelped in pain, then he pushed in front of me.

My fear level, already off the charts, went stratospheric and my stomach clenched so tight I could barely breathe. I recognised that foul maniac: Lucifer, Brother Luther's serial killer personality. The animal who'd terrorised mortals and vampires alike. The walking nightmare who'd stalked me.

With a roar, Devereux released me, his sudden movement thrusting me backwards into several guests already sent tumbling in the chaos and who were now struggling to stand. I scrambled to my feet in time to see Devereux leap towards Lucifer as the uninvited fiend grabbed two donors by their necks before all three of them vanished.

Devereux followed.

The last thing I remembered was Anne lifting me into her arms and her voice saying, 'Oh, great. Once again, Anne has to clean up the leftovers.'

CHAPTER 5

'No!' I screamed and sprang up into a sitting position. Heart pounding, sweat beading on my chest, I surveyed my environment, relieved to discover myself on my own couch, still wearing the silver dress, the sun flowing in through the living-room windows.

Daytime. No vampires.

I sniffed tentatively, anticipating Lucifer's foul calling card. Instead, all I smelled was the breakdown of my own deodorant.

It took a few seconds for my pulse to calm and my breathing to slow.

Memory fragments of the night before swam into my consciousness in disjointed pieces. My hands shook and I eased myself up against the cushions, staring down at the cross and pentagram around my neck. I lifted the cross, expecting to feel heat, but it was cool.

What did that mean? Had something happened to Devereux again? No matter how confused I was about our relationship, I didn't want any harm to come to him. He'd become important to me, even if it turned out we couldn't be together any more.

The enormity of my situation rolled over me like a psychic avalanche. I hadn't meant to make bad choices – shit! I simply hadn't acquired enough information about anything during the last three months to make any rational decisions – but I had to face the fact that both my current options stank.

How could I possibly have known the degree to which my brain was being physically changed and controlled by vampire energy? Even Devereux didn't know. I'd just thought my headaches were due to normal human reasons, like stress. I shivered, thinking about being a guinea pig in my own experiment. Dr Frankenstein ingested his concoctions on purpose. I'd thrown my brain into the undead blender without a qualm.

But what if Anne was manipulating me and her claims about my brain were lies?

What if they weren't?

I guess I'll find out eventually.

Okay, get a grip, Kismet. Options.

If I did what I wanted to – closed down my bloodsucking private practice, stopped work on the vampire-wannabe book and stayed away from Devereux – it was only a matter of time until Brother Luther's even more repulsive and evil personality Lucifer swooped in to carry me off. For some unknown reason, the fiend was obsessed with me and that kind of sick connection was almost impossible to extinguish even in humans. As a vampire, his ability to move through time and space made me unsafe everywhere. So, result of option one? Quick death. At least, I hoped it would be quick.

Option one definitely sucked.

Option two? If Devereux survived whatever happened when he and Lucifer vanished last night, I could stay with him. Let him turn me into his obedient human slave, his fast-food snack, his destined mate. I couldn't deny that I behaved strangely when I was with him. He might even deign to tell me his real agenda one day, why he *really* wanted me around. Of course, he'd be a kind master – he'd treat his pet well. But soon the physiological effects on my brain would simply stop me trying to have any independent thoughts, behaviours, or feelings. I'd just wait for instructions. He could dress me up like his goth Barbie doll. But I'd be safe. Sort of alive.

Fuck that.

My mind spun as I tried to figure out the best thing to do. The most rational decision. All my feelings about vampires in general and Devereux in particular had been upended. I didn't know what was real and what could be written off to brainwashing. According to Anne, I only had about a week to drive my own mental bus and I wanted to make good use of it.

I picked up the TV remote and clicked it onto check the time: 2:20 p.m., Sunday. CNN ran a replay of last night's New Year's Eve ball-drop in Times Square. I tapped my fingernail on the coffee table and watched the crowd celebrate. The blissfully ignorant humans who had no idea vampires really existed. The partying hoards of normals who would wake in the morning only missing brain cells they'd chosen to destroy in the name of fun.

Why couldn't I remember what happened after I left the wedding? Had Anne delivered me home? Or someone else? The scope of the possibilities made the hairs on my arms rise and my stomach roil.

The bloodsucker-free part of the day was dwindling. There was no more time to waste. I needed help.

Alan.

Regardless of any unfinished business between us, I had to call him. No matter what sticky issues we had, being two of the small number of humans aware of the existence of the undead created a bond deeper than our ridiculous personality dramas.

I was just about to click off the TV when a *Breaking News* alert flashed across the screen and the scene shifted to a reporter standing on a narrow, steep street featuring the Golden Gate Bridge in the background. 'Breaking news: not many details yet, but a source close to a police investigation tells us they're hunting for a serial killer here in San Francisco. The governor is demanding swift action. Stay tuned and we'll bring you updates as they're available.'

Three images flashed through my mind: a screaming dark-haired woman standing in an office, someone wearing a hooded raincoat lying in a wet parking lot next to a car, then a shadowy figure running down an empty street. What the hell? Why was I seeing these things?

Chilled by the horrible news and the visions, I rubbed my arms. Another serial killer? *What the hell's wrong with humans? Why do we insist on killing each other?* I tried to imagine the horror that would ensue if the world discovered the existence of even worse predators.

Guiltily grateful that the deaths hadn't occurred in Denver, I turned off the remote, heaved myself up from the couch, then stepped towards my desk before noticing my stiletto sandals were missing. When had they disappeared? I looked around to see if I'd kicked them under the furniture but didn't find them.

Deciding that mystery was low on the priority scale, I headed upstairs for a quick shower and a change of clothes. Since today was a holiday, I had no clients of any kind, so I could make a new game plan.

Figure out a way to stay alive.

A half-hour later I was sitting at my desk, drinking coffee and eating a banana-nut muffin while I fired up my laptop.

Since I was willing to do anything that might help my situation, I'd put the diamond cross back on after my shower, along with the pentagram necklace. I should have felt relatively safe because the sun was out, but I no longer had any pretence of thinking I knew what was – or wasn't – possible in the world of the vampires.

I toyed with the cross, grabbed my phone, called Alan's cell, and went to voicemail. 'Hey, Alan. It's Kismet. I need to talk to you. Please call me back as soon as you can. It's important. You have all my numbers. Bye.'

Last we'd spoken, he was still in Sedona following Lucifer's trail of drained bodies while simultaneously continuing his search for his mother – his mother the vampire. On Hallowe'en, he'd told me his childhood story of her disappearance. He'd never recovered from her abandoning him; he'd become a forensic psychologist, joined the FBI and devoted himself to exploring the strange and unusual in hopes of catching another glimpse of her.

'Come on, Alan. Call me,' I said to the silent phone. 'Where are all my alleged abilities when I need them? Seems like I ought to be able to contact you psychically. Well, hey, let's give that a try.' I held my hands out, palms up, adopting what I thought might be a mystical pose, and said, 'Ohm, ohm. Alan! Ohm, ohm. Call me now!'

I'd just taken a breath to laugh at myself when the phone rang. I jumped in my chair.

'Hot damn!' I read the caller ID screen and saw Alan's name. I scooped up the phone and answered, 'Alan? Is that you?'

'The one and only.'

'You got my message?'

'Message? No. I haven't had time to check my voicemail today. I was out all night riding with some cops and just woke up a while ago. Now I'm sitting in a coffee shop, updating my notes, and I suddenly had an overwhelming urge to call you. Weird, eh?'

Actually, it's excellent. Maybe I finally have a reliable skill!

'Yeah, weird. But I'm glad you called. Do you have a few minutes? What time is it there in Sedona?'

'As of two days ago I'm no longer in Sedona.' A small crash echoed through the phone. 'Shit!'

'What was that?' I took a bite of muffin.

'I just managed to spill my coffee on myself and drop the mug on the tile floor. That was the clatter you heard. What a mess. Hold on—'

'Do you need more napkins, sir?' a young-sounding voice said in the background.

'No. I'm good, thanks.'

'Would you like a coffee refill?'

'Sure. Why not?'

'Alan?'

'Yeah, I'm here – looking like I wet myself – but I'm here.' His mouth shifted away from the phone. 'Thanks, I'll try to hang onto this one.' He cleared his throat. 'So like I said, I left Sedona. A few days ago I started hearing rumblings about activities in San Francisco that sounded like our repulsive, bald, toothsome friend so I hit the road. I'm now staring out across the water at the notorious Alcatraz and thinking life doesn't get much better than this.'

'San Francisco? I just saw something about serial killers there. Are you involved with that, too?'

'No. I heard about it, but nobody's said anything. I've got my hands full with Stink Vamp and the six deaths I'm sure he's involved with, and as psychologically interesting as it would be to chase a real-life version of Hannibal Lecter, I can only handle one fiend at a time. Of course, none of the locals have put the pieces together about the six drained bodies yet, so I'm the only one who knows there's a supernatural angle.'

'Well, as awful as this sounds, if you have to track him somewhere, I can't imagine a more beautiful city.'

'Yeah, it's great. I've spent a lot of time here over the years. And let me remind you that you have a standing invitation to come and visit, wherever I am. I'd be glad to show you the town.' He laughed. 'And the inside of my comfortable hotel room. We could tour this side of the bed, then that side, then the table in the corner . . .'

Nope. Let's not go there.

'Gee, thanks.'

He didn't say anything for a few seconds. 'Okay. What's up? You didn't give me any grief for the hotel room remark. Is something wrong? What was your message about?'

'I saw Lucifer.'

'What do you mean?' The easy banter ended and his voice took on a serious edge. 'Where did you see him? My undead intel is pretty solid that he's primarily killing on the West Coast.'

I took a sip of my coffee to give myself time to decide what I wanted to say. 'I'm sure you're right. We both know vampires can be on the other side of the world or in another century from one moment to the next. There's really no way for humans to track them.'

'So where was he?'

'In Aspen. I went to a vampire wedding with Devereux last night and Lucifer showed up in time to ruin the nuptials. It was bad enough that he was even there, but it looked like he focused on me: he stared and pointed at me before Devereux took off after him and both of them disappeared. Of course, he stank – engulfed in his usual horrible rotting-corpse, sewer-from-hell odour. I smelled him a few nanoseconds before I saw him. But just because he was there last night doesn't tell us anything about where he is now.'

It felt so good to be able to talk to someone who understood.

'Yeah, you're right about that. You said the last time we talked that you're still getting voicemail messages from the Brother Luther part of the maniac's personality. Is he still calling?' Another crash. 'Bollocks! What the hell is up with me today? I just dropped my plate. Damn tiny tables. I'm going to gather my stuff and walk back to the hotel room. Don't hang up. So, about the messages . . .'

'Uh-huh. He calls at least once per day. Same tirades as before. I'm going to burn in hell, I'm Satan's whore, I'll be punished, washed in the blood – same demented song. Sometimes he just sobs and says *help me, help me*, over and over. But I guess that's the child part. I wonder if there are only three personalities, or if we're in for additional surprises?'

A door slammed.

'All right. I'm back in my room. With my luck an earthquake will shove California into the ocean today and I can't swim. Hey, do you know what Skype is?'

'Sure. I use it to meet with clients who can't come to the office.'

'Cool. I'm all set up for it, too. Why don't we connect face-to-face, so to speak? I've turned on my computer and now I'm adding you to my contacts.'

'Okay.' I put on my headset and made sure the camera was working. 'I'm ready.'

Alan's charming face popped onto my computer screen. Behind him was a nondescript beige motel wall with a colourful oil painting of downtown San Francisco. 'Hello there, gorgeous.' He waved his fingers.

'Hi, Alan. Nice to *see* you.' And it was. His eyes, always some variation of bluish-purple or purple-blue, really stood out today against his faded tan, messy brown hair and five o'clock shadow. 'You look a little tired.'

'It's been a rough few days. You, on the other hand, look great. So, picking up where we left off,' he frowned, 'is this the first time you've seen Lucifer since Hallowe'en? You haven't mentioned him showing up before.'

'Uh-huh.' I sipped from my coffee cup. 'This was the first time. I hadn't become complacent about him – I know he can materialise anytime he wants to. I've also thought I smelled him a couple of times. But I can't stay in a constant state of terror. My heart can't take it. I'll stroke out or something.' I adjusted my microphone. 'It's not like I have anywhere to run to. I've been wearing the protective necklace Devereux gave me, and I know he has some of his vampires watching me. Maybe even some humans during the day. Normally that would annoy me, but anything that keeps the bogyman away is all right with me. Not being able to find Lucifer has really pissed Devereux off.'

'What do you mean, he can't find him?' He glanced down at the coffee stain on his white T-shirt. 'Isn't that impossible? From what I hear, Devereux's like the vampire Pope – infallible.'

'Apparently not. He hasn't talked to me about it, but one of his vampire friends said the entire community were shocked that Lucifer bested him at The Vampires' Ball on Hallowe'en. I don't think anything has ever rocked Devereux's confidence like this. He's been very moody. Angry. Gone a lot. Searching for Lucifer without any success.'

'Really?' He moved closer to the camera. 'That's too bizarre. According to the vampire grapevine, Devereux's the biggest badass around.'

'Well, judging by what I've been hearing, there's definitely a dent in his badass reputation. Vampires are saying awful things about him. I actually heard one guy at the party call Devereux a *sissy*. Which, now that I think about it, is a pretty *sissy* word for a vampire to use. And I'll bet Devereux is trying to keep a stiff upper lip through this whole thing. No wonder he's acting strangely.'

'Wow. That doesn't bode well for the vampire community, since Devereux keeps them in check.' He paused. 'Something else is going on here. You sound weird today. You're not yourself, either. What's up? Are you two still an item?'

I unconsciously lowered my gaze for a few seconds and tried to dislodge a nut fragment caught in my teeth with my tongue. Any other time I would have found some way to change the topic or distract him from talking about Devereux, but I needed his help so I decided to suck it up and be honest. I brought my eyes back to meet his. 'I don't know what we are. I haven't told you much about the *reality* of being with Devereux.' I fell silent again for a few seconds and picked through the muffin remains on the plate.

'Kismet?' He leaned close. 'What the hell? I'm starting to get a bad feeling about this. Come on, spill. Has something happened to you?'

'Do you remember telling me when we met that you'd like to have Devereux take over your mind, just to see what it would be like? You said you'd like to experience being under a powerful vampire's control. I wasn't sure if you were kidding or not.'

'I don't remember saying that specifically,' he shook his

head, 'but it sounds like me. I probably wasn't kidding. What's that got to do with anything?'

'Well, I know exactly what it's like.'

We stared at each other for a few seconds.

'Are you talking about him being domineering and controlling, which I think is no secret to anyone, or something else?' he asked.

'All of the above. Ever since I met him, whenever he came near me I turned into a hormone-driven zombie. I simply lost control of myself. Lost myself. He said it was only a matter of time until I got used to his vampire intensity and that I'd acclimatise. Looking back, I always thought my outrageous attraction to him was legitimate – that he just rang my chimes. I thought it was exciting to be so over-the-moon about someone. But after what I found out last night, I don't know any more.'

'What happened last night?' he said sharply.

'Anne Boleyn, who's an old friend of Devereux's, apparently, told me she clearly senses that my brain has been altered. Compromised. I've been having bad headaches. She explained there's nothing to be done about it – powerful vampires simply affect and overwhelm humans that way and I'm guessing the effect is cumulative.'

Silence.

'Alan?'

He held up a hand. 'Hold on. You said Anne Boleyn? *The* Anne Boleyn? She's a vampire?'

'Yeah, and remind me later to tell you who else I met. You won't believe it.' He was quiet again for a few seconds, just staring. 'Alan?'

'Yeah.' He slapped his palm against his forehead. 'I just can't get past the Anne Boleyn part. If I hadn't seen all the outrageous bull in the vampire world that I've seen, I'd think you were lying or jerking me around. But I believe you. Damn. That's something. Anne Boleyn. So, she said your brain has been altered. That can't be good. Is that why you're so upset?'

'Well, yeah!' I sat back in my chair. 'Wouldn't you be upset if you discovered that the choices you've made weren't really your own, but rather a product of mind control? Even if the mind control wasn't intentional?'

'How do you know it wasn't intentional? Are you that sure of Devereux?'

'No!' I shook my head. 'I'm not sure of anything any more. Anne said Devereux has no idea how manipulated I am by his vampiric voodoo. He thinks he's in total control of himself. She said he's in denial. So not only am I in constant fear of Lucifer coming to snatch me away, now the head-honcho vampire I thought could protect me can't, apparently. Maybe. And even if Devereux could fight Lucifer off, being around him wigs my brain. This is a lose-lose proposition.'

'Wait a minute.' He gave me his all-knowing FBI agent look. 'Even though you're upset, you don't sound like somebody whose brain cells have been scrambled. Are you only a space-case around vampires?'

'Mostly around Devereux and other strong vampires, but Anne did something last night to clear away all the vampire influence. I'd say I feel like myself, but that's not true. I feel like a stronger version of myself today, as if all those crazy experiences strengthened me somehow. She said she's given me a few days to figure out if I want to continue in the world of the undead. But her clearing did nothing to ward off Lucifer. My choices still suck.' I braced my chin on my hand and frowned.

'Why would she want to help you? Maybe she just wants to get you away from Devereux.' He picked up a small package of crackers with an airline logo on the wrapper, no doubt acquired during his last flight, and held it up to the camera before ripping the paper open. He bit into an orange-coloured treat and crunched loudly.

I smiled at him before answering, 'She said she just likes to rock the boat. But it's equally possible she wants me to go away – she said she and Devereux spent some time together centuries ago. Maybe she isn't over him. Whatever. Regardless, my brain is my own for a little while. I don't know what I'll do when her hocus-pocus wears off.'

'Well, damn.' He licked crumbs off his fingers. 'There's got to be another answer. Maybe there's some way you can learn to protect yourself. I have to believe that each species evolves the characteristics and traits necessary to survive predators in its environment. What about that psychic you met, the one you said was talented? You told me she knows about the vampires. Maybe she's heard of something that might help you.'

'Cerridwyn? Hmm. Yeah. I guess it wouldn't hurt for me to talk to her again. I actually had a brief telephone appointment with her in early November. I asked about her knowledge of vampires. She said she has lots of vampire clients and learns through them. I was surprised by that and she asked why, what would be the difference between a vampire coming to a psychologist and coming to a psychic? She was right. She pretty much verified everything you and I talked about. Good thinking, Agent Stevens. I'll do anything at this point.'

'Huh. You'll do anything?' He waggled his eyebrows.

'Wait: let me qualify that. I'll do *almost* anything, and for the life of me I can't see how getting horizontal with you would help my current situation.'

He laughed. 'As unusual as this is for me to admit, I wasn't actually thinking about sex. Of course, we can always discuss that. But I just remembered something. Let me get in touch with someone and I'll be right back. Don't go anywhere.'

'Okay,' I said without enthusiasm.

He took off his headpiece and moved out of camera range. I lifted my coffee cup and drank, discovering it had gone cold. I pushed it aside, along with the remains of my crumbled muffin. What a perfect metaphor for my life.

I minimised the Skype screen and pulled up my email account, noticing several messages from the American Psychological Association Conference address. I'd been giving presentations annually for the last few years and had a standing slot in the programme.

I clicked open the most recent email.

Dear Dr Knight:

Since we hadn't heard back from you about your topic for this year's presentation and the deadline for taking the brochure to the printer was fast approaching, the conference committee decided to create a tentative lecture subject for you. We are aware that you've been busy with the unfortunate situation in Denver which involved some of your clients, so we naturally assumed the missing paperwork was an oversight. Since you are still working with the clients you call 'vampire wannabes' and planning to publish in that general category, we hoped it would be acceptable to assign you to speak on an aspect of that area. Please see the attached brochure for the day and time of your lecture. Don't hesitate to contact me with questions. We look forward to seeing you.

Best, Marian Teller, PhD, Conference Chair

Crap! I couldn't believe I'd forgotten to send in my topic for my yearly APA lecture. As if I needed more proof that my brain had slipped a groove.

I clicked open the conference brochure and scanned it, looking for my lecture information. There it was: *Lost Children of the Night, Dr Kismet Knight, Thursday, 4 p.m.*

Lost Children of the Night? Who'd come up with that one? My stomach tightened as I imagined the committee having a good laugh over my area of discussion. Maybe I could call and give them an alternate topic. Ask them to let me present on narcissism or borderline personality disorder. Something normal.

But then I thought, why should I? I'd gone through all the madness with the vampires in order to gain knowledge, or as Captain Picard said, 'To boldly go where no one has gone before.' Why should I give in to pressure – real or imaginary – now? I made it through the insanity at Hallowe'en and the fallout afterward. I'd come too far to allow myself to be professionally – or personally – coerced.

I was going to the damn conference. Not only to stand my professional ground, but because getting out of town sounded like an excellent idea. No vampires.

As I read through the rest of the brochure, I was reminded it started this Wednesday. Three days away.

Given how distracted I'd been for the last three months, I opened my appointment book to confirm I'd taken myself off the schedule for the days of the conference. I verified having booked my flight and hotel room months earlier, and was relieved I hadn't forgotten anything else of importance. The conference was one of the highlights of my year and I'd have been sad to miss it.

I'd just sent a confirmation reply to Dr Teller when Alan returned.

'Hello? Are you there?'

I clicked back into the Skype screen. 'I'm here.'

'So this is going to sound pretty *out-there*, but hang in with me.'

'I'd say *out-there* is par for the course for you, Mulder. Let's hear it.'

'After that bizarre ritual Bryce did to capture Devereux, with all the incantations, spells, bells and whistles, I started asking around about magic. It was a rush for me to think about that kind of power being available.'

I gave a thumbs-up gesture. 'If you liked that ritual, after things calm down I'll tell you about another one I attended with Devereux. Strange and impressive.' The memory of him dancing on a cloud, his platinum hair fanning out around him, during the protection ritual last October still gave me chills. Was there ever anything real between us? Was it all a synaptic delusion?

'I'll hold you to that. So, you probably know that most vampires have no connection to magic. It's only the blood-suckers who were involved in the esoteric arts before they turned – or who were brought over by a magician – who appear to have any kind of magical abilities. If I hadn't encountered Devereux, I might never have known magic was real. Your basic vampire wakes up with the standard package: some telepathy, vampire hypnosis, enhanced strength and speed, taste for blood, et cetera.' He tapped a pen on the table in front of him. 'For some reason, vampiric powers seem to enhance magic for those who have the gift.'

'Huh. I've never really thought about it, but that makes sense. Where are you going with this?'

'I've been doing a lot of research.' He leaned in. 'Don't laugh.'

'Why would I laugh?'

'I'm just preparing you for what I'm about to say, which is something you'll probably find amusing. I've been thinking of writing a book.'

'A book? What kind of book?'

'A novel, actually. A vampire novel. Based on what I've seen. Especially the magic parts. I could tell a fictionalised version of the truth using a pen name. I've been playing with the idea for a while and I actually have a few chapters roughed out.'

'Awesome. I think that's great, Alan. Feels like a natural fit. But I still don't understand what that has to do with me.'

'Sorry, got a bit side-tracked there. In my research, I discovered references to a group of exceptionally wise vampires – almost an esoteric vampire cult – who were skilled with magic, and they're said to have written their wisdom down, passed it along.' He ate another cracker. 'If that's true, there must be thousands of handwritten manuscripts in a secret library somewhere. There has to be something in that material that can help you.'

I sat quietly, trying to take in what he'd said.

'Kismet?'

'Yeah.'

'What do you think?'

'I don't know what to think, Alan. Esoteric vampire cult? Secret library? I appreciate that you're looking outside the box for answers for me, but how the hell would I find any such material? And if I did find it, what would I do with it?'

'Okay, okay.' He raised both palms. 'I know there are some details to work out. You could ask Devereux to help – I wouldn't be surprised if he was connected to this group – or I could try to get in touch with this character I keep hearing about, Zephyr, who has a rep as a powerful magician. It's just another line to tug.'

I sighed. 'Every time I start thinking about vampires or magic or being stalked by Lucifer, I want to crawl into bed and pull the blankets over my head.'

'I can't blame you for that. Okay, how about this? What if I make some inquiries, see if I can talk to this Zephyr guy? Can't hurt, eh?'

'Can't hurt?' I laughed and put an incredulous look on my face. 'When we're talking about vampires, everything can hurt.'

'Agreed, but you have to do something. You can't just hide out in your townhouse until Lucifer shows up.'

'You're right. And I *am* going to do something.' I folded my arms. 'I'm going to the APA Conference in New York City on Wednesday.'

'What are you talking about?' He brought his face so close to the camera I could pick out the various shades of blue-to-grey in the bags under his eyes. 'New York City? No way. You'll be alone, without any of your vampire bodyguards.'

'I doubt if Devereux will pull his protection detail just because I'm out of town. Really, Alan – I need to get away, clear my head, spend some time in an environment where I know what I'm doing, where I belong. Even if they make fun of me.'

'Why would they make fun of you?' He looked genuinely baffled.

'You're kidding, right? Didn't you catch any of the media coverage during the so-called Vampire Murders and their aftermath last October? I was the butt of jokes on every late-night TV show and the focus of insulting, never-ending stories online and in the tabloids. It was awful.'

'Yeah, you'll get no argument from me there.' He relaxed back in his chair. 'We live in a screwed-up world. But I also saw a lot of coverage of Lieutenant Bullock and other police officers stating that even though you'd been threatened by a mad psycho, you came forward as a good citizen to help the police while protecting your clients' confidentiality. I thought you came out of it smelling like a rose. The article about you in USA Today was especially positive. Do you really think your shrink colleagues will burn you at the stake?' He mimicked lighting a match.

I thought for a few seconds. 'No, I guess I don't. But it doesn't matter. I'm going to the conference and they asked me to present on the vampire wannabes, and that's what I'll do.'

'Well, damn. I wish I could be there to help you. Mind you, thinking about it now, if Lucifer's still obsessed with you, I'd probably be better off returning to Denver if I want to find him. But to my knowledge there haven't been any more drained-body murders in Denver. I'm certain the six deaths here are right up my alley.'

'So you're the official FBI agent working with the police again?'

'I am indeed.'

'And the FBI sent you to chase a regular serial killer?'

'Yep.'

'Can I ask a question about your job?'

'Sure.' He stretched.

'Do you carry a gun? The only time I've seen you use one was when Bryce and Raleigh came to snatch us from my house on Hallowe'en.'

'Yeah. It's regulation.' He lifted his carry-on bag into camera range and pulled out a gun in a clip-on holster. 'Although I rarely have cause to use it. I'm in a special category.'

'I was just wondering. Another thing – when you're working with the police, do you think of yourself more as a federal cop or a psychologist? Seems like those would be radically different philosophies.'

He leaned in close again and gave his usual excellent eye contact. 'It's interesting that you ask that question because it's been on my mind a lot lately. I've realised I don't think of myself as a cop or a shrink. I'm not interested in helping someone explore his inner child, and I don't like the rigid rules and regulations inherent in law enforcement. I mostly identify as a profiler, which comes in handy for what I consider my real job.'

'And what would that be?'

'Monster hunter.'

'Monster hunter?' I laughed, then stopped because he wasn't laughing. In fact he looked very serious. 'Monsters? Really? Are you talking about vampires specifically, or are you aware of other supernatural nightmares you haven't told me about yet?'

'I'm fascinated by monsters of all varieties, including human ones, and I'm starting to suspect that bloodsuckers aren't the only shadow residents sharing the world with humans. I think I've got my work cut out for me.'

'Well, Professor Van Helsing, I hope you're wrong. I'm not up for any more unpleasant surprises. Do you have proof?'

'Ever the scientist.' His lips spread in a friendly smile, showing his perfect dentistry. 'Not yet. But that's one reason I like working with the FBI – we get dibs on the creepiest un-explained cases first. With my quirky reputation, I usually get pulled into whatever the normal Feebs can't solve, and I have access to the Bureau's state-of-the-art resources. The trade-off works for the time being.'

'So you're glad to be part of the San Francisco police operation?'

'Definitely. In fact,' and he gave a quick laugh and brow

waggle, 'the cop in charge – Detective Andrews – is one gorgeous ass-kicking upholder of justice. She hasn't warmed up to me yet, but I'm working on her.'

'I'm sure you'll win her over.' *And why does that make me sad?* 'You're not easy to resist.'

'You think? You've resisted me well enough.'

'Are you sure? Hey, listen – I need to get off the computer. Lots to do to prepare for the conference.'

'Wait!' He angled one of his eyes right up to the camera lens. 'You can't just say something like that, then leave.'

I laughed. 'Yes, I can.'

'Okay.' He pulled away, grinning. 'I'll let you wiggle out this time, but I'm going to do that research and see what I can find out about this secret magical knowledge for you. I'll be in touch. Watch your back, Doc.'

'I will. You, too. And thanks, Alan. Really.'

We both clicked off and I slumped back in my chair, staring at the clock.

Night falls early in January.

CHAPTER 6

As the sun dropped behind the mountains, my anxiety grew. Throughout the evening, I kept feeling the tingling in my midsection that alerted me to the presence of vampires. Devereux's contingent of bodyguards had likely arrived and stationed themselves around the perimeter of my house. I peeked out through the window blinds every so often but didn't see anyone. But then again, I wouldn't.

With each sound my stomach clenched. I kept waiting for Devereux to pop in, or worse, Lucifer. I stroked a finger along the cross and pentagram, feeling half-foolish for counting on symbols to make me feel safe, yet still taking some comfort from the action. The cross's warmth was back. Did that mean Devereux was okay? Or just that he was awake?

I really didn't know what to feel about Devereux. I was torn between wanting his protection and being afraid of it. I had a hard time believing that nothing between us had been authentic – that my attraction to him hadn't been real in any way. How could that be? What about all the feelings I'd experienced?

Having completed a rough draft of my conference present-ation, I yawned, saved my work, then turned off the computer.

I'd just poured a glass of white wine and plopped down on the couch when I heard the telltale *pop* sound and Luna, Devereux's demon-in-training, materialised in the middle of my living room. 'Hey!' I started and spilled some of the chardonnay as I set it on the coffee table. 'I thought Devereux told you not to drop in unannounced any more.' My stomach lurched and a waterfall of dread cascaded down my body.

'Shut up.' She pointed her index finger at me, then sat on the other end of the couch.

Devereux's hostile assistant wasn't dressed like her usual self, which mostly consisted of the dominatrix-from-hell look, heavy on the skin-tight black leather. Tonight she was wearing a dress-for-success business suit in blood-red with a short skirt, a sheer low-cut silver top that matched her eyes, and black stilettos. Her very long dark hair was piled up on top of her head and held in place by chopsticks. Ruby and diamond earrings swung from her earlobes. This was the first time I'd seen her without her leathers and that was almost more startling than her showing up in general.

I'd never felt so much fear in her presence before. Well, except for the time she was overcome by bloodlust and almost fed on me, but thankfully she'd managed to control herself. Since she hadn't done anything in particular to warrant my fear tonight, obviously the filter was still down.

'Devereux is too busy chasing Lucifer to care about how I deliver his message,' she said, 'and I don't have time to waste answering human questions. Devereux said to tell you he's determined to find the maniac and that he'll be unavailable all night. He doesn't know when he'll see you. He said he would join you in your dreams if he can, but finding Lucifer is his priority.'

'Okay. I guess he didn't catch Lucifer last night, then?' I

breathed to calm myself. At least nothing terrible had happened to Devereux. Yet. Truthfully, I was relieved he wasn't planning to visit. I wasn't ready to talk to him.

'Obviously not,' she snarled, 'ergo the message.'

Luna and I had reached a pseudo-truce while Devereux was recovering from Bryce's ritual and I thought she'd begun to tolerate me, or at least stop actively threatening me on a nightly basis. But now it appeared we were back to square one with her hating everything about me. Hearing that Devereux hadn't captured Lucifer made my stomach clench.

'Why is Lucifer so hard to catch? Even for Devereux?'

She snorted and flicked her fingers dismissively, looking like she wasn't going to tell me, but then she did. 'There's something very strange about that demented bloodsucker. He has no signal.'

'No signal?' I'd never heard that term before, but then almost everything about the vampire world fell into that category.

'Pay attention, stupid mortal. Don't you even know that vampires have a specific brain frequency? Well, I guess if you want to be picky, humans do, too, but yours resonates at a much slower rate than vampire minds. Devereux says Lucifer gives off nothing, as if there's a void where his consciousness should be. That's why Devereux can't lock onto him and kill his ass.'

'A void?' I licked my dry lips. 'Maybe that's what happened when his psyche split into the different personalities – there isn't one dominant mind any more.'

She rolled her eyes. 'Leave it to you to discuss meaningless psychobabble even when your miserable life is at stake. Until Devereux figures out a way to trap the bastard, you're at his mercy. Even with all the vampires surrounding your house and the spell Devereux cast around you, this Lucifer asshole is still an unknown quantity.' She polished her crimson nails on her skirt. 'You might want to sleep with that sword you used to behead Bryce.' She studied her sharp fingernails. 'You never know when unexpected company will drop in.'

'Thanks for telling me,' I replied tartly. 'I appreciate your concern.' *As if.*

'Concern? Puh-lease. I'm still waiting for Devereux to get bored with you. I told you we have a date when that happens. Your human mind can't possibly imagine what I have planned for the two of us.' She gave an evil grin, stood and said sweetly, 'Sleep well.'

She vanished.

I retrieved my wine, sank back into the cushions and stretched my feet out on the table. The Luna-inspired fear rush was diminishing but I could still feel the residue like a hand clutching my heart.

So that was why Devereux was so . . . *off.* Lucifer's mental illness kept him from being able to control the situation. No brain frequency? I wondered if the same applied to humans with Dissociative Identity Disorder. Maybe there was a test that could verify the diagnosis for this very rare illness? I was sorry Devereux hadn't talked to me about Lucifer. Since the brain was my area of expertise, perhaps I could have helped him.

I sat on the couch, aimlessly clicking through the TV chan-nels and waiting for the next horrible thing to happen. Alan's suggestion that I talk to Cerridwyn kept replaying in my mind so I jumped up to look for the business card she'd given me to make an appointment. I eventually found it in my brief-case. I checked the clock to see if it was too late to call. Since it was after midnight, I'd have to wait until morning.

Too antsy and afraid to go to bed, I turned my laptop back

on and began searching for a credible professional hypnother-apist. Working with someone who could help me reinforce my boundaries as well as expand any psychic abilities I might not be fully utilising could prove beneficial. I printed out the contact information for several PhD-level clinicians and left the pile of papers next to Cerridwyn's business card.

I'd just started up the stairs to go to bed when the doorbell rang.

Terror stole my breath. I froze.

What the hell now? Would a bad vampire ring the doorbell?

I inched over to the door and turned on all the lights I'd just switched off. My vampire radar gave its familiar stomach-flutter and fear ran a fingertip down my spine. I flipped on the porch light and looked through the peephole. 'Who is it?'

'Doctor Knight? It's McKay – one of the Master's vampires guarding your home.'

I eyed the peephole again and recognised the Mohawk haircut on the quirky vampire I'd seen a few times before. He was half-Mohawk and half-Scottish. 'War paint' decorated his chest and face and a vibrant green plaid kilt swathed his lower half. 'What do you want, Mr McKay?' I really wasn't in the mood to be polite or friendly.

'A couple of your clients have shown up out here, wanting to talk to you. I didn't think you'd like it if I just refused to let them see you. Maybe you'd already arranged to meet and nobody told us. So, do you want to see them?'

Clients? I mentally sorted through my caseload, trying to figure out who might show up at my home. Since my address was protected, how could anyone know where I lived? But then the obvious thumped me on the head. It had to be vampires. No human would approach my home surrounded as it was by a herd of undead. The fear vibration – which I'd recently experienced first-hand – would make that impossible. Besides, most of my mortal clients followed the spoken and unspoken therapy rules. They'd never breach protocol by stepping out of their prescribed roles to intrude on my personal time. But vampires were a different breed in more ways than one. As far as they were concerned, rules simply didn't apply to them.

'Doctor Knight? It's me, Marvin,' a different voice said through the closed door. 'Eleanor is trying to take my stuff again. I'm having panic attacks. Please. Can you help us?'

'Please, Doctor,' a woman's voice said. 'I'm at my wit's end.'

Uh-oh. I knew a meltdown was coming, but so soon?

Marvin was a hoarder. He and Eleanor had been seeing me weekly for the last month, and as with all hoarders, progress and trust-building came slow. They hadn't even felt safe enough yet to disclose the sorts of things Marvin collected. Something big must have happened for them to take the scary step of reaching out.

I unlocked and opened the door, bracing myself for a barrage of fear.

'Hello, Marvin, Eleanor.' I breathed to calm my fluttering heart and stroked the diamond cross with a finger. 'I'm sorry you're having a difficult time. Yes, we can talk for a little while.' *As if I could force them to leave if they didn't want to. Another negative in the working-with-vampires column. But what the hell? Meeting with clients always takes my mind off my own drama.* I turned to McKay. 'Thank you for checking with me, and for protecting my home. I appreciate you all.'

He clicked his heels together and saluted. 'We're happy to serve the Master, Doctor Knight. We'll make sure you're safe and sound.' He looked at my clients. 'Just give a holler if you need us.'

'I will,' I said to McKay, then turned to Marvin and Eleanor.

'Come on in.' I stepped aside and opened the door all the way so they could enter, then closed and relocked it. 'Please.' I pointed to the living room. 'Take a seat and be comfortable.'

Marvin hurried to the couch and Eleanor chose a chair.

Barefoot and dressed in his usual jeans, T-shirt and head-band, Marvin was the quintessential long-haired hippie mu-sician. He'd become a vampire in the early 1970s and he lived in a perpetual *Woodstock* movie, even going so far as to smoke pot, though it had no effect on him. I was sure the drug had created a lot of his paranoia when he was human, which led to his need to soothe his anxiety by hoarding. He continu-ously scanned the room, darting glances over his shoulder to make sure nothing surprised him, and pulled a couple of throw pillows against himself for security. He was always nervous during our appointments, but he looked especially jittery tonight.

Eleanor couldn't have been more different from Marvin. Petite and trim with shoulder-length blonde hair, dressed in a beige sweater with matching trousers, she'd been a librarian when she was attacked and turned. Her conservative, obsessive nature followed her into the vampire realm. A compulsive cleaner, she struggled to keep herself and her environment under tight control. Living with someone like Marvin had to be her worst nightmare.

'What happened, Marvin?' I gave him my attention. 'Why did you have a panic attack?'

Hmm. The fear is diminishing. I can breathe. Is it because Marvin and Eleanor aren't very old? Or because they're less predatory?

He pointed a quivering finger at Eleanor. 'Like I said – she tried to take my stuff again. She wanted to clean up my room.' He pressed his hand against his chest, trying to calm the theatrical breathing. 'I told her it freaks me out when she

does that, but she won't listen. I caught her moving my private
. . . objects. Tell her, Doctor. Tell her she can't do that. It scares
me.'

'Eleanor,' I said, turning to her, 'give me your version of
what happened. Did you move Marvin's possessions?'

She pursed her lips and folded her hands primly in her lap.
'Yes I did, Doctor. Things have got out of hand. If I'd known
what Marvin collects, I'd never have let him talk me into
moving in with him. I had a perfectly nice basement room in
one of Devereux's buildings. Everything was neat and tidy, all
my books were alphabetised on the shelves. I was happy then.
But things are a mess now. Not only does he save musical
instruments, old vinyl records, every cassette recording ever
made and stacks of CDs, but there are also piles of news-
papers and magazines, shoes that aren't even his size, crates
of condoms – which he blows up like balloons – and bags of
cat food. He doesn't even have a cat!'

'I used to have a cat! In fact— Er, never mind—'

Eleanor gasped. 'Are you saying—?'

'I don't want to talk about that.'

'So,' I interjected, my intuition sounding the alarm, 'what
did you remove, Eleanor? What set Marvin off?'

Marvin leaped to his feet, trembling. 'Don't tell, Eleanor.
You know I need my stuff to feel safe. Everything I keep is
important to me. Don't betray me!'

Oh, great. Whatever the big secret is, it's going to be dramatic.

'Please sit down, Marvin.'

He sat.

'We're all just here to talk. There's nothing to be afraid of.'
I nodded at Eleanor. 'What was it?'

Eleanor shifted her eyes between the carpet and Marvin's
angry face. 'I was in the middle of pulling one of the dead

bodies out of the room when he came home and caught me.'

'Eleanor! Don't tell!' He pulled on his hair, his eyes wide. 'We can talk about our problems without being specific. You promised.'

'Dead bodies?' I asked, anxiety spiking. 'What kind of dead bodies, Eleanor?' *Does this clear up the cat reference?*

She shifted her gaze to Marvin. 'I know I promised, but I can't deal with it any more. There must be thirty dead bodies in there by now, unless you've hidden more I haven't found yet. They stink, Marvin! And they're filthy. They take up too much room. There's dried blood and body fluids all over the floor. I can't get the stains out. The bodies don't stay neatly piled up – a stray arm or leg always flops into my path and I trip over them.' She looked at me. 'He dresses them in costumes, Doctor. Military clothes. There are corpses scattered all over the apartment.' She returned her attention to Marvin. 'And there's nowhere to put my periodicals or my computers.'

What the hell? No, I don't want to know this! I can just get up and run away now . . .

Marvin started to cry. 'You can't take my bodies away. Please, Eleanor!'

I straightened and took a deep breath. 'Eleanor, what kind of bodies are you talking about?' *As if I didn't know. Shit, shit, shit! I don't want to hear this.*

'Dead human bodies, Doctor.'

I'm too tired for this insanity!

I grabbed the arms of the chair. 'Let's be clear: are you saying Marvin is killing humans and bringing them to your apartment?'

Holy fuckola. No way! Not even Dexter would do that . . .

Marvin threw himself face-down on the couch, sobbing wildly.

Eleanor covered her ears with her hands.

'Eleanor?' I raised my voice and she let her hands drop, looking guilty and afraid. 'Please answer me.'

'This is hard, Doctor Knight.' She twisted her hands. 'I don't want to hurt Marvin – I'm very fond of him. He did *accidentally* kill a couple of humans and then bury them in the yard next door, but that was twenty years ago. He dug them up recently and brought them home – what was left of them, anyway. Mostly he just finds the corpses – homeless people, junkies, mortals who have car crashes where nobody's around, people who kill themselves. He's quite an efficient body-snatcher.'

His mother must be so proud.

Marvin pulled a pillow over his head, muffling the sobs.

My mind spun. If Marvin was human, I could call the police and turn the entire mess over to them, put Marvin on a 72-hour psych hold so he could be evaluated and properly medicated. But what options were available for chronically mentally ill bloodsuckers? Meds didn't work on them. Who could I tell? Devereux? Maybe, but he wasn't available right now. This situation definitely pounded another nail into the coffin of not working with vampires. Nobody could be expected to cope with such insanity.

But I'm a therapist, damn it. I have to do something. Don't I?

Eleanor squeezed her eyes tight and covered her ears again. 'Marvin!' I said.

He didn't answer so I tried again. 'Marvin!'

No response. He'd told me at our last session that, in addition to everything else, he also has a phobia about being touched. His childhood had been hideous – he'd suffered sexual abuse at the hands of all the trusted people in his life, so he was unable to have *normal* relationships or intimacy. I tried calling his name again, with the same lack of reaction, then I took a risk. I hoped McKay could hear me if I screamed, because it was entirely possible my technique could backfire. Marvin might be a wimp, but he was still a vampire.

'Marvin!' I reached over and touched his arm.

He bolted up, his face a mask of fear. But he'd stopped crying.

His terrified expression made me feel guilty for doing something I knew frightened him, but sometimes we have to weigh the cost of an intervention against the price of the status quo.

'Marvin?' I spoke in a soft voice. 'I'm sorry I touched you, but I need you to talk to me. Can you do that?'

Yuck! I looked at my hand. *I just touched someone covered with decomposing-corpse cooties!*

Eleanor stared at him, still very upset, the corners of her lips quivering.

He nodded and combed shaky fingers through his tangled hair.

'Tell me about the bodies, Marvin. Why do you collect them?'

Holy shit. Did I just actually say those words?

'They make me feel safe.' He looked at the floor. 'I know this sounds stupid, but they're like the toy soldiers I had when I was a kid. I can line them up around me and keep the bad people away. I'm sure if I can build a tall enough wall with them, I'll finally be okay. I won't be scared any more.' He looked at me with sad eyes. 'And I didn't mean to kill the ones from before. I wasn't very good at just drinking a little blood back then and they were drug addicts who were already close to death. I haven't hurt anyone since, honest.'

Any minute now I'm going to wake up ...

'I'm sure that's true, but we're going to have to deal with the current situation. Are you willing to have the bodies removed from your home? Do you want Eleanor to keep on living with you? It sounds like it's very important to her that you give them up.'

He started crying again. 'I don't know what I'll do without them. I'm freaking out just talking about it. But I don't want Eleanor to leave.'

Hoarding was so difficult to cure. Marvin had a lot of work ahead of him, if he could even find the strength to begin. Maybe the thought of losing Eleanor would be the impetus for change.

'Eleanor, talk to Marvin. Tell him what you need in order to stay with him.'

She cleared her throat and a tear slid down her cheek. 'I just want to be more important to you than the dead bodies. I want you to spend time with me instead of them. I hear you talking to them. I feel left out. And I want you to empty an entire bedroom just for me. I need my own space!'

She wants to be more important than the dead bodies. That's reasonable.

'Marvin? What do you want to say to Eleanor?'

Breathe, Kismet. This is a nightmare and nobody came to the door. I'm fast asleep.

'What if I put them all in one room, so you can have your own space? Would that work?' He looked at her hopefully.

'Hmm,' I interrupted, 'I don't think that will take care of the problem, Marvin. We're going to have to discuss moving the bodies out completely.'

He looked ready to start crying again so I quickly continued, 'Would you feel safe talking to the Master about this?'

'The Master? Is he even still the Master? I heard some things—'

I cut him off. If Marvin had heard the rumours, then it was

official that every vampire had. 'Yes, he certainly *is* still the Master. Do I have your permission to tell him what you and Eleanor have shared with me? He can have some of his staff collect the . . . remains and figure out a way to have the bodies turn up somewhere so the families of the missing people will know their loved ones are dead. You can give them closure. That would be a good thing, wouldn't it? You'd like to help them, right?'

How obsessed with these bodies is he?

He pouted. 'I guess so. If I *have* to.'

I rolled my shoulders to release some of the tension there. 'That was very courageous, Marvin, and a step in the right direction. Eleanor,' I shifted my gaze to her, 'is there anything else you need to say? This is your opportunity to clear the air.'

She frowned and looked at Marvin. 'I can't stop thinking about your cat comment. I used to have several cats when I lived in my old room, and they all disappeared. I want to know if you had anything to do with that.'

His chin trembled and he stared at the floor.

Eleanor jumped up, wringing her hands. 'No! Not my cats! You knew how much I loved them. What did you do with them?'

'Please don't be mad, Eleanor! I just brought them home to play with and then I couldn't give them up. I might have forgotten to feed them, though. That's why I keep lots of cat food around now.' He wiped his running nose.

Ick. Vampire snot.

I handed him the tissue box.

He blew his nose, then brightened. 'But you can have them back! They're all in the closet.'

Eleanor stared at him for a few seconds with her mouth open, then stomped to the front door and unlocked it.

'Eleanor?' Marvin said. 'Where are you going?'

She flung the door open, turned back long enough to give him a nasty glare, then bolted into the night.

Marvin leaped off the couch. 'Oh no! She's going to take my cats!' He hustled after her.

Well, at least she's practising her assertiveness skills. That's something. And I have to give her points for a dramatic exit.

McKay bounded across the grass and met me on the porch. 'Are you all right, Doctor Knight? What happened?'

I didn't know whether to laugh or scream, but I gave him a tired smile and breathed through the heightened terror. 'I'm fine.' *Nope. I've gone insane.* 'Therapy is hard work – sometimes people have strong emotional reactions. It goes with the territory. Good night, Mr McKay.'

'Good night, Doctor. Sleep well. We'll watch over you.'

Yawning, I closed the door and locked it, grateful for my dark guardian angels.

As I shuffled upstairs, I felt a flash of optimism. I'd just survived Eleanor and Marvin's crazy session. I was strong, smart. I could figure out my mess.

But just in case, where *was* that sword?

CHAPTER 7

The sun hit me in the eyes.

I wasn't dead.

Lucifer hadn't finished me off while I slept. I stretched, luxuriating in still having a heartbeat.

Making it through the night definitely perked me up.

And since I hadn't scheduled any clients until afternoon, I could call Cerridwyn for an appointment and line up a few hypnotherapists to interview.

Feeling irrationally cheerful, I made some coffee, drank it with a light breakfast, checked voicemail messages, then took a quick shower.

It occurred to me that Devereux hadn't visited my dreams, and I was glad for the reprieve. What did it say about our relationship that having no contact with him felt liberating? But it was also true that I was worried about him. It would be harder than I cared to admit to let go of him if it came to that.

Finding a qualified hypnotherapist in my local area wouldn't be a problem. According to my Internet search, Denver was favoured with an overabundance of traditional and non-traditional practitioners. I waded through the information I'd printed out last night and narrowed the list to four candidates. I went to voicemail with the first three calls and left messages.

The fourth call was answered by an actual person: Dr Hamilton – please call me Ham – Taylor. Discovering he preferred to go by the name of a pork product gave me pause and ordinarily might have put me off. After all, there were hypnotists who led people to believe they had valid credentials when they didn't. And I wasn't looking for a stage hypnotist. No clucking like a chicken required, thank you. But Dr Taylor laughed engagingly at my hesitation and provided a long list of sterling qualifications. Not only had he earned an MD from Harvard Medical School, but his grandfather, also a physician, had worked with Milton Erickson, the famed medical hypnotherapist, and Ham had grown up with that influence. He'd followed his interest in various alternative healing modalities and was comfortable exploring subjects like psychic abilities and the supernatural. Now that I'd spoken to Dr Taylor, I vaguely remembered a young client telling me the clinician was great, if eccentric. The fact that he recognised my name from all the media attention at Hallowe'en and already knew about my vampire-wannabe clientele saved me from having to give a long explanation about my request for an appointment. By the time we'd scheduled for the next morning and hung up, I was excited to meet him, regardless of the outcome of the session. Maybe he'd be a kindred spirit.

Next I called Cerridwyn, who answered on the first ring. Before I could identify myself, she said, 'Hello, Doctor Knight.'

'Uh, hello.' *She must have Caller ID.*

'No, I don't have Caller ID. I have psychic abilities.' She gave a throaty laugh. 'Which you well know, since that's why you're calling.' She cut right to the chase. 'I can see you in one hour. I'm at 423 Maple Street. Until then.'

She hung up.

I held the phone out and stared at it, as if it could explain what had just happened. Once again I was impressed by her keen skills, and even though it was irritating to have yet another person read my mind, I couldn't argue that she'd certainly been spot-on. And I did want her help.

Planning to go directly to my office after seeing Cerridwyn, I dressed in a dark-blue wool trousersuit, answered a few emails, then drove the short distance to her address, which turned out to be a lovely Victorian-style house.

I parked and walked up onto her porch. She opened the door before I could ring the doorbell. Her long grey hair was pulled into a bun on top of her head. Instead of the flowing gypsy dress she'd worn when I saw her on the Mall, she was dressed in new-looking jeans and a lavender sweater, which matched her socks and the deep purple of her eyes.

She smiled genially and held out a hand. 'Welcome to my home.'

I took her hand and she pulled me inside. A couple of pairs of her shoes sat along the wall near the door. I took that as a cue. 'Would you like me to remove my shoes?'

'Yes, if you wouldn't mind. I appreciate the tradition of honouring someone's home by removing shoes. You can put them on the mat next to mine.'

She gestured for me to follow her into a large living room arranged with high-quality classic furniture, amazing paintings of goddesses from various cultures and a grand piano in the corner. The floors were polished wood. A huge fireplace filled one of the walls, the flames sending warmth into the room. I didn't know what I'd expected a psychic's house to look like, but it wasn't this gorgeous place. 'Your house is incredible. Did you decorate it?'

'Thank you. The house has been in my family for more than a century. My parents are responsible for the restoration and the furniture. I added the paintings, which were created by one of my coven-mates. Please,' she pointed to the burgundy brocade couch, 'sit, make yourself at home.'

A large black cat appeared out of nowhere and jumped onto my lap.

'Oh!' Surprised, I stroked a hand along the soft fur. 'You have a black cat.'

She laughed. 'Of course. Would you expect anything less?' She gently pushed the cat off my legs. 'Down, Pyewacket.'

'Pyewacket? That's an unusual name.'

'Not in some circles. I named her after the witch's familiar in one of my favourite old movies, *Bell, Book and Candle*. Have you seen it?' She sat across from me in a rocking chair.

'No. I don't think so, but if you recommend it, I'll have to pick up the DVD.'

'I think you'll like it. Of course, you'll have to take it with a grain of salt – it was made in the 1950s and the morality of the time demanded the main character make a stupid decision. I'd tell you more about it but I don't want to ruin the ending.'

'No, I'm interested. Tell me.' I had to hear what she considered a stupid decision. 'I'll still enjoy the movie.'

'If you're sure . . .' She warmed to her topic. 'Well, in order to win the love of the mortal male, the witch, played by the marvellous Kim Novak, had to give up her magic. She had to literally stop using witchcraft and become society's limited idea of a good girl in order to be rewarded with love. She had to *conform*.'

'That sounds like *Bewitched*'s Samantha, always trying to please the mortal husband by denying what she is.'

'Yes!' She clapped her hands together. 'Precisely. What would possess so powerful a woman to allow herself to be diminished? But we both know women do it every day.'

'That's true. In fact, that's sort of why I wanted to see you.'

'I suspected as much.' She rose, headed into the kitchen and came back with two bottles of water. She gave one to me and returned to the rocker. 'Let me centre myself and then we can begin.'

Suddenly nervous, I rubbed my palms against the fabric of the couch. 'Aren't you going to use your cards?' She'd laid out tarot cards before when we met in person.

'I can if you'd like me to, but they're not necessary. My intuition tells me I need to focus deeply for you, which is easier if I'm not working with the cards. Is that okay?'

'Sure. Absolutely. However it works for you.'

She closed her eyes and breathed slowly. As I watched her inhaling and exhaling and listened to the crackling fire, I began to relax, too.

Eyes still closed, she spoke. 'First, I want to mention that your brain is different today.'

I tensed, my relaxation out the window. 'What do you mean?' *Oh no – is my brain even more altered than I feared?*

'All is well, Kismet – your brain is fine. But the first time I met you, I detected a subtle influence operating, as if some of your neuro-pathways had been rewired. I recognised it because I'd *seen* it before. That's how I knew you were spending time with strong vampires – it's their calling card. Today that subtle effect is gone. Your mind is clear, powerful. You know what I'm talking about, don't you?'

'Yes.' There was no use in lying or evading. If I wanted help, I had to be open to it. 'I learned recently that being around vampires, especially old, powerful ones, affects my brain.' I took a breath and figured I might as well dive right in. 'Do you know Devereux?'

She opened her eyes and studied me. 'I do. I've met him several times. Many of Devereux's vampires come to me for readings. He's one of the most potent vampires in the world. I'm aware that you've been spending time with him. It must be difficult for you to be yourself in his presence.' She frowned. 'But what's the meaning of your state of mind today? Why don't I sense his influence? Ahhh—' She nodded. 'Something has happened to erase it from your mind. Someone intervened. Another vampire.' Surprise coloured her tone.

'Yes.' I swallowed at this demonstration of her abilities. 'She cleared all vampire effects and control from my brain and made me harder for them to read for a few days. I hadn't realised how restricted I was until I wasn't.'

She closed her eyes again. 'Anne Boleyn? How fascinating. You met the notorious queen? Why would she help you?' I started to answer and she held up a hand. 'Oh, I see. She wasn't helping – she was hoping to cause trouble and annoy Devereux. She's a little angry with him because . . . oh yes, an old romantic issue. But the end result actually benefitted you. But there's more.' She opened her eyes. 'What else is worrying you?'

Deciding not to think about Anne hoping to cause trouble, I let the idea evaporate and reminded myself that vampires were not human. 'How much do you know about the events that took place on Hallowe'en at The Vampires' Ball?'

'I know everything.'

And she went onto prove that she did.

'Out of jealousy, one of Devereux's offspring Bryce set a ritual trap for him, involving the insane vampire Lucifer who killed so many people across the country. The very same madman who became obsessed with you. Devereux wasn't able to defeat Lucifer, and it weighs heavily on his mind. He burns with the need to balance the scales. He's so caught up in restoring his reputation that he's losing perspective, no longer thinking clearly. His emotions are volatile. Lucifer still stalks you and you are afraid.'

Yep. Got it in one.

My mouth had gone dry, so I opened the water and took a long drink. 'I'd say that about covers it. At this point, I only see two choices. I can continue to spend time with Devereux, who might be the only person with any hope of protecting me from Lucifer, but my brain would become more and more affected until I eventually lose myself.'

I paused for breath, then continued, 'Or I can stay away from him and wait for Lucifer to show up and kill me. Needless to say, both those options reek. I came to ask if you can sense any other possibilities. And if you happen to see anything else I need to know, I'd appreciate if you'd tell me. I feel like I've been wandering in fog for the last three months.'

She stared at me for several seconds, her lips pressed together, before she cleared her throat and spoke. 'You've come a long way in your struggle to accept things like vampires and psychics like me. It's impressive that you're here asking the right questions and have the courage to hear the answers.'

'Thank you. I never had any problem with you – I've always believed in the validity of psychic abilities. Psychics are different from vampires. There's scientific proof that the human mind is capable of much more than we've discovered so far. I guess I didn't realise psychic abilities could be as exten-sive as yours – and Devereux's – are, but I never doubted that they're real. It took me a bit longer to process the existence of vampires, but now that I'm committed to working with them therapeutically, I have to find a way to protect myself from all of them. Can you see any other choices for me?'

'I can, but first let's discuss the one that's totally in your hands.'

'What's that?'

'You must learn to still your mind and calm your emotions. Even though you are a rational woman, a scientist with an analytical mind, you come across to others – energetically – as if you function from pure emotion. It's a paradox. Devereux told you that thoughts are fuelled by emotions and that's one reason why yours are so easy for him to read. He also told you that you have your own talents which you haven't fully explored yet.'

'Yes!' My heart leaped. 'That's what I want to know about! My supposed abilities. Vampires tell me that all the time. Can you give me any insight into what they're talking about?' If she could just do that, I'd owe her for ever.

She paused, her gaze tracking around the edges of my body. 'You have a unique energy field. There's something unusual – almost nonhuman – about you. I think that's why you attract so many supernatural and paranormal creatures and situations. It's as if you're shining out an invisible beacon and they're answering.'

It felt like she was psychically dissecting my very DNA. 'What? I don't attract a lot of anything. Just because I stumbled onto some vampires . . .' I trailed off and shifted uncomfortably.

'Not only vampires. You also communicate with ghosts. You attract witches. Even I feel pulled. The unknown world has yet to fully show itself to you. And your own psychic abilities are much greater than you think. If you spent even an hour a day *exercising* them, you'd discover the talents the vampires can't help but notice.' She leaned towards me.

'Forgive me for mixing metaphors, but now that the veil has been lifted and you've tasted the apple, what are you going to do about it?'

'That's why I came to you.' I gave her a helpless look. 'I don't know what I *can* do about it.'

'You know more than you think, and I can help you with the rest. Do you meditate?'

'I know how to meditate, but I don't do it regularly. My mind races. I can't remain in a space of *no thought* for more than a few seconds.'

'That's a sufficient beginning. I can teach you a technique that will allow you to go into a trance while fully conscious. If you can master this skill, you'll be able to reset your brain at will. Are you willing to do the work?'

That was a no-brainer. I was nodding vigorously before the words were completely out of her mouth. 'Yes. Yes, of course. I'll do whatever it takes to regain control of my life.'

'Good.' Cerridwyn seemed to relax in relief. 'The second part of finding more options comes from the realm of magic.'

'Magic?' I blurted. 'You're not going to tell me I have magical abilities as well, are you?'

She chuckled. 'Not at this point, but we'll come back to that topic in the future. Remember I told you I've encountered other humans whose brains have been taken over by strong vampires? Over the years, I began comparing notes with other witches and psychics, asking if they'd ever seen anyone who was able to resist or repair the damage caused by ongoing contact with vampires. Slowly, anecdotal stories began to emerge, tales of mortals who were not mentally enslaved, who somehow managed to remain themselves.'

My mind raced. If she'd learned this much, surely there was hope for me. 'Okay, that's good. So what did they do?'

'In every case, they realised what was happening and sought out a particular magician to cast a spell on them. Apparently there's a secret vampire library of knowledge—'

The hairs on the back of my neck stood at attention. 'That's odd. You're the second person who's mentioned that to me. My friend said he was going to research it for me.'

'Alan Stevens?'

'Yes.'

'He has strong feelings for you.' Her voice held gentle amusement.

'No, he doesn't.' *No way. I'm not talking about Alan.* 'He's just confused—'

'It sounds like he's not the only one. But that isn't important right now. Did he tell you the name of the magician?'

'Yes, something like Zoltar, or Zoloft, no, wait . . . Zephyr.'

Cerridwyn grinned. 'See how the universe is lining things up for you?' She closed her eyes and rocked for a moment. 'I see you connecting with this vampire. He will help you. In the meantime, you must work hard at the technique I mentioned. It will seem complicated but is actually quite simple. You'll learn to hum a certain pitch silently in your mind. Think of it as sound magic. I will communicate it to your unconscious now.'

This sounded like more weirdness. But she knew things – things I hadn't spoken of to anyone except Devereux. Or Alan. And I had nothing to lose at this point. 'How will you do that?'

'I'll send you a psychic soundtrack of sorts – as if I'm uploading it directly to your deeper consciousness – and I'll hum a tone out loud. Then we'll practise. Ready? Okay, close your eyes.'

For a few seconds there was nothing, then I *heard* several dissonant pitches in my mind. As I listened, Cerridwyn's voice cut through the chaotic sound, strong enough to force all the other tones to align with hers in multiple octaves.

'Hum the tone silently,' she said.

I spent a couple of seconds wondering how I could hum silently, then I was simply doing it.

'Keep going and watch what happens.'

I literally felt myself slowing, as if my brain waves shifted from beta all the way to theta. Suddenly my consciousness expanded and my body rhythm downshifted.

'Open your eyes and talk to me. Realise that you can remain in this state while functioning normally. Memorise this feeling.'

My eyes eased open. Everything looked sharper. Colours were brighter. 'Is this what a drug trip feels like?'

She laughed. 'In some cases. Keep talking.'

'So I have to do the imaginary hum any time I'm around a vampire so they won't take over my brain? How can I hold therapy sessions if I'm humming in my head?'

'Good question. The more you practise, the less effort it will take. The new vibration will become your baseline. This technique allows you to physically transform your own brain from one that's easy for vampires to manipulate by moving to another frequency that can't be altered.'

'Sounds great – sign me up.'

'Of course, this won't keep Lucifer from harming you.'

Shit! At the mention of Lucifer, my heartbeat raced and my breath caught. I was right back in normal beta waves. I blinked and drank more water. 'As soon as you mentioned him, I returned to my regular consciousness.'

'Yes, I thought you would. Without closing your eyes, start the mental humming. Become aware of the other tones I seeded into your unconscious. Remember the experience of being in that expanded place. Show yourself you can easily return there.'

It took longer than it should've because my mind kept

insisting it was necessary to think about Lucifer and what he might do, but I was soon able to imagine humming the note and felt myself changing. 'This is amazing. Sound magic?'

'Well, more accurately vibration or frequency magic, but any label will do. You must practise as much as possible, every day. Between this technique and talking to Zephyr, your choices will increase.'

'Will you contact Zephyr? I've never heard Devereux talk about him. Does he live in Denver?'

'I doubt he lives in North America and perhaps not even in current time. You know how some of the old vampires prefer to live in the past, which was a much simpler era for them.' She tapped her fingers against her knee as her eyes took on a glazed look. A minute passed before she blinked and looked at me. 'I believe Alan Stevens will arrange for you to speak with Zephyr. You and I can meet again when you return from New York City.'

'How do you know I'm going—? Oops, sorry – forgot who I was talking to for a moment. That sounds good. I look forward to seeing you again. You've been wonderful.'

We spent a few minutes haggling over the fee for the session – she didn't want to take as much as I wanted to give her – and then she walked me to the door.

'Remember, Kismet,' she said, her expression serious, 'you must practise. Everything depends on it.'

'I promise.'

We said goodbye. As I drove to my office, I wondered if I'd run my car off the road if I practised the mental hum while driving.

I didn't put it to the test.

CHAPTER 8

The afternoon proved to be highly productive.

I met with several clients, updated case files, filled out required paperwork, returned phone calls and practised the hum. It was already becoming easier. I knew my human clients had no physiological effect on my brain – although a few resistant souls often made my head feel like it was going to explode – but I enjoyed practising my new conscious trance state during their sessions. It was exciting to realise I could be as – or even more – effective functioning from a deeper level of mind.

Since the bleak winter day had been overcast – several inches of snow had fallen in the last twenty-four hours – darkness began creeping in by late afternoon. I checked the clock and arranged chairs in a circle. My Fear of Fangs group members would be popping in soon for our third meeting. I never would've suspected so many vampires had biting issues.

Sitting behind my desk, I breathed deeply to prepare myself for the increasing fear level and waited for the participants to arrive. Only four members would be attending. The other two regulars were taking the night off. One of the no-shows, Betty, a former actress and current histrionic bipolar, had called and said she wouldn't be leaving her coffin this evening due to having difficulty breathing. Apparently being dead wasn't enough of a clue that breathing was optional. And the other, Medina, a suicidal two-century-old blood-drinker with depression, kept using the same methods she'd used as a human to try to kill herself. She knew none of the familiar approaches would work, but she couldn't break the pattern. According to her roommate, she'd jumped off a skyscraper again and would be incapacitated until she healed.

Should I send a get-well card? A regenerate-your-limbs-soon card? My night-walking clients were nothing if not creative.

Chain arrived first. True to his name, he wore chains around his neck, through his belt loops to hold his baggy blue jeans up, wrapped around his biker boots and encircling his wrists. Tall and thin with long, stringy black hair and dull grey eyes, he was wearing his well-loved Harley jacket. Swaggering over to my desk, he hitched a hip on the corner and said, 'Hey, doll. Let the party begin.'

To the casual observer, Chain appeared to be one tough bloodsucker.

Looks can be deceiving.

'Hello, Chain. Remember we talked about you calling me by my professional title? You're practising being respectful, right?'

'Sure, doll – I mean Doctor Knight. Whatever you say.'

'Thanks, Chain. Go ahead and take a chair.'

Lucille silently appeared. 'Hello, Doctor Knight. I hope I'm not late.'

'Hello, Lucille. As usual, you're right on time. Please find your seat.'

'Well, if it ain't Mother Superior, come to join the sinners,' Chain said, referring to the fact that Lucille, who usually came to group wearing tight, revealing clothing with big hair, tonight sported a floor-length nun's habit complete with veil and a long rose quartz rosary around her neck. Her vivid green eyes sparkled in her pale face. A wisp of brown hair peeked from the white coif on her head. Like many schizophrenics, Lucille experienced religious hallucinations as part of her illness.

'Chain? Is that respectful?' I asked.

He slouched down in his chair, sulking. Chain's diagnosis was antisocial personality disorder mediated by extreme anxiety. While he had strong psychopathic tendencies that would normally preclude him from participating in the group, his urges were held in check by his profound fear. He'd told us he liked torturing and killing animals when he was a human child, but after every incident he hid in his closet for hours, terrified, waiting for the ghost of the dead creature to take its revenge.

'I forgive him, Doctor Knight,' Lucille said, crossing herself. 'He can't help it.'

Something must have escalated her anxiety to account for the clothing choice.

Partners in every way, the last two members appeared together, as they often did.

'Hi, Doctor Knight,' they said in unison.

'Hello, Walter, Dennis. Nice to see you. Go ahead and sit and we'll get started.'

'Hey! Bummer and Downer are here. Let the whining begin!' Chain teased.

'Chain? We had this discussion. Walter and Dennis prefer to go by their real names.'

'Yeah.' He pouted. 'But you're the only one who calls them that, so you shouldn't just yell at me. Everybody knows how they are.'

Well then, should I call you Psycho?

But Chain was right. They'd earned their vampire nicknames due to their negative outlooks; they'd elevated pessimism to an art form. No matter how many silver linings were offered, they could always find the dark cloud.

Gathering my notebook, pen and water bottle, I joined them.

'Let's go around the circle and check in. How did your week go? Any success to report? Lucille, would you like to begin?'

She burst into tears. 'Oh, Doctor Knight. I tried what you suggested. I stood in front of the mirror and tried to appreciate my fangs, to think good thoughts about them, but the longer I looked at them, the sharper they seemed to get, until I was so scared I pulled them out of my mouth again. Like before. I tried to collect the blood from the holes in my gums so I could drink it and not have to feed, but it clotted too fast. And drinking my own blood doesn't work anyway.' She covered her face with her hands and sobbed for a few seconds before plucking a tissue from the box and wiping her nose. 'When the fangs grew back in, I tried to drink from one of my regular humans, but I was so clumsy pushing my teeth into his neck that I ripped him up. He screamed and I screamed. It was horrible. He finally agreed to cut his wrist and drip the blood into a cup for me. I'm such a failure.'

'You got that right,' Chain said.

I gave him a look and he shifted his gaze to the carpet.

There definitely wasn't a Love Your Fangs class in graduate school.

'Did pulling your fangs out relieve your anxiety, Lucille? Did it make you feel better?'

'Yeah, for a few minutes. But then I felt worse.'

'That's what usually happens,' I explained. 'When we hurt ourselves, we distract from the real problem but nothing gets any better. What could you do instead?'

She thought for a few seconds.

'I know! I know!' Dennis said, bouncing in the chair, his hand raised.

'Hold on a minute, Dennis. Let's give Lucille a chance to figure it out.'

Lucille shifted her eyes from Dennis back to me. 'Like you taught us, I could try to ride out the anxiety, switch to thinking about something that makes me feel better and wait until the urge passes.'

'That's exactly right, Lucille. Are you willing to try that?'

She wrapped her hands around the rosary beads. 'Yes. I'll try.'

Since his hand was still waving in the air, I turned to Dennis. 'What would you like to say, Dennis?'

'Everyone's talking about the Master getting his ass kicked by that Lucifer guy. Ever since me and Walter heard that, we've been afraid. We thought the Master would protect everyone in his coven, that he was like the vampire Superman. But what if he can't?' He leaped out of his chair and paced, twisting his hands, his eyes wide. 'What if that bad vampire and other monsters come to kill us?'

'Yeah,' Walter said, bouncing up to join Dennis, 'who's going to keep us safe? If we're all truly dead, then it doesn't matter if we're afraid of our fangs. We'll be gone!' He jumped up and down in place, smacking himself on the sides of his head with his hands. Dennis imitated him.

Uh-oh. The Mad Hatter Vampire's tea party.

'Jesus,' Chain said. 'The fags are freakin' out.' He stood and tugged the chain from around his waist. 'Here, Doctor Knight – you can use this to tie them up.'

His expression was so sincere I almost smiled. 'Thank you, Chain, but I don't think that'll be necessary. You can put your

... belt ... back on. And please don't use that hateful word in group.'

'What word?' he asked, frowning.

'Fags. We've also talked about *that* before. Please think before you speak.'

I rose and approached the two frantic bloodsuckers slowly, then spoke very quietly. 'Come on, you two, sit down. Everything's okay. You raised good questions – let's all calm down and we can discuss them.'

They looked at me for a few seconds, then at each other, before they sat.

I guess we have a new topic for the meeting tonight. What the hell am I supposed to say now?

'Is it okay with you, Lucille and Chain, if we talk about this subject? This is your group as well – we all have to be on the same page.'

Lucille wrapped her arms around herself and swayed in the chair. 'I guess I've been afraid, too, Doctor Knight. I don't really want to talk about it, but I do want to know what's going on. I don't want Lucifer to get me. I've been having nightmares that he will.'

'Chain?' I asked. He'd become unusually quiet.

'I don't give a fuck,' he said, trying for bravado, but his voice cracked. 'I don't need anyone to protect me. You can talk about whatever you want.' He pulled his jacket over his head.

Okay, then. They're all afraid. Let's address the bloody elephant in the room.

'Dennis, you raised the issue, so why don't you tell us more about your fear of not being protected?'

He stood and scanned the group. 'The whole vampire community is scared. Nobody wants to say anything bad about the Master, but we're worried. We heard Lucifer just pounded on him, that the Master didn't even put up a fight.' His voice caught. 'We heard he begged for mercy.'

Should I give them the facts or just do therapy? I can't have Devereux's reputation ruined by lies.

'No!' I said firmly, 'none of that's true.'

Walter jumped up again. 'But it *is* true – everybody's saying it.'

'Sit down, please.'

They sat.

Lucille was crying quietly and Chain had burrowed deeper into his coat. Dennis and Walter stared at me with bug-eyes.

Would Devereux be upset if I discussed his private business with *lesser* vampires? How much difference would it actually make to the rumour machine if I told these four clients the truth? After all, it was only my word against a juicy story. Who'd believe the Master's girlfriend – or whatever I was now? No doubt Devereux's enemies were revelling in his expected downfall. No matter how conflicted I felt about him now, Devereux and I had been lovers. More importantly, we'd been emotionally intimate. I didn't want to see him hurt.

After a few seconds of mental debate, I decided to throw caution to the wind and share what I'd seen.

Determined, I took a deep breath, set my pad and pen on the floor and crossed my legs. 'Devereux didn't beg for mercy – he'd never do that. He was ambushed and he fought brilliantly.'

'How do *you* know?' Walter asked.

Chain threw off his coat and lunged at Walter. 'Because she was *there*, asshole. Everybody knows that. She's the Master's woman!'

Walter squealed in fear and grabbed onto Dennis.

'Chain, please,' I said, 'go back to your seat.'

Scowling, he reclaimed his chair, but he didn't cover his head with his coat again.

'As Chain said, I was there.' I couldn't sit still any more, so I stood up and paced around the outside of the circle. 'It wasn't Lucifer who bested Devereux. Nobody *kicked his ass* – it was the blood-fuelled death-magic ritual that temporarily incapacitated him. The magic was astoundingly powerful. Without that, Lucifer wouldn't have had a snowball-in-hell's chance of subduing Devereux. Even the intensity of the spell couldn't keep Devereux from returning. He is, and will always be, someone you can count onto protect you.'

I hope that's true.

Dennis turned in his chair to speak to me as I passed behind him. 'But why can't Devereux catch Lucifer? I thought nothing was beyond the Master's powers. Is he afraid of Lucifer?'

'Yeah,' Walter said, 'that's what we heard.'

Lucille began touching her beads, reciting the rosary out loud.

'No, he isn't afraid of Lucifer – and he's very eager to find him. Lots of Devereux's vampires are looking for the maniac. But there's something strange about Lucifer, something that makes him difficult to track.'

'What's that?' Chain asked, his voice quivering as he rubbed his arms. 'Is he some kind of major bad dude with extra powers Devereux doesn't have?'

'No,' I said, 'there's something wrong with his brain.'

'His brain? What do you mean?' Dennis asked.

'He's severely mentally ill. Whatever happened to cause the split in his personality took away the unique signal every brain has. There's an empty space where his pattern should be.'

'Signal?' Lucille asked and sucked in a breath. 'You mean like we're being controlled by aliens?'

Oh, Geez. Beam me up, Scotty.

'No, no aliens. Lucifer's brain is broken. He isn't *normal* like you.'

Normal. Vampires. What's wrong with this picture?

'Devereux can't get a fix on Lucifer's brain because there's no energy to detect, no personalised frequency. Nothing,' I continued. 'That's the only reason he's still at large. And Lucifer isn't going to hurt you – he focuses on humans.'

Dennis wiped his face with a tissue and puffed out a breath. 'Well, that's good,' he said, then looked at me and remembered I fell into that category. 'Er, I mean, not good that he hunts humans, but I'm relieved he isn't interested in us.' Worry still shadowed his face. 'Is he going to come after you, Doctor Knight?'

How much truth is too much?

Before I could decide whether that was something they didn't need to know, Chain said, 'Fuck. You guys are dense. It's common knowledge Lucifer's after Doctor K. He only wanted Devereux out of the way so he could have the Doc. Don't you know *anything*?'

Actually, Bryce wanted Devereux for himself. I don't think Lucifer cared one way or the other about him. The madman was too screwed up to consider him a threat.

Lucille cracked her knuckles loudly. 'Oh no, Doctor Knight. I've been so afraid for myself that I didn't think about you. What will I do if he hurts you? Who will be my therapist? How will I survive?'

First rule of narcissism: it's all about me.

They all started talking at once, the collective anxiety escalating. Then the tension level in the room spiked, and as if an invisible switch had been thrown, everyone went berserk. Walter slouched out of his seat, dropped to his hands and knees and crawled frantically around the room, smashing his head repeatedly into walls. Dennis climbed onto the chair, jumped up and down and screamed, 'We're gonna die!' Lucille tore off her beads, sending them ricocheting off every surface in the room, before she stripped out of her nun's outfit, exposing her nude body. Then she ran in circles as Chain chased her, laughing hysterically.

Holy shit. Here we go again.

Acting out like this was their way of not dealing with the real issue: sublimation at its most bizarre.

Chain wrestled Lucille down and sank his fangs into one of her breasts. I didn't know whether to chastise him because he'd assaulted her or congratulate him for getting past the fear of using his fangs.

But because I'd been there and done this, I knew what to do. I climbed up on my desk, pulled from my pocket the whistle I'd tucked away earlier and blew it as loud as I could.

'Stop!'

They all froze.

I pointed to the circle of chairs. 'Go back to your seats. Now!'

With sheepish expressions they all complied.

I hopped down from the desk, grabbed a jacket someone had left hanging on my coat rack and tossed it to Lucille. She draped it around her shoulders instead of covering herself.

Quick as a snake, Chain pinched one of Lucille's nipples.

Lucille giggled.

'Chain! We never touch someone without their permission. And we don't bite without an invitation. Apologise to Lucille and keep your hands to yourself.'

'Apologise? For what? She's naked, Doctor Knight. What's a guy supposed to do? And she lets me do a lot more than that outside of group.'

'That doesn't matter,' I said. *And thanks for that disturbing visual.* 'You know the rules: no physical contact with any of the other members, or with me. So go on – apologise. And congratulations on using your fangs, by the way.'

Everyone clapped.

Chain looked at Lucille, stuck his tongue out, then said in a sarcastic voice, 'I'm sorry.'

Undead preschool.

Dennis and Walter were sitting rigidly, trying not to look in Lucille's direction.

'Okay. Anyone still worried about whether or not Devereux can protect his coven?'

'No,' they chorused.

'Anyone still afraid Lucifer will get you?'

That elicited a less enthusiastic, 'No.'

None of them sounded convinced, but at least I'd given them something to think about.

'All right, that's it for tonight. Good job, everyone. Practise thinking positively about your fangs and take a courageous risk – bite someone who wants you to. See you next week, same time, same place.'

They all popped out amid a flurry of goodbyes, leaving me in glorious silence.

Bite someone who wants you to? I'm becoming as bizarre as they are.

After group I sat at my desk, writing notes. I'd just completed the last paragraph when my cell phone rang. I tensed. Lucifer's Brother Luther personality usually left messages on my business voicemail number, but I couldn't take anything for granted. There was nothing to keep him from calling my cell.

I checked the caller ID and let out the breath I'd been holding. I couldn't deny the little rush of pleasure I experienced when I read the name. Alan. But then I wondered, *Why am I pleased? Because I'm attracted to him? Or because he's human and can't mess with my head in any non-normal way?*

'Alan? Is everything okay? We just spoke yesterday – you're usually way too busy to spend much time on the phone.'

'No. Everything's not okay,' he said, his voice strained. 'Hold onto your hat.'

His tone tightened my stomach as much as his words. 'Why? What's wrong?'

'I just found out the three bodies the cops have here are Lucifer's work. Add them to the six I already knew about and he's killed nine so far.'

'Oh, Alan! That's terrible, we've got to find—'

'Wait. There's more.'

'More?' A wave of nausea washed through me.

'Four of the drained bodies we already knew about plus the three new victims had something in common: something the cops just put together.'

My body trembled. Whatever he was about to say was bad. I could feel the negative tendrils of energy crawling along the phone lines. 'What did they have in common?' I remembered the quick vision flashes of people I'd seen during the TV report.

'They're all psychologists.'

'Holy bat-shit, Robin,' I blurted, reverting to my favourite junior high expression. 'Lucifer's murdering therapists?'

'Uh-huh. Dark-haired female psychologists.'

My mouth went dry. 'He's symbolically killing me over and over? But why, Alan? Why would he do that? Why is he so fixated on me?' Even as I asked the questions I knew there wouldn't be any logical answers.

'Your guess is as good as mine. I had to tell you so you can protect yourself accordingly. We both know he'll eventually lose interest in offing people who represent you, and then he'll go right for the source. His madness has escalated. The cops haven't released the link between the victims to the media yet, but they will – and soon.'

'Oh. My. God. What am I supposed to do about this, Alan? And I'm going to a conference full of psychologists.' I knew I was in denial, but I had to ask anyway, 'Do you think that might draw him?'

'I'd say there's a good chance he'll show up, but as we discussed before, there's no way of knowing for sure where he is or where he'll go. Maybe he's back in Denver right now.'

'Damn.' My stomach clenched. 'I hope he's not here. But for all I know, he could be right outside my window.' That idea startled me so much that I walked over to convince myself he wasn't lurking on my windowsill. Devereux had so many magical protections on the office building – and on my home – that it was harder for Lucifer to simply show up in those places. But there was nothing to prevent him from attacking me in my car – or anywhere else, for that matter. Great.

'Should we warn the conference organisers?' I wondered aloud. 'Let them know there's possible danger?'

'Sounds good in theory, but what the hell would we say? How would we explain having access to such information?'

'I could tell them I heard it from you, Mr FBI – that you told me there's a crazed serial killer tracking psychologists.'

'Yeah, and then I'd have to deny saying any such thing, you'd look like a fool and the FBI would fire my ass.'

'Well, shit.'

'But maybe we can think of something we can do.'

'We?' I suddenly realised that 'you' had become 'we' a while ago.

'Yeah. I've decided to go to the conference with you. Officially. There's no way I'm letting you go alone now. If he's targeting therapists and he's fixated on you, this psychologist smorgasbord is probably too juicy for him to pass up. We might have a real chance of catching him there.'

Catching him? We? How would we do that? I'm back to wanting to crawl under the covers.

But even though hearing Alan say he'd come was an unexpected relief, part of me was still wondering whether I should reconsider going. Would the trip be a suicidal gesture on my part? But how cowardly would I feel if I didn't go? And how long could I hide from the demon even if I stayed home?

'You're right. We've got to do whatever we can. Thanks for agreeing to go with me – you're the best.'

'I'm glad you're finally realising that,' he teased, trying to lighten the mood. 'And besides, New York's my old stomping ground and I haven't been back for a while. I think I told you it's the last place I saw my mother. It wouldn't hurt to check in with some of the accessible local vampires again – see if there have been any sightings of her.'

'Yeah. I hope you'll tell me more about your mother some time. But listening to you reminds me that your life is as vampire-saturated as mine. I don't know how good that is for either of us.'

'Probably not very good, but there's another benefit to me attending the conference. After we spoke yesterday, I thought it might be nice for both of us to have a little time alone together, see what's what.'

'Alan, you know I care about you, but I'm all screwed up right now—'

'Screwed up' doesn't even begin to cover it . . .

'I know,' he interrupted, 'no commitments. No promises.

Just two friends who are attracted to each other getting together for companionship and conversation, and joining forces for the apocalypse.' He fell silent for a few seconds. 'I think we both could use a friend, Kismet. Things have been crazy for me, too. I'm under a lot of pressure at the Bureau – they want me to catch what they believe is a serial killer pretending to be a vampire or turn the case over to another agent. I don't know what I'll tell them if and when we do catch Lucifer. They'll never believe the truth. Likely I won't even have any proof he existed. When he dies, or stops being undead or whatever, he'll just rot down to bones and ashes. Am I supposed to vacuum him up and take the remains back to the FBI?'

'Crap. I never thought about that. I guess you are in a no-win situation. We can brainstorm about it if you like – can't hurt to try to generate some out-of-the-coffin ideas. But what will you do during the daytime at the conference while I'm presenting and attending workshops? There's not much vampire hunting to be done while the sun's out.'

'I can check in with the local cops, and there might be some lectures of interest to me. I'll just sneak in – or use my FBI credentials and let them think I'm undercover on a case.' He laughed. 'That always works. I never have to pay for anything. Aside from that, we can catch up over some good meals. I'll even reserve my own room in case I need it, but it might be better – protection-wise – for me to stay close.'

I imagined him waggling his eyebrows when he said that.

'Uh-huh. I'm sure you think that. Wait – what about Detective Andrews, the gorgeous ass-kicking upholder of justice? Won't she miss you if you're gone?'

'You're jealous! I love it – you just made my day.'

'I'm not jealous.' *Am I?*

'Yeah, right. You just happened to remember the way I described her, word for word. I thought *I* was the one with the tape-recorder memory. Now I *know* we've got to get together. I'm not giving up without a fight. So you're okay with me sticking close to you at the conference?'

Well, why not? Alan was the only other human who knew everything about the vampires. It would be a relief to spend time with someone around whom I didn't have to censor my words. And maybe we did need to explore our mutual interest. I'd been so *besotted* – unnaturally so – with Devereux that I'd never given myself the opportunity to stick a toe in Alan's pool.

'It's fine with me as long as you're okay that my priority will be networking with colleagues and hearing the latest research. I'm hoping that'll take my mind off the bloodsucking insanity – if only for a little while. I wouldn't want you to think I'm ignoring you.'

'I'm a big boy, Kismet. You just enjoy the conference and trust me to take care of myself. I'll be there for you.'

Hmmm. I've heard that before . . .

'So, it's a date?' he said.

'Yes. I'll see you in New York on Wednesday. Bye.'

Just as I disconnected, Devereux popped into the office.

'You will see who, where?'

CHAPTER 9

'Devereux!' I practically fell off my chair. 'You startled me – I wasn't expecting you.'

He moved towards my desk like a predator stalking prey, his eyes narrowed. 'Apparently.'

Fear shot down my spine. What the hell? He was definitely in a mood. I sat straighter in my chair, my fight-or-flight reflex engaged. 'What's wrong? Why are you acting so ... threateningly? Has something happened?'

'To whom were you speaking just now?' He circled around behind my desk, put his hands on my shoulders and began to knead the tight muscles.

I would've let myself enjoy the impromptu massage if it wasn't for the flashing red alert my intuition was sending out. Under the circumstances, relaxation was impossible. Something was very wrong. 'I was talking to Alan Stevens. You remember him – the FBI agent Bryce captured at the Vampires' Ball. The one who's searching for Lucifer.'

'Ah, yes.' His voice was cold enough to cause frostbite. 'The profiler with whom you had a sexual interlude. I do indeed remember.'

Why was he getting pissed off about that now? 'What's

going on, Devereux? Why are you so angry?' I automatically started practising the hum.

He let go of my shoulders, walked around to the front of the desk and sat on the arm of the couch, facing me. 'I will come back to Alan Stevens in a moment.' He raised a brow. 'I cannot read your thoughts, but I do not need to mind-read to sense that you are deceiving me, pretending you do not know why you are closed to me. Why would you do that? Have you decided to disrespect me along with everyone else? Do I suddenly mean nothing to you?' Hurt simmered under his anger.

Disrespect him along with everyone else?

This was getting scary. I'd never felt Devereux so emotional, so . . . unhinged. Unfiltered fear scorched my skin and I began to shake. He couldn't be this upset because I was talking to Alan. That simply wasn't like him – but then he hadn't been himself since he came out of the coma. Anne was right: Devereux was teetering on the edge. His inability to catch Lucifer had put his entire self-identity on the line.

'Devereux, please – what are you talking about? Of course you mean something to me. Talk to me.'

'I do not wish to be psychoanalysed right now, Doctor. Just tell me who cloaked your mind.' His voice was deceptively calm but it sent terror ripples through my solar plexus.

There was no getting around it. I knew I'd have to tell him sooner or later. Might as well forge ahead. 'It was Anne Boleyn,' I said, struggling to breathe through the miasma of dread saturating the air.

'I knew, of course, but I wanted you to tell me. Go on.' He crossed his arms over his chest, his gaze intense, his words ominously quiet.

My heart was pounding so loudly I was sure he could hear

it and I began gasping for breath. 'Is there something you can do to ratchet down your predatory intentions? My body's so tense my throat's choking up.'

He shut his eyes for a few seconds and when he opened them, the tension decreased. Whatever had been pressing against my chest wasn't gone, but it no longer felt life-threatening.

'Thank you.' I licked my dry lips.

'Please continue.'

I had to swallow several times before I could speak, and while I worked out what I was going to say to him next, I kept my eyes firmly focused on his forehead. His gaze had mesmerised me many times in the past and I wasn't about to lose myself again. Anne had warned me that his strong vampire energy could chip away at her clearing and I didn't want that.

'After you left me with Anne at the wedding, she mentioned that vampires alter human brains physiologically without intending to. I told her I'd noticed I felt less ... spacey, intoxicated while you were recovering from Bryce's ritual. She said that was to be expected because your power wasn't flooding my brain to the same degree while you were unconscious. She was surprised I could even remember my name. She knew as soon as she met me that I'd been having a lot of headaches. Which, by the way, you didn't notice.' I coughed to clear my throat. 'She scared me.'

Devereux leaped up and circled the room. 'That is ridiculous,' he said, gesturing expansively.

His anger flared out like a wildfire and I recoiled without meaning to. I'd never instinctively cringed in his presence before. The fact that he was acting so unlike the Devereux I knew both frightened and confused me. Apparently things had deteriorated pretty badly in the Master's world.

'I told you I am in complete control of my abilities. No harm can come to you. Anne has a tendency to be a trouble-maker and she is still holding a grudge.' The pain was back in his voice again as he added, 'You should not have listened to her. Apparently you do not trust me.'

My arms broke out in chills and I rubbed them. 'It isn't a matter of trust. I believe her when she says you don't know how negatively you're affecting me. You never intend to hurt me, but you do.'

He looked shocked at that. 'I would never hurt you. You are the most important person in the world to me. I have dedi-cated myself to protecting you, to keeping you safe.'

'I know, and I'm sure you mean well, but being around you all the time changes my brain in negative ways. Anne removed the accumulated vampire influence and somehow made me more difficult to read. I'm myself again for the first time in over two months.' I didn't share my intention to find a way to keep my brain clear. Did I really think Devereux would try to sabotage me?

He strode to the front of the desk and stood there, hands on hips. 'What did Anne do, specifically, to block my access to your thoughts? If you describe it to me I will undoubtedly recognise the method. She is quite gifted in creating new tech-niques but I am equally skilled at deciphering them. Trying to read you now is like floating through thick fog. I wish to undo it.'

Like hell! 'I don't want you to undo it – I prefer having my mind clear. Are you saying you only want to be around me if you can read and control me? What kind of relationship is that?'

'Of course not.' His expression was disgusted. 'But in order to protect you, I must have access to your mind. It is not safe for you otherwise. Stop being difficult, Kismet. I insist you tell me what she did.'

'Difficult? You insist? You don't care if my brain is altered, harmed, just as long as you have what you want?'

He paced, his platinum hair swinging. 'As usual, you are interpreting the situation in a limited way. As soon as we have restored our usual connection, all will be well, you will see.' He turned to me, his eyes narrowed again. His voice held a razor's edge. 'And what did you mean, you will see Alan in New York on Wednesday?'

So many emotions swelled up inside me that I couldn't speak. Anger that Devereux refused to see my point of view, sadness because he was apparently willing to sacrifice my brain to achieve his mysterious goals and despair that what he'd called love felt like anything but. And still, even in the face of all those feelings, part of me knew he wasn't himself – he'd been pushed beyond his limits. Regardless, I couldn't let him bully me. He wasn't *my* Master.

'I meant exactly what I said.' I sucked in a deep breath, steeling myself for more of his unleashed rage. I calmly rose from behind my desk and walked over to stand in front of him. I fixed my gaze on the space between his eyes. 'I'm going to the American Psychological Association's yearly conference. I've attended for years. Alan wants to meet me there.'

He was deathly quiet for a few heartbeats. The hairs on my arms rose and my stomach contracted. Then he laughed.

'I am going to assume you are joking, because you know I would never allow you to leave Denver without me while Lucifer is at large.' He sat on the arm of the couch again and folded his hands on his lap, as if he wasn't holding onto his temper by his fingernails. 'But I do appreciate your attempt to lighten my mood.'

Wow. I could write an entire series of books about Devereux's narcissism. If anyone would believe such an extreme case, that is. Were all vampires so self-centred? Just master vampires? Where was the line between confidence and arrogance? Devereux had definitely obliterated the distinction.

'You would never *allow* me to leave Denver?' I asked, struggling to keep the pain and fury out of my voice. I clasped my hands together behind my back to prevent them from shaking. Disappointment swamped me. Maybe everything really had been a lie. 'You actually believe you get to write my script? That I'll continue to *allow* you to manipulate me now that I'm free? You're too intelligent an individual to cling to such ludicrous ideas.'

Devereux exploded. At least that's what it looked like. He thrust his fists into the air as he moved like a blur across the room and a wounded-animal sound burst from his lips. He stood staring at me, his hair covering half of his face, the predatory energy once again exploding against my chest like a heat blast.

I clutched my throat, gasping for air. My heartbeat pounded double – no, triple-time – against my ribs. My knees gave way and I sank to the floor. Sweat trickled down my sides. I knew I was close to losing consciousness.

'Kismet!' And then I was in his arms. He sat me on the couch, said a word I couldn't understand and, as before, the crushing heaviness in my chest lightened. I sank into the cushions, willed my heart rate to slow and tried to make sense of the last few minutes.

A headache pulsed behind my left eye. The throbbing reminded me of how I'd felt before Anne's clearing and I suddenly feared Devereux had broken through. Almost panicking, it took a few seconds before I could restart the inner vibration. Keeping my eyes open, I centred myself and hummed silently. After a few seconds more I *heard* the strange sounds Cerridwyn 'uploaded' into my unconscious again. As I breathed, my brain waves shifted from beta to theta and soon the headache receded.

Okay. I'm still me – I hope – for now.

Even though I'd succeeded at bringing my mind back into a calm state, under my control, I still felt numb. All my assumptions about Devereux had evaporated in the face of his dissonant behaviour. He needed help and I was pretty sure he'd never ask for it. And even if he did ask for my help, being with him had serious physiological downsides for me. But I couldn't abandon him when he needed me. I didn't know what to do. There were just no easy answers.

He strode to the window and stared out for several minutes, then turned to me, once again the elegant, rational man I'd thought him to be. 'I understand you are worried about my *alleged* negative effect on your brain, but I can assure you there is no cause for distress.' He moved to the couch and sat next to me. His expression went flat, all emotions locked down. 'After I catch Lucifer and he is no longer a threat to you or my coven, we will discuss your concerns. And in the mean-time, you must remain here in Denver where I can have my vampires keep watch over you. You will simply have to miss this year's conference.'

He spoke as if he took for granted his orders would be followed, that I'd acquiesce to his commands.

As I listened, the numb feeling rapidly morphed into resent-ment and outrage. Devereux's expectation of my subservience brought back every awful memory of the various men – starting with my father – who'd decided they could determine what I should do or say or feel. Every situation where I'd allowed myself to be disempowered, manipulated. I fought the urge to lash out – to punch his gorgeous nose – but I wouldn't give him the satisfaction. He'd probably find me amusing.

'I'll have to miss the conference? You seriously think that's going to happen?'

He reached over and patted my hand, having completely missed the sarcasm in my tone. 'Yes. It is for the best under the circumstances. You will have to trust my judgement. I will always take care of you.'

I was stunned speechless.

Taking my silence as acceptance, he rose effortlessly from the couch and gave a quick bow. 'I do not know when I will be able to see you again, but you may rest assured you are surrounded by protection at all times. Lucifer will be contained.' He leaned down to kiss me and I pressed a hand against his chest.

'No.'

He jerked up in surprise and my hand fell away.

'Your complete disregard for my needs and desires has become intolerable. I never thought things would end this way, but don't worry about when you'll get around to seeing me because I don't want to see you. Not only am I going to the conference, but I'm reassessing my involvement with vampires across the board. Including you.' I rose from the couch, moved to my desk and sat on one corner, strangely calm. 'You need to respect my wishes, whether you want to or not. I'm exploring options for protecting my mind and I can't be around a vampire as powerful as you until I'm stronger. If you care about me at all, you'll honour my request and leave me alone.'

Yet again, the emotions he'd stifled flared out and I felt myself drowning in the deluge.

He kept his voice tightly controlled. 'It is precisely because I care about you that I will do whatever it takes to protect you. I do not want you to go to New York.' A frightened expression flashed like lightning across his face 'Nor do I wish you to spend time with Alan Stevens. We will discuss your concerns as soon as possible, but you are not to leave. I will see you as soon as I can.'

He vanished.

What the hell? I stared at the empty space where Devereux had been.

As soon as he dematerialised, the fearful energy dissipated and the concrete blocks crushing my chest disappeared.

My head spun. *What just happened?* I returned to the couch, kicked my shoes off and stretched out along its length.

Was Devereux having some kind of emotional breakdown? If I took a clinical step back, reclaimed some distance as a psychologist, I could see the signs of instability. He'd asked if I was disrespecting him like everyone else, yet he didn't share any of his pain with me, the woman he claims to love. The situation with Lucifer had obviously caused Devereux to decompensate. What the hell would happen to one of the most powerful vampires in the world if his meltdown continued? Not to mention the consequences for those around him while it was happening.

Thinking about his outrageous mood swings made me feel guilty. Maybe I should've put aside my personal feelings and listened to him with my therapeutic ears, insisted he talk to me. But that was the problem with a therapist treating those she's close to: no objectivity. Too much counter-transference and projection. There was no way I could see Devereux clearly. My own expectations, patterns and beliefs got in the way.

With a start, I realised I hadn't told him about the therapist murders. I'd been so overwrought by his unnatural behaviour that I'd forgotten all about it. But if I did tell him, he might do something other than verbally forbid me to prevent me from going to the conference. I knew he meant well but I couldn't allow him – or anyone else – to control me any more. No matter what. I had to figure things out for myself.

Suddenly everything felt too heavy. Too big. Too much. I closed my eyes to block out the memory of Devereux's frightened expression and the conference issue, and dropped into an exhausted sleep.

CHAPTER 10

The sound of the wind rattling my office windows as it roared down from the mountains woke me from my restless sleep.

I sat up and looked around, disoriented. Why had I spent the night in my office? The question had barely solidified when the answer coalesced.

Devereux's meltdown and his strange behaviour.

Tears formed in my eyes and I blinked to clear them away. My heart ached for his pain. I grieved for what I thought we'd had – for the lie it turned out to be. I plucked a tissue from the box on the table and loudly blew my nose. I sat up and straightened my clothes, trying to get a grip on myself, and gave myself a good talking to. 'He's the one who didn't care if my brain melted out through my ears. At least the control issue came to a head quickly, before I became even more enmeshed in his horrifying world. How irrational of me to think I could just step into a bizarre alternative reality and expect to navigate it.'

With a deep breath I forced myself up from the couch. 'No time to wallow in emotions! Too much to do! I can't let the fact that he doesn't care about me ruin my life.' I hadn't taken even one step before my knees gave out and I immediately collapsed back into the cushions.

'Damn it to hell!' I felt like I'd been kicked in the gut. Thinking about not having Devereux in my life hurt. My chest ached and my chin quivered as tears flowed down my cheeks. Wailing, sobbing and sniffling, I gave myself permission to have a full-fledged pity party. I threw myself face-first into a pillow and made sounds I hadn't heard coming from my mouth since I'd been a hormonal teenager.

A few minutes later, after I'd exhausted myself and stopped crying, the anger that had been waiting its turn stepped up. I sprang into a sitting position. 'How dare he tell me he loved me, that I was his *mate*, then treat me so shittily!' I grabbed one of the pillows and started pounding the couch with it, screaming all the while. 'What an idiot I've been! It was never about love, just control and some mysterious agenda.' I pounded harder. 'Once again I'm the Homecoming Queen of the Failure Prom. Well, Mister Master Vampire, you can kiss your ulterior motive goodbye!' I lost my grip on the pillow and punched the couch with my fist until the anger gave way to more tears.

I sobbed for a few more minutes while the storm ran its course, then I stopped and stared at nothing, feeling utterly empty. I grabbed another tissue, which came away black with mascara when I wiped it under my eyes. 'Great. I might as well look as bad as I feel.' I sniffled and snorted a few more times, thinking I should have known better than to believe I could attract a healthy relationship. Better to give up on men altogether.

I went through a few more tissues before it finally occurred to me that I'd been sitting there for a while and I had an appointment with Ham the hypnotherapist. Afraid I'd missed it, and disgusted with my self-pity, I jumped up and checked the clock. I was relieved to discover it was still very early –

not even 7 a.m. yet. Which was also good because probably nobody else had been in the building to hear my breakdown. I cringed at the memory.

I made a quick pit-stop in the bathroom, then gathered up my things, locked the office and rode the mirrored elevator down to the underground parking area.

There were only a handful of other cars there besides mine. Since all of the businesses in the building – with the exception of my therapy practice – were run by Devereux and his various vampire employees and they travelled via thought, few human vehicles were necessary. I shivered as I hurried to my car, my breath puffing out in the frigid air.

Thanks to several inches of fresh snow on the road, the timing of the traffic lights and morning rush-hour congestion, it took longer than usual for me to drive the short distance between the office and my townhouse. To avoid a slow-moving snowplough, I turned onto the side streets. After a few minutes, I noticed a dark-blue SUV with a dented front fender behind me. I didn't make anything of it at first – probably just a coincidence that the vehicle matched my turns and appeared to be heading for a similar destination. Odd, though, that it stayed so far back – too far away for me to see the driver clearly – and didn't approach my bumper when we stopped at red lights. Feeling ridiculous and paranoid but beginning to register anxiety, I made an unnecessary turn to see if the SUV would follow. It did.

Was someone tailing me after all?

My first thought was Lucifer, since he was the only one who'd made threats. But Lucifer couldn't be out in the daytime. Or at least I hoped that was true. And besides, a vampire would simply flash through time and space. The idea that he'd choose to drive was ludicrous. Although I did have one client who collected human sports cars – he enjoyed reliving his human past – most wouldn't be caught dead, so to speak, using such mundane transport.

I turned again and the SUV followed.

What the hell?

This was definitely no coincidence. Could the driver be someone new Devereux had hired to keep an eye on me? It was possible. But why follow me so obviously all of a sudden? Was there some additional danger I didn't know about?

Spotting a drive-through Starbucks up ahead, I turned into the driveway. The SUV rolled past. I hadn't realised how tightly my stomach had been clenched until I huffed out a breath, releasing the tension. I laughed at myself. 'Paranoid much, Kismet? I definitely need caffeine.'

Feeling like an idiot, I drove to the take-away window, ordered my coffee and pulled back onto the street. I hadn't gone half a block when the now-familiar SUV appeared in my rear-view mirror again.

The last thing I wanted was to guide some stalking stranger to my house. But if he worked for Devereux, he obviously already knew where I lived. What was I supposed to do? Drive around until the guy gave up and went away? Fat chance.

Lacking a better plan, I went home.

The SUV followed until I pulled into the alley behind my place to enter the garage. He – I had the sense the driver was male – didn't turn in behind me.

A little while later, after showering and getting dressed, I headed out for my hypnotherapy appointment. Nobody followed me this time.

Dr Taylor's office was only a few blocks from mine, in a former bungalow converted into professional space. It sat on a corner lot at the intersection of two busy streets and the cozy building looked out of place in a neighbourhood filled with coffee shops, art galleries and modern high-rises. I parked half a block down the street and walked to his entrance. Thankfully the snow had stopped falling but more was forecast for later in the day.

There was a sign on the front door that said:

Welcome to the office of Dr Hamilton Taylor.

Come in. Waiting room to the right.

I pushed the door open and was met with the aroma of cinnamon buns – or at least that's what it smelled like to me. It was probably a scented candle, but I enjoyed the homey scent regardless.

A coat rack with one lone sweater on a hanger sat just inside the entryway. I walked to the first doorway on the right and entered the waiting room. Like many clinicians in private practice who didn't want to hire a receptionist, Dr Taylor had a system to alert him to the arrival of clients. Next to a closed door on the other side of the waiting room was a panel with a lighted button and a sign that said: *Please press this button when you arrive and I'll be with you shortly.* I knew the button would turn on a light in his office, which he would turn off when he came to get me. I'd considered asking Devereux if he could install one of those systems in my office, but Victoria, resident witch and building manager, was more than happy to call up and announce my daytime human clients. The vampires needed no announcement. They just popped in.

The waiting area consisted of one tan leather couch, four chairs in various shades of brown, a large square coffee table, two shelves filled with self-help books and a wheeled cart with an espresso machine and a tall thermos of decaf coffee. The walls were covered with framed posters of Colorado mountain scenes. Soft Native American flute music flowed from speakers in the ceiling. The overall effect was a soothing, safe cocoon. Dr Taylor certainly knew how to set a scene.

I'd just taken off my coat and laid it on one of the chairs when I heard the jiggle of a doorknob. I bent to retrieve my coat.

'Doctor Knight, I presume?' the deep voice asked.

'Yes.' Straightening, I turned towards the voice. My face must have been comical because Dr Taylor laughed.

Standing in the doorway between the waiting room and his office was a tall brown-eyed man of about fifty. His long grey hair was pulled back into a ponytail and his chin was whiter than the rest of his skin, giving evidence of the recent removal of a goatee. He was wearing false eyelashes, light-brown eye shadow and rose lipstick and his cheeks were dusted with a subtle blush of pink.

My eyes tracked down his body before I could stop the reflex action.

He was dressed in a lovely black skirt and jacket with a white blouse that buttoned snugly over his impressive breasts. Conservative black pumps completed the ensemble.

'Not what you expected, I'm sure.' He smiled. 'Please call me Ham.' He thrust his hand out for me to shake.

I'd been so stunned by his appearance that I was standing speechless with my mouth open. It took a few seconds for me to grasp the hand he offered. 'Er, it's ... nice to meet you, Ham,' I managed.

He's transgendered?

He pointed to the inside of his office. 'Please, come in.'

We walked into a very nicely furnished room suffused with the same kind of cozy feeling as the other parts of the building I'd seen so far.

He gestured towards a burgundy leather recliner chair. 'Why don't you make yourself comfortable?'

I looked back and forth between the chair and Ham and couldn't make up my mind what to do. Finally, out of politeness, I sat in the chair.

Well, my client did say Ham's eccentric. Maybe this is what he meant.

Ham chose a nearby chair, sat and crossed his legs. His legs were smooth.

Did I shave my legs today?

'I suppose I should have given you a heads-up about my situation so you could decide if you were willing to take a chance on me, but I simply forgot. I guess I don't think about my outer appearance as much as I used to. I'm in the long, complicated process of preparing for sex-reassignment surgery and I've been dressing as a female for several months now. You might be aware that as part of the requirements, I must practise being the gender I'm choosing. I'll eventually have to take hormones for a while before the surgeons will agree to do the surgery.'

Not sure what to say, I simply fell into my usual role and nodded.

He smiled gently. 'I can see I've surprised you and you're desperately trying to figure out what kind of reaction to have. Please let me put you at ease. Aside from my desire to have my outside match my inside, I'm a perfectly normal person.' He chuckled. 'As normal as any clinician can be, anyway.' He picked up a notepad and pen. 'Why don't we begin and see how it goes?'

He thought I was surprised by his appearance and his decision to become a woman but that wasn't the cause of my reaction at all. I'd worked with many transgender individuals and was familiar with their challenges, and as a psychotherapist I'd also learned to expect the unexpected. No. It was that once again, I'd been presented with evidence that I'd stopped attracting humdrum situations and people and had shifted into the realm of the unique and interesting in more ways than just counselling vampires. I mean, what were the odds that I'd connect with a hypnotherapist courageous enough to appear as their true self with strangers?

I studied him for a moment. 'Okay. But I'd like to ask a question first.'

He tapped his pen on the pad nervously and appeared to brace himself for my words. 'Certainly.'

'Why did you shave the goatee? I'll bet it suited you.' I smiled.

He relaxed so much the pen fell out of his hand. He retrieved it and returned my smile. 'That's an excellent question. And the answer is, because I was finally ready to take a significant step – to remove yet another sign of my former masculinity.' He mimed stroking the missing hair in question. 'I thought it *did* suit me.' He laughed. 'It's been a babe magnet. I hesitated to let go of it until I was absolutely certain I was on the right path. Now that I've decided to become a babe myself, being clean-shaven was the natural next step. So I made an appointment with my barber, who happens to be my ex-brother-in-law, and celebrated chopping it off.'

'Congratulations. I know how difficult it can be to make such important decisions.'

'Thanks. Even harder is telling the woman I've been dating that after the operation, I'll be a lesbian.' He grinned. 'Lesbian. Saying that word is a dream come true.'

'So you're woman-centred?'

'Yes. My sexual focus has never been in question. Only the genitals involved.'

Okay. This is starting to be TMI. I'm taking off my therapist's hat now.

'Well, I hope everything works out,' I said, probably telegraphing my discomfort.

Picking up on it immediately, he straightened in his chair. 'So, back to you. How can I help?'

'I'm not sure. You told me on the phone that you're aware of my recent notoriety – the media frenzy about the so-called *vampire murders* around Hallowe'en.'

'Yes. I was intrigued by the entire situation. What an interesting clientele you have, Doctor Knight. Vampire wannabes. I've worked with some blood-seeking goths myself, so I understand a little about the demographic. There was also one client who insisted he was a real vampire. Can you imagine?'

'Yes, I can, and at the risk of sounding mysterious and paranoid, I'm involved in a situation I can't really talk about.'

'Legal issues? I don't have to remind you that everything we discuss is totally confidential.'

Okay. Legal issues sounds good . . .

'Of course, but after dealing with my fifteen minutes of fame a couple of months back, I lost some confidence. I started questioning my judgements, my ability to make good decisions about which clients to see. I'd like to utilise hypnosis to build up my intuition, my radar.'

'Are you familiar with hypnosis?'

'Yes – I'm a practitioner myself and I realise all hypnosis is self-hypnosis, but I also subscribe to the notion that sometimes it's very helpful to find a trusted professional and to allow oneself to be guided. To just let go.'

'I couldn't agree more.'

'Or at least that's the theory and what I tell clients. I've never asked anyone to hypnotise me before.'

His sculpted eyebrows rose. 'I'm honoured you chose me. I hope I can be helpful. So you don't actually know how receptive you'll be to trance-work?'

'I have a good imagination and I have enjoyed using various self-hypnosis and guided-visualisation CDs. Based on those experiences, I expect I'll become more receptive over time, as we get to know each other.' *If we get to know each other.*

'Good.' He lifted a microphone from the table and attached it to my jacket. 'I'll record the session so you can practise on your own.' He rose to turn on a small table lamp and shut off the rest of the lights in the room. He fetched a blanket from a cupboard, spread it over me and pulled a chair next to the recliner. 'I have an eye mask if you'd like one to help you cut off more sensory stimulation, but it might ruin your lovely makeup job.' He studied me. 'You'll simply have to tell me where you bought that gorgeous eye shadow.'

I grinned. 'Happy to. And I'm fine without an eye mask.'

Ham was a delightful character. I hoped he was as skilled at hypnosis as he was at putting clients at ease.

'All right. Go ahead and close your eyes,' he said, speaking softly and slowly, with pauses between each sentence. 'Turn your attention inwards and just notice your breathing. Become aware of the air flowing in and out of your nostrils, giving yourself the suggestion that you are becoming more relaxed with every breath.'

I struggled to shut off my mental chatter and took some deep breaths. Even if I wasn't able to go into a deep state of hypnosis today, the relaxation would be worth the time I devoted to the session. And so far I really liked Ham.

'Imagine yourself counting backwards from one hundred.'

I followed his request.

'At some point, and I don't know exactly when it will happen, the next number and all the remaining numbers will simply vanish. And when the numbers vanish, you will drop down ten times as deep inside . . . Just counting backwards from one hundred now.'

That was the last thing I remembered until I cracked one eye and found Ham standing over me, patting my hand and saying, his voice stern, 'Please come back, Doctor Knight. Return to full consciousness now. I will count up from one to five again, and when I get to five you will be fully back in the room. Fully aware. Fully awake. One—'

My eyes popped open.

He sank into the chair next to me. 'Oh, thank heavens.' He fanned himself, which did nothing to relieve the sweat pooling on his forehead. 'I've never experienced anything like that before. I was starting to think I'd have to pull you into the shower and turn on the cold water.'

'What happened?' I licked my dry lips and glanced at the clock on the wall in front of me. An hour had passed.

He looked at me with a worried expression. 'Oh, my dear, I'm afraid you won't have to concern yourself about the things you said you couldn't tell me. You told me everything. Every horrible detail. You poor thing.'

Terror tackled me. 'What are you talking about? I didn't tell you anything.'

'I'm afraid you did,' he said, eyes wide. 'Devereux and Lucifer and working with real vampires and murdering therapists and finding out your brain has been compromised . . . Oh my God – what a mess!'

I stiffened in dismay. *Surely* I hadn't told all my secrets to a total stranger? If I had, I was obviously more messed up than I thought. My mind spun. What should I do? I'd have to ask

Devereux to visit Ham and erase his memories. Or I could tell him the things I'd said were part of a novel I was writing. After all, if Alan could write one, why not me?

'No, you don't understand,' I said, trying to sound convincing. 'Those are characters from a novel I'm writing – I obviously wove quite a tale for you. And you know we humans can lie even under hypnosis. I'm glad you recorded me – maybe I can use some of the details for plot points in the book.' I pressed down with my feet on the bottom of the chair and it clicked upright. 'If you could just make a CD of the session for me I'll be on my way. I have clients . . .'

He watched me with compassionate eyes. 'You don't have to be afraid. I won't tell anyone. In fact, why don't you sit back and relax for a moment and I'll share something with you. Something that pertains.'

I couldn't believe I'd told him about the vampires. What was wrong with me? And he wasn't buying my novel story. No surprise there. 'I really need to get going. I appreciate your time and it's been great meeting you—' I started to get up again and he gently grasped my wrist.

'Please. I've never had anyone I could tell this to and you'll see that we have more in common than you think. Please.'

I sat back in the chair, still wary. He obviously wasn't going to let me leave without listening to him. 'Okay, I can stay for a minute.' Was he going to tell me more about his transformation into a female, or was there something else?

'Remember I told you I had a client who insisted he was a real vampire?'

I nodded.

'His name was Martin. He came to me for evening sessions, saying he wanted to remember what it was like to be human. He claimed he hadn't been alive for more than two hundred years. We were actually successful at regressing him back to his childhood and exploring his memories.'

'You're obviously used to working with delusional clients. What made you think he was the real thing?'

'He proved it.'

'How?'

'He read my mind and found my most painful memory of being beaten by my father as a child for dressing in my sister's clothes. He also discovered that my father left us because he was ashamed to have a son like me. I hadn't seen my father since I was ten, and I've carried the burden of being the cause of him abandoning his family ever since.' He sat back and smoothed the fabric of his skirt. 'Martin also picked up information about the private detective I hired to find my father and the results of that search. My father is – was – an alcoholic living on the streets in Baltimore.'

'How do you know he read all those things from your mind? Just because he told you he did?'

'No. One night he came for his session and said he had a gift for me. He said he was grateful for all the work we'd done and he wanted to repay me in a more valuable way than just giving me money. He picked me up like a child and the next thing I knew, we were standing under a highway overpass in the middle of a homeless camp. I was flabbergasted when I realised I'd been with a real vampire all that time and had just soared through space. My mind couldn't grasp it. Martin set me on my feet and pointed to a large cardboard box. He said my father was inside.' Ham got up and walked to the window and stared out.

Knowing vampires, my stomach tightened at the thought of where his story was going.

'Was he inside?'

Ham turned to me. 'Yes. Martin literally shredded the box, pulled my father out and dropped him at my feet. I barely recognised him. He was filthy and he'd lost his hair, but it was him. Of course, he didn't know me – he was too drunk even to realise what was happening. My heart broke for his miserable life and how he'd ended up. I was just about to ask if there was anything I could do for him when Martin twisted his head to the side and snapped his neck.' Ham looked horrified, his eyes glassy and his skin pale. His hands shook.

'I'm so sorry, Ham,' I said softly. 'That had to be awful for you. Vampires have their own rules. They don't pay any attention to our ethics or laws. In fact, they find them to be ridiculous.'

'So I learned. After he killed my father, he brought me back to my office and expected me to have a session as usual. He couldn't understand why I was devastated. He said he'd just got rid of someone who'd hurt me, and that he'd expected me to like his gift and be appreciative. He said I'd been a big disappointment – not much different from my father's words years before. Martin left and I've never seen him again.' Ham dropped into the chair next to me. 'But now I know they exist.' He stared into my eyes. 'How do you deal with it?'

'One day at a time. It took a while for me to accept it, even being inundated with evidence. We both know there are plenty of humans sick enough to give a convincing performance as a vampire. Now I can't deny the existence of the undead, but as I obviously told you under hypnosis, there are layers of problems. Vampires actually affect the human brain physiologically. If I'm going to keep seeing them as a therapist, I have to find a way to protect myself.'

'I can't imagine how you'd be able to protect yourself from something that powerful. But you did say something about a vampire named Zephyr who could cast a spell to help you. Are you saying that magic is real, too?'

Judging by his lost expression, I didn't think Ham could take much more reality at that moment, so I patted him reassuringly on the arm. 'Let's save that discussion for the next time we get together and I'll try to break it all to you gently. You've already got a lot on your emotional plate. But you have to tell me what you did to make me tell you everything. That's just not like me.'

'I didn't really do anything. It was you. You apparently counted yourself down then began speaking. I've never seen anyone go that deep so quickly. Your mind is truly unique.'

'Yeah, so I hear. Maybe it's due to all the vampire influence. Or maybe I'm well and truly broken.'

He took my hand. 'I don't think so. You talked about your vampire lover Devereux and your mixed emotions about him. What's it like to be with such an astounding individual? How do you keep up?'

I laughed. 'I don't. In his presence, my brain is often mush. He doesn't mean to hurt me, but he does. Except for now – did I mention the reprieve another vampire gave me?'

'You did – but I wasn't sure you were telling the truth about that part because you said it was the historical Anne Boleyn who cleared the vampire influence from your mind. Surely you were just embellishing?' He looked hopeful.

'You could believe all the other things, but Anne Boleyn was too much? It's all true. But who knows how long this reprieve will last. Despite everything, I have to say that clinically it's been the most fascinating thing that's ever happened to me.'

'I'd love to talk to you about all your experiences. I imagine you don't have too many humans you can confide in – maybe just the one FBI agent you mentioned. I'd be pleased to act as a sounding board for you, if it would help.'

'It would definitely help. I'd enjoy getting together with you regularly – let's stay in touch. I'd like to come back and work on the issues I originally mentioned, especially now that I'm apparently such a whizz at hypnosis!' I smiled. 'But I really do need to get that CD and head over to my office now.'

He jumped up and went to the computer sitting on the nearby desk. After a couple of minutes, he carried the disk over to me. 'Here. If you have any questions, please call me.'

'Thank you, Ham. Can you bill me for today?'

He held out a hand to help me up from the recliner. 'No charge, Doctor Knight. Believe me, I gained as much from our time together as you did. In fact, I'm not sure what you gained, but I hope being able to share your story with someone was beneficial.'

I lifted my coat from where he'd hung it on a wall peg and slipped into it as I walked towards the waiting room. 'Just meeting you was worth the time. I look forward to seeing you again soon.'

He accompanied me to the outer door and watched while I navigated the icy sidewalk and headed to my car.

I tucked the CD into my pocket and wondered how much stranger things could possibly get.

CHAPTER 11

After my session with Ham, the rest of the day was filled with client sessions, case notes and making sure all the arrangements had been made to cover my practice while I'd be at the conference.

My therapist, Nancy, had agreed to be on-call for my clients in case of emergency. She occasionally attended the yearly gathering with me, but this time she didn't want to travel out of town because her youngest daughter was pregnant and approaching her due date.

Since the conference started early on Thursday morning, I'd arranged to arrive in New York the night before and would be flying out tonight. The weather cooperated and my flight hadn't been delayed.

I'd dressed in my newest pair of jeans, a light-blue turtle-neck sweater and flat-heeled black leather boots. It felt great to be out of my professional clothes for a while. The cross and pentagram necklaces rode against my skin. Relaxing in a window seat, I studied the lecture notes I'd jotted down on a pad while giving half my attention to the flight attendant's demonstration of what to do in the event of a water landing. Since there wasn't any significant water between Denver and

New York, I didn't think the issue would arise, and I'd heard the talk so many times I had it memorised.

Flying was such a miraculous thing to me. I understood the science of flight, but the idea of a huge cylinder with wings hurtling through the air still boggled my mind. It was the closest thing to magic that most people experienced.

After we got the all-clear to turn on our electronics, I set my laptop on the tray table in front of me and added my hand-written notes to my official presentation.

'Excuse me.'

Distracted, I turned my head towards the voice, suddenly aware of the man sitting on the aisle. The middle seat was vacant. Had he been there all along?

Attractive, probably in his early thirties, he had amber eyes and dark-brown hair just long enough to brush his shoulders, tousled in that haphazard-by-design style. He wore a denim shirt tucked into jeans.

'Yes?'

'I know this is terribly rude,' – he bent toward me and lowered his voice – 'but I couldn't help noticing on your computer screen that you're writing about people who want to be vampires.'

Shit.

I angled the screen away, blocking his view and met his gaze. He blinked slowly and smiled.

Perfect. A nosey, chatty seatmate. The last thing I wanted to do was talk about vampires with a stranger. Was this his attempt to pick me up? Well, I didn't want any of that either. My cup of men was full and my track record awful. But why hadn't he made me nervous like all the other good-looking non-colleague men always did? Had my phobia evaporated? 'You're right. It was rude.'

He straightened, eyebrows raised. He probably couldn't remember the last time his charming overtures were rebuffed. 'Sorry. Shouldn't have blurted that out – I know better. Let's start over.' He held out his hand. 'Hello. I'm Michael Parker.'

'Mr Parker—'

'Doctor Parker. I'm a psychologist.' He continued quickly, 'That's why I noticed what you were typing – the psychological terms caught my eye. I'm on my way to the APA Conference. Is it safe to assume that's your destination as well?'

Now it was my turn to be surprised, but that explained my lack of anxiety. I must have intuited he wasn't just another pretty face. 'That's *exactly* where I'm going.' *Nicely played, Doctor Parker. You skilfully shifted my perception and took control.*

'And might I also speculate that you're giving a presentation and would really like to get back to working on it, if only the obnoxious passenger next to you would mind his own business and stop bothering you?' The charming grin was back.

'I wouldn't go that far,' I said, trying to decide how friendly I wanted to be. He was a peer, after all. Or so he claimed. 'But I am giving a lecture on a specific subculture.'

'Vampires?'

I looked around at the nearby seats to see who might be listening. All the other passengers within hearing distance wore ear buds or headphones and were plugged into personal devices or the in-flight movie.

'Vampire wannabes,' I said quietly. 'Or as the conference committee refers to them, "lost children of the night".' *He must not be as sharp as he appears if he's from Denver but doesn't recognise me after all the media attention a few weeks back.*

'Well, this is a stroke of luck for me, Doctor – er . . . I don't know your name.'

'Kismet Knight.' I waited for him to have some reaction, to connect the dots, but he didn't.

'That's a wonderful name. Kismet: fate, destiny. Is it stressful to have such a meaningful name?'

I laughed. He had no idea. Being a weird kid was bad enough. Having an unusual name was like waving a red flag at little bulls. 'Stressful? Yeah, I guess you could say that.'

He pressed his hand over his mouth. 'I've done it again. Forgive me – I tend to blurt out whatever comes into my head. That's my biggest professional challenge, and one reason I'm taking a sabbatical from seeing clients.'

The flight attendant came to take drink orders. She gave a flirty smile to my seatmate.

'I'll have a Scotch and water,' he said to her, then looked at me. 'Please, at least allow me to buy you a drink for putting up with my clumsy introduction. What would you like?'

Why not? I was off-duty. 'White wine, please.'

She scribbled on her pad, winked at Michael and moved to the next row.

I brought my eyes back to his. He wasn't hard to look at – he reminded me of actor Orlando Bloom. 'So you're taking a break from clinical sessions? What are you doing instead?'

He released his seatbelt and turned towards me. 'I'm writing a book. That's why I said it was a stroke of luck for me to meet you. My general topic is about people who are susceptible to mind control, those who believe they're under the power of a vampire or an alien, for example. '

'Mind control?' My stomach tightened for a moment. He couldn't possibly know anything about my situation, but what a weird coincidence. 'Are you focusing on the supernatural specifically?'

'No. I'm looking at everything, including followers of gurus and members of religious cults. I'm fascinated by why some people surrender their autonomy, either to authority figures in the "real" world or fantasy creations. I'm studying the underlying mechanisms.'

Our drinks came and he raised his in salute. 'To synchronicities, Doctor Knight.'

'Yes,' I replied and took a sip from my glass, appreciating the relevance of Carl Jung's theory.

'Have you discovered your vampire-wannabe clients are looking for someone to take responsibility for them?' he asked. 'Is that part of the draw?'

'Absolutely,' I said, warming to the topic. My inner nerd loves talking shop. 'In every case, clients are seeking something they don't have in their lives: structure, meaning, someone to make them feel wanted – an escape from trauma and abuse. From that perspective, wanting their old selves to die makes total sense.'

'I completely agree. In a dysfunctional way, it's a good coping strategy.'

We both thought about that for a few seconds.

'I had quite a few alien abductees in my practice at one point,' he said. 'They were interesting and creative clients. I even had an abductee therapy group, but I disbanded it because the participants were triggering each other and incorporating the stories they heard in group into their own memories. It wasn't helpful. Do you work with abductees? That appears to be a popular therapy topic in Denver, or at least in Boulder, where I also had an office.'

'Oh yes.' I chuckled. 'Alien abductees. Denver's an extraterrestrial hotspot – we have a very active chapter of the Mutual UFO Network. I think half the members are my clients. Hmm.' I paused. 'Now that I think about it, that's pretty strange. How *did* so many of them find me? I didn't do any advertising for non-ordinary clientele.' But Cerridwyn had said I attracted the paranormal and supernatural. Could that be true after all? *Maybe it's more accurate to say I attract the weird and strange.* 'I had to stop using hypnosis with them because they're very susceptible to false memories.'

He grabbed my arm and nodded excitedly. 'I'm so glad to hear you say that. I had the same experience.'

I looked down at his hand on my arm and he let go.

'Sorry. I've been so isolated for the last few months that my social skills are rusty. Plus it's such a pleasant surprise to find a like-minded therapist on the plane going to the conference. But as I was saying, I did have some iffy situations with my abductees. Even giving emphasis to a certain word in a question I asked while they were in trance could stimulate their imaginations and cause them to fabricate.' He shrugged. 'It was too stressful. I think I prefer the *worried well* – those who are basically healthy and who want to explore themselves spiritually or grow personally.'

'You're preaching to the choir here, Michael. As fascinating as I find my chronically disturbed or nontraditional clients, it's a relief to have a few metaphysical seekers along the way. Have you worked with any other unusual kinds of clients?' *I haven't had any werewolves or faeries show up yet. Do they exist? Is that something else I have to look forward to?*

He smiled. 'I performed an informal exorcism once.'

The flight attendant shoved the box of snacks she'd been carrying down the aisle in front of Michael. 'Would you like some cookies or crackers? You can have as many as you like.'

'What? An exorcism?' I asked. Bad timing.

She raised her eyebrows at me and pursed her lips.

'No thank you,' Michael said.

She didn't offer me any and hurried on past.

Michael laughed softly. 'I think our topic of discussion start-led the attendant. She probably thinks your head is going to spin around while you puke green pea soup now.'

Well, at least I'm not that bad. Yet.

'I'll try to behave myself. So, exorcism – are you affiliated with a religious group?'

'No – that's why I said it was informal. One of my attached-entity clients insisted I was the only person who could cast out the demon in his chest. One day, in the middle of a session, he threw himself onto the floor and began having a seizure. Or at least that's what I assumed it was.'

'Wow. I've never had an attached-entity client go quite that far. What happened?'

'He flailed and kicked his feet on the carpet and started speaking in tongues, something he'd told me about earlier. I was sure the massage therapist downstairs would call the building manager or the police or something, so I used my most theatrical voice and demanded the demon leave his body.'

'Did your command work?'

'Amazingly, it did.' He grinned. 'He twitched a few times then got to his feet, shook my hand and told me he felt reborn. I never saw him again.'

I shook my head. 'Never underestimate the power of suggestion. And professionals used to think hypnosis wasn't effective. Now we know better. But it can be dangerous if a clinician isn't properly trained.'

'That's for sure. I've done my share of repairing damage caused by so-called hypnotists who only took a weekend workshop.' He looked at my computer keys. 'I'm really sorry – I distracted you from the work you were doing. I'll be quiet now so you can finish.' He gave a thumbs-up and straightened in his seat.

A glance at my watch told me we were more than halfway through the flight. He'd been such a pleasant conversation partner that I hadn't given any thought to my bizarre problems. I didn't want to end the discussion.

'You haven't kept me from anything. The presentation was already finished – I was just adding last-minute notes.' I met his gaze as he turned to me again. 'I enjoyed our talk.'

'That's good.' His eyes lingered a few seconds, then he cleared his throat. 'Maybe we could meet at the conference if you have time?'

The large man sitting behind me stood up to go to the restroom and pushed my seat so far forwards I almost knocked my computer onto the floor. 'Sorry,' he said in a gruff voice.

I caught the computer and spoke over my shoulder, 'That's okay. No harm done.'

'So what do you think about hooking up?' Michael asked.

'Hooking up?' My clients usually gave those words specific meaning.

'Yeah.' He saw the question on my face and chuckled. 'Oh no – not *that* kind of hooking up. I mean hanging out at the conference.'

'I knew what you meant. I just wanted to rattle your cage a little. It's a possibility, but I'm meeting a friend there.'

'Oh, well, I wouldn't want to be in the way.'

'Not at all – I think you'd enjoy meeting him.'

'Is he your boyfriend?'

What a nosey guy!

'Just a friend. Or maybe more than that, I don't know. And why I'm telling you that, I have no idea.'

What the hell, Kismet? Just spill your guts to a stranger for the second time in a single day, why don't you?

He laughed. 'Something about me encourages people to tell

their secrets. It's one of the reasons I'm a good therapist. My former partner was going to come to the conference with me, but we broke up a few months back.'

'I'm sorry to hear that. Is she a therapist, too?'

'He.'

'Oh! I'm so sorry – how narrow of me to assume . . . So you're gay.'

Crappy gaydar you've got there, Kismet. But he was flirting with me, I'm sure of it.

'Actually, I'm bi, but the last couple of relationships I've had were with men. And now I don't know why I'm telling *you* that.'

Well, at least I wasn't totally wrong.

'I'm glad you felt comfortable enough to tell me. Let's definitely plan to meet up at the conference.'

'I'd like that.'

We sat silently for a while, each lost in our own thoughts.

The man returned from the bathroom and dislodged my seat again, but this time I was prepared and held onto the computer.

After a couple of minutes, I was unable to restrain my curiosity and asked, 'I'm wondering why you didn't recognise my name.' My infamy had spread worldwide, so it didn't matter where he was from – I'd been the media *topic du jour* for weeks in the very recent past.

He frowned, looking confused. 'Why would I know your name? Are you famous? Have I been politically incorrect yet again?'

Glad I'd chosen a Wi-Fi flight, I swivelled my computer screen around so we could both see it, called up a search engine and typed in my name. Thousands of hits came up. I scrolled down to a *New York Times* story about the 'vampire murders' in Denver last October, brought up the information, then lowered the tray on the middle seat and slid my computer over.

'Take a look,' I said, pointing to the screen.

He read through a few paragraphs, then looked at me. 'Wow,' he said, slowly shaking his head. 'That's one hell of a tale. I can't believe I missed it. I spent most of the last four months in a Buddhist retreat centre up in the mountains, meditating and working on my book.' He poked my arm playfully. 'You really *are* famous.'

I pulled the computer back onto my tray and clicked out of the article. 'Yeah. Lucky me. Are you a Buddhist? Is that why you were at the retreat?'

'No. I'm not a Buddhist – or any other denomination, for that matter – but I do enjoy meditating, and it was a great place to observe religious devotees for my research. I highly recommend it if you ever need to get away from the everyday world for a while. No phones or computers allowed – I had to write on legal pads. It was a powerful and humbling experience.'

I laughed. 'So was mine.'

'I can only imagine,' he said, his tone serious. 'Have they caught the killer yet? The article only says he left Colorado. Are you still involved with the case?'

'They haven't found him yet, but the FBI's hot on his trail, as well as every local cop in every jurisdiction where blood-drained bodies have turned up. They'll catch him eventually.' I didn't answer his question about my involvement or mention the maniac's fixation on me. The purpose of going to the conference was to get away from all the vampire bullshit. Nobody else needed to know about it. I turned off my computer, packed it into its case and tucked it underneath the seat in front of me. I momentarily wondered if I should tell him about the psychologist murders since we were about to join a large gathering of the same, but if the police hadn't informed the media yet, I didn't think I should jump the gun.

Unfastening my seatbelt, I said, 'I need to get out.'

'Get out?'

'Yes.' I pointed to the bathroom.

'Oh! Of course.' Michael jumped up and stood in the aisle so I could pass.

I hurried into the closest lavatory, turned to flip the lock and was immediately overwhelmed by fear. I leaned back slightly and pressed against something solid. Somebody was in the tiny cubicle with me. Holy shit! I'd just sucked in a deep breath, preparing to scream, when a hand clamped over my mouth and a familiar voice said, 'It is I, Kismet, Devereux. Do not scream. Please nod if I can take my hand away.'

My knees almost gave out in relief. Devereux? At least it wasn't Lucifer. The thought that the monster could material-ise inside a plane hadn't occurred to me. How the hell had Devereux found me in the aeroplane bathroom? My heartbeat tripped. Vampires really were going to give me a coronary. I nodded and he released me. Almost without thinking, I started the mental hum, pleased it was becoming automatic.

I faced him and was stunned by his appearance. His usually sleek and shiny hair was twisted up into a rat's nest, sticking out everywhere, littered with debris. His clothes were stained and shredded; dirt and various unidentifiable substances covered his face. 'What are you doing here and what happened to you? Wait – more importantly, how the *hell* did you know which plane I was on and that I'd stood up to go to the bathroom? I thought you couldn't read me any more. And *please* turn down the fear.' My stomach was roiling. 'I'm going to pass out.' *Oh God – are the effects of Anne's interven-tion already fading?* But that couldn't be, because he was giving off the same intense fear resonance I'd felt in my office last night.

He closed his eyes briefly and my anxiety eased.

'I have computer experts who can discover anything I wish to know. It was easy to access your itinerary.' He ran his fingers through his massively tangled hair and growled, 'This is the first time I have ever attempted to materialise inside an aeroplane. I landed on the wing twice, then on the roof. Even with magic spells and my enhanced strength, grabbing onto the plane was no easy feat. I suspect the mechanics will find unexplained finger grooves pressed into various parts of the plane.'

Oh my God – grabbing onto the plane? Unexplained finger grooves? He really is an undead Superman.

'Finally,' he continued, 'I was able to accomplish my intended task: to find an empty seat I could target. Once I found that, I was able to materialise inside.'

I couldn't get past the absurd image his words were creating. 'Let me get this straight: you were hanging onto an aeroplane flying at hundreds of miles per hour? How were you not blown off?' Unbelievable. Were there no limits to what he could do? No wonder his hair looked like he'd been electrocuted then thrown into a wind tunnel. It was weird to see him so ... flawed.

He held up his filthy, bloody fingers. 'I *was* blown off. Repeatedly. Actually,' he said, 'that part was rather exciting. I have heard of skydiving but have never tried it. Until today. It was an experience I do not wish to repeat anytime soon. I felt like an idiot. The lengths to which I will go for you never fail to amaze me.'

No way. He didn't really land on the outside of the plane. Impossible.

'How come nobody saw you? Your light hair and skin almost glow in the dark – you had to be putting on quite a show out there. Why didn't I hear anyone screaming when you popped into the cabin?'

'I would point out that *you* did not see me, even sitting in a window seat chatting with your handsome companion and with your mind completely unencumbered of vampire influence. But just because I cannot control your mind, it does not mean I have lost the ability with everyone else. I simply told them they could not see me.'

'Huh, okay.' *Of* course *that makes sense . . . in Bizarro Vampire World.* 'Why are you here? I really did come into the bathroom for a compelling reason and I don't want to share the experience with anyone, including you. Is something wrong?'

'Yes. We are wrong, and it is my fault. I was insufferable and demanding last night.'

Really?

'You won't get any argument from me.' I couldn't take my eyes off his wild hair. It was *so* not him. I fought the urge to lick my palm and smooth it over his hair.

'That would be a pleasant change,' he said, 'but in this case I accept complete responsibility for our poor communication and I wish to apologise. You are correct that I have no right to impose my will upon you. You are, as you said, a separate person. I acknowledge that you have every right to attend a conference and that you have your own life to live. I will not be bullheaded or domineering.' He pulled down the neckline of my sweater and retrieved the cross necklace. 'Of course, if my assistance is required in an emergency, you need only hold the heirloom and say my name, and I will come.'

I pressed my thighs together to give my bladder the 'wait' signal. 'Okay. I appreciate the apology. I know you've been under a lot of stress and if you want to talk when I get back, I'm happy to do that.'

Devereux pointed towards the door. 'There is someone waiting.'

'Well, I'm not surprised – we've been in here a while. They're probably thinking I've fallen in or I'm doing something extremely unpleasant.'

He laughed. 'I do not miss those bodily functions. But let me take care of this.' He closed his eyes briefly. 'I gave the suggestion to everyone that it has been only a few seconds since you came in here. The poor fellow who ate something disagreeable has gone to the bathroom at the other end.' He eyed the facilities. 'I can say with certainty that my mode of travel is much more enjoyable than your human version.'

He wrapped his arms around me and pulled me closer. Meeting my gaze, he whispered, 'I am sorry. I was not myself.' He pressed his lips against mine in a sweet kiss, then teased his tongue into my mouth and took the kiss deeper.

Yum.

We kissed for a couple of minutes, then reluctantly pulled apart. His skin was colder than usual, perhaps because of his frigid outdoor adventure.

It occurred to me that I was responding to Devereux without any mind control on his part. Maybe we really did have something authentic going on between us after all. I considered the possibility of asking him to whisk me off to New York himself so we could spend some alone time sorting things out.

Unfortunately, my romantic fantasy was rudely squashed by reality.

'I wish I could remain longer but the night is short and Lucifer has been sighted.' He kissed me again. 'Also, I came to tell you that you were right – upon reflection, I believe it might be best if we take a break from each other for a little while. Just until we both have time to think about the optimum outcome. Things have moved too quickly for you. I exerted too much pressure. You are correct that you need to have the opportunity to decide for yourself whether you will choose to share my world or not. I do not wish to harm you, and if it is true that my mere presence damages your brain, then I will remove myself.' He lifted a shoulder. 'Perhaps I am not ready for a serious relationship either.'

'What?' I almost choked on the word. 'What do you mean, you're not ready for a serious relationship? Since when?'

'Since you made me think about whether or not we are truly a good fit for each other. I had been unwilling even to consider the possibility previously.'

What the hell is this? He's breaking up with me? After all his bullying and saying I'm his mate? I pressed my legs together more tightly.

'Your reasoning makes sense,' he continued. 'I was not seeing the larger picture. It is wise for us to have a cooling-off period until the situation with Lucifer is settled. After that, we can talk and see how we feel.' He brushed my lips with his again. 'Enjoy the conference and be safe.'

With that, he stepped back and disappeared.

Turning towards the mirror, I stared at myself in disbelief. *What just happened?* Surely I couldn't have heard what I thought I heard. His words kept replaying in my mind as I tried to sort out my feelings. My stomach cramped.

Take a break. That's what I wanted, wasn't it?

Yes.

No.

Well, shit. I was more confused than ever now. He'd respected my wishes. He'd done as I asked. A cooling-off period was good. I should be happy, right?

Why wasn't I happy? Why did I feel miserable and on the verge of tears?

I definitely hadn't seen that coming.

But I had told him I was going to rethink my involvement with all vampires, including him. What did I expect?

After dabbing my eyes with a tissue, I took care of business then navigated up the aisle to my seat, surreptitiously scanning the other passengers along the way to see if anyone had a reaction to my camp-out in the bathroom. Nobody did.

Michael stood before I reached our seats.

My chagrin must have been written on my face because he stared at me, frowning. 'Is everything okay? You seem upset. I hope I didn't say anything inappropriate.'

It took me a moment to shake off my reaction to Devereux's unexpected decision and turn my attention back to the conversation Michael and I had before the events in the bathroom. 'Of course you didn't. I'm just festering about a personal problem.'

He raised a brow. 'Anything a new therapist friend can help with? I'm a pretty good listener.'

'Thanks.' I smiled and fastened my seatbelt. 'You know how it is – things will work themselves out eventually.'

Would they? My vision blurred with tears and I suddenly felt overwhelmingly sad.

One of the pilots broke in over the speakers, reporting we were preparing to land. I was shocked by how quickly the time had passed. Apparently the secret to a speedy journey was a charming seatmate and a vampire breakup in the bathroom.

CHAPTER 12

We landed, and Michael and I shared a cab to the conference location – Hotel Briarwood, across from Central Park. The weather was cold but precipitation-free. The East Coast had experienced a dry period for the last couple of weeks.

Hotel Briarwood was a new site for the APA conference and, after seeing photographs of the neo-Gothic building a few months back, I'd done a little online research. The hotel had a traumatic history. Fire partially destroyed it twice, once in 1900 and again in 1942, and it was rebuilt both times to match its original style. Scores of people died in those still-unexplained fires. But the building lived up to its sterling reputation: no expense had been spared to recreate the elegance and beauty of the past. Entering the hotel felt like stepping back in time.

After checking in we took the elevator, our luggage among the cases piled on carts pulled by hotel staff. The doors had almost closed when a man wedged his hand into the narrow gap between them and thrust them apart. He propelled himself into the little space remaining and swivelled his head to stare at me.

He was humongous, like a football player, dressed in a thick black anorak with a brown wool cap pulled down over his head to his eyebrows. He was carrying a small grey bag and a computer case. His nervous energy sent my intuition into overdrive – the man definitely gave off some heavy negativity.

I scooted as far from him as I could and began to wonder what was in his bag. Should I alert hotel security? But what would I say? *A weird-looking guy's walking around the hotel with a bag.* Gee, that was unusual. I'd sound like a nutcase.

The man shifted to one side to let Michael out when we arrived at his floor. We said goodbye and promised to find each other the next day.

I watched the numbers over the doors rise as we climbed higher, feeling uncomfortable and a little frightened.

The man kept slanting dark glances in my direction.

Geez. I was glad the porter was with me. Brown Hat was definitely trouble waiting to happen.

When we reached my floor, the man backed up against the wall so we could exit, then, to my alarm, he followed us out of the elevator and accompanied us down the hall as we headed towards my door.

Crap. I didn't want to show him which room I was in. I'd just opened my mouth to ask the porter to keep walking when he stopped in front of room 936 and ran the keycard through the reader. Brown Hat turned on his heel and strode back towards the elevator.

Was he just some lunatic following a random single woman or had he chosen me in particular? Now that he knew my room number, I'd have to move.

After the porter left, I surveyed the room. It was spacious and luxurious, decorated in shades of blue and green, with two queen-size beds and a sitting area big enough for a couch and two comfortable chairs with footrests. A large television screen was mounted on one wall over an entertainment unit with a fully stocked refrigerator. Lovely reproductions of famous paintings dotted the other walls. A small office desk with commonly used supplies filled one corner, while a small conference table and chairs were centred in the other. Wireless computer access was available throughout the entire hotel.

The APA always held their gatherings in high-quality digs and this year was no exception. Too bad Brown Hat had already cast a shadow on my conference experience.

The light on my telephone was blinking when I sat on the edge of the bed to call the front desk. I retrieved one message.

'Hey, Kismet. Alan here. I'm all checked in. I figure you won't get here till late and you'll be tired, so I'll come by in the morning. I look forward to seeing you. I found out a little information about the – person – and the library we discussed. Sleep well.'

I kicked off my shoes and called the desk. When I asked to switch rooms, they informed me the hotel was completely booked due to our conference and another. I explained that someone had followed me up to my room, and they assured me they would try to arrange for me to change floors. In the meantime, they offered to have their security people pass by my room more often during the night.

That would have to do.

Of course, I always had the trusty cross, even if its owner wasn't sure he wanted to have a relationship with me. Damn it. Why did that still bother me?

Yearning for a shower, I took a few steps towards the bathroom and stopped dead. 'Oh!' A woman dressed like Ingrid Bergman in the airport scene from *Casablanca* came towards me. Upset that I'd unintentionally intruded on someone, I said, 'I'm sorry – I didn't know this room was already occupied. I'll call—' I'd barely got the words out when she walked right through me, sending a shock of icy cold along my body, like breathing in death. I gasped and looked behind me. Nobody was there.

My heart hammered in my chest. Feeling clammy and nauseous, I sat on the edge of the bed and tried to consciously lower my blood pressure. That was a first. Never before had a ghost made physical contact with me.

What the hell's happening? How weird am I going to get?

'Doctor Knight?'

'Shit!' I screamed and leaped off the bed, spinning around towards the voice that had come from behind me. I clutched my chest, my heart racing again.

Standing in front of the desk in the corner was a naked vampire. A sparkling naked vampire. A familiar sparkling naked vampire.

'Esther?' I breathed deeply and deliberately to calm myself and took a couple of steps in her direction. 'Is that you?' Turned as a thirteen-year-old a hundred years ago, she'd been denied the chance to fully develop, physically or mentally. Her narrow hips and flat chest made her look more like an adolescent male than a female and her developmental challenges caused her to behave like an even younger child. She definitely had no impulse control.

'Yes, Doctor Knight.' She gave me wide brown eyes. 'I'm so glad I found you. I wanted to show you my sparkle.'

She was painted all over with glittery white body paint. Her dark-blonde hair, which she usually pulled back into a long braid, was smeared with some sort of fruit-scented glitter gel with little hearts in it and plastered flat to her head.

Back to the sparkle. I thought we'd made progress.

She danced in a circle. 'Isn't it great? I finally sparkle, just like Edward and Alice Cullen! Now I'm a *real* vampire!'

She still thinks the characters in the movie are real.

'Yes, I see. That's very creative of you. What made you think of the body paint?'

'I went to a costume shop to see if they had any new cool vampire gear and a guy was having himself painted with white glitter paint. He wanted to be Edward for a gig with his band. So after he was finished, I had them paint me, too!'

'That's great, Esther. I'm happy if you're happy. By the way, how *did* you find me? I told everyone I'd be out of town for a few days.'

'I hang out with Chain sometimes and he said you went to the shrink conference in New York City. We looked it up on the Internet and found the hotel. Then I just showed up, waited until nobody was waiting to talk to the desk person, and forced her to look up your room.' She swung her arms over her head, hopping from foot to foot and making hooting noises. 'I guess she'd never seen a *real* sparkling vampire before because she passed out cold! It was so funny!'

'Esther! You didn't drink her blood or hurt her, did you? We've talked about how dangerous it is for you to drink in public.'

'Nope, I remembered what you said. After she fell down I popped up here.' She brushed her arm with her fingers, sending some of the glitter fluttering to the floor. 'Okay, I'm gonna go now. I just wanted to show you. See you later.'

She vanished.

I stood there staring at nothing and shook my head. I'd definitely entered a parallel dimension.

In spite of dreaming about a fire and screaming people jumping out of skyscraper windows, I woke up relatively relaxed and functional. I ate my room-service breakfast in front of a window overlooking Central Park. It was a glorious sunny morning.

If Brown Hat had planned any harm he'd failed, because I'd passed an unmolested night. I wondered if he was a guest in the hotel, or a conference attendee.

After dressing in a pink silk blouse, new dark-blue trousers and a matching blazer, I went down to the conference registration desk to pick up my materials and say hello to Dr Teller, the chairperson. While I was there, I checked out the information table, scanning the new therapy-based products that assorted salespeople would be pitching during the event, then returned to my room. I spent a few minutes reading through my presentation pages again, adding a few new thoughts and noting some new research I wanted to explore before giving the lecture.

Assuming the hotel would be able to switch my room, I hadn't unpacked my bags. I'd just tucked the few things I'd removed back into the suitcase and poured a half-cup of coffee when a knock sounded at the door.

Even though I was expecting Alan, the strange experience with Brown Hat had me on edge.

'Who is it?'

'Your friendly FBI agent.'

Recognising Alan's voice, I opened the door. He usually favoured worn jeans and white T-shirts, but today he was wearing tailored dark-grey trousers with a rich purple shirt that made the blue-purple of his eyes pop. His brown hair had been recently trimmed and styled and for once he'd avoided using his fingers as a comb. Agent Stevens was a very good-looking man.

He stepped in, wrapped me in a tight hug, then planted his lips on mine.

As the only human male who knew as much – if not more – about the vampire world as I did, Alan always inspired a safe, *normal* feeling in me. I responded to his kiss and felt him slide his hand down to cup my ass.

'Wow,' I said when I had flicked his hand away and we moved apart, 'you're frisky first thing in the morning.' I straightened my blazer.

'You have no idea.' He grinned. 'Maybe we could stay here for a little while and I'll show you.' He brushed my lips with his.

Touching him caused inner turmoil, as always.

I knew this would happen. My body says yes but my brain says, 'What about Devereux?' But that isn't a consideration any more, is it? We broke up.

I pressed a palm against his chest and gave a gentle shove. 'Not now. I'm here to attend the conference and figure things out.'

'Not now?' He stroked his hands up my arms. 'I'll take that to mean there will be a later.' He pretend-punched my arm and stepped away. 'Okay. I need more caffeine anyway.' He picked up the pot, filled the rest of my cup and took a sip.

'Did the San Francisco police report the therapist connection to the media yet?' I asked.

'No. They're still holding that bit of info back, along with the fact that there are nine bodies all together. They won't be able to contain the flood much longer.'

'I'm still wondering whether we should warn everyone here that there's a mad shrink-killer on the loose – do we have a duty to report?'

'No – we should wait until the cops release the information. Come on.' He looked at the bed. 'Let's sit down and I'll tell you what I found out about Zephyr.'

Since room service had only provided one cup with the large pot, I looked through the cabinets and drawers to see if there was a make-it-yourself coffee setup with cups. There was. I grabbed one, poured more coffee for myself and stared at the couch in the sitting area before perching on the opposite bed from Alan. 'So is there such a thing as a vampire cult's secret library? Does Zephyr exist?'

Alan set his coffee on the nightstand between the beds and shifted himself up to prop his back against the headboard. He crossed his legs at the ankles and lifted his cup again. 'According to my research, it's all true, and it's even weirder than I thought. Are you sure you're ready for this?' He returned the cup to the nightstand. Cocking a brow, he looked at me expectantly.

'Judging by your body language and your question, whatever you have to say is a big deal.' I took a deep breath. 'Let me have it.'

He waggled his brows and smiled. 'Later.'

I leaned over and smacked his foot. 'I mean the information, funny guy.'

He smirked, relaxed his arms and jerked his feet out of my reach. 'Okay, so I heard there's a fortress built into the mountains somewhere in the Andes that's the real home – unlike the castle a certain government advertises to collect tourist dollars – of the most famous blood-drinking monster ever.'

'What? Are you talking about—?'

'Yep,' he interrupted, 'Dracula, who prefers to be called *Dracul*, and who actually exists. Turns out he had, and still has, a unique relationship with his biographer, Bram Stoker. Dracul does occasionally frequent that popular Carpathian castle, just to keep a fang in, and also enjoys spending time in England when he's able. The Carfax Abbey vacation home immortalised in the movies about him holds a warm spot, so to speak, in his heart.'

'You're making that up, trying to be funny,' I said, frowning. I stood, preparing to grab my briefcase and head downstairs. 'I thought you were going to help me.'

'Wait! I *am* helping you,' he said, sitting up straight. 'I'm serious – this really is what I heard, and from more than one source.'

I sat and studied his expression, looking for signs that he was messing with me. 'All right, I'll play along. So Dracula exists and lives in the Andes. What else?'

Frankly, upon second thought, that wasn't any more ludicrous than anything else I'd learned about vampires.

'Apparently he's seriously considering an offer to become involved – as a silent partner, of course – in the creation of a "Dracula Land" amusement park in London.'

'Uh-huh.' I gave him a bland look. *Right. A fictional vampire who allegedly lives in South America bankrolling a theme park in the UK.* 'So what does this have to do with a library? Are you saying Zephyr is another name the mythical Dracula uses?' Suddenly an idea occurred to me and I slapped my hand on my thigh. 'Of course! This is from your book, right? A plot idea. Very creative.'

I should have known better than to talk about anything serious with Alan.

He swung his legs over the side of the bed and took a sip from his cup. 'That *would* be a cool subplot for my book, but I didn't make it up. It's common knowledge among the older vampires. And no – Zephyr isn't one of Dracula's names.' He tapped his index finger against his chin. 'But now that you mention it, maybe I could borrow the idea for my book.'

'It's not likely vampires will sue you for lifting their story, I guess.'

'Oh, I don't know.' He grinned. 'What if lots of vampires are attorneys?'

'You're right. People always talk about lawyers being bloodsuckers. I hadn't thought of that.' If Devereux and his corporate colleagues could run multinational companies, anything was possible. 'But what does Dracula have to do with the secret library?'

'It's housed at the fortress, deep inside the mountain, in a steel-reinforced waterproof chamber. There are supposedly thousands of volumes, each one a handwritten account of members' magical experiments and discoveries, spanning millennia. Zephyr is the current keeper of the wisdom – the head librarian, as it were. Has been for longer than anyone can remember.'

'So he lives in the Andes? That puts an end to the idea of me getting in touch with him.'

'Not necessarily. He works there, but the location of his lair is unknown. I guess several vampires, including all the master vampires like Devereux, know how to contact him. But I already put the word out across the vampire grapevine that you'd like to speak with Zephyr. My source says you're well known enough that the librarian will follow through, so you can expect a visit.'

'Shit! You mean he's just going to pop in whenever he feels like it? We can't make an appointment?' I'd be a nervous wreck, waiting for a Gandalf clone to appear in my bedroom as I slept.

'Yeah. I guess he will just pop in. Even though you're associated with Devereux, I don't think vampires give much weight to human wants and desires. I'm sure he'll show up when it's convenient for him.'

Someone knocked on the door. I visibly startled and Alan

noticed. 'Geez, Kismet – it's only the door. More high-strung than usual today, aren't you?'

'Some guy followed me and the porter up to my room last night. I keep expecting him to show up.'

He immediately shifted into high alert, relaxed body posture totally gone. 'Why didn't you tell me sooner? I could have had a chat with hotel security.'

I rose and walked to the door. 'Who is it?'

'Hotel Guest Services. You asked to switch rooms?'

I cracked the door to find a tall red-haired woman and a short Asian man in hotel uniforms. No linebacker in sight.

Alan sidled over to see for himself.

'Yes. Thank you. Come in.'

The man rolled the luggage cart into the room and lifted my bags onto it. After I gave the area a last eyeball scan to make sure I hadn't forgotten anything, the four of us exited into the hallway.

As we stood in front of the elevator, Alan flashed his FBI credentials at the pair, then said to the woman, 'Which room are you moving her to?'

'1029,' she replied.

'Great. Give me thirty seconds' head start before you get in the elevator.' He pointed down the hall. 'I'm going to check the stairwell and keep watch as you enter the new room.'

He trotted off and the three of us made polite conversation about the weather for the requested time. The two employees kept their faces blank and didn't express any opinions about the clandestine operation.

The only difference between the new and old rooms was the colour theme. This one was gold and burgundy. I still had a view of Central Park.

My belongings relocated, I waited at the doorway for Alan

to return, which he did a couple of minutes later.

'All clear,' he said, strolling in. 'Nobody lurking. Damn. There's no coffee in here. Let's go down to the restaurant – I'm hungry.'

'I already ate, but maybe I can sit with you for a little while.' I opened my briefcase and searched for the conference workshop schedule. 'I don't want to miss any good presentations.' The first one I intended to catch was still an hour away. 'Okay, I've got time. Come on.'

We went down to the restaurant and joined the long line of folks waiting to be seated.

'Holy hell – look at all these psychologists. I'll never get any food at this rate,' Alan complained.

I turned to look for the toilet, and spied Brown Hat standing next to a large potted plant near the entry to the restaurant. He was dressed exactly the same as last night. Since he was still wearing his coat and hat, it wasn't likely he was a hotel guest.

'Alan.' I tugged on his sleeve and whispered, 'There's the guy who followed me to my room last night.'

'Where?' he said, still keeping his eyes on me. I looked in the general direction and Alan stuck his hands in his pockets and nonchalantly ambled towards the entrance, purposefully giving no attention to the man trying unsuccessfully to hide himself behind the plant.

As Alan approached, Brown Hat must have realised his cover was blown and took off running across the hotel lobby. He moved pretty fast for such a bulky guy. I hoped nobody got in his way because he probably didn't intend to stop.

Alan took off after him.

I'd already started running by the time Alan did and we both tromped across the marble floor, luckily managing to avoid luggage carts and hotel guests.

Brown Hat hit the open automatic door just in time to glide through before it closed and Alan and I had to pause a moment for it to activate again.

We slammed out onto the sidewalk and looked both ways. There was no sign of the stalker – if that's what he was.

My wool blazer was no match for the frigid temperature, much less Alan's shirt.

'What should we do?' I asked. 'Go get our coats and try to pick up his trail?'

'We?' Alan laughed and took my arm, pulling me back into the hotel. 'Who's the FBI guy here? You've been watching too many movies and TV shows. But for the record, I'm not a werewolf. The likelihood that I can sniff out the guy's direction is pretty low, and with all these businesses he could've ducked into, I'd say we wouldn't have much luck with that particular needle.'

We were the centre of attention as we re-entered the hotel.

'Let's go and report the guy to security. I got a pretty good look at his face. At least they can be on the lookout for him.'

Turns out we didn't have to go find security. Thanks to our dramatic run across the lobby, they found us.

After Alan showed his FBI credentials and we explained the situation, reminding them that I had asked to switch rooms due to the man following me, they cooperated and took a report. They assured us the man would be banned from the hotel and turned over to the police if he tried to enter again.

We went back to the restaurant, where the line was now much shorter, and got a table right away.

'Damn, it's cold out there,' Alan said, rubbing his arms. 'I have to admit it's always exciting being around you. Something unusual always happens.'

He was talking about today and all the chaos a couple of months ago.

'Hey, it's not my fault. I had nothing to do with that guy showing up – I just happened to be in the wrong place at the wrong time.'

'Yeah,' he said, laughing, 'that's the story of your life.'

I looked at my watch as the waiter brought our coffee. 'It's almost time for the *Working with Nontraditional Clients* workshop.' I lowered my voice. 'I'm sure they're talking about humans, but I might pick up a few tips I can apply to my population.' I took a couple of sips of my coffee. 'What are you going to do all day? Did you actually register for the conference?'

'No, I'm a gate-crasher. As I told you before, I have plenty to do to occupy my time. I still have to keep in touch with the team in San Francisco and check in with the locals here. Don't worry about me. You just go ahead and attend the presentations, consult with your colleagues and have a great day. I'll see you back at your room this evening.'

Hmm. Back at my room this evening. Room. Bed. Alan. Well, why not? I didn't appear to have any prior commitments any more.

'Okay,' I said, and stood up to leave. 'I'll be finished at five.'

'Don't I get a kiss goodbye?'

I scanned the nearby tables. 'No kisses in public.'

'Isn't perfection exhausting?'

He's right. What the hell ... I bent down, pressed my lips to his and put some juice into it.

'Wow,' was all he said as I walked away.

CHAPTER 13

My Inner Nerd was ecstatic by the time all the presentations for the day were finished. I took volumes of notes on my laptop – learning to type fast was one of the best things I've ever done – and had interesting discussions with colleagues between sessions. A few people mentioned my recent notoriety, but nobody said anything disrespectful. After expecting the worst – to be ridiculed or shunned – finding myself treated much the same as always at the conference, with maybe a little more positive attention, was a tremendous relief.

And either hotel security had done an efficient job or Brown Hat had lost interest, because there were no more sightings of the creepy guy today.

I rode the elevator up to my floor, feeling energised and tired all at the same time, and found Alan pacing frantically along the corridor outside my room. He jetted up the hallway when he saw me. Something big had happened.

'Kismet! You won't believe it.' His grin stretched from ear to ear. Vibrating with excitement, he grabbed my hand, then dropped it and raced up and down the hall again, mumbling to himself.

'What?' I trotted along behind him. Was there a break in

the case? Had someone destroyed Lucifer? Was that what the excitement was about? He was obviously caught up in some kind of manic episode. 'Alan!'

'My mother.' He sped down the corridor again and I followed. A door opened and an elderly woman poked her head out, watched Alan for a few seconds, then quickly closed and locked the door.

'Your mother? What about her?' *His mother?*

He returned to my door, pointed to his phone, then leaned against the wall and slid down to the floor. Looking stunned now instead of excited, he sat with his knees drawn up, his arms wrapped around them. With a groan, he rested his forehead on his arms, all the mania suddenly gone. His adrenalin high had exhausted itself and he crashed. I wondered how long he'd been pacing before I got there.

'Oh my God, Alan!' I knelt next to him and pushed a lock of hair back from his forehead. 'What?'

He raised his head. 'My mother—'

'Yeah, your mother. You said. Please tell me what's happened.' What the hell could it be? His eyes were filled with sadness, his expression a lost child's.

His mother? The woman he suspected was a vampire and who'd abandoned him?

I put my arm around him. 'Tell me. What about her?' Had he learned something so awful that his mind had snapped?

He held out his cell phone. 'She left me a message just a few minutes ago. I was on another call so it went to voice-mail. Let me put it on speaker—'

'Wait, Alan. Let's go inside.' Listening to a private personal message out in the hotel hallway wasn't a good idea under any circumstances, but who knew what his long-lost mother might disclose? If it was even her. He wasn't thinking clearly.

I rose and hooked my hand under his arm, drawing him up and into my room.

I led him over to the couch in the sitting area and he plopped down bonelessly, hope and fear dancing on his face. Setting my briefcase on the bed, I peeled off my blazer, then pulled a chair over from the office area in the other corner and sat in front of him.

He pressed a couple of buttons on his phone and a woman's voice came from the speaker. He locked eyes with me.

'Alan, my sweet son. It's Ollie. Your mother. I need your help. Colin and I live in New York, and I know you're here, too. I've kept track of you all these years. Please. Something's happened . . . Call me back. You have my number in your phone now. I'm waiting to hear from you.'

He replayed the message again, the muscles in his face slack, as if all the blood had been sucked out and he'd deflated. When the voice stopped the second time he sank into the couch cushions and let his head fall back, his neck no longer able to hold its weight.

I sat with him in silence and waited for him to give any subtle signal that he was ready to talk about the call. A few minutes later he blinked repeatedly, swallowed and raised his head.

'Do you think that was really your mother?' I asked, hoping the message hadn't been a hoax perpetrated by some horrible person.

He tried to speak and his voice cracked.

I went to the small refrigerator, collected a couple of bottles of water, and brought them over. I handed one to him.

He drank, then cleared his throat. 'Thanks. Yeah, that was her – I recognise her voice. She sounds exactly the same as I remember. And only those closest to her knew I called her Ollie.'

'Ollie?'

'Her name is Olivia and she hated being called Ollie, so as a kid, of course I teased her when I found out, and I started using it once in a while, just to press her buttons. It was a special thing between us, because she never let anyone else call her that.'

'Have you contacted her yet?'

He shook his head. 'I've been hoping for this my whole adult life and now that she's contacted me, I'm suddenly afraid.'

'What are you afraid of?'

He stared off for a moment before looking down at the floor. 'I convinced myself that she didn't want to leave me. That she'd been taken against her will. What if that isn't true? What if she chose to walk away?' He drank more water. 'That would mean she never loved me and the stories I told myself were lies.' He looked at me. 'If I was wrong, that changes everything and I don't know who I am.'

I leaned in and laid a hand on his knee. 'No matter what, you'll still be the same amazing man you've always been.'

'Yeah,' he said on a sharp laugh. 'Some amazing man. Fixated on his mother. Tell me, Doctor – am I a prime psychological specimen, or what?'

'You're human, Alan. And more honest than most.'

'She said she needs my help. What could that possibly mean?'

'Only one way to find out.'

'Right. And *he's* with her.'

'Colin? Is that the same man—?'

'The one who turned her.'

'She sounded scared. Said something's happened.'

'Shit.' He bolted off the couch and walked a groove into the carpet, finally kicking the leg of a chair in frustration. 'She did sound scared. I have to call her.'

'Yes. You do.'

He sat on the edge of the bed, took out his cell phone and stared at it.

'Do you want some privacy?' I asked.

'No – I could just go to my own room if I did. I'd rather have you here. Okay.' He found his mother's number and pushed the buttons to call her and to put her on speaker.

After two rings, a woman answered. 'Alan?'

'Mom? Is it really you?'

'Oh, Alan,' she said. It sounded like she was crying. 'You have no idea how I've missed you. How terrible it's been to have to watch you from the sidelines.' She sobbed more loudly now, not even trying to hold back the tears.

'Why did you leave, Mom? What happened to you?' Alan had fully regressed to his eight-year-old self.

'I can't talk about it on the phone, honey. Can I come and see you? I didn't want to just show up without asking. After all, you're probably pretty upset with me.'

'Upset? You think I'm *upset*? Try out of my mind with worry and fear. Broken-hearted. Lost.'

She sniffled for a few seconds. 'I know. I'll try to explain. Can I come?'

He looked at me, wanting – advice? Support? No idea.

'Yes. You can come. When—?'

She appeared in the room. My stomach clenched and a mild tremor of fear rumbled through me.

There was no question now about whether or not she'd become a vampire. Being able to move through time and space was a big tip-off. Not to mention the flare-up of my temporarily more intense vampire sensing system.

Alan dropped the phone.

He'd told me his mother was great-looking. That was an

understatement. She must have been in her late twenties when she became a vampire because she looked younger than both Alan and me. Only about five feet four inches tall, she was lean with curves in all the right places. Her waist-length hair was a rich shade of brown, like Alan's, and it was obvious where he'd got his purple-blue eyes. She was wearing a long black dress and matching cape.

After a slight hesitation on his part, they leaped into each other's arms and held on tightly, both crying.

When they finally pulled apart, Alan stared at her as if he thought she would disappear if he looked away.

'Let's sit down, Mom.' Alan pointed to the couch.

'Just a minute, sweetie,' she said as she turned in my direction, holding out her hand. 'I'm Olivia, Alan's mother. It's nice to meet you. Thank you for caring about my son.'

I took the hand she offered. 'I'm Kismet Knight.'

'Yes, I know. I really have stayed close to my son and I'm aware that you're important to him.'

'Mom!' Alan said the word like an embarrassed teenager.

'He's important to me, too,' I said.

'Yes, he is.' She walked over to the couch and sat.

Feeling like a third wheel, I went to the refrigerator to see what I could find. I held up bottles of beer and wine for Alan to see. 'Would you like anything?'

'Should I offer Olivia something?' I mumbled under my breath as I turned back to the refrigerator. 'How good a hostess should I actually be?'

'No thanks,' he said.

Olivia laughed and addressed me. 'I have very good hearing, Kismet. No veins are necessary. I'm fine.'

I felt my cheeks warm. 'Well, that's good.'

Talking to yourself, Kismet? Not a good sign.

I poured the small bottle of white wine into a glass, carried it over to the bed and sat. I'd been practising the hum, so the fear I was picking up from Olivia had remained manageable.

'It's been a while since I laughed. That felt good,' Olivia said, turning to face Alan. 'But this is a terrible time for me. Colin is missing. I'm sure another of his violent business partners has taken him.' She reached over to the side table and plucked a tissue out of the box.

'Colin? This is about Colin?' Alan said, anger colouring his voice.

Olivia sat up straighter and raised her chin. 'You don't know him, Alan. You were a child when the three of us spent time together. He's a fine man. Perhaps he behaves foolishly sometimes, but he's basically good. He took care of me after the attack.'

'Attack?' Alan jumped to his feet. 'Are you saying he hurt you and you stayed with him anyway?'

Olivia tugged on his arm until he sat. 'No, Colin would never hurt me. He's been trying to protect me the same way he protected you.'

'What are you talking about?' Alan jerked to attention and clenched his fists, barely able to keep his rage in check. 'He didn't do shit for me. He took my mother away. He turned you into a vampire and left me an orphan.'

She laid her hand on his arm. 'No, Alan, that isn't what happened. But my becoming a vampire is indirectly Colin's fault.'

'What—'

'Please. Let me tell the whole story.' She looked into Alan's eyes and he relaxed back into the cushions, unclenching his hands.

Impressive. She transformed his anger.

'As I said, Colin is a good man but he makes poor decisions. He involves himself with dangerous individuals. He makes lots of enemies. It was one of those enemies who turned me. Actually, he and his gang left me for dead to punish Colin. You were their next target.'

'Me?'

'Yes. Colin killed all the vampires who attacked me, then he took me to Denver to ask for help from an old friend who is Master there.' She looked at Alan then at me. 'I believe you know Devereux.'

We both stared at her, and finally I spoke: 'What a small world.'

Her expression told me she knew exactly how well I knew Devereux.

Returning her attention to Alan, she said, 'You went to live with my sister in Jersey, where you wouldn't draw the attention of any of Colin's other enemies. Devereux helped with that, too, by casting some magic to hide you and keep you safe from vampires in general. It took me a long time to recover. Years. At first I was an animal, filled with bloodlust. Eventually I regained the ability to be around humans. Without Colin and Devereux, I wouldn't exist at all.'

'Well, that explains why Devereux was willing to talk to me when I met him. The bastard already knew me and didn't say a word about it.'

'I asked him not to and he agreed to keep my secret.'

'Yeah.' He stared off into space for a few seconds. 'I'll deal with him later. But when you got better, why didn't you contact me?'

'By then I believed it was best if you thought I was dead. I didn't know you'd be so tenacious about uncovering what really happened to me, and since you were never sure I'd been turned, I just kept quiet. But as I said, I watched over you as soon as I was able.'

'What about the night in the bar here in Manhattan back when I was in college, when I saw the two of you and you ran away?'

'We ran because Colin couldn't face you. He knows what losing me did to you, and he holds himself responsible.' She looked at me. 'He always had a tendency towards depression and anxiety and has been despondent and guilt-ridden ever since I was turned against my will. He never wanted that for me.' She smiled sadly. 'He's the one who never recovered. I actually tried to get him to go and see you, but he wouldn't.'

'He *should* feel responsible. He *is*,' Alan said. 'So he's missing – what's that about?'

She stood and marched back and forth, much like her son had earlier. 'I don't know. He simply didn't come home at dawn two days ago.'

Alan made a disgusted sound. 'He probably just took off. Greener pastures. More sheep to fleece.'

'Stop,' Olivia said, her eyes narrowing, her body taut. 'I understand that you're hurt and you can be as angry at me as you like, but I won't have you disrespecting Colin. He's been wonderful to me and something is wrong. He'd never stay away by choice.'

I wasn't sure if I should interrupt, but a lot of strong emotions were about to combust between them. They'd have to cope with them all, but maybe now wasn't the best time. 'How can Alan help you, Olivia?' I asked.

They both shifted their attention to me, the tense moment broken.

She sat, and took his hand. 'I want you to find him, Alan.

You're not only an FBI agent – you've become a talented vampire hunter. Please help me.'

'Find Colin? I wouldn't know where to start.'

Olivia stood and held out her hand to him. 'I'll tell you everything. Come with me.' She pulled Alan up off the couch into a hug, and they vanished.

'Bye,' I said to the now-empty space, remembering my hope that coming to New York City would take me away from all the vampire madness. I laughed at the naïve notion. And of course Devereux was a participant in this East Coast brand of bloodsucking chaos as well.

Thinking about Devereux made my stomach tighten. He wasn't human and it wasn't likely I'd ever truly understand him. Who knew how many secrets he carried? But it didn't matter since we had decided to break things off. I kept forgetting.

Forcing myself to push him out of my consciousness, I focused on Alan again. I understood Olivia's fear about her mate, but was it safe to thrust her son into a situation involving yet more homicidal vampires? Not even close.

Restless, not knowing how I could help Alan, I wandered over to the window and sipped my wine while watching the lights of Manhattan. Despite my attempt to distract myself, a vision of Devereux's face suddenly popped into my mind and I felt overwhelmingly sad. As professionally important as the last almost-three months had been, they'd been personally disastrous. Could I step away from the vampires? As I wondered that, another question arose that took my breath away. Would the vampires *let* me step away now I knew of their existence?

I anxiously pondered that horrifying question for a couple of minutes until a stomach growl brought me back to the present. I hadn't really eaten anything substantial since morning and, with nothing to soak it up, the wine had gone to my head. At least eating was something I was in charge of, an activity *I* could control.

I shook off the fearful new possibility and focused on the reality of food. I freshened up, grabbed my briefcase and headed out for the hotel restaurant. Maybe I could get some work done.

The line for the dining room was long again and I considered going out and looking for a less-busy option within walking distance, or just calling room service, putting on my Freud pyjamas and staying in for the evening.

'Kismet!' a familiar voice said.

Michael, my seatmate from the aeroplane, trotted out of the restaurant, waving at me. 'There you are! I didn't see you all day – we must have attended different workshops. I'm just finishing up – please join me.'

Amid grumbling from the people ahead of me in the line, I accompanied Michael back to his booth, which was tucked into a dim corner. All that was left of his meal was a half-empty cocktail.

How did he see me from way back here? I suppose there is a somewhat direct line of sight to the waiting area – if you're leaning out of the booth, that is . . .

I joined him. 'It was pretty lucky you were able to see me from way back here. Who knows how long I would've had to wait for a table?'

'Okay,' he gave a charming grin, 'I've been found out. I asked for this booth on purpose so I could watch for you. I called your room earlier and there was no answer and for some reason the voicemail option was disabled. I enjoyed our conversation on the plane so much I hoped to have some time with you tonight. It's rare to find another clinician who works with the type of clients I see.'

Well, he likes guys, so we can just be friends. No drama. He still doesn't make me nervous, so I must have him firmly in the buddy column. What's the harm, right?

'I enjoyed our conversation, too.'

The waiter came and handed me a menu, then stood patiently next to the table. I ordered coffee and a big chef salad.

'Are you sure you want to sit here while I eat? You were probably ready to leave.' Actually, I was too hungry to care if he sat with me or didn't.

'I'm sure. I don't know anyone else here, so I'll try to make my company pleasant enough that you'll tolerate me.' He smiled and made excellent eye contact.

Okay, he's flirting with me, isn't he? Or is this just his personality?

'Where's your friend – the one you were meeting here? Did he decide not to come?' he asked.

Where is he? I wish I knew.

My food arrived and I dug in, glad it had come quickly. 'He's here but was called away on a case.'

'Oh – is he a local psychologist who had to have someone hospitalised, or something? Or is he so well known that his talents are in demand even here?'

How much should I say? Does it really matter?

'He's a psychologist, but he works as an FBI profiler.' The food had begun to relax me.

'Wow. That sounds exciting. I hope I get to meet him while we're here. Does he share your interest in vampire-wannabes? I'll bet he encounters all kinds of fascinating cases.'

'He's pretty open-minded.' *Time to change the subject.* 'So, tell me about the workshops you attended today.'

We spent the next hour discussing the sessions we'd attended. He was right – it was rare to encounter another psychologist with similar interests and client demographics. Talking to him was pleasant and it wasn't a hardship that he was easy on the eyes. I found myself laughing more than I had in days. Maybe he and I could schedule informal consultation and supervision with each other when we got back to Denver. It really would be great to have a professional friend. Hell, I could invite Ham and we'd have a weird little mini-coven.

'Can I admit something to you?' he said, lowering his voice.

Uh-oh. Do I really want to hear whatever it is?

I picked up my coffee cup and drained it. 'Okay,' I said, not sounding sure at all.

'Actually, I need some advice. Peer consultation.'

'What kind of advice?'

'I'm being stalked by a client.'

'What?' I almost tipped over the water glass I'd just reached for. 'Are you serious?'

'Deadly.'

'All right, Doctor Parker.' I relaxed back into the soft booth cushions. 'I'm all ears.'

He sighed and played with an unused spoon. 'A few weeks before I went on sabbatical at the meditation centre, one of my clients finally became overt in his attempt to convince me to have sex with him.'

'Is it safe to assume that kind of behaviour is part of his diagnosis?'

'Yes. I see many GLBT clients, some of whom aren't comfortable with themselves or their orientations, so it's not unusual for them to act out their concerns and insecurities in session. That's normal.'

'It's normal for all clients.'

'You're right. But this particular client was different. He exhibited the most extreme sex addiction I'd ever worked with. From the moment he walked into my office, I became his object of fixation.'

'That doesn't sound good. What happened?'

'He physically assaulted me, and afterward he begged me for forgiveness. He swore he'd stay away from me and seek treatment elsewhere if I didn't file a police report. I agreed. Looking back now, I can see he was more disturbed than I thought and I was wrong not to go to the authorities. A couple of weeks later, he filed a grievance against me, saying I'd abused him. My licence is currently in review.'

'No way!' I sat up straighter. 'That's terrible, Michael. I'm so sorry. Did he hurt you?'

'Not physically. I was able to fight him off and force him out of my office. But the fact that I missed the severity of his illness makes me doubt myself. That's really why I went to the centre – I didn't have the confidence to continue with my private practice. My partner broke up with me because of the stress.'

'Oh, Michael, I don't know what to say. Is there anything I can do to help?'

He smiled, a glimmer of the familiar charm peeking through. 'Just listening is great. I haven't told anyone – it's a relief even to say the words to someone.'

'Do you think you'll lose your licence? Can you prove your innocence? Once there's a legal proceeding involving the two of you, confidentiality is no longer a concern.'

'I'm confident I'll keep my licence. Turns out I'm not the first therapist he filed a grievance against, nor the first he assaulted. But the experience has been traumatic and overwhelming. I decided this was a good time to work on the book I'd had on the back burner for years. I'm not sure I want to work in private practice any more.'

'I can't blame you for that. What a horrible experience. Nobody recovers quickly from that sort of ordeal.' I wished I could tell him about the time bloodsucking Bryce came to my office and bit me, intending to drain me dry. Or when Lucifer kidnapped me from outside The Crypt. Or about finding a dead body in my office. He'd never believe me, which was understandable, because all those situations had been totally unbelievable. My heart went out to him, but without bringing up vampires, there wasn't much I could say.

'Okay.' He ran his fingers through his hair as he gave a bright smile. 'That's enough depressing talk. I didn't mean to turn our dinner into a therapy session.'

I patted his hand. 'You didn't. I'm glad you told me – thank you for trusting me.'

We sat silently for a couple of minutes.

'This has been so nice, I hate for the evening to end,' he said.

'Me, too.' I folded my napkin, then rifled through my brief-case looking for my wallet. He probably felt exhausted from talking about the incident again.

When I set my credit card on the table, he picked it up and handed it back to me. 'No. I insist on buying your dinner, modest as it was. Please, put your card away.'

'That isn't necessary, Michael. Really. I can write it off as a business expense.'

'Regardless. I still want to treat you – please let me.' He gave me his adorable puppy-dog look.

I laughed. 'Okay. I wouldn't think of depriving you of the opportunity to spend your money.'

'Good. Do we really have to go our separate ways now? Are you tired? Maybe we could find a nightclub or something. Go dancing.'

'Nightclub? Hmm. I haven't been dancing in, well, I don't remember the last time. Do you think there's something in walking distance? I'd really like to get out and stretch my legs.'

'Let me ask at the front desk. I'll bet there's something. I don't want you to think I'm a coward, but is it really safe for us to be walking the streets of New York City at night? I've heard stories. I'm afraid all my talents are in my head rather than my fists. I don't know if I could adequately defend you. Maybe I should ask about the safety issue, too.'

Yikes. He's really afraid. Who would've guessed? His negative experiences obviously drained his confidence. I hope I don't have to protect him. I'm too tired for that. But with Lucifer darting through time and space, I'm never safe. Is this really a good idea? Michael is both a friend and a therapist. Would Lucifer go after him? Should I tell him about the therapists being murdered in San Francisco, even though the cops haven't released the information yet?

'Okay.' Deciding to throw caution to the wind, I slid out of the booth and held up my briefcase. 'I need to go up to my room, drop this off and grab my coat. I'll meet you in the lobby in ten minutes.'

'It's a date.'

The elevator was full and the ride up was glacial and uncomfortable, someone entering or leaving at practically every floor. At one stop, a man in a World War II Army uniform walked in through an exiting couple and stood half-in, half-out of a portly businessman who gave no indication he was even remotely aware of his new appendage.

I sighed. It was going to be a long conference. Of course this had to be a haunted hotel.

Happily, Ingrid Bergman hadn't followed me to my new room and – for the moment – I was the only inhabitant.

After I refreshed my makeup, used a hair pick on my curls and changed into the flat-heeled black leather boots I'd worn on the plane – not great for cold weather but hopefully we wouldn't be outdoors long – I grabbed my coat, shoved a red wool hat and gloves into one pocket, filled my jeans pockets with money, cell phone and the room keycard, then wrapped a multicoloured scarf around my neck.

I was ready to play. Gee, having fun – what a foreign concept.

Michael walked towards the elevator as the doors opened and I spontaneously laughed. He'd dressed himself like Nanook of the North. He had on so many layers, I was surprised he could even move.

'What's so funny?' he asked, pretending to be offended. 'I just don't like to be cold. Come on.' He linked his arm through mine, once again behaving like his charming self. 'The woman at the desk said there's a great nightclub just a block down, and aside from the odd pickpocket, she thinks we should be safe enough.'

Looks like he's rediscovered his courage. Let's hope there's no reason to challenge it.

We strolled down the street, our breath clouding in the frigid air as we joked and made comments about the contents of the retail windows. It had to be near zero degrees.

Heavy bass reverberated through the walls as we approached a building sporting a neon 'Retro Dance Club' sign.

'This must be the place,' Michael said.

I listened for a few seconds. 'Sounds like the Rolling Stones – "Miss You". This should be fun.'

'How do you know that tune? It's older than you are.'

'I'd know that distinctive bass line anywhere. My parents

had a huge record collection – the vinyl kind. I grew up listening to music from the sixties and seventies.' I laughed. 'I have a photo of my geeky scientist parents taken at a disco. If I ever need to blackmail them, that's the one I'll use.'

A blast of heat almost pushed us back outside again as we entered the huge dance club. The room was packed with bodies, dancers boogying wherever they could find a spot.

We peeled off our winter gear at the cloakroom and checked it in. Then we wove through the mayhem and found an empty table in the undesirable corner near the door to the kitchen, which also happened to be underneath one of the enormous wall-mounted speakers.

The DJ, a tall African-American guy with a retro afro that stood out a good twelve inches from his head, grooved on a raised stage, boxed into his electronic universe by sound equipment of all kinds. Every few seconds he flicked some switches and coloured lights flashed on and off, illuminating a glittering oversized disco ball hanging from the centre of the ceiling.

'Wow,' Michael yelled as we settled into our chairs, 'we've entered some kind of time warp.'

The music was too loud for conversation, so I just nodded.

A waitress appeared to take our drink orders and I leaned back against the wall, watching the waiters pass our table carrying trays of bar food from the kitchen. The smell of grease oozed out every time the door opened. My clothes and hair were going to smell like a dumpster by the end of the night. At least there was no smoking allowed in the club.

'Hey!' Michael waved his hand in front of my face and pointed to the dancers. 'Wanna dance?'

We squished into the pulsing mob as the DJ segued seamlessly from the Stones to 'Stayin' Alive' by the Bee Gees, which

I viewed as a cosmic message especially for me, then into other disco hits. Michael and I danced through them all, sweat dripping down our faces, detouring over to our table every so often to chug down the wine we'd ordered. During the last song, Michael had started bumping my hip with his in some form of dance movement I wasn't familiar with. Each time he bumped, he laughed, which proved to be contagious. It was such a relief to relax and be silly for a little while.

After a couple of hours, despite the perspiration and the exercise, the wine had done its job – I was officially buzzed. I knew alcohol wasn't a good way to quench thirst or stave off dehydration, but it had been so long – maybe years – since I'd last cut loose and tied one on. After all the paranormal madness of the past few months, didn't I deserve some downtime? I was so tired of thinking about vampires. Weary of being so responsible. Maybe if I drank enough, I'd blot the undead totally out of my mind.

I tugged Michael's arm, pulling him back to the table, then pointed to the toilets. He mouthed 'okay' and sat.

I'd just turned to head towards the women's bathroom when I saw Lucifer across the room. I stopped dead, held my breath and pressed my hand to my mouth to stifle the scream that threatened to erupt. I flicked my gaze back over my shoulder to check if Michael had noticed my reaction, but he hadn't. And when I looked again, Lucifer was gone.

Shuffling around the edges of the crowd, I scanned for the bald head, but didn't find it. Had I really seen him? Or had the stress and alcohol and my altered mind made me hallucinate? Was I so afraid of him that I'd imagined him coming after me? It would be horrible if all the brain trauma I'd experienced around the vampires caused me to exhibit signs of schizophrenia. One consolation: if I developed a severe mental illness, I wouldn't have to worry about anybody else's energy warping my mind.

After looking around a bit more, I hurried to the bathroom then walked back to the table, constantly scanning the dark room for the maniac. By the time I sat down, I'd half-convinced myself I was just seeing things that weren't there. A trick of the flashing lights in my eyes.

Shaking my head to clear some of the alcohol haze, I tried to logically dissect the situation. Either I'd had so much wine that I'd imagined my worst nightmare or I'd really seen him. Since I didn't know which option was true, obviously I needed an outside opinion. I pulled out my cell phone to call Alan, still searching the crowd for the dreaded face, but I couldn't get a signal. Damn. I'd have to see if Michael's phone could pick up in here.

'Listen,' I started, hoping he wouldn't ask me to explain, 'I've just remembered I need to leave someone a message and my cell phone's dead – can I borrow yours? I'll only be a moment.'

'Sure.' He dug out his iPhone and handed it over. 'My turn for the john,' he added, leaped off the chair and headed to the men's room.

Alan must have been using his phone because I went immediately to voicemail.

'Alan?' I slurred, yelling over the music. 'Hey, it's me. Kismet. I'm at a disco down the street from the hotel and I might have seen Lucifer. He might be here in the club. I've had a little wine ... well, okay, a *lot* of wine, and I'm not sure if I saw him or if he was a figment of my pickled brain. Can you come over and see if he's here?'

I disconnected then said, 'Okay, bye.'

The full glass of wine in front of me on the table no longer held any appeal, and I pushed it away.

Too bad there wasn't a cell phone number I could call to reach Devereux. I was sure he had one, but he'd never given it to me. Why should he? He'd assumed he would always be able to read my mind and know exactly what I was thinking before I did.

Remembering the cross, I tugged it from underneath my blouse, held it in my hand, and said his name silently. I waited expectantly for him to pop in. Nothing. Then I tapped the bejewelled thing, saying, 'Hello? Devereux? Come in, Devereux.' I raised it to my ear, listening for a few seconds before shoving it back under my shirt.

'Damn necklaces! What good are they? One has to be touched directly and the other apparently doesn't work at all!'

'Who are you talking to?' Michael asked as he plopped onto his seat.

'Myself, of course. Drunk people do it all the time.' I handed his phone back. 'Thanks for this.'

He tucked it away and stood up again. 'Ready to get back on the dance floor?' he hollered over the music.

'No. I think we should go back to the hotel now.'

'What? Why? We're having fun. Aren't you having fun?'

I couldn't tell him the real reason I wanted to leave and my addled brain wasn't capable of thinking fast enough to make up anything beyond one level of truth. 'I've drunk too much. I need to go and sleep this off.'

He held out his hand. 'In that case it's even more important you dance off some more of the alcohol. Come on, just a little while longer.'

Staying really didn't sound like a good idea, but since I'd called Alan and asked him to come, maybe I should wait a bit before leaving. Might as well take Michael's advice and burn off some more of the wine while I watched for the fiend.

I nodded and he gave a thumbs-up gesture, then pulled me into the writhing crowd. We danced through several more songs. Michael was having such a good time that he didn't appear to notice my preoccupation.

The DJ was talking into his microphone and I looked up at the stage. Lurking in the corner, partially hidden by the black drapes, was Lucifer.

I stumbled and blinked a couple of times. He was gone. I hated the thought that the disgusting bloodsucker was in my brain. He wasn't the kind of fantasy image I wanted to conjure for myself.

Clearly I had to extricate myself from the madness. If I kept on stressing about Lucifer and all the other vampire crap, I'd either have a stroke or a psychotic break. If I hadn't already.

'What's going on, Kismet?' Michael said. 'You look like you've seen a ghost.'

'The lights and shadows are playing tricks on me.' That was true as far as it went.

We danced through several more songs, Michael giggling and acting like a kid. I focused on contacting Alan and wished my life was as carefree as the lives of the other dancers appeared to be.

Come on, Alan! Call me! Why aren't my mystical psychic powers working this time? And why don't you check your voicemail?

Over the next half-hour I imagined seeing Lucifer several more times. Once I thought I saw him actually imitate John Travolta's *Saturday Night Fever* dance pose from the movie poster tacked on the wall near the women's bathroom. I probably hadn't really seen that, either.

Under any other circumstance something so ludicrous would have been funny, but now I interpreted the vision as more evidence of the destruction of my brain. Each sighting lasted a few seconds then faded away – a sure sign of a hallu-cination. I grew so used to glimpsing his ghastly form in among the dancers that at one point I wondered if he'd died and become a wispy apparition and that's why I could see him. Wishful thinking.

The DJ played a slow song and Michael slid his arms around me.

'What are you doing?' I asked, leaning back.

'Don't you like to slow dance?' He pulled me close again.

'No – I mean yes – but I don't want to.' I pushed against his chest. 'I want to leave now.' Obviously, nobody was coming to help.

He released me and stared at my face. 'You do look wiped out. We'd better get you back to the hotel.'

'Thank you.' Would the Lucifer hallucination follow me back to my room?

He took my hand and walked me over to our table. A horrible odour wafted into my nose.

'Jesus H. Christ,' Michael said. 'Either the toilet's backed up or someone's had an accident on the floor.'

I spun a little too quickly to investigate, lost my balance and pushed my palms out in front of me to catch myself. They came to rest on the foul, blistered chest of the bald lunatic Lucifer. The moment I touched him, my gaze flicked up to his, which widened in surprise. Out of the corner of my eye, I saw someone who looked like Devereux reaching for Lucifer.

Then I felt the familiar sense of being in an elevator as I shifted through space.

Everything went dark.

CHAPTER 14

Incredibly cold.

That was my first realisation as I woke outside, sprawled on my back in the snow on the frozen ground, half under a bush.

My body was shaking so hard my heels were clicking against the ice.

The last thing I remembered was being in the nightclub and imagining seeing Lucifer again. No, wait – that wasn't a hallucination. It was real. I touched him. I had disgusting decomposing death-cooties on my hands. He must have taken me somewhere. What happened to Michael? Did the monster kill him? And all the people in the club? Was Devereux really there?

I scooted out from underneath the bush and sat up. I definitely wasn't in the club any more. The movement caused my headache to explode and my stomach to heave. Grabbing my hair, I leaned to the side just in time to throw up on the ground next to me.

After everything that was going to come up did so, I dragged myself a few inches away, then pulled my hair back into a ponytail and shoved it inside the collar of my blouse. I wanted to be ready in case my stomach went for an encore.

As I sat, trembling and trying to catch my breath, an old homeless man dressed in a ragged coat, gaffer-taped plastic boots and one tattered glove wandered over and stared down at me. We looked at each other for a few seconds, then he held out a filthy rag.

He'd probably seen me vomit and wanted to offer his . . . handkerchief . . . for me to wipe my mouth. I really didn't want to touch the dirty fabric, but even in my discombobulated state I couldn't bring myself to be rude.

'Thank you,' I said, reaching up for the rag.

My hand went right though it.

I let my arm drop and looked at the phantom. He continued to shake the rag in my face, a sad expression on his. Apparently he really was trying to help.

'Thanks, I appreciate it. But if you really want to help me, tell me where I am or how to get back to the Briarwood Hotel.'

He nodded vigorously and shook the rag to my right, also pointing with his other hand.

'The hotel is that way?' I said, looking in the direction he'd indicated, shivering so badly I could barely speak.

He jerked his head and pointed again.

I climbed to my feet, managed to remain vertical and started stumbling in that direction. I turned around to thank him again and he was gone.

At least throwing up and freezing had taken the edge off my intoxication and I soon realised I was in a park. The logical assumption would be that I was in Central Park, but there was no limit to how far in time or space Lucifer might have transported me. I wondered how long I'd been lying on the ground, and how quickly someone could die from hypothermia. Why had he taken me, then abandoned me? The last time he kidnapped me, he'd held me captive in an ancient crypt filled with dead bodies. This experience was anticlimactic, to say the least.

What did it mean that I was getting used to all the vampire insanity? Had I resolved myself to my doom?

But logic prevailed. I *was* in Central Park, and a short walk brought me out of the trees directly across from the night-club. Michael was standing in front, clutching my belongings to his chest.

'Kismet!' he yelled when he saw me. Dodging cars, he ran across the street, dropped my clothes in a heap, then threw his arms around me. 'Christ, Kismet – where the fuck did you go? One minute you were there and the next you were gone. Did that big ugly guy pull you out of the club? I didn't even have time to react.'

I tried to talk, but my teeth were chattering too hard.

'Shit. You're freezing.' He quickly dressed me in my jacket, then tugged on my coat, stuck the knitted hat on my head and wound the scarf around my neck. Then he wrapped me in his arms again. 'You really scared the fuck out of me. Let's go back to the hotel and warm you up.'

'How long was I gone?' I mumbled.

'About twenty minutes. I was ready to call the police.'

What the hell? Why did Lucifer snatch me if he was only going to drop me in the park? Maybe he was losing more of his mind than he'd already lost. Lucky for me.

My legs were stiff and my feet were blocks of ice, so I couldn't move very quickly. Michael pulled me along with his arm around my shoulders. Instead of trying to weave through the cars as he had before, we hurried along to a crossing and waited for the light to change, then hustled across. We made it to the hotel faster than it had taken us to walk in the other direction hours earlier.

It occurred to me that I probably didn't smell very good after hurling in the park, but there wasn't anything I could do about it for the moment.

Michael kept up a running monologue during the whole trip. 'I feel like such a wimpy asshole, not even able to keep you safe in a crowded nightclub. Some friend I am. I wouldn't blame you if you never wanted to have anything to do with me again. I was afraid New York City would be dangerous. Now I'm acting like the stereotype of a gay drama queen, but I don't care. Did he hurt you? Oh, God, I'll bet he did. We probably need to go to the hospital to have you checked out . . .'

I tuned out after that. I didn't have any idea what had happened.

We crossed the lobby, called the elevator and rode up to my floor. Nobody held their noses and ran away, so maybe I wasn't as stinky as I feared.

Pausing in front of my door, Michael said, 'Where's your keycard?'

I slowly flexed my still-frozen fingers to make them useful, unbuttoned my coat, then reached into my jeans pocket for the card and handed it to Michael. He opened the door and we were both surprised to see Alan sitting on the edge of the bed, watching television.

Alan smiled, then took a better look at me and my companion, frowned and strode over to us. 'What the hell, Kismet? What's wrong? Who is this guy? Where have you been? I've been waiting for hours.'

'I ca . . . ca . . . ca . . .' I said, unable to force my lips to form the words to let him know I'd tried to call him.

'Ca ca? What?' Alan asked, sounding exasperated.

'I'm Doctor Michael Parker, a colleague of Kismet's. You must be her FBI friend,' Michael said as he guided me over to the bed and sat me down. 'We went to a nightclub and something weird happened. One minute she was there and the next she was gone.'

Alan knelt in front of me and said in a hostile tone, 'What's he talking about?'

My teeth were still chattering so I just shook my head.

'Let's get her something warm to drink and I'll tell you what little I know.' Michael headed over to the shelves under the television and retrieved the coffee and tea supplies. He opened a teabag, set it in a cup, pulled a bottle of water from the mini-refrigerator, poured the water, and put the cup in the microwave. The height of efficiency.

Alan followed Michael's movements, scowling. 'What were you two doing at a dance club?'

'Dancing,' I croaked.

'Very funny,' Alan said, giving Michael the evil eye. 'I meant, why were you with *him*?'

I pointed to the blanket folded at the foot of the other bed. Alan grabbed it and tucked it around me.

'Thank you,' I said, starting to thaw out.

When the microwave dinged, Michael fetched the tea. 'Oh, now this is just a little too hot.' He poured some of the remaining cold bottled water into the tea. 'Okay, I think this is good. Here, Kismet.' He handed me the cup and sat on the bed next to me.

Not to be outdone, Alan sat on my other side.

Michael patted my knee and Alan made a growling sound.

'Michael, is it?' Alan said.

Michael nodded, and looked annoyed.

I wrapped my hands around the small cup and drank my

tea, wishing they'd both be quiet. I didn't have the energy to deal with a testosterone-fuelled pissing contest. I'd have to get Michael out of the room pretty soon so I could talk to Alan about whatever bizarre thing happened with Lucifer.

'Just how good a friend of Kismet's *are* you?' Alan asked, his tone unfriendly.

'We met on the plane coming to the conference.' Michael cleared his throat. 'I didn't catch your name.'

'Special Agent Alan Stevens. Doctor Stevens.'

Geez. This *mine is bigger* competition could go on all night.

'I can take it from here, Doctor Parker.' Alan rubbed his hand up and down my back.

'I really think I ought to stay for a while, Agent Stevens, just to make sure Doctor Knight is okay.'

'I'll make sure she's okay, so—'

Now sufficiently thawed and irritated, I got up, kicked the blanket out of the way and set the tea on the cabinet. I walked into the bathroom and heard Alan say my name as the door clicked shut. They were still arguing as I turned on the hot water in the shower. The sound of the spray drowned out their voices.

While the room filled with steam, I brushed my teeth – twice – then swished mouthwash. I undressed and stepped gratefully into the shower.

It took several minutes of standing in the hot water before I finally felt defrosted all the way to my bones. My hair smelled like grease from sitting so close to the kitchen at the dance club so I washed and conditioned it, then soaped my body. By the time I stepped out, I felt mostly human again. Except for the unavoidable effects of having ingested too many glasses of wine. My stomach was churning and my head throbbed. I knew I'd be hungover in the morning – if I made it through the night.

I turned off the water and listened. Surely they couldn't still be arguing after all the time I'd been in the bathroom. Silence. Maybe they were gone. I rooted through my cosmetic case, found the aspirin bottle and took four pills. The aspirin wouldn't keep me from reaping the rewards of my idiotic behaviour, but it might control the headache. I always hated the floaty, surreal feeling I got when I overindulged.

'Crap,' I said aloud, when I remembered I didn't have any clean clothes in the bathroom. I wrapped a large, thick towel around me, then wrangled a wide-toothed pick through my snarled hair.

Figuring I might as well get it over with, I opened the door and stuck my head out, expecting – due to the quiet – to find an empty room.

Alan and Michael were still sitting on the end of the bed, where I'd left them. They wore matching scowling expressions as they stared at the muted television.

They both looked at me when I entered, then their mouths dropped open. I guess they hadn't expected me to walk out in a towel.

I went to the closet, pulled the fluffy white robe off the hanger, and slipped it on. With my back to them, I released the towel and tossed it into the bathroom, then tied the robe's belt securely around my waist.

'How do you feel?' Michael asked at the same time Alan said, 'Are you okay?'

Feeling both relaxed and sleepy, I shuffled over to the couch by the window and sat. 'I'm fine. Yes, I'm okay.'

'What happened?' Michael asked. 'Do you remember?'

I shot Alan a covert look to let him know there was more to the story, then said to Michael, 'I don't know what happened. Maybe I just drank too much and wandered out of the club.

You shouldn't feel badly, Michael – it was my own fault for drinking half the club's wine supply.'

He shook his head, a clear look of disbelief on his face. 'No. I don't think so. I saw that big bald guy behind you. You pushed him and then you both . . . disappeared. You didn't leave the club by yourself, I'm sure.'

Great. I had no desire to be rude, but the last thing I wanted to do was try to make up some lame story for Michael's benefit.

Tugging my robe tighter around me, I sighed loudly. 'Maybe I'll remember more in the morning, Michael, but right now my brain's in an alcohol fog. Would you mind if we picked this up later?'

He looked at me, then at Alan. 'Okay.' He stood. 'I can take a hint – you two want to be alone. I'm not always this dense. I was just worried about you.'

Geez. Now I feel guilty. It's a pain in the ass to have such an overactive conscience. We do want to be alone, but not for the reason you think.

'I appreciate that. I promise to tell you whatever I remember when I see you at the conference tomorrow.'

'I'll definitely be there for your presentation.'

'Presentation?'

'Wow,' he said, frowning, 'you *are* impaired. I'm talking about your *Lost Children of the Night* lecture tomorrow afternoon. I can't wait.'

Is tomorrow Thursday already? Oh, shit!

'Me either,' said Alan with a smirk.

'I'm glad you're okay,' Michael said as he walked towards the door. 'I'll let myself out. See you tomorrow.' He paused and turned towards us. 'Nice to meet you, Agent Stevens.' It didn't take a psychologist to hear the lie in his words.

When the door closed, Alan bounded off the end of the bed and hurried to join me on the couch.

'Okay, cut the bullshit,' Alan said. 'What really happened? Was it Lucifer?'

'I think so.'

'You *think* so? Why didn't you call me?'

'I *did* call you. I left a message.'

He grabbed his phone from his pocket. 'No way. You didn't leave a message. I checked ...' He pressed a button and my voice, almost indistinguishable over the loud music, blared from the tiny speaker. He listened then looked at me. 'Shit. Was that you? I couldn't understand what the person was saying. I thought it was a wrong number, some drunk moron in a bar somewhere.'

'Well, you got that part right.'

He leaned in and gave me a hug. 'I'm sorry. I screwed up. I should have gone looking for you. What the hell happened?'

'I kept seeing Lucifer at the dance club, but only quick glimpses and then he was gone. I was never sure if I really saw him or if the alcohol and stress were making me hallucinate.' I rubbed my forehead, trying to remember what would happen if I took more aspirin already. 'He was usually too far away for me to tell if he was real. And I *had* sucked down a lot of wine.'

'Yeah, about that – why were you out drinking and dancing with pretty boy? I thought you'd want to hear what happened after my mother showed up and whisked me away.' A hurt expression shadowed his face.

'Hey, how was I supposed to know when – or even *if* – you'd be back? I just wanted to have a little fun. And anyway, what right do you have to give me the third degree? Why am I always attracting men who think they can tell me what to do?' I snugged my robe tighter and pressed my lips together.

'Okay, you're right – I'm sorry. I didn't call you after I left, so you couldn't know when I'd be back. Please finish telling me about Lucifer.'

I pouted a few seconds longer then picked up my story. 'Just when I'd convinced myself my eyes were playing tricks on me, I smelled him.'

Alan grimaced. 'Eau de sewer.'

'You got it. Michael said something about the toilet overflowing and I turned too fast, lost my balance and pressed my hands against Lucifer's slimy chest.'

'And then he took you?'

'I guess so. What else could have happened? But the really strange thing was that when I touched him and looked up at his face, he seemed surprised to find me there. That was the last thing I remember until I woke up across the street in the park.'

'In the park?'

'Yeah. I resurfaced lying on the frozen ground under a bush. Then I threw up.'

'Thanks for that detail.'

'You're welcome.' I smiled for the first time since I'd left the nightclub.

'How did you know where you were? Lucifer could have dropped you anywhere.'

'That thought occurred to me, but I got directions back to the hotel from a homeless ghost who came to offer assistance.'

'A homeless ghost? Really?' A grin lit up his face. 'You do have the most interesting experiences.'

'Oh yeah – ghosts and vampires. What woman wouldn't want that?'

He scooted closer and draped his arm around my shoulders. 'Don't forget psychics and witches.'

'Uh-huh. And transgender hypnotherapists. Well, one, anyway.'

'What?'

'Never mind. I'll tell you about Ham some other time.'

'Ham?'

'Focus, Mulder. Why would Lucifer snatch me then drop me in the park?'

Alan mimed stroking an invisible beard. 'You said he looked surprised. Maybe he blinked out when you touched him and you just went along for the ride. What if he hadn't intended to take you anywhere?'

That actually made sense.

'I think you're onto something. But why would he bother stalking me in the nightclub if he wasn't going to do anything?'

'Who knows anything about the behaviour of a demented vampire? But now that I think about it, why did he take you to that bloody mausoleum before Hallowe'en and just leave you there? Why didn't he stick around to do any number of things? Maybe he's conflicted, like other DID patients. One part takes charge then gives over to another, each with its own agenda.'

'That's a good thought, Alan. You might be right.' I shifted slightly and turned towards him. 'So it's possible he just wanted to scare me. Something about those actions makes sense in his fragmented mind. I'll have to think about the implications of this new information.'

When I moved, the robe spread at the neck, exposing the tops of my breasts. The pentagram and cross necklaces rested between them. So much for Devereux sensing my emotions through the cross. Unless I'd been too drunk to be a clear sender.

Alan's gaze tracked to my cleavage and he slid a finger down to my nipple.

'What are you doing?' I pushed his finger away. 'I've just had a trauma, on top of being inebriated.'

'You don't seem inebriated to me.' He tugged at the robe's belt, loosening it. 'I think the trip to the park and the stomach cleanse have sobered you up.' His eyes twinkled. 'I feel it's my duty to make you feel safe and cared-for after your trauma. What kind of friend-with-benefits would I be if I didn't?' He untied the belt and tugged the robe apart, then pushed the towelling robe down my shoulders.

'Hey, cut it out!' I said, without much conviction.

He lifted the cross and studied it. 'What's this? I didn't know you were religious.'

I pulled it from his hands. 'It's Devereux's. A family heirloom. It was supposed to signal him if my emotions shifted towards the negative. Apparently it doesn't work.'

He smiled and stared at my uncovered breasts.

'You're not seriously thinking I'll have sex with you now, are you? After the night I've had?'

'Why not? What better way to distract and soothe you?'

He stood and held out his hand, his expression serious.

Should I? After all, Devereux isn't in the picture any more. We broke up. Why shouldn't I have sex with Alan?

I let him pull me up from the couch and the robe pooled at my feet. We'd been naked together after Lucifer kidnapped me the first time. We hadn't exactly enjoyed official sex with each other then – we'd been disturbed by police letting themselves into my unlocked house – but he'd been very generous with me. I knew what it felt like to have his hands on me.

And we'd been circling each other ever since.

Gently he eased his arms around me and hugged me to his chest.

'Wait – aren't you going to tell me what happened with your mother? I really do want to know. You were so upset before.' *Am I stalling?*

'I'll tell you later.' He pressed his lips to mine.

I surrendered to the good feelings and kissed him back.

'Aren't you supposed to be looking for Colin?' I said when we paused for breath.

'I *am* looking for him. I've put the word out on the vampire grapevine. There's nothing else I can do for the moment. Except this.' He kissed me again, pulling me tighter against him. 'Maybe *I* need a little tender loving care.'

'Er . . .' *Why am I not feeling more enthusiastic about this?*

'Shall I be gallant and scoop you up into my arms and deposit you on the bed?' he said. 'Or would you rather just walk under your own steam?'

'Ah, yes. Now I remember. Still the incurable romantic.'

'I *am* romantic. Wait and see.'

Oddly reluctant, I walked to the bed and pulled down the covers. What was up with me? I found Alan attractive. He was a great guy. What was the problem? Just before I climbed between the sheets I felt a twinge of fear, thinking about Lucifer popping into the room. Goosebumps rose on my skin.

Alan came over and ran his hands up and down my arms. 'What's the matter? Your body just tensed – are you sensing something? Is your intuition sending up a warning?'

'Not exactly. It just occurred to me that Lucifer could pop in here as easily as anywhere else. Do we have any sharpened stakes or flame-throwers handy?'

He laughed. 'Let me check my coat pockets. I'm sure I

brought something to ward off insane vampires.'

'You're making jokes, but Lucifer is a violent psychopath. If he decides to take me, there's really nothing I can do. I hate feeling powerless.'

'Would it help if I said I'd protect you?'

'And how would you do that?'

'Hell if I know, but at least if we're having sex when he arrives, maybe he'll take both of us and the odds will be better. Two against one.'

'Right. Two puny humans against one maniacal blood-sucker.' I climbed into the bed and pulled the covers over my chest. 'I can't talk about this any more. My brain is going to explode.' Out of nervousness, I grabbed the remote and clicked on the television.

He stood staring down at me, frowning.

'What?'

'Television? Really? Aren't you going to watch me undress?'

'I *am* watching you,' I said, shifting my eyes back and forth from him to the political argument on the screen. *I'm stalling.*

'No you're not. You're watching idiots yell at each other. Now who's being unromantic?'

Not unromantic. Confused.

He had such an annoyed look on his face that I had to laugh.

I turned off the television and rolled on my side, facing him. 'Okay. I'm watching.'

He locked his gaze on mine, unbuttoned his shirt, slowly drew the fabric down his arms, then threw it across the room. The muscles in his smooth chest flexed.

I made hooting noises. 'Take it off! Take it all off!'

'First things first.' He pulled a condom out of his pocket, tossed it onto the nightstand, then unbuttoned and unzipped his trousers. 'I've waited a long time for this.' His expression was now serious and intense. He pushed his trousers down his long legs and kicked them aside.

I smiled at his purple Fruit-of-the-Looms.

'You like these? I bet you'll like this better.' He peeled of the underwear and stood there in all his naked glory. The memory of the last time I'd seen that erection sent a hot rush up my body.

He playfully jumped on the bed next to me, jiggling the mattress.

Suddenly the world tilted, my stomach roiled and all adult activities were forgotten. Heat rushed up my body and I knew I had mere seconds before the tea I'd drunk would be projected out onto the nearest surface.

'Oh no!' I mumbled as I scrambled out of bed and headed for the bathroom. I ran inside, slammed the door and grabbed my hair nanoseconds before heaving the remaining contents of my stomach, plus what felt like various organs, into the sink.

'Kismet?' He knocked on the door. 'Are you okay?'

I made a 'gak' sound.

'I guess not. Is there anything I can do? Should I come in?'

'No,' I moaned.

I leaned over the sink until the dry spasms stopped, then turned on the water and splashed my face. As if everything in my life wasn't already a colossal mess, I had to poison myself and fog my brain. *Brilliant, Kismet.* At least the do-I-want-to-sleep-with-Alan question had been taken off the table for the moment.

Alan knocked again. 'Are you alive in there?'

'That's open to debate. I'll be out in a minute.'

'Okay.'

I splashed more water, wiped my face with a towel, then

struggled to spread toothpaste onto the brush so I could clean my teeth. After a couple of false starts, I managed the task and stared at myself, acknowledging that I looked like death barely warmed over. 'Not one of your best days, Kismet.'

I shuffled out of the bathroom.

Alan was sitting on the edge of the bed in his purple boxers, shaking his head. 'Not to make this all about me, but we really have some shitty sex karma. I'm starting to think the planets have lined up against us.'

That made me laugh, which caused my head to throb. 'You might be right.' I crawled into bed and pulled the covers up to my chin.

'You're looking a little shaky there, Doctor Knight. Would you like me to leave so you can get some sleep?'

I thought for a few seconds. 'No. I'd like you to hang around for a little while, if you don't mind. The combination of too much alcohol mixed with too much fear is making me feel weird. I'd appreciate the company.' I pulled down the covers next to me.

'Okay.' He peeled off his colourful boxers. 'But I want you to know that not every guy's confident enough to crawl into bed with a woman who barfed at the sight of his naked body.'

I laughed, which twisted my stomach. I braced for another dash to the bathroom and was relieved when nothing happened. 'Don't jiggle the bed.'

He lifted the covers, inched himself in, and sighed contentedly. 'Smooth landing, as requested.'

'Thank you. I'm sorry I got sick. And you know very well it had nothing to do with your naked body.'

'That's good to hear. So where do we stand now?' he asked.

'What do you mean?'

'Do we still have the makings of an *item*?'

My lips spread into a spontaneous smile. 'I thought you told me a couple of months ago that you don't *do* relationships. Does being an "item" mean we're in a relationship?'

He leaned over and kissed my cheek. 'I don't know. What do you think?'

'I think you're caught up in the rush of almost-sex. We both know that neither one of us is good commitment material. We're both career-driven. I have a lot of vampire problems and you have to figure out what you're going to do now that your mother's come back into your life. I'd say that changes your focus, because up to this point you've been looking for her.' I gingerly rolled on my side and pushed a stray clump of hair out of his eyes. 'Tell me what happened after your mother popped the two of you out of my room.'

He lifted my hand to his mouth and kissed my finger. 'We went to the apartment she shares with Colin. It's immense – half of the top floor of one of those old Gothic buildings in a swanky, moneyed section of the city. She has real antiques in there. I don't know where all the cash came from, but they didn't skimp on the furnishings. And you have to see the rooftop entertainment area. You won't believe it. Every kind of perk you can imagine. I'll take you there when things settle down.'

Will things ever settle down? What does that even mean?

'How's your mother doing? She was pretty distraught over Colin going missing. Have you heard anything about him?'

He closed his eyes and flung one arm across them. 'She really loves the guy. After listening to her talk about him for a couple of hours, I had to admit I probably leaped to some wrong conclusions. He might be a fuck-up, but he'd never hurt her.' He uncovered his eyes and rolled on his side to face me. 'Mom gave me the names of some of the vampires who would likely snatch Colin because he'd done one stupid thing or another to them, or owed them money, and we went to stake them out, so to speak. I hoped she'd be powerful enough to be able to read their minds, but she's too young a vampire for that. So I'm going to have to find someone else who's strong enough to read them and see what I can find out.'

'Do you actually have vampire friends you could ask for help?'

'Sort of. At least vampires who won't automatically try to drain me.' He frowned. 'Remember my mom said Devereux had put a protective spell on me when I was a kid? Well, that explains a lot. Even that weird situation I told you about when I first encountered a real vampire – Ian, the British blood-sucker who first attacked me, then backed off. I couldn't figure out why he suddenly gave up and didn't eat me. Not to mention all the situations with evil humans who've tried to take me down. Some of the guys at the Bureau say I've got nine lives. That doesn't sound too far off. And that spell Devereux cast on me is probably why I've been able to hang around with vampires without becoming dinner.'

We need to stop talking about Devereux now.

'Nine lives can come in handy. What's your gut telling you, Agent Stevens? Is Colin still among the living – as much as a vampire can be?'

'Are you asking because you're picking up something from me? You know – using your psychic juju?'

'I did get the feeling you aren't optimistic about Colin's chances.'

'That's probably true. I tried to convince Mom that every-thing would work out, but I think even she – as much as she wants him back – didn't buy it. I do have a sense that he's toast, and I don't know what she'll do without him.'

'Did the two of you talk about your future as a family? Is she open to that idea? Or does she fear you're still in danger if you hang around with her?'

'She's starting to realise that I really can take care of myself. Well, with the help of your bloodsucking boyfriend's spell, of course, but I'm not a helpless mortal. We talked about spending some time together to get to know one another.'

'I think that's great. Are you still committed to the FBI now you've found her? You said before that you joined so you could have access to resources to track her.'

'That's a good question. I haven't had time to think about it yet. I'm just so relieved to have discovered the truth and to have her back in my life.'

He leaned in again and gave me a soft kiss. 'I hope we'll have a chance to find out if the third time is the charm.'

There was a loud *pop* sound and the blankets flew off the bed.

We both bolted up, expecting Lucifer.

'What is the meaning of this?' Devereux demanded.

CHAPTER 15

Alan and I went statue-still for a moment, then he jumped off the bed and stood in front of Devereux.

'Didn't anyone ever teach you to knock?' Alan said, his hands fisted on his hips.

Devereux ignored him and addressed me, his anger flaring like solar fire. 'Is this what happens the first time I leave you on your own? You betray me?'

'Betray you?' I said. I climbed out of the bed, picked up the towel from the floor and wrapped it around myself as I walked towards him. The fear in the room was as hot and thick as lava. 'Listen, mister. We broke up. I seem to recall you saying you weren't sure if you were ready for a relationship. That maybe we should take a break. You've got nothing to say about what I do or who I do it with. You bailed.'

Well, after I told him I was going to rethink everything. Should I tell him nothing happened?

'Kismet, let me handle this,' Alan said.

Devereux flicked his fingers at Alan, who crumpled to the floor.

Shit!

'Hey!' I said, 'you don't get to dispose of my friends. Who the hell do you think you are?'

'You are the one who suggested you needed time away from me. I was simply accommodating you. How foolish I was – now I see you had an alternate agenda.'

'*I* had an alternate agenda? This from the mysterious Master who has some dark, secret reason for wanting me to be his mate – a reason you've never disclosed, by the way – and who doesn't care if my brain explodes as long as he gets what he wants. Don't make me laugh.' I looked down at Alan. 'Did you hurt him?'

Devereux gave a quick downwards glance. 'No, of course not.'

I tightened the towel around me and tried to focus on the inner hum as I breathed through the oppressive weight on my chest. 'What are you doing here, anyway?'

Are you so lost without me you can't stay away?

'Olivia told me she spoke with you and Alan. I assume you know about my previous involvement with them.'

'Yes. You helped protect Alan when he was a boy.'

'I did it for his mother – she did not deserve what happened to her. And those responsible had to be punished.'

'Did you help Colin get rid of them?'

'I was of some assistance. Tonight she asked me to help her find Colin, so I came to offer Alan my aid.' He slowly moved towards me until he was standing very close. 'He was not in his room so I came here to ask if you knew his location.' He scowled. 'Apparently, you did.' He reached out a finger and stroked it along my cheek.

Before I could say anything, he vanished.

'If you're going to pop in without an invitation, you're going to see things you don't want to see! And it's not what you think!' I yelled at nothing and kicked one of Alan's shoes across the floor.

'Well, crap!' I said and flopped down on the end of the bed, taking deep breaths to shake off the fear haze. I pressed my palms against both sides of my head, warding off an imaginary impending skull explosion and recalling a time in my life when things had been calm. Boring, certainly, but calm. It wasn't so long ago that I could actually sit in my living room, eat popcorn and watch a movie, with nothing stranger to deal with than an occasional suicidal client.

Since I'd met Devereux, nothing was sane. Calm was an alien concept.

But I'd always stunk at relationships with men, so that wasn't new.

Did I feel guilty for thinking about having sex with Alan? Honestly, I didn't. Even though Devereux continually talked about our fated, destined connection, in reality we'd only known each other for less than three months. And he'd been out of commission for some of that time. Since he recovered, he'd been too busy to deal with me.

Was I attracted to Devereux? Absolutely. Without a doubt. Even without any of his mind-control. He could make my libido dance the cha-cha and fan my pilot light into a raging inferno. Maybe that feeling could grow into something serious over time, but now that my mind was clear, I had to take advantage of the opportunity to keep my cortex from turning into cerebral slime.

Alan moaned and flopped onto his back. He blinked a few times. 'What happened? Did Devereux attack me?'

Should I tell him the truth or save his pride? I decided to go with the truth. I couldn't handle any more complications.

'No. He just flicked his fingers and you fell down.' *Maybe that was a little too blunt.*

He was silent for several seconds, then leaped to his feet.

'Wow,' I said. 'That was a pretty athletic move there, Special Agent.'

'Yeah.' He crossed his arms. 'I felt compelled to do something to prove I'm not just an expendable wimp. Much more manly than letting Devereux flatten me by waving his fingers. I can't tell you how thrilled I am that the woman I'd just tried to seduce got to see me drop like a swatted fly.'

I couldn't even work up a smile at his indignation.

'In your defence, I don't think there was any "letting" involved. In my experience, vampires, especially powerful ones like Devereux, do what they want. We humans are just around for food and comic relief.'

He sat next to me on the end of the bed. 'So Devereux broke up with you, huh?'

I met his gaze. 'It's more complicated than that, but the short answer is yes. He dumped me in the aeroplane bathroom. How appropriate.'

'What? He was in the aeroplane bathroom?'

'Yes. He said he tried to materialise on the wing of the plane and missed a few times. He finally arrived inside.' I shook my head. 'He looked like a nuclear-blast survivor.'

'But how—? Never mind.' He shook his head. 'My brain can't deal with anything more right now.'

'See?' I wagged my finger at him. 'Now you know how I feel most of the time.'

'So he broke up with you. Does that make me your rebound guy?'

'No! You're not my rebound guy. I've known you almost as long as I've known him.'

'Yeah, but not in the same way.'

'Well, that's true, but . . . I never meant to hurt you or—'

'Hey, don't sweat it – I'm okay with being your rebound man.' He grinned. 'I can definitely live with that.'

'Really?'

'Sure. Who knows what'll happen? I told you before I wasn't just going to give up because my competition is a badass vampire.'

'But Alan, really – I told you I'm not able to have a relationship with anyone right now. I've got huge things to figure out. You deserve to be with someone who's available, who's—'

'Are you trying to ditch me? Is this the *après*-almost-sex brush-off?' He narrowed his eyes and frowned.

'No! Of course not. I just don't want anyone else getting mad at me because I'm not doing what they want me to do.'

'Okay, then – you just go ahead and figure out whatever you need to and I'll take care of myself. Deal?'

'Really? You're not going to lecture me or try to make me feel guilty?'

'Nope. I'm all out of energy for that shit.'

'In that case – deal.'

He looked at the clock. 'It's pretty late. We ought to try to get some sleep – the conference starts again in a few hours. I'll go back to my room . . .' He jumped up and started searching for his trousers.

I saw movement out of the corner of my eye and started. A woman wearing a red satin nightgown ran through the room, her clothes and hair on fire, and smashed through the closed window. The glass exploded, sounding like a bomb-blast. Her screams echoed and faded as she fell.

I stared at the imaginary wind blowing through the hole in the glass. Had I really thought coming to New York would get me away from all the madness? Little had I known this was Weird Central.

'Wait.' I stood and went to him. 'I don't want to be alone tonight. I'd like you to stay here, with me.'

He paused, one leg in his trousers. 'Are you sure?'

'Completely.'

He can be my human teddy bear.

I straightened the sheet on the mattress, then I gathered the other covers and spread them on top.

Alan shook his leg out of the trousers, tossed them aside and got back in bed. He plumped his pillow. 'This is pretty intimate, you know, actually sleeping with someone. Way more private and meaningful than having sex.'

I nestled under the blankets and turned on my side to face him. 'Yes. It takes a lot of trust.' I angled over and kissed him. 'Good night, Agent Mulder.'

'Sleep tight, Doctor Scully.'

As I turned over onto my other side, the woman in red ran through the room again.

I closed my eyes tight and pulled the covers over my head, hoping that would put an end to the ghostly horror show.

The sound of the smashed glass had barely trailed off when a thin, strongly accented high-pitched male voice said, 'Kismet Knight?'

My eyes flew open and my breath caught. That hadn't sounded like the woman in red. I slowly nudged the covers down so I could see.

What the hell now?

Standing slightly bent over in a beam of moonlight streaming in through the window was an old man dressed in a dark robe. His long grey hair was pulled back into a braid. He had a thick grey moustache, the ends of which narrowed into points underneath his chin.

He walked slowly towards the bed. 'Are you Kismet Knight?'

'Yes,' I mumbled, a jolt of fear slicing through me.

'Good.' He nodded. 'I am Zephyr. I understand you wish to speak with me.'

Chapter 16

Clutching my rumbling stomach, I sat up and subtly nudged Alan under the covers. He didn't budge. My heart raced.

Zephyr cleared his throat. 'Your companion won't awaken – my business is with you alone. We must go.'

So much for subtle.

'Go? Go where?' Terror tightened its grip around my throat. I'd never sensed such a powerful vampire.

'That is too complicated to explain, but allow me to diminish your reaction to me and the effects of your overindulgence.' He pointed both his index fingers at me and a wave of relaxation flowed through my body. My muscles softened and I almost toppled over onto Alan.

'There. I have weakened your ability to sense predators for the time being and healed your hangover. You should feel much better now.'

And I did. Straightening, I took a few breaths and felt myself calm. I glanced at the digital clock on the nightstand. Three a.m.

Zephyr and I eyed each other for a few seconds. I didn't know what the proper etiquette was for a situation like this. Should I ask him to sit while I made tea? My brain was so tired I couldn't think. The worry and alcohol had taken more of a toll than I thought. 'I should probably get dressed,' I said, remembering I was naked. 'Would you mind turning your back so I can get out of bed?'

'Please,' he said on a chuckle, 'I am so old I don't even remember what the sight of a naked woman is *supposed* to inspire in a man. I think I lost those urges hundreds of years before I even became a vampire.'

He lived hundreds of years before being turned?

'Yes.' He answered my unspoken question. 'I was an alchemist – a very successful one, by the way – and enjoyed my own form of immortality. Had it not been for some idiot vampire ... well, that is a story for another day. Hurry now. We do not have much time.

Uh-oh. He read my mind. Does that mean my brain is unprotected?

'No,' he answered, 'Anne's little fix is still in place. I am the one who taught her that trick. No one can mask their thoughts from me – it is simply one of my gifts.'

I glanced out through the window. Stars sparkled in the night sky.

'How do I know you're Zephyr? You could be anyone.'

'That is true. I suppose you will have to decide if your desire to speak with me is larger than your fear. What does your intuition tell you?'

What the hell? For some reason, I didn't feel anything particularly threatening about the old man. He felt relatively benign. Although it occurred to me that as an old vampire, he could change his appearance – and his energy – to anything he wished.

He smiled. 'I assumed this physical façade because it was what you expected. I hate to disappoint.'

Throwing the covers back, I dashed out of the bed and into the bathroom. I turned on the light, wrapped myself in a large towel, then returned to the main room to pull clothes from the suitcase.

I dressed quickly in jeans and a red sweater and, because my mouth tasted sour, I took a minute to brush my teeth. There was nothing to be done about my wild, tangled hair, so I pulled it back with a scrunchie.

My coat was still in the bathroom where I'd left it before my shower, so I dragged it with me and walked to where Zephyr was sitting on the end of the unoccupied bed.

'Very good. Go ahead and put that coat on – it is chilly out for humans.'

I tugged the coat on as he moved next to me and anchored his arm around my shoulders. Before I could even begin to fret about being so close to a stranger, a few loose strands of hair blew back from my face as we travelled via thought to . . . where?

Zephyr released me abruptly and I blinked in the twilight. I was standing on something smooth and hard, and the air temperature had warmed slightly since we completed our quick journey through the stratosphere, so I assumed we were indoors again.

He snapped his fingers and light burst forth from tall torches spread throughout the huge expanse of darkness.

It took a moment for my eyes to adjust before I realised we were inside a beautiful Greek temple, complete with soaring columns, statues of gods and goddesses and gold silk draped along the stone walls. The floor was beautiful gold-flecked marble and a long, narrow pool ran down the middle of the atrium, complete with waterfalls at each end. A golden dolphin rose out of the vibrant blue water, caught in mid-leap.

Was this the mysterious library?

'No,' he answered, and I realised he'd been staring at me.

His voice echoed through the cavernous room. 'This is just the entry hall. I designed it aeons ago to reflect my country of origin. The sacred texts are protected far underground.'

'You're Greek?'

He bowed. 'I am. I was born as a human in Delphi.'

'Delphi? The home of the Oracle?'

'Yes – a relative. Quite mad. Right up your alley, actually. Not to mention all the gods. Always fighting and killing each other.'

'The gods? They were real?'

He laughed. 'As real as vampires.'

I looked around and shifted my gaze to the extremely high ceiling, which – along with the walls – had been carved out of rock. 'Where are we? I was told the library's inside a mountain in the Andes.'

'Actually, calling it a *library* is quite inaccurate. We do house books, papers and all manner of ancient scrolls and papyri, along with the largest collection of antiques and artefacts in the world. Some of the objects prove the existence of vampires, so they had to be removed from human circulation. We have thousands of mortal-created accounts of interactions with the undead, none of which can be allowed to fall into human hands. But yes – we are inside a mountain in the Andes. In fact, the complex is spread out through several mountains.'

My mind boggled. I was thousands of miles from my hotel room in New York City, on another continent, chatting with an ancient Greek alchemist vampire. And I thought everything I'd experienced so far had been as strange as things could get.

'Do you know why I wanted to talk with you?' I asked.

'Of course. I would not have brought you here if the elders had not approved your reasons. We believe you can be of service to immortals.'

'Of service?' My body tensed and my brain was suddenly bombarded with horrible visions of myself tied to an altar while ravenous vampires sucked the blood from every part of my body.

Zephyr burst out laughing, then clapped his hands. 'That was marvellous. Very entertaining. I am afraid I was not thinking of anything quite so ... messy. The service I have in mind is your psychology practice. You can keep your finger on the pulse of the communal vampire psyche. Alert us to potential problems.'

I was so relieved my knees almost gave out. Realising I'd stopped breathing, I coughed to open my throat so I could inhale.

'Come,' he said, holding out his hand, 'let me amuse myself by showing you some of the wonders of this place. I do not often receive visitors.'

As if I have a choice.

The moment my hand touched his, we were in motion again. When we stopped, my head spun and I reached up in an unconscious attempt to catch my balance. Even though he'd muted most of the symptoms of my wine-fest, travelling via thought brought back a vague sense of discomfort. I made a promise to myself to remember how bad I felt and never to over-imbibe again. *Isn't that what all over-imbibers say?*

Zephyr smiled. 'There is no real equivalent to getting drunk for us old vampires. When we are young, some of us can achieve a drug-like effect by ingesting too much blood, and some newborns become addicted for a while, but by the time one has lived for a few centuries, we are immune to such lunacy.'

He spread his arms wide and hundreds of balls of light flicked on, suspended in thin air throughout the mind-boggling expanse.

He'd transported us to a rock outcropping. An overlook.

I sucked in a loud breath. The scene in front of me was impossible. I slowly turned in a circle. Stunned as I was, I still managed to determine that I was looking at miles – literally miles – of antiquities, stretching out in every direction. Some were so massive I had to squint to see their boundaries.

'Here,' he said, lightly touching the spot between my eyes. 'This should help.'

Suddenly the vague outlines of statues, relics and works of art I could barely distinguish from such a distance were made crystal clear, as if I'd donned super-magnifying glasses.

'Wow.' I pointed. 'Is that a . . . cathedral? An actual full-size building?' The tallest spire jutted high into the air.

'Yes. One of many.'

'But, but, but . . .' I sputtered. 'How did it get here?' I just couldn't wrap my brain around the idea of moving an entire building without any humans noticing. 'And why would vampires want a church?'

Vampires. Church. Those words just didn't go together.

He chuckled. 'I had forgotten how delightful it is to witness the appreciation of visitors. Unfortunately, it is not safe to bring many guests here, human or vampire, but I am thoroughly enjoying having you. What was your question? Oh yes – how and why?' He slid his arm around my shoulders. 'Perhaps you would like a closer view.'

In the flick of a batwing, we were standing in front of the beautiful Gothic church, complete with ornate towers and arches.

'There is a fascinating story to this particular acquisition,' he said, waving his arm in the direction of the breathtaking building. 'This cathedral was erected in France in the nineteenth century. Shortly after construction was completed, one

of our elders had a vision of its destruction due to an earthquake. At the moment the trembling began, we magically
transported it here while creating a visual illusion for the
mortals, letting them see the building actually collapsing into
a rift that opened in that spot. Which is what would have
happened had we not intervened. A day or two later we utilised
the power of an aftershock to close the opening in the earth
to prevent any enterprising explorers from noticing the lack
of residue to excavate. It was an effortless rescue of an archi-
tectural masterpiece.'

'Damn,' I said, impressed. 'But why just keep it here? Why
not find a way to resurrect it somewhere? Hardly anyone gets
to see it locked away inside a mountain.'

'You are correct, but no doubt you will soon realise that
collecting – or *hoarding* as it is called now – is a vampire trait.
We do not easily give up our acquisitions.' He gave me an odd
look. 'Things or people.'

I was tired enough to blurt out what was on my mind
without censoring it. Not a great idea when talking to
vampires. 'Why did you look at me like that? Are you saying
I'm now *your* acquisition?'

The corners of his lips rose. 'No. Not *mine*.'

'What—?'

'You asked about vampires and church. You might be
surprised to learn that many vampires are attracted to the
energy surrounding religious sites. The vibrational field is
permeated with the hopes, dreams and fears of untold
numbers of humans, not to mention an aura of death. Hiding
in churches and temples was – and is – a common occurrence
with the undead. Humans rarely have the courage to open
the coffins of historical figures or loved ones to chase away
a temporary bloodsucking lodger. Consequently churches are

relatively safe havens for vampires. And of course Devereux has informed you that religion has no effect on us, one way or the other.'

A blur of motion off to the side startled me and I gasped.

'There you are.' A tall, indescribably handsome male appeared on the other side of Zephyr. He was dressed in a modern dark-grey European business suit and matching shirt. His wavy ebony hair flowed inches past his shoulders. 'I have been waiting to meet the charming and famous vampire shrink, and here you are, monopolising her with one of your tedious tours. I should have known.'

'You are so impatient, Dracul,' Zephyr said. 'One would think that someone as old as you would have figured out the mean-inglessness of time by now.' He turned to me and nodded at the new arrival. 'Doctor Knight, allow me to introduce the infamous Dracul.'

No way – Dracula? He doesn't look anything like the pictures of the warrior he's supposed to be based on. The live version is a vast improvement.

As I hadn't been able to tear my attention away from the gorgeous man since he showed up, my gaze remained cemented to his. An exotic aroma surrounded him and I inhaled the enticing fragrance, which caused my heart to flutter. As I stared into his dark eyes, I suddenly thought about the picture I must have presented with my tangled hair pulled back into a messy ponytail and no makeup. For some reason not looking my best felt unacceptable. I wanted to please him. I had an overwhelming urge to rip my clothes off and press my naked body against him.

Uh-oh. What's happening?

He smiled and stepped towards me, displaying even white teeth and dimples. He unbuttoned my coat and pushed it down my arms until it dropped to the floor. 'In my time, there was much poverty. Women did not have the luxury of wearing makeup. I am accustomed to appreciating the natural beauty of the females under my care.' He lifted my hand and kissed it. 'You, Doctor Knight' – his eyes scanned my body, lingering on my breasts – 'are exquisite.'

'Er, thank you.' He was the most amazing-looking individual I'd ever seen: exotic, with perfect facial structure and features. I couldn't drag my eyes away from his. And as I watched, his irises changed from almost-black to blood-red. I groaned and moved closer.

He wrapped me in his arms.

'Dracul! Stop it.' Zephyr grasped my shoulder and tugged in an unsuccessful attempt to pull me away. 'We have business to attend to. I don't think Doctor Knight came here to be seduced by the Dragon.'

'Do not be such a spoilsport, Zephyr. There is plenty of time for everything. Perhaps she would *like* to be seduced. Let us ask her. Doctor Knight?'

'Yes. I really would,' I said, without conscious thought. *Did I say that?*

'You know full well she will not be able to make an informed decision. She is the prop— er ... friend ... of an important vampire,' Zephyr said. 'You have already entranced her. Why must you arouse every female within miles of you? Surely you must be satiated by now.'

Dracul rubbed his hands up and down my back, pulling me tighter against his firm chest. 'I am fully aware of whose property she is. And you know I cannot help it – I am a prisoner of my urges. You are lucky to be free of sexual desire. It can be a harsh taskmaster.'

Zephyr finally managed to pull me away from Dracul and

snapped his fingers in front of my eyes. 'Doctor Knight.' He lifted my coat from the ground and held it out for me to put on.

Startled, I came back to myself. Shit! How had Dracul done that? Was he able to override my brain's protection, too? I slipped into the coat and re-buttoned it.

'Yes,' Zephyr answered, 'indirectly. Dracul has the ability to *borrow* vampiric gifts. In my presence, he is able to use my ability to access anyone's brain. I apologise – I should have warned you. He is what would these days be called a *sex fiend*.'

'Um, probably not a sex *fiend*,' I said, grinning at the 1950s-type reference. 'That's a little dated. Maybe a sex *addict*, though.'

Dracul gave a charming smile. 'I love it when people talk about me and my idiosyncrasies.'

Zephyr sent Dracul a frustrated frown then looked at me. 'Ordinarily, perhaps, Doctor. But in Dracul's case, I believe the word *fiend* is appropriate. Come.' He eased his arm around my shoulders. 'Let us address the issue that provoked your visit.'

'Wait,' Dracul said, stepping in front of me, his expression serious. 'The reason I wanted to meet you was that I wish to make a confession and to caution you, Doctor Knight. First, I believe I may be responsible for the insanity of the human who now torments you as the vampire who calls himself Lucifer. Rather an arrogant name, yes?'

Zephyr dropped his arm from around me and sighed.

At the mention of Lucifer's name, my stomach twisted. *He knows about the psychotic's behaviour? And he's responsible for it?* 'What do you mean?'

Dracul took my hands in his. 'No doubt you have heard the story of my old friend Renfield? How he went mad as a result of my influence on his brain?'

I nodded, uncomfortably familiar with the idea.

'Of course, that was not his real name. I asked Bram to disguise everyone except me.' He bowed. 'I do enjoy being notorious. Consequently it will likely come as no surprise that I have had many human slaves in addition to Renfield over the centuries. A hundred years ago, I met a religious man when I was travelling through the mountains of the American south. Quite insightful and intuitive, actually, because he recognised my darkness immediately. He erroneously assumed I was a literal demon, but I became fascinated by his ability to sense me. I had to have him.'

'Brother Luther?'

Dracul looked up and to the side for a few seconds, remembering. 'Yes, I think that was his name. His sensitivity worked against him because he lasted barely a decade before his mind completely broke and he began displaying other personalities. Several of them. Being the mischievous bloodsucker that I am, I thought it would be fun to bring him over, to hold onto him for his entertainment value.'

'You turned him after he was insane?'

'Yes. It was very amusing, for a while. Just imagine how strong he was, since I sired him. But as so often happens, I quickly lost interest and the last time he escaped, I did not bother sending anyone to find him. In fact,' he squeezed my hands, 'I forgot all about him. He only came to my attention again a decade ago, when the elders met to share future visions.'

'Lucifer was in the elders' visions? Does that mean you'll be able to help capture him before he kills more innocent humans?'

He leaned in and kissed my cheek, his eyes still deep red. 'We did see him, but no – according to the vision, everything must unfold as foretold. I'm merely giving you this information to help you understand the roots of his derangement, for your own edification. I thought it was the least I could do since my offspring has become obsessed with you and caused you so much trouble.' He released my hands.

'Do you know why he's obsessed with me, or is that some mysterious secret?'

'I know exactly why he is interested in you, and it is not a secret at all. In fact, the reason is quite banal. It happens all the time.'

'*What* happens all the time?'

'Familiarity. When I met Lucifer in his human form as the religious man, he was already slightly mad. His wife had just died in childbirth, along with the babe.' He chuckled. 'The poor sod actually sought me out, and believing I was a literal demon, asked me if I could bring her back. By the time he invited me to her body, it was too late. Her form was cold and her crimson essence congealed.'

'That's horrible.'

'Yes, it was. I would have enjoyed drinking her blood. What a waste. But the wife was quite lovely, even in death. She had dark hair and blue eyes.'

'You mean—'

'Yes, you look quite like her. So when Lucifer saw you, it was undead déjà vu. He does not know *why* he wants you, since he is unaware of his other personalities. He only knows he does. Long ago, Brother Luther convinced himself that his wife and child had been taken by God for some infraction on her part; consequently Lucifer is not only attracted to you, he also needs to punish you. He has no idea why.'

'So,' I said, mostly to myself, 'he's just reacting to a memory.'

'Yes. Unfortunately for you.'

'You're just going to let him continue murdering people? You don't care about that?'

Zephyr answered, 'As a rule, we never involve ourselves in the affairs of humans. Vampires have always preyed upon mortals – it is simply the way of nature. But we do try to control situations that might bring unwanted attention to us.'

'Although some of us long for the olden days when vampires ruled the food chain,' Dracul said. 'As so often happens, visions of many possible futures were explored and it is just as likely as not that vampires will triumph.'

'This is not the appropriate time or place for such a discussion, Dragon,' Zephyr said, his tone hostile.

'Ah, yes – we should not discuss vampire politics in front of Devereux's human toy, but I doubt very much if she is aware of his work to keep the undead cowering in the dark, pretending to be humans with fangs.'

'Enough, Dracul!' He turned to me. 'Come. We must conclude our business.' He clutched my shoulders again.

'One more thing,' Dracul said. 'Most people believe I am the oldest vampire on Earth because I am the most well known, but that is not the case. There is one who is much older. He is my maker. You would do well to ensure you do not come to his attention in the future.'

He bowed, then vanished.

'What does that mean?' I said just as Zephyr tightened his grip and we moved through time and space. Had Dracul said that last thing about his maker to scare me? I didn't see how I could be any more frightened than I already was. After meeting him, I definitely preferred the movie versions to the real thing.

This time we landed in a vast area that actually looked like a library, a closed-up, musty smell thick in the air. Thousands – millions? – of bookshelves filled with all manner of books, scrolls, papyri and loose pages, each tome or collection enclosed in a glass box, filled the area as far as the eye could see.

After my head cleared from the trip and I was confident I could remain upright, I walked to the closest shelf and peered into one of the clear containers. I stared at the non-English text. 'Is this where the special ancient vampire knowledge is kept?'

'Yes. This is the small library.'

I looked at him to see if he was joking. If there was a larger room than this, I couldn't imagine it. 'Really? This is *small*?'

He laughed. 'Comparatively speaking.' He pointed to a nearby round wooden table and two chairs. A large book with an ornate jewel-and-silver-encrusted cover filled the centre of the table. 'Please sit. Be comfortable.'

I did as he asked, pulling my coat more tightly around me. We must have been further underground because it was colder than at the previous locations. I could actually see my breath, like being in a meat locker.

Meat locker. Am I the meat? That thought sent a shiver of fear through me that had nothing to do with the cold.

Zephyr claimed the other chair and waved his hands over me. I immediately felt warmer.

'No, Doctor Knight, you are not the *meat*. Not that meat plays any role in a vampire's diet.' He smiled at my frown. 'But you were thinking metaphorically, of course. You might as well relax.' He pointed to the edge of the seat where I was perched. 'We are going to be here for a little while.'

I scooted back in the chair, suddenly nervous about the magic spell I'd apparently signed myself up for.

'We will not be performing a magic spell today.'

I tensed. 'I don't understand. I thought you'd decided to

help me so I could benefit the vampire community. Has some-thing changed?' Knowing I was broadcasting my thoughts to him as clearly as if I was speaking them aloud, I tried not to give vent to all the worst-case scenarios crowding my conscious-ness.

'I should have said, we will not be using *only* a spell. I will help you, but first I must explain why your situation is compli-cated. Please continue to breathe – I would hate to have to give you mouth-to-mouth resuscitation.'

He was right. I had stopped breathing, so I shuddered out a burst of air, feeling dizzy. 'Complicated?'

'Yes.' He pulled the book across the tabletop and patted the cover. 'There is a spell in here, one I created myself, which works perfectly for *ordinary* humans.'

'Ordinary humans? Are you saying I'm not one of those? I keep hearing that and I wish someone would explain—'

'Yes, yes. I know. You are unique, but that is not what I am referring to in this instance. For us, your non-ordinariness comes from the fact that you've already drunk the blood of several very powerful vampires, including Devereux. That changes everything. And it constitutes a large part of your difficulty.'

'My brain is being destroyed because I drank blood at the ritual? I thought it was because all vampires give off a vibra-tion that's damaging to humans. I'm so confused.'

'Merlin's Fangs!' Annoyed, he slapped the table. 'I am not accustomed to speaking with humans. You all ask so many questions! Let me begin again. Perhaps I can be more succinct. It is true that all vampires negatively affect human brain physi-ology over time. The stronger the vampire, the more profound the effect. Not to be indelicate, but this has not been a big problem in the past since most vampires did not keep their humans alive long enough for the damage to become apparent. And in the rare cases where the mortals were exposed longer – as Dracul mentioned – they all lost their rational minds. Do you follow?'

My stomach tightened at his blunt reminder. Whatever I decided about my future work, I couldn't let myself forget who – or what – I was dealing with. If there was no way to keep my brain safe, I would be out of the vampire counselling business. 'Yes. I understand. Go on.'

He nodded, no doubt having heard my inner debate. 'Let us use the example of Renfield. Had Dracul come to me and asked that I use the spell on his . . . associate . . . he would have been able to retain his faculties. He could have served his Master for as long as Dracul wished, since the human was controlled by him mentally and not through blood sharing. Of course the Dragon would do no such thing, since he enjoys being sadistic and liked watching Renfield go mad. But since you have shared blood with vampires, and your energy field already had unique qualities that enhance you – making you sort of a *human-plus* – you are in a different category.'

Yes! Finally, someone who knows.

'Human-plus?' I leaned forward. 'I really want to hear more about that. What—?'

Zephyr shook his head. 'I will consider your request for additional information at another time. Right now we have enough to deal with.'

Pouting, I sat back in the seat. I knew I was acting like a child, but I was so tired, I didn't care.

'Okay. So is there anything I can do to protect my brain? Anything in addition to the technique a friend taught me?'

'Ah, yes.' He stroked the long ends of his moustache and looked at me. 'Cerridwyn: she is a personal favourite. Very talented. I am glad you followed through on the suggestion I planted in Agent Stevens' mind and called her. I made sure the sound magic she taught you was potent. It makes things much easier for me.'

'You know Cerridwyn?' *Am I caught up in some vampire conspiracy?*

'No conspiracy, and no, I have not had the pleasure of meeting her in person, but I intend to. Anyway, back to your dilemma. The elders spent quite a lot of time discussing the best way to keep your grey matter healthy despite all the challenges you present. It finally came down to a single solution: you must drink the blood of the elders yearly.'

'What? Oh my God!' My heart tripped. I leaped out of the chair and backed away, bumping into the nearest bookshelf. 'That's ridiculous. Why would I do that? Wouldn't that change me into a vampire?' Instead of helping, this meeting with Zephyr was pushing me over the edge. All the fear he had diminished earlier now came rushing back.

He sat silently for a while, watching me. 'Please.' He pointed to the empty chair. 'Come back and sit. I probably should not have said that quite so directly. I do understand that humans have many misunderstandings about the transformation process.'

When I didn't move, he smiled gently. 'Sincerely, you will feel better after you learn the facts. I know that is how your mind works. Let me remove your fear again.'

Trembling, I inched over to the chair and sat. What else could I do? There was no way for me to get out of the underground cavern without vampire aid. Where the hell was Devereux when I needed him?

Zephyr traced his finger across my forehead, then touched it to the centre of my chest. The relief was so powerful and immediate, it made my eyes water. I sat just breathing for several seconds, feeling perspiration gathering under my arms.

'There. That is better. Your heart is slowing. Now let me explain.'

I licked my dry lips and nodded.

'Even with your unique energy frequency pattern, had you not taken any vampire blood the spell alone would protect your brain from physiological damage for the rest of your mortal life. But because you drank from Devereux and others, and you intend to spend a lot of your time in close proximity to such a powerful Master, that *normal* solution will not work. We all agree that the only way to safeguard your mind is to make you a little less human, by casting the spell on our blood and having you drink small amounts of it regularly.'

Will this nightmare never end?

A jaw-cracking yawn reminded me how utterly exhausted I was. Struggling to focus, I said, 'But why do I need to drink blood? Why will that make a difference? Isn't there some other magical remedy?'

'That *is* the magical remedy. Blood is the most powerful magic of all.'

Shit! This is lose-lose-lose. If I do nothing and keep working with vampires, my brain will disintegrate. If I do nothing and walk away, Lucifer will get me. If I take the remedy, who knows what I'll turn into?

'That's really the only way? What will it do to me, exactly?'

'The main purpose of the blood is to allow the spell to be effective. The combined strength of four elders will override the control Devereux has exerted, in addition to adding protection, which will include not being overwhelmed by fear in the presence of vampires. You will probably be a little stronger, your intellect a little keener and your inherent abilities more substantial.'

'That doesn't sound so bad. What's the downside?'

He stroked his moustache again. 'Since this particular situation has not arisen previously, we are not sure what the side effects might be. Although according to our visions, there is no obvious change in you or your life if you take our offer.'

I gulped. 'No *obvious* change? I guess that means I don't grow fangs or sprout batwings. What are some not-so-obvious possibilities?'

He raised a shoulder. 'It is likely you will continue to attract the supernatural, perhaps to an increased degree. Whatever it is about you that appeals to the otherworldly might continue to grow, which could mean you will find yourself in more non-ordinary situations.

'Another benefit might be that your tendency to psychically know things will extend to vampires. Thus far, you have been limited to sensing humans. You might view such an ability as a professional asset.'

'What about strong vampires being able to read my mind? Especially Devereux. Would that ability be blocked?'

'It would be ... mediated. As you learn to perfect the technique Cerridwyn taught you and create healthy boundaries for your thoughts, most vampires will be unable to read you. Young ones cannot, anyway. Strong vampires like Devereux will still be able to plunder your safeguards if they choose to, but even Devereux will not be able to pick up your thoughts if you remain unemotional and practise the sound trance. It is emotion that unlocks the gates to your interior world. With our spelled blood, all your barriers will be reinforced.'

I sat quietly, trying to sort out all the conflicting thoughts and emotions. Assuming my brain would be healthy, the decision finally came down to whether or not I wanted to continue working with vampires. And whether I wanted to try to sort things out with Devereux. If so, I had little choice but to accept Zephyr's bizarre offer.

'You said you've looked at my future.'

'Yes. The most likely future if you drink our blood.'

'Can you tell me if I'm still with Devereux then? If—'

He shook his head and held up a hand. 'No. That is not something we can discuss, only whether you wish to accept our solution.'

'Can I sleep on it?'

'You must decide now. The elders applied the spell to the blood we collected a short while ago. It is best to drink it while it is fresh and the spell is potent.'

Yuck. Drink. Fresh blood. I never thought I'd think those words together.

'But wait – can't you give me some time to mull over the options then bring me back to this moment again afterward? The spelled blood would still be fresh.'

He gave a quick grin. 'Very good, Doctor Knight. That is absolutely true. But,' he leaned in and frowned, 'how do you know we did not do that already and this is your agreed-upon decision point?' He chuckled. 'Besides, as important as your brain's health is to you, I do not share your feelings in the matter. I have given as much time to this situation as I care to.' He sat back in his chair, touched the table with his thumb, and a beautifully crafted silver cup appeared, about the size of a small to-go coffee. He lifted it, turned the handle towards me and offered it. 'Drink and save your brain, or walk away and take your chances with Dracul's servant Lucifer.'

Thoughts pinged across my mind like the metal ball in an old pinball game. I tried to see another way out, but there wasn't one. Nobody, including me, believed I had a prayer of surviving Lucifer's fixation without help. Devereux's help. I met Zephyr's eyes, then grasped the cup and brought it close enough to see the contents. The cup was half-full of dark liquid.

I looked up at Zephyr again, my lips already pursing in anticipation of the thick, coppery taste. 'Really?'

He nudged the cup to my mouth. 'Really.'

I closed my eyes, held my breath and slammed the blood. The taste was as unpleasant as I remembered from the ritual. As soon as I swallowed, my entire body began to tingle and I experienced a burst of energy – my exhaustion suddenly becoming a vague memory.

He took the cup from my hand and it disappeared. 'Good. Now I will return you to your world. Come.' He rose and guided me up from the chair. I barely stood before the air blew against my face and we were once again in my hotel room.

I quickly looked over at the bed to see if Alan was still there. He was. And the clock showed the same time it had before I left. Still feeling remarkably energised, I smiled at Zephyr. 'Thank you. I appreciate your help.'

He took a step back.

'Can I call on you if I have questions or if something else weird happens?'

'Absolutely not.'

'No? Why not? What would be the harm?'

'As I said before, we rarely intervene in human affairs. Had there not been a benefit to vampires, we would never have contacted you. You must figure out the rest yourself.' He bowed again, then held up his index finger. 'Do not forget to practise the sound magic. Without it, there will always be a weakness in your boundaries.'

And he was gone.

Unsettled, I went to the window and stared out at Central Park. I'd just turned and bent to remove my shoes when the woman in the red nightgown ran through me. I gasped at the freaky sensation, surprised again that a ghost had touched me physically. 'Help me! You've got to help me! I don't want to die!' Startled by the sound and forgetting for a second that it was an illusion, I covered my head with my hands to protect it from the shattered glass as the apparition leaped out into the night.

Not only had she touched me, she'd talked to me. That was new, and definitely unwanted. Obviously the elders' blood had kicked in already and opened me to expanded madness.

In the sudden silence afterward, I laughed, sounding crazy to myself.

Well, what else is new?

I shuffled over to the bed, climbed in without taking my clothes off and listened to Alan's snores for a few seconds before I sank into oblivion, dead to the world.

Chapter 17

The phone ringing jolted me into wakefulness and I grabbed the handset and mumbled, 'Hello?'

Someone breathed for a few seconds, then hung up.

'Great. My morning pervert wake-up call.'

Alan snorted, then rolled over and went back to sleep.

I replaced the phone and sat up, waiting for the expected hangover to wrestle me down. There was no getting around the fact that I'd drunk a disgustingly unhealthy amount of wine last night, and by rights I should feel terrible.

But I didn't. In fact, I felt great. Thanks to Zephyr and the blood.

Oh, hell. The blood.

I didn't want to think about the blood, so I shifted my focus and stared at my bed companion, trying to sort out all the different feelings I had about him and our almost-sexual encounter. I had to admit I'd been relieved by not having to make the decision. I guess I just wasn't ready emotionally to let go of Devereux yet. I tugged the sheet up over Alan's arm.

Was I attracted to him? Absolutely. Did I love him? Apparently. I stroked a finger through his hair. Was it the same kind of love I felt for Devereux? I didn't know how to answer that. Love was different in every relationship, wasn't it? That's what I told my clients.

Being with Alan was comfortable and fun. He made me laugh and we had so much in common – plus he knew about the vampires and all that entailed. If he ever decided to become less of a workaholic and settle down with one woman, I could do a lot worse than share my life with him. At least he didn't try to control me and he wasn't hazardous to my mental health.

And there was no way for me to be sure how much of my former lust for Devereux had been due to his influence on my brain versus authentic emotions. What would happen now that Zephyr had given me the elders' blood to drink and told me the hum would keep my brain safe and less readable? Did I want to find out what was real between Devereux and me?

The flutter in my stomach said yes.

But it didn't matter what I wanted. Devereux and I had broken things off and then he'd found me with Alan and leaped to all the wrong conclusions. I didn't expect him to show up anytime soon. Besides, he had no idea I'd discovered a way to protect myself, and he was in denial about his effect on my brain anyway.

Once again, everything had changed. My life felt like an unsolvable puzzle. Or a mass of tangled Christmas lights.

A heavy sadness settled in and my eyes teared.

Light snow was falling. The overcast day was cold enough to etch frost around the edges of the glass. I eased out of bed and padded over to the window, appreciating the early-morning stillness and glad the woman in the red nightgown had taken a break.

Her expanded manifestation last night after I drank the foul blood concoction had been an unpleasant surprise. In fact, now that I thought about it, my reawakened ability to see ghosts hadn't really been fully revived until after I drank the blood at that ritual last October. Great. If things kept going the way they were, I'd be able to give James Van Praagh and John Edward a run for their money. I didn't *want* to see dead people.

I turned and strode towards the bathroom to shower and dress. A newspaper had been shoved under the door and I picked it up, noting the date. Thursday. The day for my vampire-wannabe presentation to my peers at four p.m. My heart tripped. Even though nothing unexpected had occurred with my colleagues, I was still anxious about their reaction to my lecture. I hoped I could find a way to make an academic paper on bloodsuckers sound professional.

When I tossed the newspaper on the foot of the bed, something white floated out and landed on the floor. A piece of paper. I bent to retrieve it and read the message printed in large type: *You aren't fooling anyone. I'll expose you. Wait and see.* It was unsigned.

What *now*? Fooling about what? The paper must have become stuck to the newspaper and gone to the wrong room. Or it was just a stupid joke.

I flung the note onto the bed, dashed into the bathroom and closed the door.

After I finished my shower and got dressed, I walked back into the main area to find Alan talking on his cell, watching television. He gave a thumbs-up to my black silk trousersuit, then pointed to a table holding a carafe of coffee and cups. He must have called room service.

'That's horrible news. I'm sorry to hear it. Thanks for contacting me. What? No. I don't know exactly when I'll be back. I'll let you know as soon as I can. Yeah. Thanks, Detective. Me too.' He disconnected.

I sat on the edge of the bed, looking at him. 'What?'

'Fuck.' He sighed and let his head drop back against the headboard. 'That was Detective Andrews from San Francisco. There's been another murder.'

'No! Another therapist?' Was anyone ever going to be able to end Lucifer's killing spree?

'That makes eight therapists.'

'Another dark-haired woman?'

'Yes. Andrews said the governor is demanding they hold a press conference and release all the details later today. It's really going to hit the fan.'

Holy shit! I didn't know any therapists working in San Francisco, but regardless they were colleagues – colleagues who looked like me – who'd been murdered by a supernatural monster. They were symbolic representations of me! How was I supposed to live with that?

'Are you going back there?' Even though I was ambivalent about us, the idea of Alan returning to the ass-kicking detective made me itchy.

He must have heard something in my voice. 'No. There's no reason to – I already know who the bloody perp is, but I can't tell them. I'm better off here playing bodyguard to the monster's obsession.' He gave a wicked grin. 'Love the jealousy, though. Nice boost to the old Stevens ego.'

I didn't bother insisting I wasn't jealous. I had no idea what I was, so I just glared at him for a few seconds. 'I met Zephyr last night.'

'What?' He jerked the cup he was raising to his lips, splashing coffee down his chest. 'Damn! That's hot.' He grabbed some tissues from a box on the nightstand. 'You met Zephyr? Where was I?' He sipped from the cup then set it down.

I rose and fetched a cup for myself before answering. 'He

popped in after you went to sleep and he did something to you so you wouldn't wake up until this morning.'

He narrowed his eyes. 'I can't tell you how tired I am of being *managed* by vampires. Devereux merely flicks a finger at me and I'm out of commission on the floor, then Zephyr renders me unconscious while he absconds with my room-mate. You must think I'm one useless son of a bitch.' He scowled.

It really was difficult to win pissing contests with vampires.

'I don't blame you for being angry – I'd feel the same way – but you know it's impossible for a human to have an equal playing field with a vampire. I'm actually grateful you finally understand what it's like to be a pawn on their undead chess-board. It really sucks.'

He picked up his cup again. 'Yeah, I know. Did you see the library? Tell me everything.'

And I did, while he listened with his mouth open.

When I finished talking, he remained silent for a minute, then bolted off the bed and paced, butt-naked. 'Holy fucking cow. I can't believe it.' He combed his fingers through his hair while he roamed around the room. 'Every time I think I've got a grip on the basic level of weirdness we humans haven't been privy to, the floor drops out from beneath my feet and I'm free-falling again.' He plopped down on the edge of the bed next to me.

Good thing my cup was empty or I'd have been covered in coffee. I tried to keep my eyes on his face. Apparently when Alan got excited, all of him got excited.

'Okay, so there's a motherfucker of a secret place under the mountains in the Andes filled with a mind-blowing array of artefacts, buildings, et cetera. Zephyr told you about an old group of vampires called the elders, which includes

Dracul.' He slapped his hands on his thighs, causing what was now an impressive erection to bob in his lap. 'Shit! Dracula! The real article! And he hit on you! Wow! I wish I could have just five minutes with him. I have so many questions.'

'Yeah.' I stood and walked to the couch under the window, shifting my field of vision. 'He borrowed Zephyr's über-ability to control minds and he made me lust after him. I actually remember thinking it would be a good idea to roll around on the floor of the cavern with him before Zephyr snapped me out of it. You'd better be careful what you wish for. I got the sense that Dracul's sexuality is pretty flexible.'

Alan followed me over to the couch and stood in front of me, hands on hips, legs apart, proudly posed like a nude un-Caped Crusader, totally oblivious to what he'd centred in my line of sight. He grinned. 'Damn! And then you drank their blood. Holy hell!'

As enticing as his equipment was, I just wasn't in a frisky mood. 'Alan?'

'Yeah?' He continued shaking his head, now staring out through the window.

'Would you mind putting your trousers on?'

'What?'

I pointed to his crotch and he looked down, then he burst into laughter. 'Oh, sorry! I didn't notice.'

'Yeah, I got that.'

His grin changed from friendly to wicked. 'But since we're all up and in a hotel room, why don't we—?' He leaned down and kissed me.

As much as I wished I could be distracted from the crazy events of the night before, even Alan's charms couldn't divert me from the confusion or my fears about my upcoming presentation. I broke the kiss. 'Can I have a rain check? I'm not really in the mood right now.'

He stepped back and examined my face. 'Sure. I'm sorry – I guess that was pretty insensitive of me. I wasn't thinking about how everything must have affected you.' He moved to the other side of the bed where he'd kicked his discarded boxers and trousers and stepped into them. Then he returned to the couch, sat next to me and patted my hand. 'So, do you feel any different after drinking that supercharged blood?'

'A little. I guess my engine is revving at a slightly higher RPM and my hangover is gone. He said I might experience more supernatural crap and my abilities could be heightened.'

'Just what you wanted, eh?'

I slumped into the couch cushions. 'Yeah.'

'And Dracul is the reason Lucifer is off his rocker?'

'Uh-huh. Dracul is totally demented and the acorn hasn't fallen far from the tree. He talked about wanting vampires to be the top predators again and became very upset about it. His energy grew fangs. I definitely had the psychic sense that he's very screwed up. But I do appreciate knowing that Lucifer is fixated on me because I remind him of his wife – or Brother Luther's wife. That explains a lot. The answer is much more psychological than metaphysical. More . . . normal.'

'Have you considered how insane you'd've gone if you kept hanging out with powerful vampires without protecting your brain? Maybe you'd wind up a female Renfield. Or a Lucifer.'

'Thanks for mentioning that horrifying possibility. I hadn't got quite that far in my speculations. What a pal.'

We sat without speaking for a few minutes, then he stood. 'I guess I'll go back to my room and shower. I have to meet with the NYPD and call San Francisco. What are you going to do all day until your lecture?'

'There are lots of workshops I want to attend and I'm meeting my former thesis advisor for coffee. Are you coming to the presentation?' It would be good to have a friendly face in the audience.

'I wouldn't miss it. I'll be the one in the front row screaming, '"Tell us the truth! Tell us the truth!"' He snickered.

'Thanks. Perfect.'

He bent and gave me a quick kiss on the cheek. 'You'll be great.'

'Hey! Did you open the door to room service naked?'

'Nope.' He gave a wide smile. 'I grabbed a pillow to cover the family jewels and signed your name to the bill.' He hurried across the room. 'See you later.'

The door closed and I was finally alone with my fearful thoughts.

After attending several lectures and catching up with my thesis advisor, it was nearly time for my own presentation. I had about fifteen minutes until I had to begin and I wanted to settle in and do some breathing exercises before standing in front of all my peers. I hoped at least a few people would attend.

Since everyone had been great so far, I was pretty sure nobody would heckle me about my topic or say anything awful, but I had to prepare myself for all contingencies.

Taking a deep breath, I reminded myself that as long as I remained professional, everything would be fine.

My hands coated with nervous sweat, I pulled out the conference workshop schedule to determine the location of my talk and made my way down the main hallway, searching for Room A-1. When I arrived I stared at the plaque by the door that read 'Maximum Occupancy 500.' I peeked inside and was surprised to see it was an auditorium instead of one of the regular conference workshop rooms, and that half the seats were already full.

Swell. They printed the wrong room in the programme. Now somebody was going to have to stand out here and direct the few participants who were looking for my talk to another location. Obviously some big hotel event was taking place here. Maybe a performance. I'd been attending lectures for two days and none of the previous gatherings had been held in this room.

I backed away from the door, intending to head to the conference information desk to ask about the real site for my presentation, when a voice called out from behind me, 'Doctor Knight! Kismet! There you are. I was hoping we'd have a few minutes before your lecture. Everyone is so excited to hear about your fascinating research,' said Dr Marian Teller, conference chairwoman, with a friendly smile.

'Hello, Doctor Teller. I'm glad to see you. I'm afraid I've come to the wrong room. Can you tell me where I'm supposed to be? There seems to be an error in the programme.'

Several small groups of people walked past us into the auditorium.

'Error?' She sidled next to me, studied the programme I was holding and shook her head. 'I don't see any errors.' She shifted her eyes to mine. 'Why do you think you've come to the wrong room?'

I turned, opened the door and pointed inside. 'Obviously there's a large event going on in here. I'm sure I'm supposed to be in a smaller workshop room.'

Her lips curved and she patted my arm. 'Why, no, my dear – this is definitely your room. We received so many calls and emails about your talk that we made sure there would be enough seats for everyone. Vampires are such a hot topic these days. Your FBI friend said you'd be thrilled to discover the level of interest in your work.'

'He did, did he?'

Shit! I'm going to be on a stage in front of hundreds of psychologists, talking about vampire-wannabes. Shoot me now.

'Yes, he seems very supportive,' she said. 'We saved him a seat in the front row. Come on.' She reached around me and opened the door. 'Let's go inside and let you get organised.'

Unsteady on my feet, I followed her down the gently sloping aisle, looking more closely at the gorgeous room. It was clearly a theatre, complete with dim lighting, reclining seats and a full stage with a red-curtained backdrop that probably concealed the movie screen.

She guided me all the way up the stage stairs to the large podium and indicated a small wooden table that had been placed next to it. 'Feel free to spread your materials out here so they're within easy reach, and you can use either the hand-held microphone or the clip-on – they're both ready to go. Let's do a quick sound check.' She lifted the small microphone, attached it to the lapel of my jacket and stood waiting. 'Go ahead and give it a test.'

'Testing, testing, test—' I stopped speaking as sharp, high-pitched feedback screeched through the speakers, like an auditory ice pick to the eardrums. The audience, who now filled almost all the seats, moaned their displeasure.

'Sorry,' I said, trying to smile between shallow breaths.

Dr Teller leaned in and spoke into my microphone. 'Timothy? Are you back there in the sound booth? Can you fix Doctor Knight's levels, please?'

A male voice floated over the speakers. 'Keep talking, Doctor Knight. We'll get you squared away.'

'Um, okay, testing, testing.' No feedback this time. The audience applauded.

Dr Teller moved off to the side and stood waiting with her hands clasped in front of her. 'I'll introduce you when you're ready.'

I felt the sweat trickling down my sides and beading on my forehead. Not only was the room hot due to the stage lights, but my newly discovered stage fright threatened to render me unconscious from lack of breath if I couldn't calm myself soon. I focused on arranging my papers on the podium and adjusting the reading lamp, then I poured a glass of water from the pitcher on the table. How absurd was it that I could handle meeting powerful vampires and drinking blood, but I was undone by standing in front of a large crowd?

'Kismet!' a familiar voice said from the area below the stage. 'It's me – Michael. Can we get together for a drink after? I haven't seen you all day.'

It was difficult to see the shadowy area below me but I aimed my eyes in the general direction of the voice. I covered the microphone with my hand. 'Michael? Yeah, sure, that sounds good. Alan will probably be with me.'

'Alan? Oh, well. Okay. I'll see you later. Break a leg!'

I laughed uneasily. With my luck, that wouldn't just be a superstitious saying.

My heart was pounding against my ribs. Since I'd never done it before, I had no idea I'd be so afraid of speaking to such a large crowd. All my previous talks had taken place in small rooms. It was a good thing I hadn't known about the scope of my phobia in advance because I wasn't sure I'd have been able to convince myself to show up. Now I wished I'd given my presentation a little more pizzazz, added a little more entertainment value, maybe opted for a multimedia approach rather than the dry academic treatise I'd planned.

I kept the glass of water nearby. My lips were so dry they kept hermetically sealing themselves.

'Kismet!'

'Alan?' I covered the microphone and squinted into the shadows in front of the stage again.

'Yeah, I'm here. You'll do great. We'll hook up afterward. Looks like it's standing room only.'

Oh, crap! Really? I wondered if I had time to sit down and put my head between my knees. Wait! The hum! Maybe the benefits of altering my brain waves could help me, whether vampires were around or not. I lowered my head so the audience would think I was reading then closed my eyes for a couple of seconds. I *heard* the familiar interior sound and imagined replicating it. My heartbeat slowed.

As I opened my eyes, Dr Teller moved next to me, lifted the hand-held microphone from the podium, and began her introduction.

'Good afternoon, everyone.' She walked to the edge of the stage, shielding her eyes with her hand as she scanned the audience. 'I can't really see with all these lights up here, but it looks like all the seats are full. Please could those of you standing at the back keep the aisle open for safety reasons?' She stepped next to me. 'It is my great privilege to introduce someone who has become a bit of a celebrity over the last few months. I'm sure some of you are aware of her interesting research and the chain of events that caused her to become involved in a murder investigation. She has graciously agreed to begin her presentation with a little of that history to bring us all up to date.'

I did? When did I do that?

'Without further ado, please welcome Doctor Kismet Knight.' She replaced the microphone and moved to sit in a chair at the side of the stage.

Thunderous applause exploded.

Oh. My. God.

My hands were shaking so badly I was sure the rattling of the papers could be heard through the speakers. I cleared my throat. 'Thank you, Doctor Teller. I'll admit I wasn't expecting such a large gathering.' Soft laughter flowed through the audience and I took a deep breath to relax my stomach muscles. 'But I'm happy to be here. The APA Conference is always one of the highlights of my year.' I lifted the water glass and drank. Since I wasn't starting the lecture where I'd expected to, I didn't need to follow my notes yet and could ad lib.

'As Doctor Teller said, I've had a series of unusual experiences over the past few months. I want to preface my talk by stating that the young client who was the instigator for my research gave me full permission to discuss her in general terms using a pseudonym.' My eyes had begun to adjust to the dim light and I could see Alan in front and the people seated in the next few rows. I decided I could pretend they were the only attendees in the room, which helped to calm me. 'Last October, *Mary*, a nineteen-year-old woman, came to my office and reported she would like to become a vampire.'

Murmuring broke out in the audience. I waited until the room was quiet again.

'She talked about the large goth and vampire-wannabe group she was involved with in Denver. Of course, her desire to belong to such a group, to be *special*, gave evidence to the disconnection and challenges she faced in her everyday life. She'd lost interest in education and was highly influenced by her peers, especially one of the males. Her parents were very concerned. At that point, I hadn't discovered whether or not my client was involved with alcohol or drugs, which turned out not to be the case. There was also an element of fantasy involved, as Mary insisted many of the people in the group were real vampires.'

Gentle laughter rolled through the room again.

Heavy footfalls pounded down the aisle and a deep, raspy male voice yelled from somewhere near the middle of the auditorium, 'You're lying! Trying to pretend you don't know about the vampires. Selling out humanity to meet your greedy professional goals. You're a traitor!'

'What?'

A louder buzz rippled through the audience.

The footsteps came closer and a bulky male dressed in a black coat and a brown knit cap propelled himself up the stairs and onto the stage. He strode towards me holding his cell phone aloft until he got close, then he shoved it into to my face, obviously filming me.

Brown Hat! The creepy stalking football lineman!

Startled, I backed up. The audience erupted into chaos as Dr Teller hurried over and gamely tried to tug the huge man away from me. 'Alert hotel security!' she yelled. He shook her off and pushed her across the stage.

Outraged voices filled the air.

Alan leaped out of his seat and practically flew up the stairs.

'I'm Jack Kent, of *Rolling Rock Magazine*,' Brown Hat yelled, his words clearly picked up and amplified by the microphone clipped to my jacket. 'I've been following and watching you since all the vampire murder stuff started in Denver before Hallowe'en and I know you're bullshitting. There really are vampires. I have proof.' He held up his phone.

I walked towards the edge of the stage. Somebody had turned

on the main lights. Alan raced over and tackled Brown Hat, who went to his knees but quickly recovered and regained his footing, then shoved Alan off the stage.

'I've recorded everything,' the big man said, his face red either from excitement, exertion or madness. 'You not only know about the vampires and their plan to take over the world, but you're hanging out with one of the most powerful bloodsuckers. I saw you.' He thrust his phone towards my face and smacked it into my forehead with a loud *whack*!

I saw stars, lost my balance and fell on my ass.

Alan's swearing got louder as he struggled to return to the stage. He must have been hurt in the fall.

Brown Hat leaned down to yell at me again. 'I've got sources who told me about your part in the murders—'

When he bent close enough for me to get good leverage, I planted my feet against his chest and pushed with all my strength. He flailed backwards and went over the edge. He might have been hefty, but he had a weak centre of gravity.

Alan jumped off after him, and like hungry vampires he and other audience members piled on top of Brown Hat, restraining him.

Holding my bleeding forehead, I climbed to my feet.

The crowd rose, trying to see what was happening in front of the stage, while simultaneously hotel security and several camera-carrying members of the media streamed into the auditorium and hustled down the aisles, filming as they ran.

'Ten people, eight of them psychologists, have been murdered in San Francisco, their bodies drained of blood!' yelled one anonymous head in the media herd.

'We got a tip that one of your members was just killed the same way here in the hotel!' a female voice bellowed. 'Comments?'

The audience gave a loud collective gasp and then surged for the exits in a panic.

My knees went soft and I grabbed the podium to keep my balance. The monster had not only taken the bait, he'd killed a conference participant, just to show that he could.

I feel sick.

The media scattered through the departing crowd, shouting questions.

A tall thin woman with short, spiky red hair and lips that were too small for her sun-damaged face surged through her colleagues and bolted up the stairs to the stage, followed by a tiny Asian woman with a camera. 'Doctor Knight.' Spiky Hair shoved a small microphone into my face. 'Do you have a comment on the dead therapist here or the latest round of drained bodies found in San Francisco? What does it mean that they're mostly psychologists? No blood was found at the scene, just like the cases in Denver. Are these more vampire murders?'

I might have been temporarily stunned and senseless, but I remembered the drill from a couple of months ago. 'No comment.'

'Leave her alone,' said a firm, authoritative voice. I looked over to find Michael standing next to me, scowling. 'You can interview someone else. Go on. Get off the stage.'

Surprisingly, they did what he said. And then, of course, they detoured over to investigate the guy wearing the brown cap writhing on the floor while being held down by six men in business attire.

Sirens wailed as police cars converged on the hotel.

'Come on, Doctor Knight, let's move over to the side until everyone clears out. I'd guess your lecture's over for today.' Michael unclipped my microphone, which had, amazingly, withstood the chaos of the last few minutes and took my arm. He guided me to the far end of the stage and Dr Teller's empty chair.

I sat and gingerly investigated the blood dripping down my forehead.

'Damn, you're still bleeding,' Michael said. He walked over to the podium, retrieved a box of tissues from one of the inside shelves, and handed it to me.

'Thank you.' I patted my forehead with a tissue.

I looked around at the madness in the auditorium. Audience members continued to pour towards the exits in a frenzied attempt to vacate the room as quickly as possible now that murder was involved. Various media people latched onto the slowly departing psychologists, like mountain lions scanning a herd of deer, waiting for the weak ones to fall behind.

And now a dozen police officers pushed their way inside, some jumping over seats, finally inching their way to the area in front of the stage and handcuffing the still-struggling stalking linebacker.

A couple of minutes later, Alan stood talking with one of the officers, and they both came over to where Michael and I were waiting.

'How's your head?' Alan asked, lifting the tissue to check.

'I think it's okay now.' If only the rest of my life healed that quickly.

The officer, whose identification tag read Martinez, said, 'Do you want to file charges, Doctor Knight? You have about five hundred witnesses who saw the accused hit you in the head with his phone and then knock you down.' He raised a brow, waiting.

I looked at Alan and shrugged, letting him know I wasn't sure what to do.

'I think you should, Kismet. The man is deranged. He needs help and he'll only get it if you press charges.'

He knew exactly what would motivate me to take action.

'Oh, in that case I do want to press charges.'

'All right. I'll be back with the paperwork. Just hold tight here for a bit.' Martinez ran down the stairs.

'Oh, Doctor Knight!' Dr Teller limped up the stairs, looking decidedly worse for wear. Her short blonde hair was standing up in clumps, dirt covered her blouse and one of her shoes was missing a heel. 'I'm so sorry about this. I don't know what happened to hotel security – they should never have let that man in. I hope this doesn't tarnish your opinion about our conference. I feel so responsible.' She plopped down on the top step. 'And now we've had a murder. I can't believe it!'

'None of this is your fault, Doctor Teller. What happened to you? Why are you limping?' I asked.

'I twisted my ankle when that asshole pushed me aside. I'm going to file charges too, just to make sure he gets locked up.'

'Good,' Alan said. 'And you're right about hotel security. I gave them a clear description of him after he followed Doctor Knight up to her room the day she arrived. They dropped the ball.'

'Oh my God!' said Dr Teller. 'I wish I'd known!'

Alan nodded. 'In retrospect maybe I should've told you, but I thought the hotel would take care of it. Apparently I was wrong.'

'I'll definitely be talking to the head of security. This has been a fiasco!'

'None of that matters now,' Michael said in a soothing tone. 'The police are taking the attacker away, neither Doctor Teller nor Doctor Knight is badly hurt and we don't have any information to share about the murder here or the ones in

San Francisco. We're all safe and sound and have a lot to be grateful for.'

Alan gave Michael his angry fish face.

Dr Teller sighed. 'I guess you're right.' She studied her swollen ankle. 'I'd better get this looked at or I won't be able to walk for days. And I need to find out what the police need from me about the member who was killed. Draining all the blood from her body, can you imagine? What sort of sick monster . . . Although, it is a rather odd coincidence, considering the topic of your research. Well, I'll check in with you later to see how you're doing. I'll have a couple more chairs sent over for you.'

'Thank you, yes, it is odd.' I said, holding out my hand for hers, which she squeezed, then rose and hobbled down the stairs and up the aisle. I hoped she was too distraught to put the puzzle-pieces together about my unintentional connection to the murders. I knew exactly what kind of sick monster killed the psychologists and all the others. But Alan and I couldn't tell anyone.

'Take care, Doctor Teller,' Alan said.

The police jerked Brown Hat to his feet and half-walked, half-dragged him to the aisle. He looked back over his shoulder at me, and with what could only be described as an evil glare, he stumbled out with his four-police-officer guard. At least one problem had been solved.

A hotel employee brought the promised chairs and Alan and Michael sat on either side of me, just as they had last evening in my room. I hoped they could get along better now than they had then.

'What was all that ranting the big guy was doing about you hanging out with vampires?' Michael asked. 'Was he talking about your wannabe clients?'

Shit. I'd hoped everyone had forgotten about the accusations in the midst of the fracas.

'I don't know. Maybe. He wasn't making any sense. Vampires taking over the world? That's crazy.'

What if he really does *know?*

Alan gave me a covert glance, communicating that we needed to talk privately as soon as possible. 'He said he's been following you since Hallowe'en – did you have any idea someone was tailing you?'

'Not until a few days ago when someone followed me home from the office. I thought it might be a bodyguard Dev–' I looked at Michael and remembered I had to censor myself.

'A bodyguard?' Michael asked. 'You didn't mention anything about bodyguards. Have you been threatened before?'

'Yes!' I looked up at him, happy to be able to talk about something suitable for public consumption. 'I received lots of threats after the business at Hallowe'en. The police assigned plainclothes officers to me for a while, so I thought it might be one of those guys.' I turned my attention back to Alan. 'Anyway, nothing came of it, and it was only the one time. Of course, who knows how often he staked out my house without my knowledge?'

Officer Martinez returned with the promised paperwork and I signed it. 'How long will you be staying here at the hotel, in case we need to reach you?' he asked.

Did I really want to stay at the conference after all this mayhem? Would it be better to go home? 'I don't know for sure. I'd planned to fly back to Denver on Sunday, but I'm going to have to think about whether or not I want to stay that long.' I reached into my pocket for one of the business cards I'd been passing out all day. 'Here's my contact information – feel free to call if there's anything else I need to do.'

He nodded at us, then turned and strode away.

'Come on, Kismet, I'll walk you back to your room.' Alan offered his hand. 'I'm sure you'd like to have some time to yourself.'

I stood and straightened my clothes.

'Hey, guys! Wait! Don't go. I don't want to be alone.' Michael fisted his hands on his hips. 'After all, there's some psychologist-killing whacko loose in the hotel. Can I hang out with you for a while?'

Alan frowned and opened his mouth to speak, but I stopped him with a look. It was important that he and I process the latest information and figure out what we could do, but Michael was right. There *was* a murderer on the loose, and he was in particular danger because Lucifer probably knew he was a friend of mine.

'Why don't we find some coffee and decompress?' I suggested. 'How about that little restaurant downstairs?'

Michael hugged me. 'Yeah, that sounds great. Thanks!'

Alan pressed his lips together and gave Michael the stink-eye. 'Whatever.'

What the hell was Alan's problem? Why did Michael piss him off so much? I didn't think I'd ever seen him be so disagreeable with someone.

'Great. Let's go.'

CHAPTER 18

It took a while for us to wade through the impromptu media interviews in the auditorium and atrium, and we stopped for a few words with therapists who wanted to express their frustration about my presentation being ruined, but we finally pushed through, saying 'No comment' to reporters every few seconds.

I detoured towards the restroom to wash the blood off my forehead and take care of business. Of course one of the reporters followed me in, so I had to pee while she stood outside the stall door lobbing questions as I repeated 'No comment'. Since she effectively held me captive, I took some pleasure in pushing the door open with a little more force than was actually needed. The reporter stumbled backwards and dropped her cell. No doubt she'd say I attacked her. I washed my hands, then smiled and waved goodbye.

The cozy bistro was dark and quiet, decorated with 1940s memorabilia, posters of movies and movie stars and World War II souvenirs. We found a circular booth in the back, ordered our coffees and sipped them, each momentarily lost in our own thoughts.

I dropped my head against the cushion and closed my eyes,

allowing the severity of the situation to sink in. It was simply a fact that until Lucifer was eliminated, my life would continue to be a nightmare. And nobody was safe.

The sound of Michael's voice brought me out of my unhappy reverie. 'I need you to tell me the truth.' He looked serious.

'About what?' I lifted my cup and drank.

He narrowed his eyes. 'I think vampires really exist, and that you know about them.'

I choked on my coffee and he gently pounded me on the back.

'Sorry. I didn't mean to startle you, but I just had to get it out.'

Dammit to hell! What now?

'Why would you think such a thing? Because of what the stalker said? I work with vampire-wannabes, that's what I know.' The incredulity in my voice was authentic because I'd never given Michael any reason to suspect the truth and his unexpected statement was a total surprise. Although if I hadn't been so preoccupied and stressed out, I might have been able to pick up his suspicions sooner.

Alan scooted to the end of the booth and started to get up. 'Holy fuck, Parker, you're as delusional as the stalker. Do you think she needs any more of this garbage right now?' He rose. 'What's your angle? I know you have one.'

'I don't think I was asking for your opinions, Agent Stevens. Why don't you take off? Kismet and I have lots of things to talk about.'

His eyes narrowed, Alan stepped towards Michael's end of the booth, a dangerous look on his face. 'Why don't *I* take off? The last thing I'm going to do is leave her alone with you. But if you'd like to step outside with me, I'm sure we can straighten things out.'

Instead of backing down, which I would've expected from someone who said he was afraid to walk the streets of New York at night, Michael showed his teeth in a disturbing smile. 'Sounds good to me—'

Tired of the drama, I slapped my hand on the table and spoke louder than I meant to. 'Stop it, you two! I mean it. You can both leave if you're incapable of having a civil discussion. I'm so sick of all this vampire bullshit!'

People in nearby booths turned their heads to look at us.

'Sorry,' I mouthed to them.

The two men glared at each other for a few seconds before Alan returned to his seat. 'You heard her,' he said in a stage whisper. 'No more talk about vampires.'

'Unfortunately, I can't accommodate her.' Michael played with a napkin on the table. 'I have my own evidence – not unlike our bulky friend – and I'm going to talk to Kismet about it now. That's the only reason I came to this conference. After I read the newsletter article a couple of weeks ago about her presentation, I made my reservations. I knew if anyone could help me sort things out, it was her.'

Newsletter article? What article? That's what I get for not opening all my email.

'Hey! Hold on.'

He shifted his gaze to me.

'You said you didn't know about my involvement with the murders in Denver until I showed you the newspaper reports on the plane. Why did you lie?'

What does he really want from me? Why does everyone have an ulterior motive?

He had the grace to look embarrassed. 'I just couldn't believe my luck. Not only were we on the same plane, but you were my seatmate. What were the odds of that? I didn't want to make you uncomfortable, so it was easier to let you think I was hitting on you – which wasn't entirely untrue.'

'You're a real sack of shit, Parker.' Alan raked his fingers through his hair and slouched back into the cushions. 'I knew there was something phony about you.'

Other customers were looking at us again, so it was clearly time to take our discussion elsewhere.

Michael half-rose out of his seat, preparing to launch himself over the table at Alan or do something equally stupid.

I scooted towards the end of the booth, pushing at Alan. 'Move!' I stomped out, wanting to get away from them as much as to leave the restaurant.

They followed me.

'Where are you going?' Michael asked. 'I'm serious about getting some answers from you.'

I looked back at him over my shoulder. 'Yeah, so you said. Where's this so-called proof?'

Michael lifted his laptop carrying case into the air. 'Right here.'

'All right. We'll go to my room and you can show us.'

'No way!' Alan trotted up next to me. 'Why are you indulging this guy, Kismet? He's obviously fucked up. And he lied.'

'Yes, he did, and he's confused. The least we can do is listen to him and educate him about the fallacies of his beliefs.' I shifted my eyes to his, silently asking him to play along. He obviously hadn't thought about the likelihood of Michael being a target for Lucifer. Or maybe he just didn't care.

Obviously pissed off, he thrust his hands into his pockets and kicked an imaginary can down the hall. 'Whatever.'

We waited for the elevator in silence, and when the door opened several people walked out. Alan and Michael stepped inside. I froze at the entrance. The doors started to close and

Alan grabbed the edge and forced it open. 'What's wrong? You look like you just saw a ghost. Did you?'

'Uh-huh.'

Stretched out on the floor of the elevator was a partially dressed couple wrapped in a passionate embrace. Her fur coat lay crumpled in the corner and her light-brown hair flowed under Michael's shoes. Her companion's white Navy uniform shirt hung from one of the handrails. Alan was standing on his arm. They were moaning and groaning. Loudly.

'Hey, lady – are you getting on or not?' asked a man waiting behind me.

'Sorry.' I stepped in, trying to find a spot to stand in where I wouldn't interrupt the phantom reenactment.

'That was weird,' Michael said after we stepped off the elevator.

'Yeah. Welcome to my world.'

'There was a ghost in there? Are there really ghosts, too?'

'Shut up, Parker,' snapped Alan. 'What are you, twelve? You're really getting on my nerves.'

Michael spun towards Alan and raised a fist. 'Yeah? Why don't you try to make me shut up, ass-wipe.' He moved towards Alan.

'Bring it!' Alan raised his fists.

I quickly wedged myself between them and pushed them apart. 'Stop it, you two! I'm not spending one more minute with either one of you if you don't get a grip.'

I studied Michael's contorted, angry face, looking for any signs of the person I thought I knew and found nothing. Who the hell *was* this stranger?

They backed away from each other and I pulled my keycard from my pocket, opened the door and we silently filed in. The atmosphere was thick with anger.

'Okay.' I set my briefcase on my bed and walked to the sitting area under the window. 'Let's see what you've got.' I sat, waiting for Michael to unveil the mysterious proof on his laptop.

As Michael started to sit next to me, Alan raised the corner of his lip and actually snarled.

'Fuck you, G-Man,' said Michael, but he took the chair instead. He opened his laptop, clicked some keys and a video began playing. He turned the screen towards us.

The first thing I noticed was the building in the background. Devereux's club, The Crypt.

Uh-oh. What could he have seen?

Michael stopped the film and looked at me. 'Over several months, I paid hundreds of individuals for accounts of vampire encounters. The project started as a lark after I met with a few clients who swore they'd met real vampires. Of course, like you, I thought they were nuts. Then I began visiting known goth hangouts. Most of the people I talked to were full of shit, but there were a few stories I couldn't ignore. I kept hearing about The Crypt, so I decided to zero in on those people. The first night I was there, the staff confiscated my phone and I was unceremoniously tossed out. How the hell had they known what I was doing? But that only made me more curious, so I started talking to people as they left the club. And then I saw your classified ads, offering therapy for vampires and actually met a couple of your clients in front of the club.' He started the video again.

We watched for a few minutes, then Alan laughed.

'What faeces, Parker.' He slapped his thighs. 'Are you so stupid that you don't recognise when people are playing you? You offer them money and they'll say whatever you want to hear.'

'It's not faeces! I know when people are lying to me, and

they weren't. It's good research. You're not even a *real* psychologist, so what the fuck do you know about collecting data?'

'Well,' Alan laughed again, 'if you're an example of a *real* psychologist, I'm glad I took a different road.'

'Stop it, both of you!' I said, relieved and surprised that Michael's *proof* was so lame. 'Michael, is that all you have? There's no evidence on the video that proves such things as vampires exist. It's all hearsay and drug- and alcohol-fuelled fabrications.'

He looked so disappointed I almost felt sorry for him. Almost. He'd lied and tried to use me, so I couldn't work up any real sympathy.

'What about the guy who admitted to being a vampire? His fangs were real.'

'Well, not so much. But they were pretty good fakes ...' I said, trying to be kind.

Alan leaped off the couch and danced across the room with his index fingers jammed up under his upper lip. 'I'm a vampire, I'm a vampire. Look at my long pointy fangs.'

I had to cover my mouth to keep from laughing.

Michael slammed the lid down on his laptop and rose. 'Oh yeah, asshole. You and me. Right now.' He strode towards Alan, who was holding his hands out in front of him now, making 'come on' gestures.

Shit.

Michael leaped on Alan and they hit the floor, flailing and pounding on each other. They smashed into the entertainment centre, sending all the hotel materials flying and a water pitcher sailing through the air.

'Fucking asshole!' Alan yelled as they tumbled into the desk.

'Cocksucker!' Michael said with a bloody lip.

'You wish—'

The pitcher gave me an idea, so I scooped it off the floor, bolted across the nearest bed and headed for the bathroom. I knew it would piss them off, but a faceful of water might slow down the mayhem. I'd just crossed the bed again with my liquid weapon, preparing to take aim, when a young voice said, 'Doctor Knight?'

I stopped and turned towards the speaker, my heart in my throat. 'Esther?'

'Esther?' Alan said, raising his head.

Michael punched him in the jaw. 'Pus-head.'

'Ow!' Alan said, sitting up. He pushed Michael off him and wiped away a trickle of blood that was flowing into his eye.

'What?' Michael also sat up and looked at the visitor.

Esther was barely recognisable, and she smelled horrible. Her fruit-scented hair gel had hardened into a foul, nauseating paste that was flaking off in chunks. The glittery white body paint had cracked, exposing several areas of her naked body. Dried blood covered her lips and chin and dribbled down her chest.

'Esther! What happened to your sparkle?' I set the water pitcher on the bedside table and moved towards her, my pulse hammering. 'Did somebody hurt you?'

She thrust out her lower lip in a trembling pout. 'No. I found out the sparkle paint comes off with water, so I bought some shimmer body lotion to cover up the cracked places in the paint and it just made everything worse. It really made me stink. But I didn't want to take a shower, 'cause I've waited so long to sparkle. I didn't want to ruin it. I want to be a *real* vampire.'

Holy crap.

'How did she get in here?' Michael asked as he slowly and apparently painfully rose from the floor. Blood trailed down his face from a cut on his cheek.

Damn! So much for there being no such things as vampires.

Alan moved to stand beside me.

'What should I do, Doctor Knight?' Esther sniffed at the two men. 'Blood – oh, wow. I've been on a feeding frenzy 'cause of being so upset.' She cocked her head. 'They're human.' She took a step towards Michael. 'They smell so good, and I'm hungry.'

My stomach clenched and I shot Alan a frightened look. What the hell were we supposed to do now? Neither of us could fight off a vampire.

'Esther!' I stepped in front of her. 'Look at me! These are my guests. You can't drink from them.'

Her irises had morphed to glassy black, showing little of their usual brown. She was lost in bloodlust, a very dangerous situation for humans.

'Esther! Come back!' I wanted to shake her, but if I did she wouldn't be able to stop herself from attacking me.

Attacking me? Wait!

I remembered the pentagram necklace and reached into the neckline of my blouse to tug it free.

Esther kept inching towards Michael, who clearly had no idea what was going on.

I jumped in front of her and bared my neck.

'Kismet! What the hell are you doing?' Alan made an attempt to grab my arm.

'Wait, Alan.' I jerked out of his reach. 'Esther!' I yelled as loudly as I could.

She shifted her gaze from Michael to me and leaned in, her fangs elongating.

I forced myself to hold still, to ignore all the primal voices in my head urging me to run, and clutched the pentagram in my hand.

As I hoped, when she bent to pierce my skin with her teeth, she raised a hand to steady my jaw. Just as her hand closed in, I pressed the pentagram against her palm and the protective talisman flared as she touched it, causing an almost electrical burst.

'Hey! That hurts!' Roused by the shock and moving vampire-quick, she dropped her hand and backed up. Immediately her eyes returned to their usual brown and she woke from her blood-trance, transforming back into her familiar self.

Alan and Michael closed ranks around me. Michael's eyes couldn't have been any bigger.

Esther slumped. Her shoulders caved in, she dropped her head and began to cry. 'I didn't mean to bite you, Doctor Knight. Now Devereux's going to kill me.'

Shaking off Alan's new grip on my wrist, I took a step towards my client. 'Esther, look at me.'

Sobbing louder, she wiped her eyes with the sides of her fingers, making herself look even more like a decomposing zombie. 'No. I'm bad.'

'You're not bad, Esther. And you didn't bite me. See?' I bared my neck again, this time hopefully just to make my point.

She blinked and studied my neck. 'I didn't bite you? But I really wanted to.'

'I know, but you touched the necklace Devereux gave me to protect myself and it kept you from harming me. So everything is okay.'

Everything is okay? In what universe?

'She's a vampire,' Michael whispered. Then his lips curled in a wide grin. 'I *knew* they existed.'

Alan gave me a look. 'Fuck it.'

I needed to get Esther out of the room, so dealing with Michael had to wait.

'Esther, I'll be back home soon and we can make an appointment to talk about the sparkling vampires again. But in the meantime, I think it would be a good idea for you to take a shower, wash your hair, let your feeding frenzy calm down and be the non-sparkling kind of vampire for a while. Are you willing to do that?'

'But Doctor Knight, I want to be a *real* vampire like Alice Cullen.'

'I know, and I promise we'll look at the options. But right now I'd like you to go home and do as I asked.'

She stuck out her bottom lip again, then whispered. 'Okay.'

With a tiny *pop*, she was gone.

I threw myself back onto the bed, not sure if I wanted to scream or cry.

Alan and Michael stood looking down at me. Michael's grin still stretched across his face. An equally big frown filled Alan's.

Michael crossed his arms. 'You tried to convince me there are no vampires. I don't think you can give me grief about my little pretence after you lied so blatantly! In fact, I think you owe me an apology!' He pursed his lips.

'Yeah, jerk-ass. Why don't you go ahead and hold your breath until one of us apologises to you?' Alan stroked his puffy lower lip. 'I wouldn't mind picking up exactly where we left off.'

Michael spun towards him, lifting his fists. 'I'm ready, butt-wipe.'

'Jesus!' I sat upright. 'Stop it – I mean it. Stop. It. Now.' Too much insanity! I grabbed my head to keep it from exploding. 'Michael, if you want to hear anything about vampires, you're going to have to talk to Alan. I'm done. Finished. Wiped out. So go away, both of you. Kill each other if you must. Just give me some peace!'

'No fucking way! I don't want to talk to this FBI idiot. You owe me an explanation and I'm staying here until you give me one.' Michael plopped down on the edge of the bed and re-crossed his arms. 'And if you don't, I'll just have to chat with the media and tell them what I've seen tonight.' He smirked.

Alan leaned his face close to Michael's. 'I knew there was something off about you and your cover story, Parker. I'm not nearly as nice as Doctor Knight. I'm not sure I'm willing to spend one more moment with you, so you'd better shut up and stop being a dick, or you'll find yourself neck-deep in vampires. I have a lot of friends of that persuasion.'

'Are you threatening me?' Michael jutted his chin into the air.

'Fuckin-A I am!' Alan straightened. 'So what's it gonna be? You can politely talk to me, or you can be dinner for my undead pals. I'll tell them exactly where to find you, and since some vampire is already draining psychologists, another dead one would be no mystery.'

'It's a *vampire* who's killing psychologists?' Michael went pale.

'Yeah, how about that?' Alan moved over to me, leaned down and kissed my forehead. 'Are you sure you want to be alone? It's been a crazy day.'

'Yeah, I'm sure. Thanks for handling Michael.'

'Hey! What do you mean, "handling Michael"? I'm not something to be handled!'

'Come on, fuck-wad. Let's go and set some ground rules.' Alan strode towards the door, opened it and waited.

Michael straightened his hair and rose to his feet. 'Okay. But we need to talk tomorrow, Kismet.'

The silence after they left was wonderful.

Feeling numb and wanting nothing more complicated than a shower, I went to the bathroom and turned on the hot spray. It had been that kind of day. Incredibly thirsty, I pulled a bottle of water from the refrigerator and chugged it. Peeling off my clothes as I went, I left them where they fell, entered the steamy bathroom, closed the door and stepped into the shower.

I washed my body and hair, standing under the water so long my skin pruned. The steam was thick enough to ski on.

'Kismet?'

My knees went soft. *Oh my God! What now?* I held onto the side of the shower to keep myself upright.

'Do not be afraid. It is I – Devereux.'

I squinted through the moisture on the glass, wiped my hand across it and saw a vague form. 'Devereux? Is it really you?'

'Yes.'

Suddenly elated, I started to open the door, then hesitated and steeled myself. He'd been pretty angry the last time we saw each other – the whole Alan thing. Why would he come here after that? 'Why are you in my bathroom?'

There was silence for a few seconds.

'Devereux?'

'Yes. I am still here. I simply could not think of an easy answer to your question. But if you will come out, I will try to explain.'

His voice sounded strange. Subdued. Sad, even. That made me nervous.

I opened the shower door and stepped out. He handed me a towel.

'Thank you.' I dried myself, then wrapped my hair in the towel and selected another to cover my body.

He opened the door and the steam escaped, mimicking the

output of the fog machine at The Crypt.

Stalling for time, and because I was sure it was necessary, I squeezed toothpaste on my brush and cleaned my teeth. Then I swished mouthwash, shifting my eyes every few seconds to where he stood, watching me. If I hadn't known he was in the room, I'd never have been able to sense him. There's no stillness like vampire stillness.

Devereux shows up and suddenly I want good breath? What does that mean?

And after thinking that, I remembered that I hadn't practised the hum since right before my aborted presentation earlier that evening, so I went through the steps and gave myself some small sense of being in control of my brain.

'It is odd not to be able to read you,' Devereux said in that sad voice, moving to look at me in a clear spot in the mirror. 'I feel separated – abandoned.'

'You feel abandoned?' That surprised me. I'd never heard him make such a deeply personal remark. I felt my eyes tearing as I stared at his beautiful reflection and blinked to clear the moisture. Why did that touch me so?

'Yes. I had not admitted, even to myself, how important my connection to you had been. How it made me feel alive and gave my existence meaning.'

He was speaking in the past tense and my heart was breaking.

We stared at each other in the glass for several seconds before I broke eye contact.

'I see you are wearing the pentagram necklace.' He looked at me. 'Where is the cross? Why did you remove it?'

I looked down between my breasts where the cross used to be. 'I always take it off when I shower. But you've reminded me.' I moved my hand over the counter, retrieved the cross and held it out to him. 'I have been meaning to give it back to you.'

'Why? Do you not want any part of me close to you?'

'What?' *What is up with him?* 'Why would you say that? No. I just don't feel comfortable wearing a fortune around my neck. Plus it didn't seem to work very well – I've been upset lots of times and you never came.'

'I am sorry for that. Whatever Anne did to your brain and your energy field appears to have affected the cross as well. Even magic fails occasionally. But please keep it for now.' He looped it around my neck.

I tightened the towel over my breasts, then walked through the door. I sat on the edge of the bed and he joined me.

'Has something bad happened?' I turned to him, watching the soft light play over his platinum hair. 'Is that why you're here? Is there some news about Colin?'

'No.' He brought his blue-green gaze to mine. 'I did not come for any reason but my own. There is no word on Colin yet, and I have not captured Lucifer.' He said the last five words with less energy, as if even speaking them was exhausting. He studied the wall in front of him.

I didn't want to rush him, so I remained quiet. Apparently something important was going on. I used the time to appreciate his perfect profile and practise the hum.

'I have existed for more than eight hundred years. For most of that time, I have explored outer knowledge. I studied all the great philosophies, learned the wisdom of the world, became a Master in every sense of the word ... except one.'

'And what sense would that be?'

He turned to me, his expression serious. 'Until I met you, it never occurred to me that the inner world – the emotional realm – might be an untapped universe. Like many men throughout history, I valued logic over feelings. Rationality over empathy. I devoted no time to learning about the depths of myself, my patterns, my fears. In fact, I repressed them. Denied them. I had been taught that a Master never showed or acknowledged his fears.' He paused.

'And now?' *Whoa. Where's he going with this?*

'Now I realise I was incomplete. I had disregarded the most fascinating and worthwhile arena of all. And thanks to you, I have been forced to leap into that void. To face myself.' He laughed.

'What's funny?' *Yikes. This is even stranger than usual – is he really having a meltdown?*

The corners of his lips curved up gently. 'I was merely thinking how grateful I am to you for holding my feet to the fire, so to speak.'

'Devereux, are you okay? You don't sound like yourself today. Or maybe I don't really know your true self well enough even to compare.'

'Yes. I am *okay*. Maybe a new version of *okay* that will take me a while to get used to, but definitely *okay*.' He laughed again. 'Even using the word *okay* is different for me. It is so American. So . . . you.' He rose and held his hands out to me.

As he stood, my eyes trailed down his body and went wide. He was wearing blue jeans. European-cut, designer jeans, to be sure, but jeans nonetheless. And a black Crypt T-shirt. My brain boggled. I couldn't remember ever seeing him dress so casually.

Smiling, he tugged me to my feet. 'Do you approve? I thought it was time for me to see why my jeans company is so successful.' He looked down at himself. 'I have to admit they are very comfortable, but they do not repel blood half as well as leather.'

Surprised by his sudden playfulness, I opened my mouth and let it hang open.

He pushed my chin up with a finger, closing my lips. Then he loosened the towel around my hair and pulled it away, tumbling my damp hair down my back. He looked into my eyes. 'I am so sorry I did not understand the importance of what you were trying to tell me about the harm I was doing to your brain. I have since investigated – and have spoken with Anne – and it appears you are correct. Without protection, your brain would have been altered even further and you would eventually have lost yourself. I also understand that you have taken steps, which I completely support, to rectify the situation.'

'I'm glad you understand. It was upsetting to me that you didn't seem to care.'

'I always cared, but it has been impossible for me ever to admit I did not have all the answers, that I could not fix everything. That felt like failure. So it was easier to stick my head in the sand, as the saying goes. Especially in the midst of all the other problems I am currently dealing with.'

'Problems?' *Is he finally going to tell me about Lucifer?*

He pulled me close and pressed my head against his chest. 'Despite my futile attempts to keep you from hearing about my difficulties, I am aware that you have been informed. Repeatedly.'

It was odd hearing his words echo through his chest, so I raised my head to look at him. 'I wish you would've felt you could tell me yourself. Maybe I could've helped.'

He still isn't saying the maniac's name.

'Perhaps. I was under the impression that it was my job to protect you from such things, that I had to resolve the issue myself in order to keep the respect of my coven and all the other vampires in the world.'

'All the other vampires? Really? You're responsible to all the vampires in the world? How can anyone deal with such an outrageous burden? Did you actually volunteer for that? Are you some kind of Vampire Master of the Universe?'

'No. That has never been one of my titles,' he answered with his usual seriousness, totally missing the reference to the old comic book and movie franchise. His eyes locked onto mine.

His energy was so intense, my stomach fluttered and my mouth went dry. 'What's going on, Devereux? What aren't you saying?' I stepped back so I could study his face.

He rubbed his hands up and down my arms. 'I know you do not wish to be with me, that you have turned to Alan, but I have to ask: now that I cannot harm your brain and your control has been restored, do you miss me at all?' He sounded like a very small child.

'Of course I've missed you.' I gave him a look that I hoped conveyed the truth of my words. 'Alan and I are friends. Our relationship is very different from what you and I have shared. I don't want to have to choose between you – you each play a unique role in my life. And if you think we had sex last night, you're wrong. I was sick from drinking too much and he stayed to keep me company.'

He stared at me for a few seconds then kissed my forehead. 'I am glad to hear that.' His voice went soft. 'Did you ever have any true feelings for me?' I'd never seen him so vulnerable.

I briefly considered giving a vague answer, so as not to hurt his feelings, but then decided to forge ahead with the truth. 'That's the million-dollar question. I'm still sorting it out.'

'What do you mean?'

'After Anne removed all the vampire influence from my brain and I was no longer unduly affected by your energy, I didn't know how much of my attraction to you had been caused by *what* you are, rather than *who* you are. I needed to stay away from you so I could figure it out.'

'And have you "figured it out"?'

'Not totally, but judging by how happy I was to discover it was you in the bathroom – and not only because you weren't Lucifer come to finally finish me off – and how much my body is still sending out the welcome committee even though I'm still in charge of my mind, I'd say most of my attraction to you is authentic.'

'That is good to know. Perhaps we could begin again. Would that be possible?' He pressed his lips to mine in a sweet kiss, then took it deeper.

I wrapped my arms around his waist and held on tight. I really had missed him.

We broke the kiss and I stepped back, looking into his gorgeous eyes. 'Definitely possible.' And as if to underscore the point, my towel chose that moment to fall to the floor.

He raked his gaze down my body and smiled wickedly. 'I could not have planned that better myself.'

I brushed my lips against his. 'Are you sure you didn't put a spell on the towel?' My answering smile morphed into a jaw-cracking yawn that made my eyes water. 'Wow. Yikes. Sorry. I don't know where that came from.' Then I yawned again. The long, hot shower must have done me in.

He raised a brow and stroked a finger along my lip. 'You are exhausted. Our new beginning can wait a little while. Sleep is what you need now.'

No doubt he was right, but I didn't want him to leave. Being with him felt good. And we had a lot more to talk about. 'I guess I *am* tired,' I admitted, yawning yet again. 'But will you lie in bed with me until I fall asleep?'

'It would be my pleasure.'

I crawled into bed, burrowed under the covers and watched his hair flow like a silky curtain as he leaned forwards to remove his boots.

'Shall I turn off the lights?' He moved towards the lamp.

As nice as it would have been to keep enjoying the view of his amazing face and body, my eyes were heavy and I could already feel myself drifting away. 'Yes, please.'

He clicked off all the lights, flipped the deadbolt on the door, then slid into the bed, spooning me from behind. He pulled me against him, kissed my cheek and whispered, 'Sleep.'

CHAPTER 19

I woke up to a sun-filled room, feeling rested and inexplicably happy. My first thought was of Devereux, and my lips curved into a smile all by themselves. The clock on the nightstand showed 9:20 a.m. I'd slept longer than I meant to, but apparently my body had needed the downtime. No wonder, since everything in my life had been such a mess for the last few days. Hell, for the last few months.

Luxuriating in the quiet, I replayed my conversation with Devereux. A trickle of joy washed through me as I recalled our decision to reconnect. It was wonderful to be sure my feelings about him hadn't been illusions or vampire juju – that fundamentally they'd been real. Not knowing had dented my confidence and made me second-guess myself about everything.

I knew I'd have to think about Alan and what role I wanted him to play in my life, but for the moment, I simply revelled in feeling good.

Treating myself to a few more moments of blissful relaxation, I rolled onto my back, stretched, and bumped against something solid next to me. 'Devereux?' I said, forgetting for a moment that he couldn't possibly be there since it was daytime. He would have left before dawn. I reached out a hand to investigate the hard mass. It was cold. I snatched my hand back, bolted upright and turned towards the huge covered lump in the bed.

What the hell's that? I scrambled out of bed, tiptoed around to the other side and stared down at the bulge.

Okay, wait. What happened last night? I was in the shower. Devereux popped in. We talked. I fell asleep.

I definitely heard him lock the door.

Unless the bundle under the covers simply grew out of the mattress like a mushroom on steroids, something was very wrong.

Slowly grasping the corner of the blanket, I tugged it away from what turned out to be a face. And screamed. I jammed my knuckles into my mouth to muffle the sound until I finally ran out of air.

Lying in the bed was a very dead Brown Hat, still wearing his headgear. His terrified eyes were wide, frozen open for ever in death.

I lifted the blanket higher and gagged. His throat had been torn out.

Backpedalling fast, I slammed into the wall and slid down hard on my ass. My brain spun. How could the angry guy be in my bed? He'd been arrested at the presentation yesterday. I watched the police take him away.

I stopped breathing as the realisation hit me.

Lucifer.

Cold chills swarmed through my body and I began to shake. The fiend had been in my room. Actually in my physical space. He must have been waiting for Devereux to leave, timing it just right so that he could drop his package before the sun rose. My stomach churned as I thought of him standing over me as I slept. Once again I wondered why he hadn't just taken me if I was so important to him. And why had he killed Brown Hat? Did he know the man had threatened me? Did he think he was helping me? None of his actions made any sense. Maybe his illness was more complicated than I'd thought.

I jumped up and ran for my phone to call the police, picked it up, then stopped. What was I supposed to tell them? Obviously Brown Hat had been taken from jail. Wouldn't they assume I had something to do with breaking him out? And killing him? After the events a couple of months back when I'd been a suspect in the Denver murders, I didn't want to do anything to shine the media or police spotlight back on myself.

Glancing at the dead body, I shuddered at the thought of having slept next to it.

Alan. He would know what to tell the cops. I dialled his cell and immediately went to voicemail. Unwilling to wait for him to get off the phone, I threw on my robe, tied the belt and headed towards the door. At the last second, I remembered I didn't have my keycard and grabbed it off the entertainment centre. The last thing I needed was to be locked out of my room, wearing a bathrobe, with a dead guy in my bed. I raced out of my room towards the elevator. Alan was one floor down.

The elevator was empty of humans when the doors parted, but the ghostly couple, now engaged in acrobatic sexual intercourse on the floor, took up so much room I had to squish myself against the side wall to avoid the woman's flailing legs. I punched the button for the floor below mine. 'Yes! Yes! Benny! Harder! Faster! Don't stop!' the woman screamed.

Having to see ghosts was bad enough, but being forced to listen to them was extra irritating.

I didn't get a chance to find out if Benny followed his partner's commands and everybody had a happy ending because thankfully the doors opened. I leaped out and speed-walked down the hall to Alan's room. I could hear him talking on the phone through the door. 'Alan!' I knocked loudly.

'Hold on. Somebody's at my door,' he said a few seconds before he opened it. He was dressed in his usual white T-shirt and jeans, his hair standing up in tufts. Dark smudges shadowed his eyes. He took one look at me and his expression became even more serious.

'Kismet? What the hell? Come in!' He pulled me inside and barked into the phone, 'I'll get back to you as soon as I know anything.' He ended the call and shoved the cell into his pocket.

By this time, the shaking that had started out as a slight trembling in my room had morphed into bona fide quaking. Suddenly freezing, I hugged myself.

He wrapped his arms around me. 'What the hell's happened? Did somebody hurt you? You're ice-cold.' He released me for a moment to rush over to the bed and grab a blanket, which he wrapped around me before pulling me against him again. 'Why are you wearing a robe?'

'I tried to call you. You need two phones.'

'Yeah, sorry about that.' He ran his hands up and down my back, trying to generate heat. 'I've been talking for hours. Seems our beefy friend escaped from jail last night. I spent some time at the precinct, helping them search for him.'

'He didn't escape.'

'Yeah, he really did. They think he somehow managed to crawl out through a bathroom window. I can't believe the cops let him go to the can by himself. Anyway—'

'No, really – he didn't escape. I know where he is.'

He grabbed my shoulders and held me at arm's length, studying my face. 'What do you mean? How could you know where he is?'

'Let me show you.' I tugged him towards the door.

'Kismet, you're acting crazy. What the hell's going on? Has all the stress of the vampire crap finally pushed you over the edge?'

'Probably, but I still know where he is.'

'Wait.' He hurried to his bedside table, lifted the gun-in-the-holster he'd shown me via Skype and clipped it onto his belt. 'Okay.'

'Come on.' I opened the door and pulled him into the hallway. Not wanting to watch the sex show in the elevator a third time, I headed for the stairs.

'Why are we taking the stairs?' He stopped and spun me around to face him. 'Talk to me. You're making me nervous. I don't want to have to put you on a seventy-two-hour psychiatric hold,' he joked.

'As if.' I tugged him again. 'I'm okay, really – it's just easier to show you than to tell you, and I don't want to deal with the ghosts in the elevator right now.'

'Ghosts in the elevator?'

He let me drag him into the stairwell and we raced up to my floor, exited into the hallway and found my room.

I let us in and pointed to my bed. 'This is what I found when I woke up this morning.'

He edged over to the bed, raised the blanket and then shot his gaze back to me, eyebrows raised, mouth open. 'Holy fucking shit. It's him!'

'I know!'

We both stared down at the corpse of my former stalker.

Alan lifted the blanket further and leaned in to examine the visible area. 'There's no blood anywhere, so he was killed – and drained – somewhere else.' He looked at me. 'Lucifer?'

'Has to be.' Points to Alan that he never considered for a

second that I'd had anything to do with the intruder being in my bed.

'Why would the lunatic bring him here? Do you think it's like when a cat brings a mouse to its owner? Sort of a sick gift?'

'That's what I thought.' I sniffed. 'We'd better do something quickly – he's starting to smell. We have to call the police.'

Alan hurried over to the other bed and sat on the edge. He shook his head. 'The cops are never going to believe this.'

I paced. 'What if we tell them the truth? I woke up and found this dead body lying next to me and I ran to your room for help?'

'Yeah, except they're going to want to know how Jack Kent was able to break into your room, or if he didn't break in, why you'd let him in voluntarily, or how someone else could dump his body in your bed while you were sleeping without waking you up.'

'Who's Jack Kent?'

'That's Brown Hat's real name, remember? He yelled it out at the presentation. He's a journalist. Which reminds me – I should try to find out what he was going to print about you.'

'Oh, yeah, Jack Kent. Do the police have his cell? Maybe it could mysteriously vanish from evidence. He kept holding it up, implying his *proof* was there.'

He threaded his fingers through his unruly hair. 'Too bad you and Devereux are on the outs. If you were still speaking to him, we could ask him to erase the memories of all the cops involved and to grab Kent's phone. I wouldn't involve him except I don't think all vampires are as good at mind-clearing as he is.' He rose, walked to me, and gave me a quick kiss. 'But I'm okay with him being out of the picture. I like having you all to myself.'

I frowned. Alan didn't know about my time with Devereux last night, and now things were going to get a whole lot more complicated.

'What did I say?' Alan tapped my nose with his finger. 'Your mood just tanked.'

'Devereux isn't exactly out of the picture.'

He backed up, scowling. 'Oh yeah? I know I'm not going to like this, but lay it on me anyway.'

'Devereux came to visit me last night. We talked.'

'You talked?' He gave me a sceptical look. 'And?'

'And we worked some things out.'

'Worked some things out. Is that a euphemism for *had sex*?' The veins on his forehead and neck suddenly became more noticeable, and his face went red.

'No!' But I didn't say sex might have happened if I hadn't been so tired.

'Right. I'm supposed to believe that?' He returned to the edge of the bed and sat. 'I thought *we* were working things out.'

I joined him and took his hand. We both stared at the carpet for a few seconds. 'I've been honest with you, Alan. I care about you *and* Devereux – you're both important to me – but I'm not going to make a commitment to anyone right now. I don't know what I want to do because the dilemma is still the same: if I work with vampires, I'll have to drink the blood of the elders yearly and do other things just to keep my brain healthy. If I don't work with them – supposing they would even let me walk away – how do I have a *normal* life, knowing what I know?' I looked at him. 'And until Lucifer is caught, my life is shit. This really isn't the time for a love triangle.'

Looking sad, he met my eyes, then shifted his away quickly.

'You're right. We didn't make any promises to each other. We said no attachments, just one day at a time.'

I leaned over and kissed his cheek. 'Yes.'

'I can still do that.' He straightened, and lifted his chin, his skin returning to its normal colour. 'And getting back to business, I have an idea for what we can tell the cops about why you didn't hear anyone come into your room.' He leaped up and trotted towards the bathroom. 'Didn't you tell me you sometimes have trouble sleeping so you occasionally take a sleeping pill?'

'Yeah. Very occasionally, if I haven't been able to sleep for a few nights. Why?'

I heard him rummaging through my toiletry bag.

I didn't want to pass Brown Hat – I couldn't get used to thinking of him as Jack Kent – again, so I waited on the edge of the bed instead of checking to see what Alan was doing.

'Yes!' He returned a few seconds later carrying a prescription medication bottle. 'This will work.' He held out the bottle.

I took it. Zolpidem, otherwise known as Ambien. 'My sleeping pills? How will these help?'

'You can tell the cops you were so upset by what happened at the presentation last evening that you came back to your room and took a sleeping pill or two, which knocked you out until this morning.' He walked to the nightstand and set the pill bottle there. 'Let's call the police and get this over with. Why don't you get a glass of water – half-full – and put it by the pills, just to make things look more realistic?'

While he dialled the police on his cell, I averted my eyes and walked past the dead guy into the bathroom to get the water.

'Lieutenant Fitzgerald, please. Yeah, this is Special Agent Alan Stevens. Thanks. LT? I have some news about Kent. You're not going to believe this . . .'

I closed the bathroom door, deciding to take the world's quickest shower before I slipped on some jeans and a light-blue sweater. When I came out with the glass of water, Alan was standing over the corpse again, which he'd re-covered with the blanket. I set the glass on the nightstand then settled on the other bed.

'The police will be here any minute. You're going to have to be a great actress, because they're already suspicious.' He moved to the couch and sat. 'You've got to admit this is pretty fucked-up. If we take vampires out of the equation, how could a dead body end up in a locked – occupied – room in a busy hotel?' He tapped his fist on his knee. 'Maybe we can sell them on the possibility that Kent had an unhappy accomplice here in the hotel – someone who broke him out then killed him, dumping him in your room to make you look guilty.' He leaped up and paced. 'Damn. I'd never buy that.' He sat next to me. 'Really, Kismet, this is all going to be on you. I'm just the person you told first, so it won't really help if I come up with any possible scenarios – I can't make it look like I have any agenda or that I'm trying to shield you.'

There was a crisp knock on the door. 'Police.'

Alan and I shared a look. I crossed my fingers and held them up as I moved to the door.

'Doctor Knight?' A tall, muscular, olive-skinned officer held out his badge. His uniform must have been custom made. He looked like a body builder. 'I'm Officer Angelino.' He pointed a thumb at the average-height wiry man with the crew cut standing next to him. 'This is Lieutenant Fitzgerald.'

'Please, come in.'

Lieutenant Fitzgerald took the lead. 'Where's the body?'

I stepped inside the room and pointed. 'There. On the bed.'

Officer Angelino handed a pair of latex gloves to his

lieutenant, and they both gloved-up. They already had little blue paper covers over their shoes. Fitzgerald narrowed his light-blue eyes and fixed them on me. 'Did you touch anything?'

'Only the top of the blanket.'

He lifted the blanket, assessed the situation and moved around the bed to me. 'Agent Stevens said you discovered the corpse when you woke up this morning.' His not-quite-a-smile was cold. 'Is that what happened?'

There was another knock on the door and Officer Angelino went to answer it. 'That'll be the medical examiner and the forensics guys. I'll get them started.'

Lieutenant Fitzgerald pointed at the furniture under the window. 'Let's move over there.'

Alan and I perched on the couch. The lieutenant took the chair in front of us.

Officer Angelino escorted several men into the room. 'Lieutenant? I let the ME and the forensics techs in. The homicide guys are waiting in the hall, along with a couple of hotel managers.'

Fitzgerald locked his gaze on me. 'So, Doctor Knight, Agent Stevens told me about your event in the hotel auditorium yesterday evening. He said the deceased, Jack Kent, burst in, made outrageous accusations, then attacked you on the stage. The police were called to the scene and you filed charges, as did another woman who was allegedly hurt. Is that correct?'

'Yes.' *Doesn't this guy ever have to blink?* I turned to Alan. 'Could I have some water, please?'

Alan went to the refrigerator, pulled out a bottle and handed it to me.

The men examining the body and surrounding areas went about their business silently. The only noise in the room was the click of the camera as the crime scene was photographed.

'Thank you.' I opened it and drank, shifting my eyes back to Lieutenant Fitzgerald, whose lizard stare was sucking all the moisture from my cells. It occurred to me that if he ever wanted to become a vampire, he already had the hypnosis down.

He waited until Alan resumed his seat, then continued, 'What happened next?' He leaned back in the chair, looking deceptively harmless.

'Then Agent Stevens, a psychologist friend – Doctor Michael Parker – and I went to the little World War II restaurant downstairs for coffee.'

'Michael Parker, you say? The same Michael Parker who was with you when you gave a statement to the police yesterday in the auditorium? Do you know how I can reach him?' He pulled out a pad and pen, prepared to record my answer.

'He's here for the American Psychologists' Conference, so he's a guest at the hotel.'

'This hotel?'

'Yes, of course.'

He tucked the pad and pen back into his inside pocket without shifting his eyes. 'We've checked the hotel's registration and there's nobody here by the name of Michael Parker, nor has there been for the last few weeks. There isn't a Parker with any first name. We also checked nearby hotels with the same result.' He leaned forward. 'How do you explain that, Doctor Knight?'

'I can't.' I looked at Alan.

'No way, Fitzgerald, he's here somewhere.' Alan shook his head. 'He must be using another name.'

The lieutenant barely spared Alan a glance before riveting his icy-blues back on me. 'Are you aware of another name your friend might use, Doctor Knight, or why he'd do that?'

'No. I only met him on the plane coming to the conference. I don't know a lot about him.'

'I see. So he wasn't actually a friend, more of an acquaintance – would you say that's accurate?'

'Yes.' I saw the corner of Alan's mouth quirk up and I knew he was weighing the consequences of letting Lieutenant Fitzgerald think Michael might have had something to do with the murder. As fun as that would be for Alan, he couldn't pursue it, because neither one of us trusted Michael to keep his knowledge to himself under pressure. It would cause more trouble than it was worth.

The examiner stepped away from the bed. One of the techs pulled out a black body bag and he and his partner quickly lifted Kent inside and zipped it up.

Lieutenant Fitzgerald paused for what felt like a full minute, unblinking. He was very good at using silence to intimidate. I wasn't even able to pick up his intentions and emotions intuitively. All I sensed was the image of a blank wall. He had to be very well trained in protecting himself.

Maybe he just blinks too fast for me to see? If he didn't blink, wouldn't his eyeballs dry up?

'What, exactly, is the relationship between you and Agent Stevens, Doctor Knight?'

'We're friends.' I drank more water.

'Friends? Have you known *him* longer than just since the plane ride to the conference?'

'Yes.' I figured I couldn't get into any trouble if I kept my answers short.

'How long?'

'What's this got to do with anything, Fitzgerald?' Alan asked. 'You're getting off-track here.'

The lieutenant ignored Alan. 'How long, Doctor Knight?'

'We met last October.'

'Hmm. According to my research, you were involved in another murder case in Denver last October. Was Agent Stevens there to investigate you?'

Uh-oh. I don't like where this is heading.

Another tech guided a collapsible gurney into the room, helped lift the body onto it, then wheeled it into the hallway.

'Fitzgerald, what the hell?' Alan straightened, his eyebrows contracted in the middle.

Lieutenant Fitzgerald held up his index finger and finally gave Alan his attention. 'I just find it odd, Agent, that you are *friends* with a woman who was a suspect in an earlier homicide. But we'll leave that line of inquiry for now.' He looked at me. 'After you, Agent Stevens and Doctor Parker had coffee in the restaurant downstairs, what happened next?'

'We came up here to my room to talk. Doctor Parker had some research interviews he wanted to show us.'

'You came to your room? All *three* of you?' His lips curved up into something that didn't look anything like a smile.

I didn't bite, although the visual of the ménage à trois he was suggesting might have been interesting if I could've stopped imagining Alan and Michael pounding each other bloody and rolling across the floor. 'Yes. All three of us.'

'What kind of *research interviews* did you watch?'

'Fitzgerald? You're definitely crossing a line now.' Alan stood.

'Okay, okay. Sit down, Agent.'

'No thanks.' Alan, still standing, clenched his hands and rested them on his hips. 'Let's just get this over and done with.'

Lieutenant Fitzgerald relaxed back in his chair and brought his intense stare back to me again. 'All right. So, Doctor Knight, after the three of you watched the *research* videos, what did you do then?'

'Agent Stevens and Doctor Parker left, and I went to bed.'

'You went to bed? Did you let Jack Kent into your room before going to bed, or did he awaken you at some point?'

Alan rolled up on the balls of his feet, looking like a street brawler. I answered quickly, 'To the best of my knowledge, Jack Kent was being held in the NYPD jail following his arrest. I went to bed alone, and woke up with a dead body next to me. I have no idea how he got there.'

The lieutenant leaned forward, shaking his head. 'Come now, Doctor – do you really expect me to believe the body simply appeared in your bed by magic? That someone managed to break into your room and deposit a large man right next to you without waking you? How do you explain that?'

He really was trying to pin the murder on me and I wasn't going to have it. 'Lieutenant Fitzgerald, the only logical explanation, since Agent Stevens tells me the lack of blood around the body means Kent was killed elsewhere and brought here, is that I slept through whatever happened. Since the deceased was such a large man, it would make sense that more than one person transported him. Maybe they had a keycard to my room. I don't know.'

'Is your keycard missing?'

I jumped up and walked to the entertainment centre. My keycard was there, right where I'd left it when Alan and I returned to my room earlier. I held it up. 'No. It's here.'

'Did the hotel give you more than one card?'

'No – I only asked for one. Of course, it's impossible to know if other copies were made.' I returned to my seat on the couch.

'Are you a particularly heavy sleeper, Doctor Knight? I'm having a hard time imagining this body was brought here in complete silence.'

'I'm not usually a heavy sleeper, Lieutenant, but after Kent interrupted my presentation and then the media arrived, I was running on adrenalin. When I was finally alone in my room, I wanted nothing more than to sleep. I took a shower, then crawled into bed. After tossing and turning for a while because my mind was spinning, I took a couple of the sleeping pills I use occasionally. They tend to knock me out.'

He rose, moved towards the nightstand and picked up the pill bottle. 'Are these the sleeping pills you're talking about?' He shook the remaining pills into his hand then read the label. 'The prescription says there should be twenty pills, but I only count twelve. Did you take eight pills last night?'

'No, of course not. The prescription's dated last October. I've taken a few since then.'

'You had difficulty sleeping last October? During the murders? I'm sure you know, Doctor, that sometimes people with guilty consciences have trouble sleeping. Not that I'm implying anything about you, of course.'

'Fitzgerald, this is bullshit.' Alan moved to stand in front of the lieutenant. 'You know she didn't do anything, so why are you treating her like Public Enemy Number One?'

'I don't have to answer any of your questions, *Agent*. This murder and the death of the psychologist in the hotel yesterday both took place on my turf and the Feds have nothing to say about my investigation. I'll conduct it any way I please and right now your *friend* is the only one with a motive for the homicide.'

Alan stood straighter, stepping into his official persona. 'On the contrary, *Lieutenant*, the psychologist murder here is part of an investigation that started in San Francisco. Since two states are involved, it definitely falls under the auspices of the FBI, so I'd say this is just as much my investigation as yours. As for Jack Kent, no one knows yet how he might be involved.'

'Lieutenant?' Angelino moved towards us. 'Forensics is waiting for everyone to leave so they can continue their jobs. The hotel manager is here, ready to move Doctor Knight to another room.'

Alan and the lieutenant glared at each other for a few seconds. 'All right.' Fitzgerald turned to me. 'Leave everything in the room as it is. You can return after forensics are finished. In the meantime, go ahead and talk to the hotel manager and get your new room keycard. Then you'll be coming downtown with me.'

'What?' Alan stepped in front of me. 'You've already heard her statement. What's the point of dragging her downtown?'

Fitzgerald's lips curved into that unfriendly smile. 'Well, as you said, I heard her statement, but nothing was written down. We'll do that at headquarters. I suppose you'll be joining us?'

'Damn right!'

CHAPTER 20

Several miserable hours and what felt like endless police cross-examinations later, Alan accompanied me back to the hotel. We went to my old room, packed up my things and called a porter to transport everything to the new room – an exact duplicate of the last one – which was on the same floor as Alan's.

I was exhausted and wanted nothing more than to jump on a plane to Denver and fly home. The conference was over as far as I was concerned. I sat on the edge of one of the beds in the new room and listened to Alan as he paced.

'I can't believe they held you there so long without any charges. And that they kept us separated. I'm going to have a word with Fitzgerald's captain. Not an FBI matter, my ass. We'll see about *that*.'

The police *had* treated me like the main suspect, based only on circumstantial evidence. Specifically, the body in my room. I mean, how stupid would I have to be to kill someone, plant them in my own bed, then call the police? And after the long, gruelling interrogation, they suddenly let me go. With no explanation. I hoped Alan could find out what had caused the quick change.

He finally stopped talking and crouched in front of me. 'You look like hell.' He tucked a lock of my hair behind my ear. 'I think a nap is called for. Why don't you come to my room and sleep while I do some paperwork?' He looked as tired as I felt. The whites of his blue-purple eyes were red, the shadows underneath darker and wider than usual, and the lines running from his nostrils to the corners of his lips were cut deeper than before. After all, he had been up most of the night.

'I think you're right about sleeping, but I'll just stay here. I don't think I could even walk down the hall at this point.'

He rose and stepped towards the door. 'Are you sure? I could have room service bring you something to eat. You must be starving.'

I wondered if he'd heard my stomach growl. 'I am hungry, but I'll get something when I wake up. Thanks, though.' I tried to smile. 'If I had to be grilled by New York's finest, I'm glad you were in the vicinity. No telling what would've happened if you hadn't been there.'

As he reached the door, I saw a movement from the corner of my eye. A child – no more than five or six years old, ran towards me, holding a doll. She was dressed in a floor-length yellow nightgown and held her other arm out. 'Momma?' As I watched, the bottom of her gown caught fire. 'Help me, Momma!' she screamed as the flames engulfed her.

Shit! A talking child ghost. No way. I had no intention of watching her little body burn in the illusory flames. I preferred the woman in red and her crashing-through-the-window routine. And who knew what other spectral nightmares awaited in this room?

'Alan, wait! On second thought, I *will* go with you. Hold on.' I squinted, trying not to see anything that wasn't directly in front of me, slipped on my shoes and hurried to the door.

He gave me a surprised and confused look. 'Er, okay.' He glanced at my face then scanned the room, no doubt guessing there was more going on than met the eye. 'Let's go.'

We shuffled down the hall like newly minted zombies. He opened his door and I fell face-down onto one of the beds, and that's the last thing I remembered for a while.

The sound of voices woke me from my nap. I must have slept for a couple of hours because I could see daylight through the window when I'd conked out and now it was dark. I rolled over onto my back then sat up, trying to find the source of the angry sounds.

I crawled to the end of the bed and heard Alan's loud voice booming from the bathroom. 'That's bullshit, Devereux. You had no reason to keep the truth from me.' The closed door didn't muffle the sound at all – in fact, it echoed in the tiled room. 'You must be one heartless bastard to be able to look me in the eye and not level with me about my mother. Who put you in charge of other people's lives?'

'Your mother did.' Devereux's tone was calm. I had to strain to hear.

'Yeah, well, I suppose she was confused after being attacked and then going through the transformation, but afterwards you couldn't possibly believe it was in my best interest not to know she'd survived.'

'Alan, your mother's transition was very difficult. Many times we thought she would not make it. It took years for her to acclimatise, to be able to control her violent urges. She was a danger to you. She made me swear to keep her secret. She was convinced you would have a better life without becoming involved with vampires.' He laughed. 'She was quite upset when she discovered your professional area of interest. Knowing the undead as she does, she thought it would be hazardous for you. She asked me to fortify the spell I had cast on you when you were younger.'

'So I owe you for all the times I didn't die over the last couple of decades? Your magic protected me?'

'That, and your mother's vigilance. We both watched over you.'

'And you think that made up for me believing I was an orphan?' Alan said belligerently. 'I was such a lost kid. I dreamed about my mother all the time, lived out imaginary fantasies of us being together.'

'Some of those were not dreams. At least not *only* dreams.'

'What?'

'One of the first skills your mother asked to learn was how to visit you while you slept. She joined your dreams often. It was a great joy to her.'

'Really?'

Silence.

'Well,' Alan said, his voice softer, 'I still think you should've told me.'

'I could not betray your mother's trust. I had given my word.'

More silence.

'What about Kismet?' Alan said.

'What do you mean?'

'Are you going to keep trying to bully her into being with you? Even after she's told you how confused she is?'

I leaned further out from the bed, eager to hear.

Devereux didn't answer right away. 'I have been as I am for a very long time. While I would not call myself a *bully*, I do tend to be aggressive about getting what I want. Kismet has made it clear she needs time to sort things out. I have promised to give her that time. The likelihood that I will be able to change my fundamental nature is very slight, but I am becoming more conscious of my tendencies.'

'You know *I'm* not going to give her up without a fight.'

'I would expect no less.'

'Good. Then we understand each other. Quite frankly, I hope you keep lying and manipulating because that's going to push her away.'

'As abnormal as it is for me, I am making an effort to be more forthcoming. You must understand that during the previous centuries, it was dangerous for me to disclose any information about me, or my intentions. The world was a much more hostile place, and vampires did not have even the *illusion* of safety, as Kismet refers to it, that we have today. As long as vampires remain hidden, that is.'

'Yeah, but you're not living in the past now. Wait – I forgot who I was talking to. Kismet says you still refuse to join the twenty-first century.' He laughed. 'That's another point in my favour. I know for *damn* sure she has no interest in the bad old days.'

'As I mentioned, I am making an effort to be less . . . mysterious and guarded. There is only one piece of the current situation I have not yet disclosed to Kismet, but I intend to.'

'What piece is that? Hey, what's going on?'

There was a pause and I nearly fell off the bed trying to listen.

'I must go – your mother has a lead on Colin's whereabouts. You should awaken Kismet and bring her with you to your mother's apartment. She continues to be protected by my security force, but I also ask that you remain with her until Lucifer is captured. She trusts you.'

Devereux must have vanished because Alan yelled, 'Hey! Wait!'

I scrambled back into the position I was in before the

argument and waited for Alan to come out of the bathroom. The toilet flushed and water ran in the sink.

There was no reason to let him know I'd heard the discussion. What hadn't Devereux told me yet? Did he plan to clue me in before we start our *new beginning*? Probably not. As he said, he'd been this way for a very long time.

The door opened and Alan came and sat on the edge of the bed next to me. 'Kismet?' He shook my shoulder gently. 'Wake up.'

I rolled over and blinked my eyes. 'What?'

His cell rang and he answered. 'Stevens. Mom?'

I sat up.

'Yeah. Okay. We'll be right there.' He stood, ended the call and pocketed his phone.

We'll be right there?

'What?' I flipped my legs over the side of the bed.

'Mom said she got a lead on Colin through the vampire grapevine. Devereux went to check it out. She wants us to come over.' He peeled off his shirt, reached into the carry-on bag he hadn't unpacked from his flight and grabbed a fresh white T-shirt. 'Do you need to go to your room first?'

'Yeah.' I rose off the bed and patted my pocket to make sure my new keycard was still there. 'Why didn't your mother just pop in like all the other vampires do? It seems odd that she uses the phone.'

'She said she isn't very good at travelling via thought yet. I guess it takes a lot of practise, and she can only bring one person back with her.'

'Well, that's okay – she can come and get you. I don't really need to be there, do I? How can I help?' I knew Devereux had told him to stay with me, but I wanted to hear how he would spin it.

He paused for a few seconds. I could see the wheels turning in his head as he tried to think of a convincing cover story. 'She's pretty upset and you're good with that. She'll appreciate the support.'

'Uh-huh.' Not bad. Some general truth with no real explanation. Well, it didn't matter. I was going, regardless – even if he hadn't wanted me to. 'Okay, let me go and brush my teeth and freshen up. Come to my room when you're ready.'

I hurried down the hall, but the sight that greeted me inside my room when I opened the door with my new keycard stopped me dead on the threshold. 'Shit!' The child-on-fire had been joined by several other people, all in various stages of incineration. The entire room – or an echo of it – was a roaring blaze. I could even smell the smoke and burning flesh. My eyes watered. I reflexively raised my arms over my face and closed myself into the bathroom where for some reason everything was calm.

Heart pounding, I leaned against the door, trying to catch my breath. How was I supposed to function if I constantly had to deal with horrors from the past? Zephyr had been right about my abilities increasing, but he'd neglected to say anything about what I could do to control them.

Since my clothes were in the other room, I eventually had to step out of my refuge. After I did everything I could in the bathroom, I steeled myself to open the door, briefly hoping that my clothing wouldn't smell like smoke. I shook my head as I remembered the scene was an illusion. On a count of three, I pulled the door open and dashed out. The fiery nightmare was still raging and one of the older female victims approached me with her hand reaching as I grabbed clean jeans from my suitcase. 'Stop!' I yelled, desperately not wanting that hand to touch me.

The entire scene vanished.

I was so stunned I dropped the jeans.

'Yes!' I thrust my fist into the air and danced in a circle. Apparently, I could control it. There was an *off* switch.

I had no idea *how* I'd done it, but I definitely needed to figure it out so I could *keep* doing it. Was it the word I used, or the emotion behind it? Or simply my intention? Regardless of how it happened, I was relieved and grateful it had. I'd take any boring normalcy I could get!

Still twitching my hips, I retrieved the jeans, chose a dark-blue sweater and dressed quickly before anything else could distract me.

A knock sounded on the door and I opened it, expecting Alan.

'There you are.' Michael grinned, looking like he'd stepped from the pages of a men's fashion catalogue, not a hair out of place, wearing a gorgeous burgundy sweater and black trousers. 'I didn't know why you'd switched rooms and nobody would tell me.' He pointed a thumb at Alan. 'Luckily I was on my way to Stevens' room when I ran into him in the hallway.'

'Yeah. What luck. As I was just explaining to the ass-wipe, we're on our way out.' Alan gave him a malevolent glare, then looked at me. 'So say goodbye to the conniving bastard, grab your coat and let's go.' Alan cut in front of Michael, stepped into my room and tried to close the door.

Uh-oh. They're at it again. I backed away.

'No fucking way!' Michael shoved his body against the door so hard it almost toppled Alan. Face flushed, he pushed his way inside. 'You're not getting rid of me. I know you're doing something involving vampires and I'm serious – if you don't let me in on it, I'll go to the media.'

'Is that so?' Alan's calm tone was contradicted by the bulging vein on his forehead, eyebrows contracted so tightly they almost met in the middle and the most evil smile I'd ever seen him display. 'Come on in here and tell me about it.' He pushed imaginary sleeves up his arms.

Testosterone madness. Again.

I wedged myself between them and pushed their bodies apart.

They both looked at me in surprise and took a step back.

Wow. Enhanced strength, too. How cool is that?

'Stop!' Well hell, it worked for the ghosts. Maybe it would work for the Y-chromosomes. 'Michael, the police have been looking for you – apparently you aren't registered at the hotel. You want to tell us what's going on?'

'Why are the police looking for me?'

'I had to account for my whereabouts last evening and you're part of my alibi. Nobody could find you.'

'Your alibi? What the hell went on last night?'

'Don't change the subject. Why aren't you registered at the conference hotel?'

He shrugged. 'I am, but since the business I told you about with the client who stalked me, I never use my real name if I don't have to. I have a whole other set of ID to keep me off the radar. I'm registered under another name.'

'So you're an even bigger liar than we thought?' Alan said. 'What's this mysterious name? Wait – is it Ass-Wipe? Dumb Fuck? Shit-Head?' Alan grinned maniacally and crossed his arms. 'What a waste of space you are.'

'I'm not telling you my other name, dick-breath.'

Alan burst out laughing. 'Wow, wishful thinking or what? Don't be casting me in any of your X-rated fantasies, butt-face.'

'In your dreams, you homophobic fuck.'

Alan shook his head. 'Nope. Not a homophobe. I'm an asshole-phobe.'

Ack! Maybe I can just jump in a cab and head to the airport.

When in doubt, repeat what worked. 'Stop!'

They looked at me but still held their adversarial poses.

'Alan, aren't we supposed to be somewhere?'

He attempted to smooth his wild hair. 'Yeah. Let's go.' He turned to Michael. 'You're not coming. This is personal business. Nothing to do with you.' He opened the door and sailed a hand towards the hallway. 'After you, Doctor Parker.'

Michael walked into the hall, suspiciously calm.

I lifted my coat off the chair and slid into it.

Alan and I hurried to the elevator. I turned to see if Michael was following us, but he just stood there, a thin smile on his face.

Miraculously, there were no ghosts – fornicating or otherwise – in the elevator, and we rode down uneventfully, both of us lost in our own thoughts.

'I'll find a cab.' Alan left me at the entrance to the lobby and hustled out into the clear, frigid night to hail a ride. Just watching the doorman's breath steam out as he spoke to departing guests made me shiver. I was glad we'd both worn heavy coats.

When the next available taxi pulled to the kerb, Alan flagged me over. I dashed into the back seat; he joined me and gave the driver the address of his mother's building. I pulled the neck of my sweater over my nose. The cab smelled like feet.

The ride was mercifully short and soon we pulled up in front of an incredible Gothic building.

'Wow.' I climbed out of the cab, took a breath of fresh air and stared up the length of the building, which reminded me of Devereux's club, The Crypt. Same basic architecture and building materials with lots of gargoyles and demon carvings. 'Is this the *Rosemary's Baby* apartment building?' It didn't look exactly like the structure they'd used in the film, but close enough. Something about the vibe was similar. That movie had scared me so badly when I watched it on late-night TV about a year ago that I couldn't sleep for a couple of nights.

Alan took my arm and guided me to the entrance. 'No – you're thinking of the Dakota over on West Seventy-Second Street, the place where John Lennon was murdered. That alone marks it as a horror site for me. It was built in the late eighteen hundreds. This building is a little older and a lot bigger.'

A middle-aged doorman dressed in a black military-type uniform with gold buttons, tassels and trim, plus a jaunty matching hat opened the door for us and saluted. 'May I help you?'

We stepped inside. 'Hello, Wesley.'

'I'm sorry – I didn't recognise you, sir. Your mother is expecting you and your guest.'

He escorted us across the spcaious marble lobby past a bank of elevators, but instead of stopping there as I expected, we kept moving towards what appeared to be the double-door entrance to a room. Wesley inserted a key and unlocked the door, revealing a private elevator.

Alan responded to my unasked question, 'This is a special elevator for the penthouse residents.'

'Have a good evening, sir, ma'am.' Wesley tipped his hat and waited for us to enter the elevator.

We stepped inside and Alan punched the only button available. The door shut. We rode up to the top floor uneventfully in the wood-panelled box and I released the breath I'd been holding. I guess I'd expected to see some kind of apparition in a building this old and I wondered if I hadn't seen anything because there wasn't anything to see, or if my cutting off the action back in the hotel wasn't associated with any specific place. Maybe I'd ended all the ghost-viewing. At least for today. I could only hope.

Olivia was waiting for us when the door opened on the penthouse floor. She ran to Alan and hugged him. 'I'm so glad you're here.' She looked at me. 'Both of you. Come inside.' She released Alan, hooked her arms through ours and walked us into her apartment. Although the word *apartment* didn't do it justice: it was a combination of antique store, museum and movie set – a wealthy-client-focused real estate agent's wet dream.

The moment we entered, I was overwhelmed by a heavy, bad feeling.

'So what's the news about Colin, Mom? Has somebody found him?' Alan turned to face her.

'No, but one of his friends said that several piles of ash and skeletal remains were found in the lair of one of Colin's enemies. Apparently somebody killed them.'

Alan hesitated, clearly thinking the same thing I was. 'I don't suppose there was any way to identify the remains? Was Colin there?'

I knew he'd died there.

'I don't know yet. Devereux went to check.' She started to cry. 'But I'm sure he's not there. He'll be found alive. He wouldn't leave me.' Her emotions belied her words. She covered her eyes with her hands and sobbed.

I looked around for tissues and found a box on a nearby antique desk.

'Come and sit down, Mom.' Alan guided Olivia towards a small couch and sat next to her. He took the box I offered, and handed her a couple of tissues.

Sensing someone standing behind me, I turned to apologise for stepping in front of him or her and found a man holding his finger against his lips in a 'don't talk' gesture.

'Don't let them know I'm here,' said the attractive man with a British accent. He was average height, maybe five feet, ten inches, slender with dark eyes and pitch-black hair pulled back into a short ponytail at the nape of his neck. His European-cut light-grey suit, black shirt and silver tie were dishevelled.

I glanced back to see if Alan, who was still patting Olivia's arm and trying to soothe her crying, had noticed or heard the man. Apparently not.

'Tell them you need to use the bathroom. I'll meet you there.' He gazed longingly at Olivia.

If I needed any proof that Colin was dead, or no longer undead, this visit put paid to it. I wasn't happy to realise that I'd been selected to break the horrible news to Olivia that her mate was gone, but I didn't see what choice I had. Yes, I could hold back the information, watch her suffer in the not-knowing, let myself off the hook. But all those options were unacceptable.

I looked at the ghost of Colin, set my resolve and moved towards Alan and Olivia. 'Excuse me – I'm going to find the bathroom. I'll be right back.'

'It's down that hallway.' Alan pointed.

'Thanks.'

I found the bathroom, which was large and luxurious enough to be an upscale spa, turned on the light and closed the door.

'I'm sorry we didn't get a chance to meet under happier circumstances.' Colin walked over to an actual gold toilet, lowered the lid and sat. 'Now I wish I'd fulfilled Olivia's request that I visit you professionally. Maybe I wouldn't have continued to make such poor decisions. Please,' he pointed towards a chair at the nearby makeup table, 'have a seat.'

I pulled the chair close to him and eased into it. 'So you were murdered by people you owed money to, as Olivia believes?'

'Yes.' He shook his head slowly. 'And no.'

'I don't understand.'

'I did owe them money but that wasn't the reason I went there.'

'It sounds strange that vampires can control each other with money. I mean, why would it even be an issue? Couldn't you all just take as much as you want by materialising in a bank or having humans give it to you?'

'You're right – we can have whatever we want, but there are those among us who still cling to the fears and beliefs about money we had when we were human. Especially the younger vampires. They haven't figured out yet that mortal notions of wealth no longer apply. And some of them simply enjoy the sport of acquiring money.'

'So, if it wasn't about money—?'

'It was about Olivia. And Devereux.'

'What?'

'They were preparing to abduct her to get at Devereux.'

'What's Devereux got to do with this?'

'It's well known that he's been Olivia's protector and mentor for a long time, and he's very rich and powerful. They assumed Devereux would do whatever was necessary to get her back. Thanks to my own connections, I heard about their plan. I stupidly went to confront them, thinking I could negotiate or distract them long enough to consult with Devereux about a way to keep Olivia safe, but there were too many of them. I was out of my league.' He gave a sad smile. 'As usual, I made the wrong choice.'

Listening to him made me wonder if I could counsel ghosts,

because Olivia had been right about Colin's depression. Why couldn't I treat them, too? Ghosts weren't any more unnatural than vampires. But I doubted ghosts had a source of income, so maybe I'd be doing some pro bono work with the immaterial.

'And they killed you?'

'Yes. They ripped off my head and tore out my heart. The standard vampire assassination.'

I'll have to remember that.

I couldn't think of a tactful way to ask the question that immediately sprang to mind, so I just blurted it out. 'But if they did those things to you, how is it that you're . . . whole . . . now? You're not missing your head or your heart.'

He didn't appear bothered by the question. 'I can manifest as I wish. I don't know if that's because I could change my appearance as a vampire or if it's a ghost thing, but I assumed you'd prefer this form.'

'Er, yes. Thank you.' I tried not to think about what I would do if some apparition appeared in its most grisly aspect. 'What about the piles of ash and skeletons that were found? Is one of them yours?'

'Yes. They'll be able to identify me by my clothing. That's one reason I wanted to talk to you alone. I want you to speak to her for me, to tell her what happened and how sorry I am. Will you do that?'

'Yes, of course.' I stood, preparing to return to Alan and Olivia. 'Wait – you said they killed you, but there were other remains present. Who do they belong to?'

'That's the other thing I wanted to tell you. After they took my heart and before I was beheaded, a tall bald man wearing a long black coat appeared in the room. I heard someone scream, then I was gone. I'm sure that man destroyed the others. You should tell Devereux.' With that, Colin vanished.

'Colin!' *Lucifer? How the hell can he be everywhere, all the time? Exactly what kind of mutant vampire is he?*

I hurried back into the main room where Olivia was still sitting on the couch and Alan, his face red and his hands in fists, stood arguing with Michael.

CHAPTER 21

My surprise had to be apparent on my face. 'What are you doing here?'

They both looked at me.

'I followed you,' Michael said. 'I saw the doorman use a key to let you into the private elevator. As luck would have it, he left the keys on his desk while he went to the bathroom and I came up.' He pulled a ring of keys from his pocket. 'I'll bet he's going crazy looking for these right about now.'

'You *bastard*. I told you this was private business.' Alan reared back and punched Michael in the jaw, then followed with a blow to his stomach. Michael crashed to the floor like a downed tree in the forest. 'I'm going to make you sorry you're alive.'

Michael sat up, clutching his midsection. 'Oh yeah? Well, I'm not holding back any more, dick-brain. You're toast. Burned toast.' He leaped to his feet and came at Alan.

Olivia and I shouted, 'Stop!' at the same time, and both men stopped dead. Olivia was obviously skilled at using her vampire voice to good effect.

She stood and walked towards the two men. 'Step away from each other. Now!'

And like puppets on her string, they did.

She looked at Michael. 'Who are you – or perhaps the better question is *what* are you – and why are you here?'

Before he could speak, Devereux appeared and strode over to Olivia.

'Master! Master!' Michael said and fell to his knees, looking up at Devereux with wide-eyed adoration.

'Silence!' Devereux said.

Alan and I looked at each other, and said in unison, 'Master?'

What the hell? Michael and Devereux know each other?

'I have painful news, my friend,' Devereux said gently to Olivia. 'Come and sit.'

'No, Devereux, no – don't say it. Please.' Olivia went to the couch and covered her ears with her hands. 'I can't bear it.'

Alan quickly sat next to her.

Devereux claimed the other side and waited until she could listen. 'We found Colin's clothing, Olivia. I am so sorry.'

She threw herself into his arms and wailed. He patted her back and rocked her gently, a profoundly sad look on his face.

Michael moved to sit at Devereux's feet, trying to mimic his Master's heart-broken facial expression.

Alan glared at him, then looked helplessly at his mother.

'What happened? Who killed my Colin?' Olivia extricated herself from Devereux's arms, plucked a tissue from the box and wiped her face.

'We do not know yet, but I promise you will know as soon as I do. There were six other vampire skeletons in the room.' Devereux sighed. 'How they died is a mystery.'

I figured that was my cue. 'It was Lucifer.'

All eyes turned to me.

'Why would you say that? How do you know?' Alan asked.

'Colin told me.'

Simultaneously, everyone rose and continued to stare at me.

Colin appeared right in front of me, close enough for his nose to touch mine, and I jumped back a few inches. 'Hey!'

'Tell her,' the ghost said.

'I will. Give me some room here.'

'What's going on, Kismet? Who are you talking to?' Alan inched closer to me.

'Colin is here.'

Olivia looked around the room, her hand pressed to her chest, a hopeful expression on her face. 'Where is he, Kismet? Why can't I see him? Is he hurt? He sent you to fetch me?'

'Mom, he's not here physically. Remember I told you that Kismet can see ghosts?'

Olivia covered her mouth with her hand and fresh tears rolled down her cheeks. 'You're saying he's really gone – that he's a ghost now?'

Colin glided next to me and cleared his throat.

'Okay, Colin, what do you want me to tell Olivia?' I turned towards the man only I could see and nodded, encouraging him to speak.

Alan pointed to the empty beside me. 'Is he there?'

'Yes. Olivia.' I held out my hands to her and angled us so that we were facing Colin. 'He wants to talk to you.'

'Tell her I'm so sorry. I never meant to leave her. I promised her I never would. The vampires who killed me are dead themselves. Some deformed-looking vampire in a black coat took them out. Tell her she's safe for now and that I'll always be with her, even if she can't see me. The promise I made to stay with her will bind me to her for ever.'

I repeated his message, plus everything he'd told me in the bathroom.

She cried harder.

Devereux's eyes locked onto mine when I mentioned the guy in the black coat.

'Tell her I'll figure out a way to communicate with her. I only have so much energy right now, but I will practise and grow stronger in the future. Tell her I love her.'

He vanished as I shared the rest of his words.

Olivia grabbed my hand. 'He's gone?'

I squeezed her fingers. 'For now.'

She walked back to the couch and sat, weeping silently. Alan went to her, braced his arm around her shoulders and let her cry.

'That was very moving,' Michael said in his most compassionate-therapist tone. He sat on the floor at Olivia's feet, ignoring Alan's pointed scowl.

Apparently, Michael had told a lot more lies than I'd realised. He'd never been who he said he was – not any version – and now he was acting like Devereux's lapdog. Reality had shifted. Again. As much as I wanted to confront the lies, it felt tacky to be pissed off about this latest deception in the face of everything Olivia was dealing with.

Devereux walked to me. 'Thank you for helping Colin communicate with Olivia.' He lifted my hand and kissed it. 'I do not know how she is going to cope with the loss of him. I hope you do not mind if I encourage her to come and see you, professionally.'

'You're welcome.' I decided to be polite. For now. 'You made things easier by telling her before I had to. I'd be happy to counsel her.'

He glanced at Alan. 'I am glad she has Alan now. He might be her saving grace.'

I frowned at him, not wanting to ruin our new beginning or argue with him in front of the others, but I couldn't disguise the fact that I felt angry about whatever he was keeping from me.

'I do not have to read your mind to know you are upset with me about Michael. Come.' He pointed to the adjacent library. 'Let us speak in private. I will disclose everything. I told Alan earlier there was only one thing I had not explained to you yet, and this is it.'

Okay. That's consistent with what I heard back at Alan's hotel room.

We sat on a loveseat in front of giant aquarium filled with exotic fish. Remembering what Zephyr had said about the importance of practising the sound magic Cerridwyn taught me around strong vampires, I rehearsed the hum. Since I'd apparently decided to stay in the world of vampires, I didn't want to be overwhelmed by Devereux's innate energy – or anyone else's – any more.

'Why did Michael call you "Master"? How does he even know you?'

He stared at the fish for a few seconds. 'He calls me Master because it is appropriate for him to do so. He is a member of my coven.'

'Your coven? Are you saying Michael is a vampire?' I jumped up from the seat and circled around the aquarium. 'No way. I couldn't have missed sensing a vampire that close to me. And besides, I saw him eat and drink human food.'

Devereux remained seated, relaxing into the cushions as if the story could take a while. 'I masked his energy. Michael is an aberration, neither vampire nor human.'

I stood over him, my hands clasped behind my back to keep me from throwing something. 'I've never heard of any such thing. You're making that up!' *No! No more insanity!*

'Unfortunately, it is very real. You will find that there are many things you have not yet heard of. No doubt you *do* remember hearing that the transformation process does not always go easily or well. Many do not survive. Michael, for lack of a better explanation, got *stuck* in the middle of the process.'

'How is that possible? As far as I understand, if someone doesn't survive the transformation, they die.'

'Usually that is the case, but there have been rare occurrences of this particular outcome. Michael was attacked by a client who left afterwards, thinking he'd merely feasted and the mortal would die. The vampire in question, who had a bad habit of leaving drained human bodies lying around for the authorities to find, was already being followed by members of my coven who keep track of such things. After disposing of the offending vampire, they found Michael, almost dead, and brought him to me. We gave him a blood transfusion in an attempt to retain his humanity.'

'Wow. You routinely give humans blood transfusions?'

'Yes. It is often necessary. I did not know until Michael regained consciousness and I read his memories that he had been bitten repeatedly many years earlier when he was a teenager. At that time he was saved by the quick actions of paramedics and another transfusion he received at the hospital. During both attacks, because he had fought back as long as he could, he ingested small amounts of vampire blood. That, when blended with all the additional human blood he was given, created the half-creature he became.'

'Seriously? But he seems so human. Is he always going to be ... stuck?'

'No. He is becoming one of us. He needs to drink blood – vampire and human – and he can no longer go out in the daylight. Although he can still remain awake during the day if he wishes, he becomes lethargic. He can eat solid food, but it does not agree with him. It is impossible for him to be fully human again, so he has asked to become completely vampire, and he is transitioning slowly in that direction.'

'Wait.' I plopped onto the couch. 'Are you saying that Michael actually was a psychologist? That wasn't just something he lied about to get close to me?'

'Indeed. That was not a fabrication. It is probably the only thing he told you that is true. He got a little carried away with the pretences he created for you and Alan.'

'You think? So what was the plan? Have him befriend me so he could spy on me for you?'

'No, not *spy* on you – rather, keep watch over you and provide you with another human – a fellow professional – you could talk to. I know how difficult it is for you to be the only human among so many vampires.'

'Well, he wasn't very helpful, was he?'

'No, I suppose not. But sending him to you was as much for his benefit as for yours.'

'And how's that?'

'Michael is not in control of himself enough to work in his chosen field now. He cannot spend unsupervised time with humans, and vampires are dead to the world during the day. He was behaving like a bored child, so I thought it wise to give him something constructive to do. Since both you and Alan have extra protections, I hoped it would be safe for him to spend time with you.' He stroked a finger along my cheek, then leaned in and brushed his lips against mine. 'I did not mean to deceive you.'

I gazed into his blue-green eyes and wanted to believe him. 'I hope that's true.'

'I realise it will take time for you to trust me and I am willing to do whatever it takes.'

'No matter how long?'

'No matter.' He grinned. 'Time is something I have plenty of.'

'Would you mind if we change the subject for a moment?'

'Of course not.'

'What's going on with Lucifer?'

Devereux looked away for a few seconds before returning his attention to me. He was obviously still uncomfortable with the topic.

'Dracul told me why Lucifer is interested in me,' I continued. 'I remind the Brother Luther personality of his wife.'

'Yes. Zephyr informed me about the content of your discussion with Dracul. I am glad the Dragon chose to be helpful.' He frowned. 'That is not always the case. In fact, it is amazing that he was so cooperative as he has recently become so radical in his opinions. It is good to finally know the reason why the demented bloodsucker is so obsessed with you.'

'And you've had trouble catching him because something is missing from his brain.'

His eyes narrowed. 'How do you know that? Who told you?'

'Luna. Why? Didn't you want me to know?'

'I had informed everyone that I would be the one to tell you that.'

Yes! Maybe he'll be so upset at his snarly assistant for flapping her lips that he'll get rid of her. Yeah, right. That'll happen.

'But you are correct. Lucifer lacks consciousness. I have never encountered anything like it. It is as if he is simply not there. Normally it is easy for me to get a fix on a particular vampire's – or human's – wavelength, for lack of a better word, and to immediately zero in on them. With Lucifer, it is as if his essence is cloaked. Or gone.'

'I don't understand what he's doing. I can't see the pattern. How did he get so powerful? Dracul said Lucifer isn't that old.'

'He is insane. You know better than anyone how incomprehensible a lost mind is. There is probably no rhyme or reason at all to what he is doing.'

'I'm not sure I agree with that. He obviously has some kind of plan. No doubt a nonsensical plan – a depraved plan – but a plan nonetheless, something that makes sense in his bizarre reality. Why is he killing psychologists? I get the obvious association, but why would he bother? I can't imagine what purpose could be served by their deaths. Is he acknowledging my line of work? Trying to eliminate what he perceives as competition? I don't understand the point of killing random dark-haired female psychologists.'

'I think he's just acting out every loose association that enters his feeble brain. If you were a construction worker, he'd be offing them.' Alan strode into the room carrying a steaming mug, pulled a chair over from a nearby desk and sat at my end of the loveseat. The shadows underneath his eyes had darkened even more and his lids looked heavy.

'Hey, you look tired. Maybe you should go and lie down for a little while,' I said.

'I *am* tired. Being up all night is finally catching up with me. But no nap. Too much to do.' Alan lifted his mug. 'Strong coffee's the answer.'

'How is your mother?' Devereux asked.

'She's doing as well as can be expected. She and Ass-wipe—'

'Ass-wipe?' The words sounded comical in Devereux's precise European-accented English.

'That's what Alan calls Michael. They aren't getting along very well.'

'Ah.'

'Anyway, she and *Michael* went into the kitchen to scare up some food for the humans. Busy work to help her cope.' Alan sipped from his mug.

'Food! How thoughtless of me,' Devereux said. 'I forgot that Olivia and Michael would need nourishment.' He closed his eyes for a few seconds then opened them. 'I have instructed my staff to bring a few donors for them.'

'Ass-wipe's a *vampire*?' Alan nearly fell off his chair. 'What?'

'Sort of,' I said. 'I'll fill you in about that later.'

'I knew there was something off about that guy but I never would've guessed he was a vampire. Damn – I'm losing my edge.'

'No you're not. So, back to Lucifer. You don't think there's any special significance to him killing the psychologists?'

'Not in any normal way,' Alan said, 'but he might be presenting them as gifts for you, as I believe he did with Jack Kent. I've interviewed human serial killers who did the same thing.'

'Michael told me you met the journalist who had been stalking you.' Devereux stretched his arm out along the back of the loveseat. 'We have had surveillance on him since October.'

My jaw tightened. 'You knew he was following me and you didn't say anything?' I felt myself getting angry all over again.

'I know.' He sighed. 'I must take full responsibility for the lapse in judgement. I considered him harmless, and he actually *was*, but he became a nuisance. You are correct – I should have told you. I had intended to alter his memories at some point and make him forget about you. I am afraid he got lost in the chaos. I apologise.' He dropped his hand onto my shoulder, pulled me against him and kissed my cheek.

Alan scowled.

'Hmmm.' What good would it do me to be angry? He'd apologised and his explanation made sense. Being upset required too much energy. 'Okay. I forgive you.'

LYNDA HILBURN | 345

'Thank you.' He kissed me again and looked at Alan, ignoring or disregarding his glare. 'You believe Lucifer killed Mr Kent and placed him in Kismet's bed as a sick gift? An offering?'

'Kismet?'

We all looked towards the new voice.

'Would you like some coffee or tea?' Olivia stood at the entrance to the library wearing a frilly red apron over her dress, dark mascara streaks lining her pale cheeks. 'I would be happy to bring you something.'

'Coffee would be great, Olivia,' I said. 'Thank you.'

She smiled and headed back to the kitchen.

We were all silent for a moment, out of respect for Olivia's pain. Then Alan returned his attention to Devereux and picked up the conversation where they left it. 'It's possible he offered the bodies as gifts. But I'm confused about why he'd kill the vampires holding Colin. Since he always seems to be hovering around whatever's going on, why did he wait to step in until Colin had been snuffed? Why not before?'

Devereux shook his head. 'Madness has no reason.'

'Or maybe we just can't see his whole plan from our vantage point.' I scrunched down to rest my head against the top of the cushion. 'It's possible he wanted to make sure we would have to come over here and comfort Olivia.'

'What do you mean?' Alan straightened in the chair, his gaze bouncing back and forth between Devereux and me. 'Do you think Lucifer's watching my mother?'

'Thanks to the power of his sire, he appears to have an almost mystical ability to be everywhere at once, and his primitive skills are amazing,' Devereux answered. 'I would like to say that my spellcasting is keeping your mother safe, but I have come to believe that Lucifer's lack of a coherent psyche keeps him from being compelled by magic.'

'Well, that sucks,' Alan said, looking at me. 'And why the hell did he kill the psychologist in the hotel?' He set his mug on a nearby table. 'Did he just roll the vampiric dice or throw a dart at the conference roster?'

'Shit! I forgot to even check the name of the victim,' I said.

'It was Doctor Patricia Kraft. Long, dark hair. She was on the APA board.'

I bolted upright and opened my mouth. 'No!'

'What is it?' they both said simultaneously.

'I found out the first day I arrived that Pat Kraft was the only member of the conference committee who voted against my presentation topic. She said it reflected badly on the organisation, that I wasn't the kind of psychologist she wanted representing the APA.'

'So there was some connection to you.' Devereux relaxed back against the cushions and folded his hands in his lap. 'That is interesting. Perhaps the monster simply overheard her expressing an anti-Kismet opinion and took action.'

'What do you know, Doctor Knight?' Alan said. 'Looks like you've got your own personal avenger.'

'That's horrible. But it also makes me wonder why he hasn't tried to kill you or Devereux or even Michael. If he's acting out his jealousy, why hasn't he targeted the men who are around me the most? That doesn't make sense.'

'Maybe he hasn't been able to get us alone long enough,' Alan suggested.

'I doubt if that would have stopped him, had he wanted to kill you,' Devereux answered.

'I agree. He could've just popped in, incapacitated you and Michael, sucked you both dry and been off to the next adventure.'

Alan frowned. 'Your faith in my ability to take care of myself is underwhelming.'

'Sorry, but it's true. And why hasn't he simply snatched me away if I'm his focus? He's had ample opportunity to do so.'

'No clue. But what I *really* want to know,' Alan stood and moved behind the aquarium to Devereux's side of the loveseat, 'is how long *you* are going to fuck around, whining about Lucifer's brain not having a frequency you can track? When are you going to figure out a way to catch the bastard? I thought you had a rep as a major badass. Either the rep's been inflated or you've lost some of your shine, so to speak.'

Suddenly, fear saturated the room – *ours*. Devereux's usually repressed predator nature exploded and even with our protections, our old-brain memories of being prey kicked in full-throttle.

Holy crap! Had Alan lost his mind? Was he trying to push Devereux's buttons on purpose? But why? Did he have a death wish?

My heart pounded. I looked over at Alan and saw the pulse in his neck racing like a cheetah on speed.

Quicker than my eye could register, Devereux was standing in front of Alan, close enough to startle him and cause him to stumble backwards a few steps before he caught his balance. He stared into Alan's eyes, a dangerous edge to his voice. 'Have a care, Agent Stevens. My affection for your mother will keep me from killing you, but there are many other ways I can make a lasting impression. Because you are under duress and worried about Olivia, I will ignore your disrespect. Once.'

I knew Alan had voiced Devereux's worst fear: that he wouldn't be able to destroy Lucifer. Alan was sometimes oblivious, but I couldn't believe he'd missed the sensitivity boat to that degree and had simply goaded Devereux because he was pissed off.

And from previous experience, I knew that we were both going to pass out pretty soon if Devereux didn't lighten up.

'Master?'

'What is it, Evan?' Devereux said, answering the man in the doorway while still staring at Alan, who had begun to shake. Sweat was running down the sides of his face.

'Devereux, please stop. You're going to scare us to death.'

He turned his head slowly towards me, so slowly it looked alien and unreal – as if he'd become someone – or something – else. He raised his head and his nostrils flared as he breathed in the fear that perfumed the air.

'Master?'

He looked at the man – Evan – still standing in the entryway and shook his head a couple of times, snapping out of whatever vampire trance had overcome him. 'Did you take the donors to Olivia and Michael?'

'That's what I need to talk to you about, Master – Olivia and Michael aren't here.'

'What?' Moving so fast I saw only a blur, Devereux left the room.

When he'd shifted his focus to Evan, his intensity waned and Alan and I were set free from the paralysing terror. We ran after him.

I heard him calling Olivia's name as he moved through the huge penthouse.

Evan and another vampire stood in the large living room with the human donors: two women and two men. They waited, fidgeting, looking ill at ease and unsure of what to do.

Devereux thundered back into the room like a vengeful

god, his long leather coat and platinum hair fanning out behind him, his face a mask of ferocity, now aroused not only by Alan's taunt, but likely by the knowledge of what had happened to Olivia and Michael. 'They are gone, and we all know who has them.'

Alan began to ease towards Devereux, then stopped. 'I'm sorry for what I said before. I thought I'd try a little reverse psychology. I didn't really mean it. I just wanted to rattle your cage, to motivate you. To piss you off, so you'd go and rip his ass. Hanging around with vampires who are civilised made me forget the truth of what you all are.' He looked down at the front of his trousers. 'I'm surprised I didn't wet myself.'

'You need not have reminded me of my duty to find Lucifer. I am aware of it always, and being unable to find him has been a humbling and enraging situation.' Having reassumed his debonair, cultured persona, Devereux looked at each of us and gave a quick nod. 'I apologise for scaring you.'

I rubbed my arms to warm the chills that had broken out after the fear decreased. 'We'll live. So what now?'

'Yeah, my little standoff caused you to have to deal with me and you weren't able to hear Lucifer abducting my mother and Ass-wi— er, Michael. I really am sorry. If anything happens to her, it will be my fault.'

'Do not blame yourself. I am glad he took Olivia.'

We both goggled.

'You're glad?' Alan asked, his expression somewhere between shocked and incredulous. 'Why?'

'Because even though I cannot search out his specific signal, I can easily track your mother's.'

'So you know where he's taken them?' I pushed sweat-drenched hair off my forehead.

'I do.' He turned to the vampires and donors waiting with wide eyes. They probably hadn't expected to materialise into so much drama. 'Evan, take the donors away.'

'Yes, Master,' he said, and with a little *pop* sound, they all vanished.

'You aren't planning to leave me behind, are you?' Alan edged closer to Devereux. 'If you don't let me help rescue my mother, I'll never be able to live with myself. I can understand making *her* stay here,' he thrust a thumb over his shoulder at me, 'but—'

'Hey! What's so understandable about that? Aren't I the crazy vampire's fixated object? Who's to say that he won't come back here as soon as the two of you are gone? In fact, that might be his plan – lure the bodyguards away so he can enjoy the spoils at his leisure. I can tell you for sure that I don't like that plan!'

'You may be correct, but in any case, I never intended to leave either of you behind.' He looked at me. 'After speaking with Zephyr, I accept it is important that you be there.'

'Uh, good? But why?'

'I have no idea.'

Damn! The blind leading the blind.

'So what's the plan?' I asked.

Devereux looked around the room and pointed to our coats lying on a nearby chair. 'Fetch your jackets and we will be off.'

'Do you know where we're going?'

'Not specifically, but I am clear we are going to Olivia.'

Alan and I bundled up and Devereux opened his arms.

Familiar with the drill, I grabbed on around his middle and motioned for Alan to join us.

'Really? I have to hug Devereux? Isn't there another way?'

'You may hold onto me or remain here. The choice is yours.'

'Come on, Alan. What are you, twelve? Don't be an ass-wipe.' I smiled.

'Shit.' Alan hooked his arms around Devereux's chest.

Devereux tightened his grip on us and I experienced the now-familiar sensation of riding a free-falling elevator.

CHAPTER 22

My feet hit hard ground and Devereux released us.

Alan stumbled a few steps and leaned over, bracing his hands on his thighs. 'That's an awesome mode of transport, but it really messes with my head.'

I breathed for a few seconds to calm the queasy, discombobulated feeling. 'Yeah, mine too.' I looked around at what appeared to be a regular suburban neighbourhood. Wherever we were, they'd received a lot more snow than New York City had. We stood in the shovelled driveway of a two-storey traditional house in an endless sea of traditional houses stretching as far as the eye could see in all directions. This one was on a corner. The curtains were closed and lights blazed in every room.

'Where the hell are we?' Alan huffed.

The block was lined with bright streetlights. I walked over to the intersection to read the road signs. 'We're on the corner of Blue Bird Lane and Sunshine Way.'

Alan raised his eyebrows. 'Seriously?'

I scanned the area. 'Are you sure this is the right place, Devereux?'

'Yeah, this looks like Mr Rogers' neighbourhood. Why the hell would Lucifer bring my mom here?'

'I do not know this Mr Rogers,' Devereux said gravely, 'so I cannot verify whether or not he lives near here, but I am certain your mother is inside that structure.' He pointed to the house. 'And it is protected by magic.'

We heard footsteps clomping behind us and we all turned towards the sound.

Shit! What now?

'Well, hello! I'm Sherry,' said a woman hurrying up the pavement from the house next door. Zipped into a long puffy white coat, dark Ugg boots and a fluffy fur cap, she carried a covered casserole dish in one hand and a half-full martini glass in the other. 'Are you friends of Mr D's? I was just heading over to bring him some dinner and see if he'd like some company. He's an insomniac, you know.' She looked at me. 'I'd shake your hand, but you can see mine are full.' She opened her mouth wide and gave a full-throated, almost-hysterical laugh that brought to mind one of the dinosaurs in *Jurassic Park*.

Who the hell's Mr D? Jesus. We're all bozos on this bus.

Alan and Devereux bunched in next to me.

'Hello. Yes! We are Mr D's friends. I'm Kismet.'

'What an interesting name. Are you Middle Eastern?'

'No. My parents are musical theatre fans.' I pointed to Alan. 'This is Alan.'

He stepped forwards and lifted an imaginary hat. 'Hi, Sherry.'

'And this is Devereux.'

Her eyes travelled up his body to his face and I watched all the muscles in her jaw go slack. Her mouth sagged open and her eyelids fluttered.

He bent a finger under her chin and lifted her face so he could bring his eyes closer to hers. 'You thought about going to visit your neighbour tonight but decided against it. It is much better to stay home where you are safe and warm. You will return the food to your refrigerator, take off your winter clothing and sit in your living room enjoying your drink. After that, you will retire for the night and will sleep soundly until your usual waking time. Go now.'

Stiff-legged, entranced, she spun around and shuffled back the way she'd come.

Devereux looked at Alan and then at me. 'We must enter the house before anyone else notices we are here. The magic only prevents vampires from manifesting uninvited; it does not prevent a human from kicking open the door.'

'Now you're talkin'!' Alan said, rocking heel to toe in his eagerness to blast into action.

'But won't the whole neighbourhood hear if we do that?' I asked.

They both looked at me as if I was the biggest wet blanket in the universe.

'You are correct.' Devereux grinned. 'While it would have been very satisfying to kick in the door, I will simply push against it, quietly, and break the lock. Then Alan can actually open it. Come.' He grabbed the doorknob with one hand and braced his other over the dead bolt. With a quick *crack*, the lock broke.

Alan turned the knob and quietly opened the door.

We walked inside and scanned the empty living areas to our right and left. The rooms were furnished and decorated in a fussy Colonial style, not currently popular, but apparently still available. Low flames burned in the fireplace and several lamps shone brightly. Magazines lay fanned out neatly across the wooden coffee table next to a plastic floral arrangement.

The place looked like a page torn from an early 1960s edition of *Suburban Homes Magazine*. Did anyone actually design their houses this way any more? Had we stepped into a time warp?

'Do you hear that?' Alan whispered. 'It's coming from up there.' He pointed up the stairway directly in front of us.

'Yeah,' I whispered back, 'I'd recognise that ranting voice anywhere.'

'Get behind me, both of you.' Devereux climbed the stairs and we followed.

If Brother Luther's familiar braying voice and lecture topics hadn't provided enough proof of his presence, his signature smell would have. But there was another energy in the house. Something powerful. My solar plexus tingled.

We rushed up the steps, following the wild harangue, and froze at the doorway of a bizarre bedroom. Or what used to be a bedroom.

Devereux spread his arms across the entryway, blocking us from stepping inside.

The walls of the entire second floor had been gutted and opened up. Curved archways replaced the original interior drywall, creating an enormous master bedroom decorated in what could only be described as Tacky Brothel.

'Welcome to my home!' Dracul rose from the bed where Olivia, dressed in a black teddy, lay unconscious and bound at wrists and ankles, her long hair spread out across the pillows. Blood pooled around holes in her neck and upper thighs. Her very white skin was smeared with it.

Dracul stood like a fanged superhero with his hands on his hips and licked his bloody lips.

'Mom!' Alan started forwards, but Devereux held him back. 'Wait,' he whispered.

'Did you hurt her?' Alan demanded.

'Not yet,' Dracul purred.

Our eyes shifted back and forth between Dracul on one side and the hysterically ranting Brother Luther on the other.

The curtains, bedding and wallpaper were black and red, embellished with more tassels than I'd ever seen in one place before. Red scarves covered Tiffany-style lamps, casting crimson light. Photographs of naked men and women, flexibly posed in various sex acts, lined the walls and the fireplace mantel-piece. An impressive collection of sex toys sat on display in a lighted cabinet. All in all, it was a successfully updated rendition of an old-fashioned bordello.

The fire-and-brimstone diatribe increased in volume and we shifted our eyes to Brother Luther.

Secured to a heavy wooden chair with his mouth taped shut, Michael fought against his gaffer-tape restraints as the crazed former preacher screamed in his face. His eyes watered, which was a natural reaction to the toxic odours wafting from the disgusting vampire. I knew from personal experience that it was impossible to determine which was worse: his breath or his body odour. I hoped Michael was far enough along in the changing-into-a-vampire process to need less air because his nose appeared to be so clogged up it couldn't be easy for him to breathe.

Dracul pointed at Michael. 'Such an interesting specimen, this half-thing. I have, of course, seen many before. This one is particularly weak. All it took was one suggestion that he could not get loose and he began struggling against imaginary bonds even before I wrapped the tape around him.' He smiled. 'I *love* gaffer-tape! What a wonderful invention!'

Even from the distance of the doorway, I felt a headache threatening thanks to the stench. It was as if the fiend was rotting from the inside out. The quintessential ghoul.

'Demons! Sinners! Minions of Satan! You will be punished! You will be washed in the blood!' the walking nightmare raged with a Southern accent as he flailed his arms through the air, spittle flying from his decaying mouth.

The ever-present long black coat hung loosely on Brother Luther's emaciated, wiry body like a child wearing his father's clothes. Oozing, bleeding sores covered his white corpse-like face, and his deformed round head hosted maggots, which crawled over his blue-veined scalp like a ghastly toupee.

'When I commanded my offspring to appear, I did not expect him to arrive with two such marvellous gifts for his Master, but I am ever the genial host.' Dracul wore black silk lounging pyjama bottoms under an untied red silk robe. He strolled around the bed, the pale flesh of his chest gleaming in the soft light. 'In fact' – he pointed at two naked women lying on the floor near the walk-in closet – 'I already had company for tonight, but I cut our time short so I could enjoy the new arrivals.'

Oh no! I looked over at the women. 'Are they dead?'

Dracul raised his chin and glanced at them, then shook his head. 'No. Pity, that. They are merely entranced. Basking in the afterglow. While I would prefer to kill them – and rest assured I certainly will, at some point – if I drain them dry now I get only one use from each of them, and so many missing mortals would draw attention, which displeases some of my comrades. That will soon cease to matter, but for the time being, my neighbours are never sure *why* they feel the need to come and visit me, but they do. Regularly.' His lips spread, showing the tips of his fangs. I remembered the power of that smile and his ability to manipulate. I hoped my protection was strong enough to resist his charms.

'You know why I am here, Dragon.' Devereux stepped towards him.

'Yes, I certainly do. The entire vampire universe has been talking about your search for my insane child.'

'Why have you imprisoned two of my people? Did you ask Olivia's permission before you drank from her?'

'Permission? *Moi?* What a strange question, Devereux. I require no one's *permission* for anything. Ever.'

'You know I must challenge this disrespect.'

Dracul pretended to yawn, tapping his open mouth with his palm. 'Yes, I suppose so. But I did not keep your coven members out of disrespect.'

'No?'

'No.' Dracul folded his arms. 'There was no disrespect intended. In fact, it is out of respect that I created my elaborate scheme to convince you to come to your senses. You are my biggest interference.'

Alan stood next to me, tensed to spring. I touched his arm, reminding him to wait.

Devereux looked over his shoulder at Alan. 'Go and awaken your mother.'

Alan hesitated, probably afraid of what Dracul would do if he tried to rescue Olivia.

What Dracul *did* was flick his fingers, causing Alan to hit the floor, unconscious.

Poor Alan. Always losing control of his legs. I knelt down to feel his pulse, just to make sure he was still alive. He was.

'You do not give orders here, Devereux. If you do not join my cause, you will never give orders again, anywhere.'

Brother Luther's, 'You'll burn! You'll burn!' screamed at ear-shattering volume as he marched in front of Michael drew my attention. I didn't know which was more horrible: watching Michael's nose and ears being tortured, or trying to control my fear and confusion over what was brewing between Devereux and Dracul.

'I have waited patiently for this moment.' Dracul relaxed

his arms and stared into Devereux's eyes.

'What moment, Dragon?'

Devereux hadn't mentioned a personal problem with Dracul, but I didn't sense any surprise coming from him either.

Dracul gave a leering glare. 'I am providing you with an opportunity to alter your stance about the future of vampire-kind. Instead of simply destroying you, I decided to give you incentive to join me. I am going to hold onto your female for a while. Just until you cooperate.' He turned his gaze to me. 'You know your woman drank the elders' blood, which included mine. I now have a strong connection to her.'

Dracul stepped around Devereux and held his hand out to me. 'Shall we, Doctor Knight?'

I could feel the compulsion he'd woven into his voice and his energy, so I began practising the mental hum with a vengeance. What was I supposed to do? Of course I wasn't about to go with him. I didn't know how resilient my protections were, or whether I could withstand a vampire brain of his intensity. I probably wouldn't last five minutes before I'd be tearing my clothes off and thinking it was a good idea. And Devereux needed to kill Lucifer before he escaped again and went back on the rampage.

Devereux peeled off his coat, threw it onto an antique dresser and reclaimed the space in front of Dracul. 'She is off-limits.'

'No one is off-limits to me.'

The two vampires approached each other slowly, eyes locked, barely repressed violence radiating from both of them.

'You are standing in the way of my plan for the world,' Dracul said. 'You have grown too strong for your own good.'

'You have me at a disadvantage, Dracul. Please explain. I am holding the same position I have always held. Are you saying I am keeping you from fulfilling your agenda?'

Dracul laughed, his sharp fangs extending. 'That is amusing. You are pretending not to be aware of how you are obstructing my desires, when we both know you have set yourself against me on purpose. You obviously see yourself as the humans' saviour.'

'As I have often said, I am not saving humans – I am protecting vampires. You have been stirring up the more blood-thirsty among us for decades, trying to convince them they will have more authentic existences if they go back to hunting mortals freely, that it is their right to feed instinctively.'

'Do you dispute the truth of that?'

'Yes. It is no longer necessary. This is not the Dark Ages. We need to evolve with the times. We are not animals.'

'Ha! What nonsense, Devereux. Vampires will always be primitive creatures, no matter how much you resist accepting that truth.'

'But why, Dracul? You have wealth, power, immortality – why would you pine for a life where you are pursued again by the hunters?'

'Because it was exciting. Invigorating. Now life is boring. Empty. Killing the hunters before they could destroy me gave my life panache.'

'If Mina had not died—'

Dracul's face transformed into a mask of rage. 'Do not speak her name!' He leaped on Devereux, snarling and growling, his long fangs flashing.

They slammed to the floor, slashing with their sharp fingernails and biting at each other. Blood spurted against the walls and pooled around them as they rolled across the rug. Their bodies, clothed only in tatters of their previous outfits, defied gravity as they soared up to the ceiling, smashing each other's heads through the pressed-metal tiles before crash-diving to the floor in impacts that would have pulverised mere mortals.

Hurling what sounded like obscene epithets in many languages, they attempted to wrestle their fangs into each other's necks, arms and legs.

I tore my eyes away from the shocking war between Devereux and Dracul and caught a movement out of the corner of my eye. Alan had awakened from Dracul's mental knock-down punch and, sliding on his belly, was inching himself out of the room, heading for the stairway.

Watching everything from the sidelines, I felt useless and frightened. My heart pounded and my brain spun as I tried to think of anything I could do. Even with whatever extra abilities the elders' blood had provided, I was still a puny human. I called out to Devereux a few more times, knowing he couldn't hear me. I'd just considered following Alan down the stairs – going for help – when suddenly the ranting stopped.

I turned to look at Brother Luther. He was moving towards me, silently.

Shit!

My entire body clenched in fear and my heart tripped. Would this ordeal never end?

He lasered his gaze on me and screamed, 'Jezebel! Whore!'

Then, like the eerie stillness before an impending storm, the energy in the room thickened and it became difficult to breathe. The flames in the fireplace surged through the grating, singeing the thick rug under Michael's chair.

Dracul and Devereux remained lost in their preternatural trance. I'd seen this kind of vampire madness before and I knew they were no longer aware of anything about the outer world. Once the predatory urge to fight became engaged, the logical parts of their vampire brains simply shut down.

Brother Luther began transforming into the Lucifer personality before my eyes.

As I'd witnessed before, he grew in height and width. The coat that had hung loose on his bony frame only seconds earlier now stretched tight across his chest, shoulders and upper arms. It flapped open to reveal an even more decomposed and festering body than when he'd frightened me at my house last Hallowe'en. The horrible red erection had become even more forbidding and disgustingly hideous, if that was possible.

Michael bounced in the chair, making grunting noises, trying to loosen the gaffer-tape securing his body. His eyes were wide. I was pretty sure he was trying to be supportive.

I shifted my gaze back to the vampiric standoff between Devereux and Dracul. Their faces had morphed into inhuman alien versions of their former appearances. Fear, stronger even than when Devereux had scared Alan back at Olivia's apartment, flooded the room like toxic psychic quicksand.

'Devereux!'

The floor creaked behind me and I spun around to find Lucifer within arm's length. I covered my nose and mouth with my hand and backed away.

Lucifer stepped towards me, his hands outstretched. 'Come to me.'

Thanks to the elders' blood and the sound magic, I no longer had the same reaction to his hypnotic voice as the last time he'd used it on me. Then the words had felt like insects invading my ears – they'd pulled me like auditory magnets. Now his voice had no effect on me at all.

I looked around frantically to see if there was any kind of weapon I could use – something to at least slow him down. The only thing I could see was an ornate letter opener on the desk a couple of feet away. Hoping it would be better than nothing, I lunged for it and held it behind my back.

'Come to me.'

I cringed at the sight and smell of the troll standing in front of me. He breathed his noxious odour into my face and my eyes began to seriously tear. My stomach roiled.

'No!'

The sound of my voice must have roused Devereux from his trance, because he called my name. Looking back over my shoulder, I watched Dracul pull a velvet cord hanging near his collection of sex toys and yell, 'Hold him!' as at least a dozen vampires materialised from nowhere. Most of them were abnormally large and dressed in full warrior gear, including armour plates over their chests.

'My servants will keep you secure while you watch your woman die. I had them stashed in the basement awaiting my signal. It appears my offspring has claimed the pleasure of draining her. Oh, well. The outcome will be the same regardless. Clearly you do not intend to lend your support to my popular idea.'

Devereux gave a primal scream and began thrusting and kicking, combining what looked like various martial arts techniques with street fighting to dislodge the vampires holding him. As soon as he knocked down one, another took his place, and he became more and more enraged.

'Kismet!' he yelled, fear saturating his voice.

Dracul surveyed the bloody, torn-up room, an expression of disgust on his face. 'I will never get my security deposit back now.'

Lucifer stepped so close his horrendous stink overwhelmed me and I gagged. Had there been anything in my stomach, I would have vomited, which he probably wouldn't have noticed.

I held my breath and squinted. His face, almost totally rotted away, was an unidentifiable mass of twisted bone, festering, pus-dripping sores, maggots and other crawling things. Chunks of decomposing flesh oozed down his chin and onto his chest.

I raised the letter opener in the inches between us. 'Stop or I'll stab you!'

He used his partially intact hands to push his coat off his shoulders and then shucked it onto the floor, exposing his entire putrefying, loathsome naked body. Pressing himself against me, his hell-fire red eyes stared into mine. 'She must be punished.' His sharp yellow-and-black fangs jutted out at odd angles from his mouth, which was missing a portion of the bottom lip.

His touch thrust me into a state of hysteria. I knew the foulness of the thing that was pressed against me: the nightmare-come-to-life. My brain refused to grasp the horror of the moment – it was incomprehensible that I'd die in such a ghastly manner. I screamed again for Devereux, who was fighting to free himself from his captors. I could hear him calling my name.

I pushed against Lucifer and my hand slid uselessly along the slime coating his skin. 'No! Stop! Let go!' Trying again, I managed to startle him into leaning back just enough for me to stab him in the general area of his heart with my makeshift weapon. The blade sank all the way into his body, causing several pieces of tissue and bone to crumble onto my arm.

Ignoring my words and the letter opener buried in his chest, he lifted my head and angled his mouth to my neck. With a growl, he struck, piercing my vein with his filthy teeth. Devereux's voice faded into the background.

Lucifer held me close as he fed. I could hear the loud sucking sounds and the moans he made as he drank from me. I struggled against him with every ounce of strength in my body, which had been increased due to the elders' blood, but even with the extra muscle, I couldn't budge him. As I fought, an idea kept circling my mind. Something about a song. I disregarded the idea, thinking it was just a reminder to practise the hum, which obviously wouldn't do me any good now. A woman's voice – whose voice? – said, 'No, not the hum. A lullaby.'

What? My knees gave out and I hung limply in the monster's grasp.

The voice began singing bits of various lullabies in my head. 'Lullaby and goodnight, hush-a-bye, go to sleep, don't you cry, through the night, lay you down and rest, gentle light . . .'

Then I remembered: the lullaby CD at the blood-ritual, where I had chopped off Bryce's head. The song made Lucifer transform into his child personality. Understanding the message of the mysterious voice, I started singing, very faintly at first, because I couldn't get any breath. I kept repeating the same melody and random words over and over, and within seconds I felt Lucifer's mouth release from my neck. Hoping that was a good sign, I tried to sing louder. 'Close your eyes, sleepy tight, may your coffin be comfy . . .'

He lifted his head, stared at me with eyes that had gone dark, and collapsed us both onto the floor.

I kept singing, louder and louder, making up words and coughing as I gasped for deeper breaths now that my face was no longer pressed against the hideousness of what passed for his physical body.

He let go of me completely, curled into a foetal position with his head in my lap and made bizarre, haunting sounds as he tried to sing along.

I didn't know how long the reprieve would last. My body

shook as the realisation of how close I'd come to dying slammed into my brain, along with the fact that I'd probably have to keep on singing until Devereux could get away from Dracul's thugs.

'Call me to you,' the same woman's voice said.

I stopped singing. 'What? Call who?'

'No, do not stop singing. Call me in your mind: Nettie.'

Nettie?

Picking up the song again, I thought, *Nettie, come to me.* What harm could it do? She'd saved me so far.

Coalescing in front of me was ... me. Or a woman who looked very much like me, dressed in a long, full-skirted grey dress covered by an apron. She knelt down and said, 'My Luke is not to blame. He was sick.' She pointed towards Dracul. 'It was that devil who brought this about. I will take him now.'

'What do you mean? How can you take him? Aren't you a ghost? Can ghosts do that?' Lucifer began to stir as soon as I stopped singing. Panicking, I quickly started up again.

Nettie gave a soft smile. It was weird, looking at my face on another body. 'There are many levels of ghosts. You will learn in time. We must go now. I must free his soul.'

His soul? Do vampires really have souls?

'Wait! Why do we look so much alike?'

'I am your ancestor.'

What? Oh. My. God.

She stood and extended her hand towards Lucifer, who was still croaking out very unappealing sounds, and he gasped, then fell silent. A wispy outline of a nice-looking young male – body intact – floated up from the thing lying in my lap and offered his hand to Nettie. They vanished, and immediately, Lucifer's body began to disintegrate.

Holy fuck. How the hell had that happened? Not that I was complaining.

I scrambled out from under the rotting corpse and glanced at Michael, who was sitting stunned in his chair, his eyes impossibly wide. Looking down at myself covered in slime and gore made my stomach churn. I took some deep breaths and thought for a few seconds about all the ways I could decontaminate myself before I noticed the room was silent. The fighting had stopped. Everyone was staring at me – even the behemoths holding Devereux.

Dracul moved with supernatural speed and stood over me. 'What did you do?' Almost naked and dripping blood, he squatted down and studied my face. 'How did you make him let go of you, and why did he die?' He poked at the bones and ash on the floor then brought his narrowed eyes back to me. 'He was a vampire. He could not die.'

Since nobody could see Nettie but me, and they probably hadn't heard me singing to Lucifer, the entire incident must have looked inexplicable and strange – strange even for vampires.

Snake-fast, Dracul dragged me up, pressed my back against his chest and hooked his arm around my neck. 'Looks like I will have the pleasure of draining your woman after all, Devereux. You will die next, of course. In any event, I believe it is even more important that she be eliminated now because she appears to be a powerful witch and I have never trusted witches.'

Devereux redoubled his efforts to escape and the vampires holding him had to struggle to keep him restrained. 'Do not give up, Kismet. I will find a way.'

I didn't see how he was going to do that, but I hadn't expected to survive Lucifer's feeding frenzy, so I was willing to hope for another miracle.

'It was never my servant Lucifer, you know, Devereux.' Dracul tightened his grip on me, causing me to have difficulty breathing. 'He was merely doing as I commanded. He wasn't smart enough to kill all those people or arrange to work with your offspring Bryce without my help. I enhanced both Bryce's and Lucifer's abilities the night they trapped you in the magical circle, and I borrowed some of your own sorcery abilities to use against you.' He laughed. 'You know how good I am at borrowing skills. The fools thought their own combined powers overcame you. Instead, it was my clever plan to either enlist you to my cause or get rid of you.'

He lifted my arm and bit down.

I screamed from the pain.

After a few sucks, he dropped my arm. 'Just a taste of things to come, my dear. Humans really have only one purpose.'

'Release her, Dracul. We can discuss your plan. Perhaps you can persuade me yet,' Devereux said.

With a wild whoop, Dracul threw me down to the floor and easily pinned me there. I barely had the energy left to fight.

'Excellent try, Devereux. I believe that ship, as they say, has sailed.'

'But Dragon, why was Lucifer so focused on Kismet? Was that your doing, too?'

Devereux's trying to keep Dracul talking. Brilliant man. Dracul loves to brag. But I'm not sure what we're buying time for.

As expected, Dracul didn't disappoint. 'Oh yes! I expanded Lucifer's memory of his wife who looked like your mate so he would become more obsessed with her. It was a marvellous coincidence. He'd found the good doctor's photo in an advertisement for her new vampire counselling practice and was already stalking her. That incredible opportunity fell right into my lap.' He licked my neck where Lucifer had fed. 'The addled fool kept forgetting he knew where your woman could be found. Instead, he attacked anyone who vaguely resembled her. He left scores of dead therapists – and humans he mistakenly *thought* were therapists – across the country.' He laughed, exerting pressure on my lungs with each guffaw. 'Of course, I also had assignments for him, like killing the reporter and the vampires holding Olivia's mate, just to confuse everyone. And sometimes Lucifer would find his beloved, only to switch to another personality and forget why he wanted her. What an entertaining few months it's been!'

Oh my God! My mind spun. It was Dracul all along! No wonder Lucifer's powers appeared extra-supernatural and he seemed to be everywhere. My heart pounded and my stomach muscles contracted. I feared I would lose control of my bladder. And I knew with certainty that Dracul really did intend to kill me.

'Well, as enjoyable as this evening has been, I really need to finish up and move to another location. I fear this one has been compromised. Say goodbye to your playmate, Devereux. You should have cooperated.'

Without further pause, he struck, sinking his fangs into my neck with such fury that I screamed, pushing against him until he gathered my hands into one of his and held me fast. His other hand was fisted in my hair, holding my head off the ground for his dining pleasure. His sucking hurt, as if he took great enjoyment in giving me as much pain as possible. I began to feel light-headed, my vision clouding as I saw Devereux struggling to break free of the iron grips of his captors. He bellowed words in his strange language.

As Dracul drank, my eyes became heavy and my bones dissolved. I'd almost drifted away when the sound of feet pounding up the stairs startled me and I jerked back to consciousness.

With a grunt, Dracul lifted his face from my neck, blood dripping from his chin. His red eyes blazed. 'What the hell?' He unceremoniously dropped my head onto the floor with a thud and leaped to his feet.

I was able to turn my head just enough to see what all the stomping and screaming was about. If I hadn't recognised Alan's white T-shirt and his unintentionally spiky hair, I'd have thought I was hallucinating. I gathered all that remained of my energy and managed to use my body weight to flip myself onto my side. The wound on my neck throbbed.

'No!' Dracul howled, his voice sounding more like the demon in *The Exorcist*.

A herd of vampires clamoured up the stairs and fanned out into the room. They jumped on Dracul's servants, which freed Devereux to lunge for Dracul.

'What took so long?' Devereux yelled at Alan. 'I read in your mind that you were going for help. Didn't my security receive the command I sent?'

'No,' Alan said, bobbing and weaving to stay out of the way of the hissing and flailing vampires as he pulled me out of the centre of the room and back to the corner where Michael was bouncing in his chair, still trying to free himself. Alan propped me up against the wall. I could feel the blood dripping down my chest from the wounds in my neck. 'I guess it was part of the magical protection deal: no vampires could pop in and no mental messages could go out. I was going to use my cell, but it was dead, so I had to run from house to house until I could find someone I could badge and convince to let me use their phone. I finally got through to The Crypt and told security to come. They had to enter through the front door. The rest is history.'

Dracul slashed what looked like claws across Devereux's

face. 'You have gained nothing bringing them here. None of you will get out alive.'

I figured that was a true statement if you didn't count Alan and me and maybe Michael since the rest were already dead anyway. The jury was still out on the survival chances for us humans.

As Alan, Michael and I watched, yet more vampires stormed into the room and within minutes, Devereux's forces had Dracul's restrained. They waited in a circle around the two master vampires who continued to slash, bite and jab at each other.

'You have changed, Dragon. When Mina was alive you did not have such rigid ideas about humans. If she had not died—'

Dracul lunged at Devereux again, as he had the first time Mina's name was mentioned. 'I told you not to say her name. She did not *die*. I killed the ungrateful bitch. I offered her immortality, to live for ever, with me. I would have given her *everything*. But she turned me down – rejected *me* – for a miserable *human* male. I could not allow her to cast me aside.'

'So that is why you want to exterminate humans? Because of your love for Mina?'

Dracul screamed and pressed his hands to the sides of his head.

He was truly mad.

'I did not love the whore.'

'You lie, Dragon. I was there. I know better.'

The two powerful vampires were so evenly matched, I didn't see how Devereux could overcome Dracul and end this nightmare.

Then I remembered the unexpected arrival of Lucifer's Nettie and wondered if I might be able to summon another ghost. What good was it to have my weird abilities if they couldn't help in an emergency? If I could summon her, maybe Dracul would be distracted and Devereux would have the edge he needed to win. Of course, I didn't know what I was going to do about the fact that Dracul probably wouldn't be able to see her.

I repeated, over and over in my mind, *Mina Harker, come to me. Mina Harker, come to me . . .*

A form shimmered in front of me: a woman with brown hair pulled back in a bun wearing a floor-length black dress with a full skirt and a high neckline. She stared at me with wide green eyes as if she didn't know what to make of her arrival.

Shit! It worked!

'Are you Mina Harker?' Just like all the times I'd used the Ouija board, I never knew for sure who would show up.

'Yes. Where am I?' Her voice quivered.

'Who are you talking to?' Alan asked.

Now that I had her here, I didn't know what to say to her. Dracul *had* killed her, after all, and now I was asking her to try to attract his attention again. I doubted if she'd be recpetive to the idea. But I had to convince her to help. 'I'm sorry. I wouldn't have summoned you if it hadn't been an emergency.' I braced myself for a negative reaction. 'Dracul is here.'

Instead of the fearful or angry outburst I expected, she lit up with joy. 'Where is he?'

I pointed behind her.

She turned and ran to him, saying his name.

Dracul paused for a second in battle, just long enough to give Devereux the opportunity to slam in a head-cracking kick. 'Who called my name?'

Damn. Could he hear her? That was more than I'd hoped for.

'Mina?' I wheezed and crumpled further down the wall. Taking as deep a breath as I could, I struggled to sit up straighter, trying to retain the little bit of strength I still had. 'Can you let him see you?'

'Yes.'

She stepped between the two fighters and Dracul's eyes went wide. 'Mina!'

In that moment, Devereux reached through the apparition, knifed his fingers into Dracul's chest and pulled out his heart, which he crushed in his hand. Then he reached over, twisted the famous vampire's head off and threw it against the wall, where it exploded, sending blood and brain matter oozing onto the floor. The rest of the Prince of Darkness's body crumbled into bone and ash.

Everything went deathly still. In the silence that followed, I saw Dracul's wispy soul form take shape as Mina grasped his hand. She paused and turned to me long enough to smile before they disappeared.

Suddenly Devereux was there. He knelt down next to me, leaned over and laved the painful place on my neck to stop the bleeding. 'You need blood, but you will be all right. I will take you home now. It is all over.'

He lifted me into his arms. My head flopped against his shoulder, my neck muscles no longer reporting for duty.

'Transport Alan and Olivia to The Crypt,' Devereux said to a couple of the waiting vampires and they untied Olivia, lifted her from the bed and carried her out of the bordello bedroom. Alan followed them.

'Free him.' Devereux pointed to Michael, and another vampire hurried over and tore away the tape.

Michael jumped up from the chair, ripped the tape off his mouth and fell at Devereux's feet. 'Oh my God – what a horrible experience! Master – please take me with you. Don't leave me here!'

'Come.' Devereux tugged Michael to his feet and drew him close. I must have shut my eyes because the next thing I knew, we were in Devereux's private rooms under The Crypt.

CHAPTER 23

Whispered voices and shadowy figures greeted me when I cracked an eye.

'She is still very pale,' a male voice said. 'We may need to resort to our regular procedures if she does not awaken soon.'

'Should we prepare the blood?' said a woman.

'Wait! Her heart is beating more strongly.' Devereux leaned down and kissed my forehead, his soft hair trailing across my arm. 'She is awake.'

As I opened both eyes and they adjusted to the dim light, I recognised a few of the vampires surrounding me. In addition to Devereux, Zephyr, Valentino and Anne Boleyn studied me with solemn faces. Devereux's assistant Luna stood off to the side, checking her wristwatch. Behind the vampires I knew were several others I'd never seen before.

Since they were all there, it had to be dark still, so I must not have been unconscious for long.

'How do you feel, my love?'

I tried to speak, but all that came out was a croaking sound. My lips and throat were so dry I couldn't form words.

Devereux poured water from a nearby pitcher into a glass, slid his hand under my back and raised my head high enough to be able to drink. The water tasted wonderful, as if I'd gone without it for a long time.

I cleared my throat. 'Better now.'

Relaxing back onto the pillows, I looked down at myself, expecting to see the bloody remains of the clothes I'd been wearing, but they were gone. Instead, I was wearing a sheer white gown. I did a double-take, looking up at the vampires and then down at my body clearly visible through the transparent fabric.

Ack! Bride of Dracula!

Oh my God! What the hell happened while I was out?

'Devereux, can I have a blanket, please?'

He looked at me, a confused expression on his face. 'But you are sweating – are you sure you wish to be even warmer?'

'Er, yes.' I looked at the faces peering down at me. 'Definitely.'

Nola, one of Devereux's devotees I'd met around Hallowe'en, brought a satin duvet and spread it over me.

'Thank you, Nola.'

She curtsied and stepped away.

Anne Boleyn sat on the edge of the bed. 'We thought we'd lost you. Your heart stopped beating more than once. But you came back.'

'What do you mean? I thought Devereux said I needed blood, but I'd be okay.'

'You did need blood – human blood,' she said, 'but we were afraid to give it to you.'

Vampires afraid of blood? What an odd statement. 'I don't understand. Why?'

'Do you remember what I told you about Michael and why he became *stuck* in between being human and vampire?' Devereux asked. 'How he drank vampire blood, then had human transfusions?'

'Yes.' A very bad feeling washed over me.

Zephyr leaned in. 'We could not determine whether or not the same thing would happen to you. Even though the assembled elders sought visions, the results were unclear.'

'So we decided to use magic alone to see if your body could heal itself,' Anne said.

Valentino gave a wicked, fangless grin. 'Luckily, we were eventually able to locate a spell Zephyr created a century ago for a similar situation. And it worked, which I'm especially pleased about. Not only because you're recovering, but because – had you died – Devereux probably would have lost his mind.'

'Well, we will never know.' Devereux brushed his lips over mine. 'I am glad you clung so stubbornly to life. It is true,' he whispered, 'I would have been lost without you.'

'But we did give you a little more of the elders' blood,' Anne said, 'just to make up for the amount Lucifer and Dracul sucked from your body, so you will continue to have the brain protection you discussed with Zephyr.'

'I need to tell you what happened with Lucifer and Dracul . . .'

'We already know,' Devereux said gently. 'Zephyr read your mind and saw how the events unfolded from your point of view. We know about Nettie and Mina.'

'Yes, sister! You really kicked some ghost-summoning ass and saved the day!' Anne said, and punched her fist into the air.

It was good they thought they knew what had happened. I hoped someone would explain it to me.

'You were also having bad dreams after being so close to Lucifer's foul body,' Devereux said, 'so Zephyr muted those memories. They should not trouble you as much now.'

Even hearing those words caused my stomach to cramp.

They were making it sound like they'd held a long vigil,

which made me nervous, so I figured I'd just ask and get it over with. 'So how long have I been here?'

'Seven days,' Anne said, and I finally noticed she was wearing an 'I'm the Queen' T-shirt and jeans, which somehow just didn't fit for the former wife of Henry VIII.

My brain ground to a halt. 'Seven days? Wait a minute. We went over to Dracul's house on Friday night. Are you saying that a week has passed since then?' I tried to spring up into a sitting position, but Devereux pushed against my shoulders, forcing me down onto the bed again. 'I had clients scheduled – and my groups – oh no!'

Anne smiled smugly. 'You will be happy to hear that I took care of everything.'

Uh-oh. Anne Boleyn taking care of everything? That could be a disaster. 'What exactly did you take care of?' I had visions of my non-vampire clients lying drained in the waiting room.

'That was very good. You are such a creative worrier,' Zephyr said.

'I went to your home, found your appointment book and called all your clients.' Anne polished her fingernails on her T-shirt. 'I told them I was your answering service and you'd come down with a very bad case of the flu. I said you would call to reschedule as soon as you were able. I cancelled your entire week's clients. And, brilliant actress that I am, I mimicked your voice and changed the messages on your phones to tell callers you were unavailable due to illness. I feel like such a profes-sional!' She grinned and took a bow. 'You may thank me now.'

Under any other circumstances, I'd have been concerned about the confidentiality issues raised by having someone other than me contact my clients, but I doubted Anne knew anyone who cared about a human psychologist's client list or such humdrum mortal activities.

'I do appreciate it, Anne. Thank you. I'm glad I still have the weekend to recuperate.'

'All right!' Anne stood and clapped her hands to get everyone's attention. 'I think we can leave Kismet in Devereux's capable hands now.' She grinned at me. 'If you know what I mean.'

Suddenly the room was empty except for Devereux and me.

He leaned down and pressed his lips to mine in a sensual, lingering kiss. I looped my arms around his neck and pulled him close, taking the kiss deeper. He eased his tongue into my mouth and I opened for him, giving as good as I got. Breathing in his delicious aroma and enjoying the brush of his soft hair on my skin helped my rejuvenation more than anything the elders had done.

Much too soon he broke the kiss, his expression serious. 'Not knowing how to assure your survival devastated me. I do not remember ever feeling more afraid in my long life.'

I pulled him in for another quick kiss. 'I'm glad you figured it out without turning me into a half-thing like Michael. What would you have done if I hadn't regained consciousness?'

He sat up and shifted his eyes away. 'That is not important. All that matters now is that you did return, and you will recover.'

I peeled the blanket off and slowly rose to a sitting position.

Devereux lifted his hands to push me back down and I grabbed hold of them before they reached my shoulders. I didn't want to lie down any more. I wanted to confront his evasive statement.

'No! I want to sit up and talk about this. I know enough to recognise when someone is lying to me.'

'I am not lying.'

'Yes, you are. You're lying by evasion. Apparently we need

to have another discussion about the level of truth-telling between us. Let me ask you again: what would you have done if I hadn't awakened?'

He finally met my eyes, the blue-green of his simply lovely rather than entrancing. 'If there was no way to bring back your humanity, and to avoid turning you into a half-creature, I would have given you my blood and performed the transformation ritual to change you into a vampire.' He watched for my reaction.

I thought silently for a few seconds. 'I see.' I couldn't say his admission surprised me because it was actually the most logical course of action. Literally dead or undead. I didn't know how to feel about either choice. 'Thank you for telling me.'

'That is all you have to say? You are not angry? Horrified?' He pressed his palm to my forehead, then against my neck. 'Perhaps you are still feverish. I will call one of the healers back—'

'No.' I took his hand again. 'I'm fine. I didn't have a reaction because I really don't know what I think. Would I really rather be totally dead than be a vampire? After treating so many undead clients, I know there's nothing black and white about the issue. Each vampire is different and there are no easy answers. At this point, I'm pretty sure I don't want to die.'

'Perhaps we should discuss this again in the near future, so I can be aware of your wishes in case something ever happens where that decision must be made.'

'Yes.' I brushed his hand with my lips. 'That's a good idea. I'm nothing if not pragmatic.' I raised my arms over my head, stretching the unused muscles. 'So, fill me in on everything. What happened to Alan and Olivia? How about Michael? And – oh my God – the conference!' My heart rate increased. 'I never said goodbye to Doctor Teller and all my things are still in my hotel room, unless they tossed them out after I ran off—'

'There is nothing to worry about. Let me begin with the easiest. All of your things were retrieved from the hotel and taken to your home. Doctor Teller's memories were altered so that she believes you told her you were leaving and said goodbye.'

'Thank you for that. I appreciate it. What about the New York cops? They thought I killed Jack Kent. What did you do about them?'

He raised a shoulder. 'I merely planted a suggestion in all their minds that you had, indeed, slept through someone bringing the dead man into your room, and that there were others involved – a group of organised criminals Kent had been involved with. The police are now searching for that underworld crime connection. They have completely forgotten about you.'

'Gee. You're pretty handy, aren't you? I'll have to think of a way to reward you later.' I kissed him.

He gave me a come-hither look straight out of a vampire romance novel. 'Your servant, my love.'

'And Alan and Olivia? Are they okay?'

'As well as can be expected. Alan has moved in with his mother for the time being and said to tell you he will speak to you as soon as you feel better. He would like you to call when you are ready. Olivia is experiencing profound grief and she has hired several mediums to come to her apartment to connect with Colin.'

'I guess that isn't totally unexpected, since they were so dedicated to each other. Have any of the mediums made contact with Colin?'

'I believe so. Apparently, a couple of them have been able

to actually channel him – to allow him to reside in their bodies. Olivia is very excited about that development. She has become obsessed with forcing the mediums to allow Colin to communicate at her command. For hours and hours at a time.'

'Really? Does Alan know?' Wow. Olivia really did need therapy.

'I do not think so. But I am concerned about where she might be taking this activity. It cannot be good for the mediums in question to constantly host another being without their consent. And at this point, Olivia is not willing to listen to conflicting views. I do not wish to force my will upon her, so I am hoping therapy can help.'

'Shit, Devereux, this is bad – really bad. She's grieving and in no state of mind to make decisions. We don't know how long the mediums can act as channels without harming themselves, and if they die, or Olivia decides to keep them, they'd be listed as missing persons and the police would become involved.'

'Yes, you are correct. One of the men already collapsed and had to be taken to the hospital.'

'Oh no! Is he okay? You changed his memories, of course.'

'Yes, I altered his mind and he is recovering well. But, thankfully, I believe Colin will help us with this troubling situation. He has expressed his unhappiness about being forced to appear on command. He says it is not pleasant for him or the hosts. He has begged Olivia to come and see you. He said he will only speak with her in your office until she returns to her senses.'

'I'll be glad if she decides to come for therapy. It sounds like she really needs it. Do you think telling Alan would help? Maybe he could talk to her?'

'I have used Alan as a tool in my discussions with her. I

have said if she does not pull herself together and control herself with the mediums, I will tell her son. So far, that appears to have been effective because this evening she is in London with Alan for a change of scene.'

'Well, I can say one thing for sure. Life in the vampire world is never dull.' I indulged myself in a good look at his face. 'What about you? How are you feeling now that Lucifer and Dracul are history and you know what happened? It must be strange to have had to kill such a world-renowned vampire as Dracul.'

Yes. Let's talk about Dracula like it's a normal thing.

'I have been so concerned about you that I have not given much thought to what happened, but I can say now that I am relieved it is over. Being unable to capture Lucifer brought out the worst in me, and that was humbling and upsetting. I knew Dracul's mind was deteriorating. Sometimes really old vampires simply choose to die.'

'Really? I'd like to hear more about that later, because it might come up with my clients.'

'Certainly.'

'He really did love Mina, despite what he said?'

'Yes. I believe that unfortunate situation accelerated his madness. He discovered soon after killing her that she had not chosen the mortal after all. He was devastated, and repressed the memory.' He stroked his hand along my hair. 'How do *you* feel about Dracul's death?'

'I can't get past the fact that so many innocent people were murdered just so he could make all of us – and the police – run in circles for his amusement. He really was a monster.'

Devereux gave me a serious look. 'He was a vampire, Kismet. Vampires do not behave like humans, or hold similar values. I know this is hard for you to hear, but to most of the undead, humans are merely food. Those of us who wish to live parallel, hidden lives alongside you are in the minority. And this is an issue that will not go away simply because Dracul has been destroyed.'

'So things are getting stranger in the vampire universe?'

'You could say that.' He sighed. 'But regarding myself, I acknowledge that I behaved badly with everyone, especially you. I have discovered that I possess a robust ego, as you have often said, and I am not sure what to do about it. Or what I *can* do about it. I fear it is such an ingrained part of my nature that I might never be able to moderate myself. And if I cannot, I wonder if you will put up with me.'

'I'm already impressed by the level of introspection and insight you just shared. That's the first step towards change. Maybe simply being aware of your challenges will help.'

'That is good to know. I will endeavour to explore my interior world more thoroughly.' He grinned. 'Perhaps I will seek out a psychotherapist, if I can find one I am not in love with.'

'Master?' Luna popped in next to the bed. 'I'm sorry to bother you in the midst of your *important* business' – she rolled her eyes – 'but Valentino's being rowdy in the club. Do you want to come upstairs and deal with him?'

Devereux gave her a hard frown. 'Of course not. You are in charge in my absence and you have dealt with him before. Go and take care of it and do not disturb me again.'

Appearing properly chastised, she bobbed her head, then vanished.

Yes! Another indication of trouble between the Master and his obnoxious assistant! Dare I hope?

'What was that all about?'

'I do not know what is wrong with her. She has not been herself lately.'

Which, to my mind, would be a vast improvement.

My stomach growled, and I realized I hadn't eaten actual food in a week – and come to think of it, I hadn't showered either. Yuck!

'You are hungry. Allow me to arrange for food—'

'Wait, Devereux.' I grabbed his arm. 'I'd really like to go home. I want to take a shower, check my emails and messages and start to feel normal again. Do you mind?'

A disappointed expression flashed over his face before he regained control and once again looked charmingly neutral. 'Not at all. You have gone through a miserable experience and you wish to return to your life. I completely understand. I am sure you have had enough of vampires for a while.'

Unaccustomed to being able to sense the essence of Devereux's feelings and thoughts, I was surprised by a burst of clear knowing. *He thinks I want to get away from him. He's still acting vulnerable. I wonder what's up with that?*

Well, Zephyr did say the elders' blood would probably make me able to sense vampires now, too. I guess he was right.

'I guess I *am* tired of vampires in general.'

He gave a tight smile. 'Of course. I will take you home.' He tucked the blanket around my body and lifted me into his arms.

'But *you*' – I looked up at him and playfully batted my eyelashes – 'are not vampires in general.'

With a joyful laugh, he sailed us through space.

CHAPTER 24

Devereux thought us to my townhouse and I invited him to return in a couple of hours, which seemed to make him happy.

Before he left, I kept picking up that he felt insecure about us, but I didn't know if it was because he couldn't read me as a matter of course any more, which threw him off his game, or if he really thought I'd chosen Alan over him. Or perhaps there was some other mystical vampiric reason I couldn't possibly fathom. Nothing I could do about it at that moment, so I left it alone.

Everything at home appeared to be just as I'd left it, except cleaner. The cleaning fairies – or vampires – had not only scrubbed and vacuumed my place to perfection, but someone had shopped. There was food in the refrigerator and cabinets and a stash of my favourite wines sat on the counter.

There were definitely perks to hanging out with a rich guy.

After inhaling a couple of sandwiches, a bowl of soup, several chocolate cookies and a large glass of wine, I headed upstairs. More than ready to discard the filmy white nightgown, I stepped out of it in the bathroom and took a long, luxurious shower. I lathered up with an amazing-smelling soap that hadn't been there when I left and washed my hair with a new French shampoo.

Feeling totally spoiled and indulged, I wrapped up in my familiar pink towelling robe and let my hair air-dry.

I ambled to my desk, turned on the computer and reached for the telephone. I was eager to check my voicemail messages and emails to make sure my entire private practice hadn't evaporated while I was away. Not that I didn't believe Anne Boleyn about her efforts on my behalf.

True to her word, the message she'd recorded sounded like me, and it was exactly as she'd described. As I studied my appointment book, I was pleased to see she'd done an excellent job rescheduling all my clients. Of course, I had no idea what had become of some of the vampires who never made appointments in advance, but no doubt they'd heard about what *really* happened through the vampire grapevine.

I'd just finished answering the emails that couldn't wait until morning and started towards the stairs to get dressed when I walked through a clammy, frigid spot. It felt like stepping into the cold storage at the morgue, which I'd experienced in grad school. I recognised the feeling from when the ghost at the hotel walked through me and I jumped back, then froze, confused that I couldn't see anyone. I retreated a few more paces and a form materialised into view.

'Doctor Knight?'

Brown Hat – er, Jack Kent! I gasped and grabbed the front of my robe, making sure it was closed, and looked around for something to use as a weapon.

'Don't be afraid. I can't hurt you. And I wouldn't anyway. Probably. I remember being angry all the time when I was alive, but now I don't know why.'

He was still wearing his usual wool cap and dark coat.

Could ghosts lie? I didn't see why not, so it wasn't likely I was going to lower my guard.

'Sorry about scaring you. I'm not so good at the ghost stuff yet. It takes me a while to manifest.'

'Why are you here? What do you want?' I rubbed my arms, which had broken out in chills from walking through his ecto-plasm or whatever the hell it was.

'I'm not sure. I think I need to apologise to you.'

'Apologise? For what?'

'For stalking and threatening you?'

'Er, okay. Why were you doing those things? What did I ever do to you?'

'Nothing. I'm not sure why I targeted you. I don't remember.' He fiddled nervously with the zip on his coat. 'I think I had the idea that you were helping the vampires take over the world, but that sounds stupid when I say it now.'

'How did you know about the vampires?'

'I started following you last October and I trailed you and a couple of guys to that club, The Crypt. I watched the blond man, who I now know is the head vampire, join the three of you at the table. I figured you'd stay put for a while, and there's no smoking in the bar, so I went outside to light up a joint. Actually, I'd smoked quite a lot that night. While I was toking, I was approached by a beautiful woman, the kind who never pays any attention to guys like me.'

'Are you saying she was a vampire?'

'Yeah.' He stuck his hands in his coat pockets.

'How did you know?'

'She told me. She said she wanted to drink some of my blood and in exchange she'd do whatever I wanted.' He shrugged. 'I guess she thought I'd want sex, but I wanted to interview her and she said okay.'

'You used your cell to record the interview?' I shifted my weight from foot to foot, noticing I was still cold, as if a dank breeze emanated from where he stood. It made me feel like I was walking through a graveyard. I shivered.

'Uh-huh. This one was just audio. But she didn't know I was recording. I have a small mic that nobody can see unless they're looking. Anyway, after we talked I let her suck my neck then she tried to welch on the deal.'

'What do you mean?'

'All of a sudden, I felt bad – dizzy – and had to sit down. She showed me her bloody fangs and said she'd entranced me and I wouldn't remember anything about her in the morning. I don't think she knew I'd recorded her. But when I woke up the next day, I *did* remember, and I had the official recording. I think smoking so much pot must have messed with the effects of the vampire hypnosis.'

Really? That information could come in handy.

'Anyway, after that I started filming vampires and their victims in the alley behind the club. I have a password-protected secret website where I downloaded all the video that only I can access. Since I'm dead, I guess I won't need them any more. What a waste. I had entire documentaries about the vampires. And about you.'

Swell. Fifteen more minutes of fame.

'So you're saying all your video about me is safe? Nobody can find it?'

'Yeah, that's what I'm saying. Nobody knew about it but me. And after I died, I saw the blond vampire take my cell from the NYPD evidence room. The web address where I stored all the videos is on the phone in a text, so you can go to the site and destroy the videos if you want. You should get the phone from him. But before you wipe the videos, you ought to watch them.

You might really enjoy the stuff I taped. It could help you with your vampire counselling practice. Lots of good details.'

'Okay, thanks. What's the password?'

'Kismet.'

Great.

Thinking I might not get an opportunity like this again anytime soon, I decided to ask the questions we humans all want answered.

'So, what's it like, being dead?' I tugged the belt on my robe tighter.

He scratched his head and frowned. 'I don't really know. I still feel like the same person, except my memory is a little fuzzy and none of the stuff that used to piss me off does any more. And I'm not hungry or thirsty.'

'Did someone *say* you had to apologise to me?'

He thought really hard. 'That's a good question. I'm not sure but I think so. I remember a woman telling me I'd be carrying anything I didn't heal.' He rubbed his hands together, then blew into them, as if they were cold. 'Shit. I don't even know what that *means*. And then I showed up here.' He gave me wide eyes. 'Who knows where I'll end up next?'

We just stared at each other for a couple of minutes. I tried to think of something meaningful to ask, but he didn't seem to have any answers, and he'd looked as surprised to be in my house as I was to see him. Then he began to fade. 'Do you forgive me?' he said, with what sounded like panicky sincerity.

'Yes.'

As soon as I said that, he vanished.

I stuck my hand out, feeling for the cold place, and it was gone. 'Well, damn!'

'Damn what?'

I clutched my chest and twisted sharply to face the opposite direction. 'Shit, Devereux, you've got to stop sneaking up on me. You scared me! My heart's going to explode.'

'Sorry.' He wrapped his arms around me. 'I was sure you had heard me arrive, but since you were talking to someone I could not see, I assumed you had ghostly company so I did not disturb you. You have never mentioned a spectral guest visiting your home before. Is this the first time?'

'Yes.' I sniffed the air, breathing in his enticing aroma. 'And I hope it's not the start of a new trend. I liked having a lunacy-free zone.'

'Was it Colin?' He gave me a quick squeeze, then released me, moved to the couch and sat.

'No.' I joined him. 'It was Brown Hat – er, Jack Kent. The reporter we talked about. He said he came to apologise for harassing me.'

'That is interesting. What else did he say?'

'He said you have his cell phone and I should ask you for it.'

I almost told him about the vampire documentaries Jack had recorded, but then decided against it. That probably fell into the category of things vampires wouldn't want humans to have access to, and I wanted to see them. Better to keep that bit of information to myself for now.

'I do have it. I liberated it from the police station in New York City. As a matter of fact, I almost destroyed it, but simply forgot in the ongoing chaos. I will bring it to you tomorrow night. Or I can have a mortal deliver it during the day if it is important.'

'No, tomorrow night is soon enough.'

We sat in awkward silence for a couple of minutes, each of us looking at anything but the other. I took advantage of the time to practise the hum.

I couldn't remember ever sensing discomfort from Devereux before. I was pretty sure he had no idea I could read his emotions so much more clearly than before I drank the ancient vampire cocktail. I looked at him, deciding on full disclosure. 'Do you know what effects drinking the elders' blood had on me? Did Zephyr tell you?'

Surprise flashed across his face, so fast I barely caught it, and the unease radiating from him increased. He met my eyes. 'He said they did not know exactly what consequences would come from you ingesting such powerful old blood, but he suspected all your abilities would expand over time. He also explained that the blood would keep any vampire, including me, from reading you, the exception being when you are in a high state of emotional arousal. He suggested that I help you remain as calm as possible in my presence, so that your brain is not affected. Why do you ask?' A muscle in his face jumped ever so slightly.

Why does this topic make him nervous?

'I was wondering if he told you about the likelihood that I'll now be able to sense vampire emotions. Previously, that skill only worked with humans.'

'No.' He erased all expression from his face. 'He did not mention that.' He looked away.

What the hell? For some reason this discussion is distressing for him.

I rested my hand on his arm. 'What's wrong, Devereux? Apparently I can sense your emotions, because I know this topic upsets you, no matter how much you try to disguise it.'

He didn't answer for a couple of minutes, then he looked at me, tapping his finger against his leg.

Is he actually fidgeting? I've never seen him show anxiety before.

'There are not many vampires who can read my thoughts

unless I wish them to, and I am not aware of anyone who possesses keen enough empathic skills to be able to know my feelings – beyond the normal ways of accessing that information through facial expression, body language, words, et cetera.'

Where is he going with this? He's not acting like his usual self.

'Okay. You still haven't told me what's wrong.'

He frowned. 'I feared something like this might happen.'

'Feared?' Since when does he fear anything? 'What do you mean?'

'If you can sense my emotions whether I allow it or not, you can use that information against me. You will know when my defences are assailable.' He looked away and went very still.

'Wait!' I interrupted, clutching his arm. My stomach knotted. I felt like I'd been socked in the gut. Did he really trust me so little? 'What are you saying?'

'I have learned never to make myself totally vulnerable to another individual.' He brought his eyes back to mine. 'This ability you have gives you too much power. I will have to trust you to an extraordinary degree, and I have never done such a thing.'

'Too much power? How in the world could I use your emotions against you? They're just fleeting feelings, like clouds floating across the sky. I don't understand. Do you think I would hurt you?'

'Not on purpose.'

'I don't understand. I've never heard you worry about someone having power over you.'

He raised a shoulder. 'Of course not. In the past, if someone threatened me, I merely killed them.'

I swallowed. 'You killed them?' I really didn't want to hear that I was in a new category for him.

'Yes. And since I do not wish to kill you, it is a dilemma.'

'*I'm* a dilemma?'

'Yes.'

'Well, I'm glad you don't want to kill me.' *Am I really having this conversation?*

'But the fact remains that one of my enemies – and some of them are very impressive – could compel you to share what you know about me, giving them an edge. I suddenly feel unsafe, for the first time in ages.'

Oh my God. He's a vampire *and he doesn't feel safe with me.*

I didn't know what to say to that, so I just stared at him for a while before trying to explain. 'I'm used to sensing feelings – it's something I've been able to do my whole life. It's part of what makes me a good psychologist, so being able to sense vampires will help me in counselling my special clientele. But even before this ability expanded, I was getting better at reading you. I haven't known you very long, but you've shared a lot of yourself with me and I was starting to recognise many of your moods. The only difference now is that rather than having to speculate about what specific emotion you might be feeling, I know.'

'I did not realise how vulnerable I had already become to you. Perhaps you are right. Maybe nothing is different.' He looked hopeful.

The tight muscles in my neck and shoulders relaxed. I hadn't noticed how tense I'd been. 'That's what I'm telling you.'

'But I must admit I find our situation disturbing. Before you took on the elders' protection for your brain, I knew your thoughts. I felt in control. Now I do not.' An edge of anger infiltrated his words and he scowled. 'And on top of that, now *you* have the advantage. I am at a loss to know how I feel about this. Perhaps I should ask *you* how I feel about this, since I do not know?'

Okay, a little healthy anger is a good thing.

'I don't blame you for being upset, and I know you'll *acclimatise.*' I repeated the same word he had used – it seemed like weeks ago – when he was talking about me and his vampire intensity. 'You'll see that nothing important is different.'

He didn't look convinced.

I had to grin. He was so out of his comfort zone. If he were a client, I'd be very happy about this development because it meant he was ready to explore unknown territory. But I didn't think an 800-year-old master vampire would really like the idea of change much. I pretend-genuflected. 'You're still the almighty vampire king of the universe.'

The corner of his lip tugged up until a full, brilliant smile blossomed. 'Well, as long as we are in complete understanding about that.'

We lapsed into silence again. This was, without a doubt, the most awkwardly uncomfortable time Devereux and I had ever spent together. It was my turn to fidget. I played with my hair and stared at the floor. The rules had changed. Neither one of us knew what was going on and until we figured out our new roles in our relationship – or whatever it was we were having – we'd feel insecure.

I felt sad that things had become so strange between us, because I really did care about him, vampire insanity and all. I guess I hadn't let myself think about how much I wanted us to work out our issues.

He cleared his throat and stood. 'I imagine you are tired and would like some time to yourself. I will go.'

I held out my hand for him to pull me up and when he did, my robe, clearly acting out my unconscious desires, came untied and draped open. I started to close it, to cover myself, but then chose not to. 'Don't go.' I suddenly felt shy with him, but wanted to take the risk of reaching out. I took a deep breath and threw back my shoulders, momentarily afraid he'd choose to leave.

His mesmerising eyes tracked down my body. 'Are you sure?'

Relieved, my nipples hardened and my hormones, dressed in cheerleader costumes, formed a conga line and began calling out the letters of Devereux's name, flailing their pom-poms across the landscape of my mind. My libido did a backflip. Apparently I was sure.

'Yes.' Warmth radiated up my body. 'All I've done is sleep for the past seven days. I'm not tired at all.' I took his hand and pulled him towards the stairs. 'Besides, I've missed you.'

'And I, you.'

We climbed silently. I felt jittery, on edge, as if I'd never been with him before. I glanced at him out of the corner of my eye. His beautiful profile looked serious, but I sensed his excitement and uncertainty.

Instead of turning on my bedroom light, I went to the nightstand, pulled out a lighter and lit the wicks of several candles I'd kept in my room since the last time Devereux and I had spent time there. I closed the door and dropped my robe to the floor.

He peeled off his black leather coat and tossed it on a chair, his eyes never leaving mine, then he tugged off his boots, pulled the silk shirt over his head in a smooth motion and shook his lustrous hair. His expression ravenous, he unsnapped the waist of his leather trousers and drew down the zip. With vampire speed, the trousers were off and kicked to the side.

We moved slowly towards each other.

My heart pounded and my body heated, as if the candles were giving off a blaze instead of tiny flames.

When we were standing close enough for my nipples to

touch his chest, he wrapped his arms around me and nodded at the candles, extinguishing them. The room went dark and immediately wind blew against my face as we soared through space.

'Hold on!' he said.

'Hey – it's cold out here! I'm naked! Where are we going?'

'You will see.'

'Devereux, really,' I yelled over the sound of the wind. I loved his surprises, but his mood had been so odd I wasn't sure I was ready for another mystical adventure. 'Where are you taking me?'

'Wherever I wish.' He laughed.

We landed gently in an incredible room that looked like my fantasy version of *Arabian Nights*.

He released me and I scanned the immediate area, dazzled by the gorgeous layers of multicoloured silk and satin fabric which covered the walls and draped randomly and luxuriously across the expanse.

I wandered, touching and rubbing the layers between my fingers, very aware of his gaze on me.

A massive bed topped with a bold red, purple and blue silk spread dominated the room. Unobtrusive music drifted from hidden speakers and rich, exotic incense burned in a small bronze tray sitting on a low table surrounded by large pillows scattered across the floor. Candles atop tall holders arranged throughout the space created a soft golden light.

'Wow, this is quite something.' I felt like a kid in a candy store. 'Is it another one of your properties?' I knew he had hundreds.

'Yes.'

Hmmm. My previous enthusiasm drooped. No confusion about the purpose of this opulent sex den. I tried to keep my voice neutral. 'Do you bring women here often?' Fearing what he would say, my stomach muscles contracted. I was surprised by how much his answer mattered to me.

The corners of his lips rose. 'I do not need to read your mind to know the response you wish me to give.' He moved to me, lifted my chin and brushed my lips with his. 'I am petty enough to be happy you are jealous.'

Was I jealous of the other women he'd brought here? Hell, yes! I imagined the truly gorgeous specimens he might choose and shifted carefully out of his reach. 'I'm not jealous. Just curious.'

'You are a bad liar.' He grinned. 'But I can give you the answer you desire: no, I do not bring women here. This suite is part of a fantasy-based business I own. The company offers multi-themed buildings all over the world for the purpose of romantic escapes. The business is very successful.'

'Oh.' I looked away as relief swamped me.

'I chose this destination because I thought we both could benefit from a little positive fantasy and some time without interruptions of any kind.'

My pulse quickened.

Devereux walked to a veiled window.

I admired his long, toned nude body as he moved gracefully across the room. The dim candlelight subdued the paleness of his skin and brought out the diamond highlights in his hair. Watching his ass and legs made my mouth water again.

He pulled back the curtain and motioned for me to come and look.

Finally tearing my gaze from his tasty physical attributes, I strolled to the window.

Pyramids!

'Where are we?' I heard the awe in my voice and knew he could hear it, too.

'Egypt.'

I goggled. I'd never been to Egypt, I'd only seen photos of the pyramids, all taken in the daytime, not enhanced as they were now by a colourful lightshow and the star-filled sky above.

'So beautiful,' I whispered, staring at the ancient structures. My heart squeezed again.

'Yes. Beautiful beyond words.'

I shifted my gaze to him, eager to admire again another natural wonder, and found him looking at me in the intense way he often did. Realising he'd been referring to me and not the pyramids, heat warmed my face. No matter how many times I heard them, his compliments could still reduce me to an insecure schoolgirl. I studied the silver-speckled marble floor. 'Thank you.'

He raised my chin with his finger and pressed his lips to mine.

Overwhelmed by the opulence of the room, with the pyramids outside the window and knowing he'd planned it all to please me, I wrapped my arms around his waist and kissed him back enthusiastically. I revelled in the feeling of his hard, sculpted chest and ... other things, one of which had risen to the occasion. His skin was hot against mine. He must have fed recently.

We broke the kiss and looked into each other's eyes. 'Let this be the start of our new beginning.' His velvet voice caressed my ears.

'Oh, yes.' More than willing, still lost in his blue-green gaze, I looped my arms around his neck and we kissed again, more deeply, our tongues dancing. Hunger leaped between us. He ravished my mouth as I melted into him, the sensuousness of his tongue just a taste of what was to come, and a wave of pleasure and desire washed through me. I didn't know if it came from Devereux or from me.

It briefly occurred to me how weird it was that I didn't seem to mind being naked. I was actually oddly comfortable. Maybe after spending seven days in a sheer white gown, total nudity wasn't much of a leap.

When we finally pulled apart, me slightly lightheaded, he pointed towards the wall. 'There is a cupboard and a refrigerator built into the wall behind the drapery, stocked with all manner of things humans enjoy to eat and drink, including champagne. Would you like some?'

'No.' I gave him a smouldering look. 'I'm intoxicated enough just being with you.'

Judging by the wattage of his smile, that statement pleased him.

'Well, then.' He walked to the bed, opened a panel behind it, and pressed a button. The background music stopped abruptly and 'Stranger in Paradise' from the musical *Kismet* began to play.

I couldn't believe he'd remembered. I'd mentioned to him, while he was unconscious after the abortive blood-magic ritual a couple of months back, that not only had my parents named me for that particular musical, but I'd heard the soundtrack so often in childhood that it had become one of my personal favourites. Especially this song. I guess some part of him really had been conscious.

'May I have this dance?' He moved towards me and opened his arms.

Thinking we'd go straight to the gorgeous silk-covered bed, I felt momentarily awkward. Dancing wasn't one of my talents, and Devereux and I had never been in a situation where it was required, but I was so touched by his romantic gesture that I simply walked into his arms. Hopefully, one of us would know how to lead.

I needn't have worried. He was magnificent. The vampiric Fred Astaire. He guided me with ease and grace in circles around the room, holding me gently yet firmly, as we gazed at each other, both adrift in the wonder of the moment.

Stranger in paradise? Was that what I was? A stranger to Devereux's supernatural world, certainly. Or maybe a stranger with a visitor's pass? Perhaps some would call living almost for ever, and having all one's earthy desires fulfilled, paradise. Others might call it a curse. I didn't know what I thought.

When the song finished, ambient music once again flowed from the invisible speakers. Devereux scooped me up, walked to the bed and held me with one arm while he pulled down the covers. Then he lowered me onto the plush mattress and climbed in next to me, lying on his side.

He leaned over and kissed me lightly at first, then more deeply. I slid into his heat, into his rhythm, wrested control of the kiss until he took it back. Finally pulling away, his mesmerising eyes on mine, he gave a gentle smile. 'Listen.'

The quiet music, barely discernable, was all I could hear. I didn't want to talk or to listen. I just wanted to kiss. I raised my eyebrows. 'To what?'

'The silence.' He tugged one of the curls of my hair until it straightened, then watched it bounce back into a spiral. 'No telephones.' He circled one tight nipple and I moaned. So much for staying cool. 'No one popping in to demand our attention. Not even any street sounds due to the excellent soundproofing.' He gently squeezed my breast in his palm before smoothing his hand slowly down past my stomach, and combed his fingers through the dark hair covering my genitals. 'Soft.'

His touch sent anticipation and pleasure through my entire body. I moaned again.

'I hope you are enjoying this private time together as much as I am.'

'Oh, yes.' I was pretty sure the unconscious sounds I'd been making gave a good indication of my level of enjoyment. 'I'm loving it. This is the most relaxed I've felt in quite a while.'

'Well,' he grinned. 'Let me see if I can expand your repertoire of feelings.' He trailed his fingers down my breasts to my stomach again, launching ripples of energy through my skin. Then he returned to my breasts, using his clever fingers to pluck and pinch and stroke my nipples into hard, aching points.

'Mmmmm ...' My legs parted without any conscious thought.

He angled over and tortured me by taking each nipple into his mouth, sucking and twirling his tongue around the tender flesh until I was drowning in bliss. Each tug of his wet lips on my nipple directly stimulated my clitoris, sending me into ecstasy overload, my body growing tight with need. It felt like he was touching both parts of my body at once, but I could see he wasn't.

He raised his head and eased his hand down my stomach then nudged my legs further apart before easing one finger into the wet heat of my core and gently stroking. He circled my pleasure centre with his thumb.

My heart pounded and my mouth went dry. I lifted myself up to him, wanting more of his thumb, more of his fingers deep inside me, wanting even more connection. All my senses burst alive with need and desire.

'Do you like this?' he whispered, watching my face.

'No,' I groaned, 'I really hate it. I'll give you an hour to stop.' My pelvis lifted again.

He gave a wicked laugh and homed in on the perfect spot on my clitoris. 'Let yourself go. Come for me.' His dazzling eyes sparkled in the dim light.

My body wanted nothing more than to do that very thing. Within seconds, any thought of frivolity drifted away and I felt myself building towards peak. But part of me thought I should hold off, wait for him to roll over and fill me with the impressive erection straining against his stomach. Then he increased the pressure of his finger and all restraint was gone. I gasped as the orgasm crested and it was impossible for me to stop the momentum.

He plunged his fingers in deep, his thumb circled me again, and I was lost.

My muscles contracted and I thrust myself against his finger, looking into his amazing eyes, seeing his light, his concern, his care. As if our energy fields had interwoven, the boundary between us disintegrated and our spirits merged. All the incredible feelings were multiplied and deepened by each of us and sent back to the other.

He rubbed his hardness against my leg and groaned.

Rushes of pleasure surged up and down my body as his relentless fingers worked their magic. My heart pounded, my breath came in quick pants and my hips spasmed as yet another powerful rush of excitement crashed through me.

After the radiating tremors subsided, he leaned down and took my mouth as deeply as his fingers had plunged into my body. I felt his heart beating fast, knew mine was thundering in time with his even as my body recovered from such bliss.

Reluctantly, slowly breaking our kiss, I circled his neck with limp arms and gazed into the unfathomable depths of his eyes, where I imagined it really was possible to see for ever. Wanting to give back to him as much sensual pleasure as he'd given me, without warning him I clutched his upper arms and somehow flipped him over onto his back, reversing our positions.

'Wha—?' His eyebrows shot up and his eyes went wide as he surveyed his unexpected new position. 'Enhanced strength. Interesting.' He growled deep in his throat as I sprawled over his body. 'It appears I am yours to command.'

'Oh yes, you are.' I angled my body slightly, sliding off to lie on my side next to him. I wanted access to all the glorious vampire flesh formerly hidden underneath me. His eyes shining and his perfect face radiant in the glow of the candles, I skimmed my hands slowly across his chest before trailing my fingers down his tight midsection.

He gave a barely perceptible groan as I continued my southern journey, watching his face for cues on how to proceed.

When my seeking hand reached its destination, I curved my finger around the head, then wrapped my hand around it and stroked its length, enjoying the feel of the silky skin over the taut muscle.

He wove his fingers through my hair and held my head in place as he pulled me in and captured my lips with his. He thrust his tongue inside to dance with mine, moaning into my mouth as I stroked faster.

I raised my mouth just enough to run my tongue over his lips and slid my finger through the warm liquid beading on the head of his penis. He gave a long groan and dropped his hands from my hair.

He mumbled words in that strange, exotic language he often used. Judging by the reflexive movements of his hips, whatever he was saying was some version of *wahoo*!

'This is wonderful' – his voice sounded strangled as he eased his fingers through my hair again – 'but if you do not stop, I will not be able to restrain myself.'

I elevated my head just long enough to say, 'Good,' and went back to driving him crazy with my hand. I cupped and caressed his sac and increased the friction with my fingers.

Feeling him building towards climax made my body vibrate with anticipation. My nipples felt hard enough to burst and my clitoris ached. The more attention I lavished on him, the more my own body responded, returning me to a highly aroused state, growing wetter, needier.

He gasped, his hips bucking as he exploded.

I kept up the rhythm until I felt him shudder through all the aftershocks, then I let go of his erection and gave him an enthusiastic grin, my own body shivering with a mini-orgasm in response to his.

He caressed my hair and pulled me close, pressing his lips to mine as he wrapped his arms tenderly around me.

The kiss became deeper, slower, and our tongues danced together in sensual movements. I threaded my fingers through his glossy hair, loving the scent and the feel of him. I felt him harden against my abdomen and my body bucked involuntarily. *Yes, please!*

He rolled us over, aligning me underneath him, and used his knee to spread my legs wider. His erection nudged against my opening.

I ran my hands up and down his back and cupped his ass, pressing him close to my heat. I wanted nothing more than to feel him inside me.

His lips on mine, he pushed slowly into me and we groaned our pleasure into each other's mouths. *At last.* I let out a heartfelt sigh of relief even as he whispered, 'So hot. So wet. All mine.'

I lifted my legs and wrapped them around his waist, tilting my hips to take him deeper.

With a smooth motion, he filled me.

Nothing had ever felt better.

He began thrusting and I matched his rhythm, clutching his back with my fingers as rising tension crawled through my body and I felt the stirrings of a powerful orgasm. He released my lips and raised his head. 'Will you allow me to take your blood, my love?'

Just those words sent me close to the edge. I remembered how it felt when he fed while we had sex. I closed my eyes and whispered, 'Yes,' eager for his fangs to pierce my neck, my clitoris throbbing in agreement between us.

His warm breath raked my skin a second before he pressed his sharp incisors into my vein. I gasped and tightened my legs around his waist, contracting the muscles of my vagina in time with his tempo.

Heat radiated from both points of contact, sending ecstatic rushes along my neural pathways. My skin tingled and my toes literally curled.

'Yes, yes, yes . . .' I pulled him tighter against me, wanting our physical bodies to melt into each other as his thrusts intensified and I felt myself ready to implode.

He sucked harder, and groaned.

'Now, Devereux. Now—' My orgasm detonated through my body so forcefully I screamed and grabbed his hair.

He lifted his mouth, coated with my blood, and pressed his lips against mine as he spasmed inside me.

We clung to each other, hips jerking, tongues exploring until the last wave diminished and I collapsed, limp, underneath him. My arms and legs were useless, my heart racing. Still shuddering with aftershocks, the bliss I'd known only with him stole through me and rendered my over-practical therapist's mind senseless with satiation.

No matter what happened in the future between Devereux and me, for this moment, everything felt just right.

CHAPTER 25

Anne had done a great job of rescheduling my clients while I recovered. She'd eased me into my routine gently, setting up only a few human clients for my first day back. She'd make a pretty good secretary if she wasn't dedicated to finding another king to bedazzle.

As darkness fell, I began arranging the office chairs in a circle for the Monday night Fear of Fangs group. All six members were due tonight. No doubt they'd have lots of questions about the events at Dracul's suburban home, and we would spend most of the session time talking about Devereux's heroic handling of both insane monsters. According to Anne, Devereux had reclaimed his title of Lord High Supreme Vampire Grand Wazoo – metaphorically speaking, of course. I wasn't sure how much discussion I wanted to have regarding my own part in the surreal tableau.

I'd just lined up the last seat when the Pooh-Bah himself popped in.

Usually fond of leather, tonight he was wearing a handsome midnight-blue European-cut suit over a silver shirt and a tie featuring several shades of blue, black and silver. Stunning.

His light-blond hair was pulled into a long, shining ponytail at the base of his neck.

'Hey! What are you doing here?' I looked at the clock. 'You know I have a group tonight and if they see you, they'll swarm all over you and we won't get any therapeutic work done!'

He smiled wide, glided sensually to where I stood, scooped me up into his arms and thought us out of my office.

'Devereux – I can't leave – I have clients coming!'

'Just for a moment. I wish to show you something.'

We rematerialised in the living room of my townhouse.

He wrapped me in his arms and pressed his lips against mine, softly at first, then with increasing passion. We must have lip-locked for a good five minutes.

I melted.

'Oh. My. God,' I said when we reluctantly pulled apart. 'If there's something more you want to show me, I don't know if my heart can take it.'

He grinned. 'No. That was it. For now.'

'Really? You whisked me away from my office just so you could kiss me?'

'Yes.'

'Well, okay, that works for me. Now what?'

He kissed me again.

My knees buckled and he tightened his grip on me.

And I'd been worried about whether or not I'd still be attracted to him after his influence on my brain was gone.

We finally broke the kiss and he lifted me into his arms again.

'We had better return to your office. You have a group.' He winked and sent us soaring through space and time, into the hallway outside my office.

I noticed he was awfully playful tonight.

'Why did you bring us out here in the hall?'

'I do not know.' He opened the waiting-room door, took my elbow and walked me inside.

'You don't know? What's going on, Devereux. You're acting weird.'

'Weird?' He opened the office door and we stepped into a dark room. I could've sworn there were lights burning before we left.

'Surprise!' The overhead lights flashed on.

Devereux nudged me ahead of him.

My office was filled with vampires – vampire clients, that is. Lots of them.

I covered my mouth with my hands. I really *was* surprised. And a little nervous. This many vampires could be extremely unpredictable.

'Hey, doll – er, I mean, Doctor Knight.' Chain hurried over, wearing his usual baggy jeans and Harley leather jacket. And his chains, of course. 'We wanted to throw a little surprise celebration to welcome you back after you almost died.'

'Yeah, Doctor Knight,' Lucille said, crossing herself. 'We heard you were actually dead. They even buried you and you resurrected. They said the Master had his head ripped off.' She'd gone back to her usual mode of dress: a tight micro-mini, a too-small red bustier and hair so big it must have taken an entire can of hairspray to erect it. In honour of the occasion she'd layered on extra-long false eyelashes, one of which had started to come loose at the corner of her eye. She didn't notice.

'Come on, Lucille,' Chain said, grabbing her breast. 'Let's go mingle and give the doc a chance to check out the guest list.'

'Okay,' she said. 'We'll be back in a minute, Doctor Knight. We're so glad you didn't die.'

Me, too.

'Thanks, Lucille, Chain.'

'Oh my God. The Master's here,' Dennis said, staring at Devereux with his eyes wide.

'The Master's here,' Walter repeated, clutching Dennis's arm.

Devereux moved in front of me, lifted my hand and kissed it. 'I agreed to steal you away for a few minutes so your clients could enter your office. I hope you will forgive the small subterfuge. My choice of activity was purely selfish.' He grinned. 'I will leave now, so that everyone can feel comfortable and have a good time. May I see you after the gathering?'

I hugged him. 'Yes. Thank you.'

He gave a quick bow and vanished.

'Oh no! The Master's gone,' Dennis said.

'The Master's gone,' Walter echoed.

'Doctor Knight! Doctor Knight! I want you to meet Wanda!' Nicky raced over pulling a short, ample red-haired woman by the hand. She was wearing a uniform from a well-known Mexican fast-food restaurant. 'This is Wanda, Doctor Knight. Isn't she beautiful?'

'Hello, Nicky. It's nice to meet you, Wanda.'

'Same here, Doctor Knight. Nicky talks about you all the time.' She looked at Nicky, who had wrapped himself around her. 'Nicky, could you give the doctor and me a minute to talk alone?'

He pouted, but reluctantly let go of her. 'Okay. I'll go and look out of the window and chew on myself.'

Great.

She waited until Nicky had walked away, then grabbed my arm. 'Doctor, you've got to help me.' She let go of me. 'He won't go away. I've been trying to get him to move out for years but he's too afraid to make the change. Please! As you can see' – she pointed to her clothing – 'I have a career. I work the night shift and I'm up for a promotion to taco-maker. That's a very important position. I'm so stressed out all the time about Nicky's neediness that I'm afraid I'll lose my job.'

Oh, geez. So Nicky hasn't been levelling with me.

'I'm sorry you're feeling so stressed, Wanda. What would you like me to do?'

'Hi, Doctor Knight. I got rid of all my dead bodies – even the cats. But it's so hard. I miss them. I had a small relapse yesterday and Eleanor got so mad—'

'Hey, buddy, I'm talking to the doc. Beat it,' Wanda said, shoving him aside.

Marvin, who had a fear of being touched, screamed at the top of his lungs.

'What's wrong? Are you all right, Doctor Knight?' Apollo, my very first vampire client, rushed over. He'd made great progress in his ability to deal with the sight of blood. 'Why is he screaming?'

Everyone in the room closed in.

'I'll get more chains, Doctor Knight. We'll take care of this.'

'We're gonna die, we're gonna die—'

Medina, who hadn't completely grown her leg back since diving off a skyscraper, hobbled over on crutches. 'Who's going to die? *I* want to die—'

'I can't breathe in here,' Betty said, dramatically resting the back of her hand on her forehead. 'Someone open a window—'

'Everything's okay, Betty,' I said. 'You really don't need to breathe.'

'Doctor, Marvin brought home another body yesterday. Can I talk to you privately?'

'Let's make an appointment, Eleanor—'

'Hey! I'm standin' right here! Don't push in front of me. I need to talk to the doc.' Wanda, who appeared to have quite a bit of muscle under the padding, started pushing everyone away from me.

Walter and Dennis jumped up and down, slapping themselves on the head, as was their habit.

All at once, vampires started punching and kicking each other. Arms and legs flailed. Blood dripped and spewed from cuts, scrapes and amputated limbs.

As I backed away, I saw Wanda leap into the air and throw herself down like a professional wrestler on top of Eleanor, who surprised me by holding her own against the much larger taco-maker.

I backed into the waiting room and listened to the carnage.

'Are you all right?' Devereux asked.

I started. 'What are you doing here? I thought you left.'

'I thought I should check back in a few minutes. I had no idea Chain was going to invite quite so many vampires. And Nicky's friend Wanda seemed especially ... energetic. I can see I was right.'

'I know they meant well.'

'Yes, they did. Would you like to leave now?'

'Leave? But they're trashing my office.'

'Never fear.' Devereux glanced off to the side for a moment and several vampires dressed in Crypt security black leather popped into the hallway. 'Take them all home, then arrange for the office to be thoroughly cleaned.'

The men – er, vampires – in black rushed into my office, grabbed two or three fighting vampires each and disappeared. Within a minute, the office was empty.

Beautiful silence.

'It appears you have finished work early, my love. What shall we do to celebrate?'

'I know just the thing.'

Epilogue

February really is the dreariest month, even in the magical Rocky Mountains. Despite the fact that we had a couple of seventy-five-degree days last week, when Denver inhabitants donned shorts and T-shirts and sunbathed on roofs, now the front range is socked-in by low clouds, impending snow, and below-zero temperatures. But still, there's no place quite like Colorado.

After all the events of early January, it took me a couple of weeks to sort myself out and to begin to feel somewhat normal again – well, as normal as someone who counsels the undead, drinks the blood of ancient vampires, has stellar sex with a master bloodsucker and communicates with ghosts can feel.

Thankfully, my unexpected vacation left no permanent scars on my private practice. It's as busy as ever. Many human clients told me they appreciated the 'chatty' call they got from my answering service representative. I shudder to think what Anne Boleyn might have 'chatted' about, so I didn't ask, and nobody volunteered the information. I imagine I could ask her, but she and I have created a connection of sorts and I wouldn't want her to think I don't trust her. Even though she'd be the first to acknowledge that she's usually less than trustworthy. But is any vampire?

To my surprise, Anne asked recently if she could come to see me as a therapist. With my new ability to sense vampires' emotions, I got the clear hint that, rather than coming for actual therapy, she thought it would be amusing to shock me with tales of her wild life – not that I can really be shocked any more. Well, never say never. But perhaps underneath her quest for a good time is a need to be listened to – who knows? Maybe we'll try a session or two and see how it goes. I hear she's been visiting a certain European monarch's castle late at night, teaching the twenty-something grandson her own version of the *Kama Sutra*.

Anne tells me that despite my ongoing relationships with vampires, my brain is still unharmed and, for the most part, uninfluenced.

Cerridwyn says the same. I went to her house for another reading and she verified that not only is my brain healthy, but it's stronger. She said I've done a good job practising the hum. I've discovered that sound magic is a potent, fascinating branch of the occult and I haven't even begun to utilise the possibilities. Of course, Cerridwyn knew about my drinking the elders' blood before I mentioned it and she agreed it was a necessary precaution. She also said I would be surprised by the new manifestations of my abilities over time – of course, she wouldn't be specific – and that I should prepare myself for another personal and professional challenge thanks to my affiliation with vampires. Besides sounding ominous, it strikes me as exhausting. Challenges because of the vampire world? So, what else is new? She agrees that it's a good idea for Devereux and me to start over, to take things slowly. She says both of us need to learn more about ourselves before trying to forge a union – or whatever it is we're forging. I couldn't agree more.

Nicky disappeared. Since he'd been so disciplined about keeping all his appointments with me, I became concerned when he missed one. After all, he *had* been actively suicidal and self-destructive. But even taking his mental state into account, I strongly suspected that Wanda had found a way to get rid of him. After watching their interpersonal dynamic the night of the gathering at my office, it didn't take my new ability to guess what had happened. Unfortunately, I was right. At my request, Devereux assigned a few members of his security force to search for the young bloodsucker and they easily read the murder details (is it murder if an already dead creature is killed again?) from Wanda's mind. She'd beheaded and staked him in the basement of the fast-food restaurant where she worked. Apparently she'd desperately wanted the job as head taco-maker, and was more than a little insane herself. Nicky was young enough that his remains could still be identified. At Devereux's command, Wanda was destroyed on the spot – not because the Master has any particular interest in the fate of any random individual, but as a gift to me. I still don't know how I feel about that. I'll miss Nicky.

Esther has discovered an unscented sparkling body paint that she can wash off every few days and have a new friend reapply for her. The friend – Fred, a gangling boy who suffered a catastrophic brain injury right before being turned – shares her *Twilight* addiction. They're both joyfully sparkling.

Marvin and Eleanor broke up. Despite Devereux's insistence that he stop collecting dead human bodies, Marvin's compulsion prevails, and Eleanor refuses to accommodate him. She has moved back into her old apartment in one of the Master's buildings and has adopted a few cats. Well, actually, a lot of cats. We might have a new therapy issue to confront.

Marvin's depression has increased since he lost both Eleanor and all his hoarded bodies, but he comes to individual therapy regularly and is exploring the underlying causes of his addiction. We experienced a setback recently when Marvin lost control of himself and brought a couple of his favourite – particularly ripe – dead bodies to a session. He'd dressed them like Civil War soldiers, one in blue, one in grey, and he threw such a panic-driven temper tantrum when I said he couldn't keep them that building security had to be called. He was held at a 'vampire jail' that nobody will explain to me, and kept in solitary confinement in a coffin for days. I don't know yet if his switch to talking about his fear of the dark is a positive change from his dead-body fetish or not. I suppose we'll find out.

My Fear of Fangs group celebrated recent biting breakthroughs for Chain and Betty, who has also been practising not breathing. Chain was so proud of himself that he got carried away and bit everyone in the group last week. I had to schedule individual sessions for everyone to manage the fallout. I'm thinking of putting the group on hiatus for a month to give them time to recommit to the process. And besides, after the last bloody session, my office needs new carpet.

Olivia kept her word about counselling. She's still grieving the true death of Colin, and she will be for a long time, but she has begun to venture out of her penthouse occasionally. At Colin's insistence, she has stopped inviting mediums to channel him, because he told her it felt like a violation – a psychic rape. But as he promised, he joins us regularly for our psychotherapy sessions, sometimes listening as Olivia pours out her heart about losing him, but more often giving encouragement and suggestions for her healing and growth. He makes quite a wonderful co-therapist. He has asked if he can have his own private consultation with me in the near future. Apparently, he has some otherworldly decisions to make. I'm hoping he'll answer a few questions I've come up with about the afterlife – or as he describes it, the parallel dimension he inhabits now.

Despite saying he wouldn't be available to me in the future – that he didn't interfere in the lives of humans – Zephyr has shown up in my dreams a few times. I suppose it's possible that he's only a figment of my nocturnal imagination, but I think it's really him. Each visit, he takes me back to the vast underground caverns in South America and shows me yet more priceless artefacts and treasures. I get the feeling that he likes having an appreciative audience. Sometimes I go to bed early, just in case he wants to play tour guide that night. He informs me he'll collect me on the same date yearly so I can drink the elders' blood. And he did drop a bit of a bombshell: it turns out the magical concoction slows my ageing process – so what will that mean for me?

Speaking of effects from the ancient blood, my ability to communicate with ghosts is definitely increasing. They're everywhere, some more intrusive than others. Mostly they show up as re-enactments of previous events – loops that play again and again. It has been very gratifying to verify that I can stop those replays with a combination of my words, emotions and intentions. Discrete manifestations aren't as easy to control. Discovering I'm being followed by a dead person – as opposed to an *undead* person – is becoming a regular occurrence. Some don't speak to me; others do. So far, there's no rhyme or reason. My not-really-serious question to myself when

I met Colin, about whether or not I'd be counselling ghosts, was answered because the spectres are showing up in my psychotherapy office now – whether there's another client already present or not. I need a new game plan. Vampires and ghosts – what's next?

Brown Hat's videos – I just can't get used to thinking of him as Jack Kent – are as educational and intriguing as he said they'd be. He gathered hours and hours of interviews with various vampires, including anecdotal accounts of their transformations, very powerful and evocative journalism. If he'd gone public with the recordings, the lid really would've been ripped off the coffin. If even only a few mortals believed them, the wall of secrecy protecting humans from vampires would have been breached, encouraging the bloodthirsty Dracul-sympathisers who want to return to being visible predators again. As horrible as it is to even contemplate, Brown Hat's death was probably a good thing. He was right that the record-ings would help me understand my blood-drinking clients better. I made a copy of the videos for Devereux, because he needed to see what some of *his* vampires are up to. Apparently, his coven is harbouring many traitors who were captured on tape, draining humans regularly behind The Crypt. He isn't happy.

Dr – call me Ham – Taylor and I have begun meeting every other week to discuss all things paranormal. He was flabber-gasted to learn about the 'reality' of ghosts and magic. His view of the world has definitely been upended, but he's coping. As much as I enjoy his company, I'm not sure meeting me was such a great thing for him. He said he has scheduled his sex reassignment surgery and has decided to keep Hamilton as his first name. He said he'll tell clients he is named after both sides of his family, which is true, and he'll change the nick-name from Ham to Hammy. I'm hoping I can persuade him that another nickname might be more appropriate for a professional. I wonder how long it will take me to remember to refer to him as she?

Devereux surprised me last week by organising a film retrospective of several well-known vampire movies at the site of last October's Vampires' Ball. He invited so many real bloodsuckers who'd played the roles that my head spun. Not only was Valentino there, but also the two actors I'd seen at the wedding – including the gorgeous Latin heart-throb – plus a very young, intense dark-haired Broadway performer who'd added new levels of sensuality to the genre in the early 1980s. My mind boggled as I was introduced to more and more actors who turned out to be the real deal. I'm still star-struck!

Michael continues his transition from half-thing into full vampire. He came to visit me at my office one night to apologise for telling so many lies. He said it would probably take months more before he was completely reborn. He offered to talk to me about his experiences and his knowledge of the vampire world, and I readily agreed. Since we're both being honest now, spending time together is pleasant. We actually talk more about 'normal' therapy issues than the madness of the undead. Once he transforms, he'd like to hang out his shingle again as a therapist to the bloodsucking community. I'm looking forward to it.

Alan has been so busy reacquainting himself with his mother and dealing with the FBI that we've hardly spoken. Since he'd focused his life on exploring the truth about his mother and he now has most of the pertinent facts, he isn't sure what he wants to do any more. He and Devereux came up with a plan to satisfy the FBI's demand that Alan find the human serial killer pretending to be a vampire or turn the case over to someone else. Alan alerted the San Francisco police, including Detective Andrews, his gorgeous, ass-kicking upholder of justice, that he had tracked the killer to an abandoned warehouse there. An unnamed source contacted the local and national media and the scene was set for a showdown. Devereux acted the role of the killer and swapped gunfire with Alan, who took a slug in the arm, just for appearance's sake. By the time the police and FBI gathered to storm the building, it burst into flames. Alan, who'd apparently barely made it out alive, staggered clear, bloody and hurt – and a hero. Devereux had liberated an unidentified corpse from a Canadian morgue to be the remains found at the scene, and he also altered the minds of everyone he encountered, making sure they were all on the same page as far as Agent Stevens' bravery and dedication to his work were concerned. Alan, triumphant, took a leave of absence from the Bureau to figure out the rest of his life. He told me he spent a couple of days in San Francisco with Detective Andrews. Non-business days. I know I don't have any right to be jealous, but I still am. He told me he'll be in touch soon. I hope that's true.

Devereux is still struggling with his concerns about my ability to sense his emotions more distinctly – not to mention the fact that he can no longer read me as a matter of course, thanks to the elders' blood and the hum. He was correct when he said he probably wouldn't be able to curb his ego after so many centuries. Even though he tries very hard, he's bossy, secretive and certain he knows what's better for me than I do. He's still not telling me why I'm so important to him – I mean the *real* reason – but despite his domineering tendencies, I find him irresistible. There have been a couple of times that he infuriated me and raised my emotions to the point that my thoughts became available to him, and he took full advantage of the moment. He's unrepentant about working to regain the upper hand. For some reason, that doesn't bother me. Since dispatching Dracul and Lucifer – I didn't want my part in the deed to be widely known, so Devereux gets credit for every-thing – he has once again assumed mythic proportions and has become the Penultimate Badass Master of the Vampires. He has reaffirmed his role as protector of the secret world of the undead. Needless to say, we don't get to spend as much time together as we'd like. But we've agreed there's no hurry. After all, I'm just starting to adjust to my strange, new reality. Surely, things can't get any weirder than this ... ?

THE END

Follow Kismet's continuing adventures in
Book Three of

Kismet Knight, Vampire Psychologist

Coming September 2013

ACKNOWLEDGEMENTS

There are so many people to thank for the publication of this book, that it would take pages to acknowledge them all. Here are a few I'd like to send special appreciation to: Jo Fletcher, editor extraordinaire and publisher of Jo Fletcher Books, an imprint of Quercus Books, UK. She has been patient, kind and supportive throughout our time together. I am very lucky to have her as my editor. My agent, Robert Gottlieb, Chairman of Trident Media Group, who continues to help me navigate through the ever-changing world of publishing. Michael Fragnito, VP, Editorial Director of Sterling Publishing, USA, who has worked hard to keep my books moving forward in the face of professional challenges. And of course I can't forget my writing/author friends and brainstorming buddies who kept me afloat during some unexpected rough seas. Many thanks and much love to Betsy Dornbusch, Esri Allbritten and Laurie Hawkins. To all my critique partners and beta readers, I send continuing gratitude. You are the best! Most important of all are the wonderful fans who love Kismet and her world and who bombard me with emails, asking for the next book. Thank you, thank you, thank you! This book is for you.